RIPPLE EFFECT

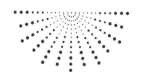

TRACEY JERALD

xoxo!
Tracy
Jerald

Love,
Jeremy
xoxo!

RIPPLE EFFECT

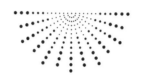

Turtle,
For accepting the girl who smashed LT's class curve.
Whiskey tango...
All the love, brother.

1

PRESENT DAY

ELIZABETH

I've tried to leave this part of my life behind so many times. Over and over, I'm dragged back to rehash the memories of the worst days I've ever endured. *How many times can I do it before I say no more?* I think wearily. I'm proud to say I've moved on. It took years for me to get to where I am right now.

My husband, recognizing the tension whipping through my body, offers with complete seriousness, "We can leave."

I snicker. "'Cause that will go over well." I rub my hands up and down my arms, trying to warm myself.

He turns me to face him, and my slight baby bump brushes against his muscular abs. "Like I give a damn about that. Especially now." His hand drops to caress my stomach tenderly.

I reach up and cup his cheek. Smoothing my hand back and forth over the bristles that tickle the inside of my palm, I murmur, "You need to shave."

"I ran out of time. This gorgeous pregnant woman had her way with me this morning. I was a wreck when she was done." His smile, the very first thing I noticed about him, makes my stomach flutter. Then again, maybe that's our baby kicking. Either way, I'm flooded with gratitude.

Now.

"I didn't notice you complaining," I tease.

He gives me a look rife with disbelief. "I may be called many things, but I hope I've grown out of my idiot stage."

Brushing my lips against his, I whisper, "I occasionally have to check. It took you a little longer than the average male."

Just as my husband's about to retaliate with some smart-ass comment, a door opens behind us. "Mrs. Sullivan? Dr. Powell is ready for you."

Cal doesn't let me go right away. "I'm right here, Libby. I've got you."

"I know." And I do; he's more than shown me that.

Concern flashes over his face. He opens his mouth but closes it just as quickly.

"What is it?" I ask. I don't have a lot of time before I need to be on the other side of that door.

Crushing me to him, he whispers directly in my ear, "You had a nightmare last night."

Surprised, I lean back in his strong arms. "I did?"

He nods solemnly. "And I know today's going to make things worse." The tick in his jaw betrays his calm demeanor.

Knowing I'm putting the schedule at risk, I wrap my arms around him and hold him as hard as I can. Cal buries his head in my neck. "Even if they try to get to me in dreams, there's nothing for you to be afraid of."

"Why's that?" His voice is raw with remembered pain.

I search his tired eyes, which I can now see reflect his lack of sleep. Probably because he was standing guard over his family. Kissing him briefly, I pull out of his warm embrace and make my way to the door. I pause there and look back. "Because just like the first time I woke from my nightmare, you were there for me."

"I always will be. No matter what."

Without another word, I follow the young intern down the hall. Another person greets us before saying, "I'll take Mrs. Sullivan from here. How are you today?"

I smile and nod, but inside I'm screeching in maniacal laughter. Is anyone ever ready to have their emotions dissected like they're a frog in science class?

It takes another few minutes before I'm settled facing Dr. Powell. "It's a pleasure to see you again, Mrs. Sullivan."

"Libby, please," I correct him. I can't do this if we're going to stand on formality.

"Libby," he returns. "We left off yesterday talking about your background; you're an interior designer in the Washington, DC, area, correct?"

Smoothing a hand over my stomach, I nod. "Yes. A little less than four years ago now, my husband's company was bought out. We decided to relocate with the new owners."

"How does it feel to be back in Charleston?"

My eyes drift out the window overlooking the harbor. Sunlight glistens off the water. I shudder.

"Is strange an acceptable answer?"

"It is."

"Then let's go with that." The laugh I receive is appreciated, so I begin to relax.

Maybe it's too soon to do that.

"Libby, I can't help but notice you're expecting. "

"It's getting harder and harder for me to miss too," I joke, earning another chuckle.

"Is your family excited?"

"Beyond belief." I smooth a hand over my stomach, pulling my dress tighter.

"After everything you've been through, it must feel like a miracle," Dr. Powell says gently.

"Yes." I don't elaborate more because I suspect he will.

And I'm right.

"We're here for a reason, today, Libby. And this miracle is a perfect conclusion to it. I hate to take you back..."

"You don't have to," I tease. "We can just talk about how I plan on decorating the nursery."

He smiles. There's an edge of determination covered by a layer of sympathy to it that I abhor—not that I'd let him see. I don't need the sympathy; the families of the people who didn't survive do.

What I need is peace.

"I'd like to go back, Libby."

I shake my head, still wearing a smile. "What's the good in that?" For me, for Cal, for any of us?

"Context." Dr. Powell's words come back at me so succinctly, I want to roll my eyes, but I can hear Cal's voice in my head telling me to calm my sass.

Reaching for the unopened bottle of juice on the table next to me, I twist the cap off and take a small sip. Just a small one. I still can't consume liquids any faster than a tiny drink at a time. "How far back would you like to go?"

Flipping through the notes on his lap, he lifts off his glasses before asking, "What made you decide to take a trip on your own on the luxury cruise liner, *Sea Force?*"

Even knowing the question was coming, my heart sinks because I know of all the subsequent questions that are going to follow.

Cal was wrong. I was wrong. To keep raking this over the coals punishes more than just us.

Taking a deep breath, I admit, "Because I was certain my marriage was over."

After all, when a communication breakdown occurs in most marriages, there's always a ripple effect. But when it occurs on the international stage, and it involves a coordinated military rescue, well, the ripples are the size of a tsunami.

Plucking at my dress, a dress I chose to wear because it has sunflowers scattered on it, I remember the days leading up to when Cal gave them to me for the first time. It was right at the end of college, and every day seemed as beautiful outside as this one.

ELIZABETH

FIFTEEN YEARS AGO FROM PRESENT DAY

Calhoun Sullivan. Just thinking his name sends tingles through my body the likes of which I've never understood.

It all started a few months ago when after months of being in his class, my cousin Sam brought Cal out to dinner when he met up with me at the local diner on campus. "Libs, Cal," he introduced us before dropping into the seat next to me.

When our hands touched for the first time, a frisson ran up my spine. My body locked as I met his brown eyes beneath furrowed brows. It was in complete contrast to the abrupt "Libby" he gave me before sitting.

Sam and Cal began talking—no, debating—about politics in earnest that night. Tuning their words out, I instead listened to the lazy cadence of both of their voices, wondering exactly how quickly I could manage to escape without being rude. Finally, I shifted uncomfortably in my seat. "Don't take this the wrong way—" I offered them both a smile. "—but I have an exam to prepare for tomorrow."

"Crap, Libs. I was going to..." Sam was utterly contrite as he was going to help me study.

Pushing at his shoulder gently, I grabbed my bag and slid out of the seat. "Nothing to apologize for. You're not always going to be there for me to lean on."

A flash of something crossed Sam's face. "No, but I'm here now."

Leaning upward, I brushed my lips across his cheek. "And after I pass this test, you can take me out to make it up to me." Looking over my shoulder, I tossed a "Nice to meet you" to Cal with a smile.

He didn't say anything. His dark head just tipped in my direction with a murmured "Libby."

That was the first time I saw Cal, but it wasn't the last. Over the next few weeks, Cal would accompany Sam to our weekly dinners. Then, as I was not so subtly trying to play matchmaker between my cousin and my roommate, Cal would be at dinners, on hikes, around concerts. It became obvious to me that my cousin, who didn't have many close friends growing up, had found someone he trusted and liked in Cal.

And if I fell in love just a little more every moment I had to spend in his presence, well, that became my problem.

We've laughed, joked, teased each other for months. As friends, we've argued current events, talked about sports, and made plans with no indication he's ever seen me as anything more than what I am—Sam's cousin. So, it's my fault if I lie in my bed late at night dreaming of what it would be like to have his dark caress on my skin. It's not like he's helping himself to a smorgasbord of undergraduates. As much as I might want him to with this undergrad, I think glumly.

It doesn't matter—it's never going to happen. At least, there's nothing giving me any sort of hope it will.

Shifting, I lift a glass of less-than-stellar wine to my lips. At least now that I'm old enough to drink, I can drown the agony of the rumors of how he fucks like the end of the world is coming before he rolls out of whatever bed he's in.

I smile into my glass before an elbow to my ribs almost causes me to upend the entire thing. "You rang?" I ask my best friend, Iris Cunningham, drolly.

"Is it just me, or is Sam taking on more and more of Cal's behavior traits?" Iris has had a crush on my cousin since the day she met him, not that it's stopped her from dating half of the male population on campus.

I, on the other hand, took one look at Cal and felt like time stood still. When we're all together—which is more and more of late—I feel like it's my mission to make the somber-faced man crack a smile. I've yet to succeed, but hey, at least Iris appreciates my efforts as she normally collapses on Sam howling. I still have time, I think determinedly, as there's still a few weeks before I graduate and head home to Charleston.

Turning to answer Iris, I ask, "Do you mean the man-whoring?"

Iris grins. "Your cousin has a way to go for that," she teases, inadvertently sending a swift pain in the region of my stomach. Pushing my wine aside, knowing I'll be ill if I drink any more of it, I ask, "Elaborate, please."

"Look at them." She tips her head to the side. Glancing over her shoulder, she continues. "They're a pair of matched emo bookends holding up the collective honeypot of campus."

I burst into gales of laughter. "Lord, deliver me," I wheeze out. My drawl is more pronounced than it normally is.

The devil that dances in Iris's eyes is more wicked than normal. "You know you're going to miss every second we're not doing just this."

"Too true, darling." I lift my glass to toast the best part of my college experience when I feel a mysterious pull from the far side of the room. Allowing my eyes to flicker in that direction, they clash with Cal's. This time there's something different about them.

They're crinkled around the corners, and one side is hitched up. He's not looking down at the woman he'll likely take home later, I think with my heart pounding. He's watching me. And whether it's wishful thinking or not, he lifts his beer in my direction to toast me.

Without thinking, I send a beaming smile in his direction. Taking a deep breath, I lift the glass to my lips and manage to swallow a little more of the lighter fluid they pass off as wine.

"What was that all about?" Iris demands. She starts to turn around, but I stop her by pinching her. Hard.

"I...I'm not really sure," I admit.

"What do you mean?"

"One minute, I'm laughing with you and the next, Cal's..." I don't get to finish my sentence because Iris has whipped around.

Cal's gone and so's the cute blonde. I'm not shocked neither by their departure nor by my feelings of disappointment. Iris prompts, "Cal was?"

"Nothing. It's nothing." I wave my hand to indicate the subject's closed, but I didn't take into account the subject sliding into the booth next to me. Iris's eyes bug out.

What the hell's happening here? Am I asleep and this is a beautiful dream? Surreptitiously, I pinch my arm. Nope. I'm awake.

"Hey, Libby. Iris. You both seem to be having quite the evening over here." Cal's dark voice sends every nerve ending on red alert.

"Well, you know us, Cal. We know how to enjoy ourselves." As soon as the words pass her lips, Iris looks like she got goose-egged herself when Sam slides into the booth on her side.

He smiles easily at me. "Cousin, do you know what to do with the trouble sitting next to you?"

"Who says I plan on doing anything?" I drawl, earning a loud guffaw from Sam and Iris.

Cal just looks thoughtful.

"I have big news," Sam announces.

"Oh, what's that?" I lean forward eagerly. Although I have an older brother, Sam and I being mere months apart in age, we were raised practically as twins.

"I got a job," he announces proudly.

A thrilled gasp escapes my lips. Suddenly, I'm shoving at Cal. "Get out of my way," I demand. "I need to congratulate him."

"Don't you want to hear what it is?" Cal asks with a bemused expression.

I'm still shoving at his shoulder even as I contemplate climbing over the table. "It doesn't matter. Look at him." I beam when I do. "He's so happy right now, he's lighting up the room."

Cal hesitates for just a second, murmuring, "I think that's you who's doing that, Libby." But he slides out of the booth so I can make my way over to Sam to hug him.

"I am so, so proud of you. Was it that government contractor you were telling me about? The one with offices overseas? Confederation?"

Sam chuckles as he squeezes the breath out of me. When did the scrawny boy who used to fish while I read on the banks of the Cooper River grow up? I bury my head against his shoulder to avoid those memories right now, knowing we'll never have those carefree days again. "Alliance, and yes. That's the one."

"When will you tell the family?" He lets me go. I turn to slide back into the booth only to be startled. Cal's been standing waiting patiently for us to finish. Slipping past him, I sit back down.

It must be my imagination that he slides a little closer when he sits back down himself.

"I wanted to tell you first. I'll call Mom and Dad sometime tomorrow," Sam tells me.

"Good." I flash a grin at him. "I want to be able to tell my parents I knew before they did."

Sam leans over and tweaks my nose. "What about you? Are you still heading back to Charleston after graduation?"

I nod. I've known what I've wanted for my life since the first day I ever entered Stafford Antiques with Nonna. Miss Julie gave me cookies and a tour of her store, telling me where all the beautiful treasures were from. And I imagined if I had all the money in the world, where I would put them in my house. It wasn't long after, I began to redecorate first my room, then my parents' home, and eventually Nonna's home on the estate with an emphasis on our family heirlooms.

"I've been waiting for this moment since I was six, Sam." We both exchange grins at the truth of my statement. "It's time."

"Time? Time for what?" Cal's demanding question forces me to turn toward him.

I shrug before picking up my drink. Wrinkling my nose, I attempt another sip. "I'm a dual major, fine arts and business. I've got plans of my own."

Pursing his lips at my nonanswer, Cal plucks my drink out of my hand—my drink! Taking a swallow, he mutters, "You need to be drinking better than this."

I shrug. "It's what I can afford." At least on a student budget, which I'm determined to live on while I'm here.

"I can afford better." Flagging down a waitress, he orders me a glass of wine—the brand I would normally drink at home. Before she can escape, he asks Sam and Iris, "Anything else?"

Iris holds up her almost empty beer. "I'll take another."

Sam shakes his head. "I'm driving."

"That will do it, then. Thanks." Cal dismisses the harried woman before turning his not-insubstantial attention back to me.

I'm stunned and a little taken aback. "I was okay with what I had."

Flicking a stray hair away from my face, he shrugs as if it's no big deal. Then again, to him, it probably isn't, I remind myself. He brings us back around to what we were discussing as he polishes off the dredges of the drink I'd been nursing. "So, a dual major? That's impressive. Do you already have a job lined up back in Charleston?"

I duck my head. It's not something I share with a lot of people. "Less of a job, more of a dream."

"I like the idea of you having dreams, Libby." My head snaps up. An arc of something different moves between us. We're butting up against a line I stopped daring to toe up against.

Then I know I'm not imagining the brief flit of a smile that crosses his lips after the new wine is put down in between us and he takes a sip before I can even reach for it. Handing it to me, his voice drops as he says, "Much better. It tastes like something the sun actually kissed versus something it killed."

The comment is so outrageous, I toss my hair back and laugh. When I finish, Cal's still smiling. I reach for the wine and declare flippantly, "You should smile more. You're incredibly handsome when you do."

Even though Cal's smile fades—a terrible shame—the words he whispers in my ear will make me remember that smile forever.

"Since you're going to be leaving soon, I suppose it's safe to tell you the only time I ever think about smiling is when I'm around you."

He sits back and rests an arm over the back of the booth, leaving me frozen in place.

Why would he say that to me? Why now when we've got less than two weeks left until I leave?

Picking up the wine, I take a long drink and hate that he's right. It does taste like liquid sunlight. And I'll never be able to drink it again without thinking of him.

3

CALHOUN

FIFTEEN YEARS AGO FROM PRESENT DAY

Libby Akin is causing me to lose sleep and not in a way that gives me any sort of satisfaction.

I roll over and punch my pillow in the off-campus apartment I live in, unable to stop thinking of her mahogany-brown hair and gem-colored eyes. While I'm recovering from a few injuries I sustained on my last assignment, I was sent here to scout out and recruit candidates for Alliance. Both of our time here is almost over.

It's why I haven't touched her the way I've been dying to.

But God, what I wouldn't give to have her beautiful smile warm the cold dark parts of me. It's impossible not to know when she's in the vicinity, and that's not simply when I'm around her cousin. All I have to do is walk out the political science building where a former Alliance employee contacted the Admiral six months ago about a few potential recruits and wham! I know she's there when her laughter peals out above the melee of students.

When she touches me, even if it's in the most innocent of ways, my skin tingles. My heart rate starts to accelerate faster than if I've just clocked five miles. And my cock? It's harder than if one of the women I've fucked since I've been here has lavished attention on it for hours.

Because it's just Libby. And the truth is she's the only thing I've ever wanted in a life where I've been given nothing.

Rolling onto my back, I make out the whirring blades of the ceiling fan in the dark. At least this assignment comes with a bed, I think ruefully. The last one involved sleeping bags and sand for much longer than I enjoyed. Rubbing the heel of one calloused foot up my leg to feel the scar, I remember the blisters I suffered as the fine sand of the Middle Eastern desert found its way into my combat boots. Pain in the ass. Sand doesn't come out of anything. I'm certain I was still shitting it when the Admiral told me I was coming here; I ate so much of it. But it was worth it. We managed to rescue the Bahraini ambassador's son without starting an international incident.

At twenty-eight, I've done more than I ever expected to do in this life. I've visited more countries on the map than most people have heard of, many of which I couldn't even identify in my youth growing up in a foster home after my mother decided she'd had enough of motherhood after three short days and abandoned me in a gas station in nowheresville Georgia.

While my resume officially reads I'm a member of the National Guard, the reality is I've worked for Alliance since my junior year of college. At the beginning, I interned for the Charleston-based company doing nothing but admin work. It was one of our former team leaders who noticed me staying late and studying mission reports with hungry eyes. "That mission was completed FUBARed," he drawled. "See anything you would have done differently, Cal?"

My guard was up, because I was uncertain if I was in trouble for reviewing the materials. But I was cleared to read them. After all, part of my job was to make certain they ended up in the right hands. But still, I answered honestly. "Your point man gave away your position, whether he intended to or not. You need to rework your signal process," I told him bluntly.

He acknowledged my feedback with a brisk nod before walking out the door without another word. I was certain I was fucked the next day when I was called into Ret. Admiral Richard Yarborough's office. Yarborough, the owner of Alliance, was and is not a man to fuck with. A former SEAL, he was taken out due to a shot to the leg that shattered his kneecap. Unwilling to sit on the sidelines, he brought together a coalition of the best civilians to operate with permission of the government to go where they can't due to negotiated treaties and peace agreements.

Alliance has never been limited by such boundaries.

"So, I hear I have a mole, Sullivan?"

"What...what do you mean, sir?" I stuttered. He spun his chair around to face me.

"Byers called me last night and said you spotted what he didn't. The signals were compromised—we could have lost brave men and women out there." He gestures to a chair in front of his mammoth desk. "Please sit."

I did, not because he asked me, but because my legs were so filled with jelly, I was afraid I was going to fall down. "Maybe it's because I'm removed from it all," I offered.

He snorted. "Bullshit, son. It's because you have an aptitude for this business. Now, have you ever heard of OCS?"

My face paled. "Is that another company?" Alliance was the only family I knew. I didn't want to leave.

"Officer Candidate School, Cal. We're going to get you in as soon as you graduate. Then"—Yarborough's eyes gleamed with unholy amusement—"we're going to get you out."

I finished college at twenty, OCS by the time I was twenty-one. And by the time I was twenty-three, there was an "accident" that required a medical discharge requiring me to be released out of my five-year commitment to the Navy. At least that's what Yarborough arranged.

Since then, I've traveled the world anywhere Alliance has sent me—including my current assignment on this college campus. Here, the "professor" became the student in so many ways, and I begin to wonder if Yarborough didn't arrange for that knife to slice into me. Before, I never understood when we'd try to rescue families with the guarantee of asylum, they would elect to live in the bowels of poverty. "You no understand. Wife gone." Then they'd turn away, asking only for the food and medical supplies we'd readily offer to leave when we were willing to offer them so much more. I witnessed people crying over loved ones, and while I felt compassion, I never understood their heartbreak.

Not until a smile more powerful than the sun started lighting the dark corners of my heart.

For the first time, I understood why men would break allegiance, disregard political survival, and beg for mercy. But I know better than to reach out for it. After all, as Yarborough once said, "Peace is a facade we convince our families of so they can sleep at night. Right, Sullivan?"

My laconic "I don't have a family" earned me a slap on the back. It might be the first and last time being an orphan was a bonus. Forget about the years of looking at the door every time there was a knock wondering if it was someone coming to claim me—as if I meant something to someone.

For once meaning nothing to anyone seemed a bonus when Yarborough said, "Good. Then there's nothing anyone can hold over you."

Rolling to my side, I realize it was a mistake to touch the silk of Libby's hair tonight. Now, I'll never forget what the strands felt like between my fingers. Angry, I grab my phone, determined to find a way to forget her.

But even as my finger hovers over the buttons, I find myself going to my photos. Flipping through, I find a picture I snapped of Libby when she was sitting on the walls of the quad. Someone had just dropped a pile of leaves over her head. Instead of being angry and seeking retaliation, something I likely would have done, she reached down and threw them up in the air again with a laugh. God, her beauty hurts my heart. Her smile is the kind that would bring me to my knees if I'd met her in a different life.

"Somehow you're always seeking the sun. It's too bad I live in the shadows." Closing the phone, I toss it onto the nightstand, determined to get some sleep.

I need to be up early for a run with our newest recruit tomorrow at 0500.

❀

"You're a sadistic bitch, Cal," Sam pants next to me. He's running in wingtips per today's instructions. I have little doubt his feet are going to be blistered later.

I smirk, my breathing easy as we take another hill. No one's up this early to hear his suffering. "What if you had to run for your life, Sam? You're not always going to be in running sneakers and compression socks."

"That's not why you suck," he mutters.

I'm unperturbed when I ask, "Not that I care, but curiosity has me now. Why am I a sadist?"

"A sadistic bitch," he corrects. I'm pleased to see his breathing has evened out. He doesn't answer me for a few as our shoes slap along the old gravel road I chose specifically for its rough terrain. "It's because you make this look so easy," he says.

I jolt to a stop, so of course Sam does too. "Sam," I reply carefully. "I've been doing this for seven years, three of those in the military. You're coming straight into Alliance because you're a fucking genius with a computer. We just don't want you to end up dead in the process of working out in the field."

"I know. That would piss Libby and our family off to no end."

Shaking my head, I begin running again with Sam keeping pace. "You're the oddest person I've ever recruited."

"Yeah, but I bet I'm the only one who has a family member you've got the hots for," he says cheerfully.

And I trip. Fortunately, I catch myself before I go down on the sharp stones lining the trail. "Jesus Christ," I growl.

Sam laughs at me. "So, what are you going to do about it?"

"Nothing."

Disappointment etches his face. "Why not?"

16

Rubbing the back of my neck, I glare at him. "Because it's not a good decision."

"Hmm." Sam stretches.

Smart man, I think approvingly as I begin to do the same. But the silence that stretches out between us starts to annoy me. "What?" I finally ask.

"I never took you for a coward," he says offhandedly.

My muscles all lock. "Excuse me?"

He backs away. "Now, Cal, I just meant in terms of matters of this. You're a badass."

Fucking right I am. "Better run, Sam. If I catch up, there's going to be hell to pay," I warn him in a lethal voice.

He takes off in a sprint.

I take a moment to rub my hand over my chest where the shot he landed aimed true. I am a coward when it comes to Libby Akin. I want her so damn much, I'm afraid of what will happen when I have to leave.

And I always do. There's always more risk, another mission, another life to protect.

I just wish I could take a piece of her with me.

Jogging after Sam, I see him a few hundred yards ahead with his head between his legs. When he sees me, he straightens before sprinting away. Even though I hadn't planned on educating him on evasive techniques this morning, it looks like Sam's about to get a small lesson in it.

EVERY SUNDAY SINCE I STARTED WORKING HERE LAST SEMESTER, THERE'S been a local farmer's market in town. Normally, I go first thing in the morning so I can beat the students who end up coming down later in the day. But now that I'm training Sam, I don't make it until 10:30. I race through, picking up fresh fruit and vegetables for the week, before I make my way for the exit.

I freeze in place when I see Libby. Juggling my packages, I manage to get my phone out and snap a picture of her surrounded by flowers. It may be my imagination, but she laughs at something the elderly woman says, and the sunflowers seem to reach for her. "Beautiful," I murmur aloud.

Libby accepts a bouquet of purple flowers wrapped in cellophane with another smile before turning her back and walking away. In her arms she's also managing a cake box with a carefully wrapped present on top.

Dialing quickly, I hear, "Didn't you torture me enough this morning?" growled by Sam in my ear.

"Is it a special occasion for Libby?" I ask without answering him.

"Not that I know of." He sounds confused.

"Birthday, anniversary of an important date? I can find out, but I'd prefer you think."

"It's not her birthday, Cal. That's October 1st."

I commit the date to my memory and then ask, "Then why is she carrying a cake, a bouquet of flowers, and…"

With a yelp, Sam yells, "What kind of flowers?"

"I don't know. They were purple."

"They were irises, Cal. It's Iris's birthday! Shit, I can't walk, and I need to go to her birthday dinner at Libby's."

"Go take a shower. I'll pick up some flowers for you to bring to her and drop them by with some Tiger Balm." His relieved sigh worries me a bit. "Are you going to be able to let her go?" Sam's growing feelings for Libby's best friend are starting to concern me.

"Let her go? I don't have to. You tagged her to be recruited as well. Remember, one of your colleagues is training her" is all he says before he hangs up the phone.

Huh. I forgot we don't have a no-fraternization policy. But now I'll have to do some deeper digging on Ms. Iris Cunningham when I get back to my apartment to make certain recruiting them both isn't going to be a colossal mistake. In the meanwhile, I approach the same flower vendor Libby just vacated. "Hello. I need a bouquet of flowers for a birthday."

"Seems to be the specialty of the day." The woman smiles. "Do you know what kind of flowers?"

"Something unique but lovely." The woman nods before turning away. Soon, she presents me with a bouquet that Sam will be proud to give Iris. I'm pulling out my card to pay when suddenly I ask, "Can you also make me up a bouquet of sunflowers?"

I must be crazy. That's the only way to explain it.

"Of course. Give me just one more moment." Soon, I have a gorgeous bunch of sunflowers in my arms. A smile spreads across the woman's face as she runs my card through. "They're such a happy flower."

"Hmm?" I'm too busy looking at the bright cheerful flowers in my arms. In their own way, it's like holding a piece of Libby.

"Sunflowers. They symbolize adoration, loyalty, and longevity, but overall they just make people happy," I'm informed.

A little stunned, I scrawl my name on the receipt and pocket the card. "That they do." But my mind is on Libby, not the flowers. "Thank you."

"Anytime."

4

ELIZABETH

FIFTEEN YEARS AGO FROM PRESENT DAY

"Y̶ou're the best friend ever, Libby Akin." Iris throws herself into my arms after reading my card.

I hug her back fiercely. "Love you."

"Love you more." She wipes her eyes. "Now, are you going to tell me who you've been cooking for all day?"

Standing, I shake my head no. "Do you want me to put your flowers in a vase?"

"Yes. Just tell me this: do I need to change?"

I give Iris a once-over. She's wearing a backless T-shirt and ripped jeans. Without betraying who's coming over for dinner, I shrug. "You look hot." And she does. Iris has black curly hair and dancing hazel eyes. Her beauty is only eclipsed by her natural ability to speak languages, something she picked up from her native-speaking Lakota grandmother and Irish grandfather. To date, she speaks five fluently and is determined to conquer Mandarin.

One of the many reasons I wish Sam would stop looking at the computers that have captured his devotion his whole life and broaden his horizons to see what's waiting right in front of him is because I don't think I've ever met anyone with as big of a brain as his until I met my roommate. Then I let it go. If they're meant to be, they're meant to be. I was only mildly surprised when Sam and Cal came to sit with us at the bar last night. If Sam's interested, tonight's dinner will be a dead giveaway.

And just as I reach the kitchen, the doorbell rings. "That must be our surprise guest," I tease Iris.

"You're such a brat," she accuses from her place on the couch.

"You've lived with me for four years and you're just getting that idea?" I glide to the door to open it—and receive the shock of my life. Because it's not just Sam there holding flowers, which fills me with joy.

Cal's with him. I swallow my jealousy when I see he's holding a bouquet of flowers as well. "Come on in, gentlemen. I hope you both like shrimp and grits." I accept Sam's kiss on the cheek.

Even as he makes his way over toward a stunned Iris, Sam calls out, "Nonna's recipe?"

I cross my arms over my chest. "Is there any other way?"

He lets out a whoop that causes a bubble of laughter to escape. But a sigh of pleasure escapes when Sam leans down, brushes his lips across Iris's cheek, and lays the flowers in her arms. She flushes before her eyes drop. I watch her lips form the words "Thank you" before she crushes the flowers between them, giving him a hug.

Cal steps up behind me. Without turning around, I swallow my ridiculous jealousy and say, "It's a good thing you brought her more flowers." Facing him, I force the smile on my lips to reach my eyes. "I have a feeling she doesn't realize the ones she just got from Sam are getting crushed."

I step to the side so I can check on the food in the kitchen when Cal's arm hooks around my waist, reeling me back to stand in front of him. I tip my head back. "If you don't let me go, dinner's going to burn," I tease gently.

He cocks his head to the side before murmuring, "These are for you, Libby. Thank you. Sam invited me to crash dinner tonight." He lays a bouquet of sunflowers in my arms. The beauty of the bright yellow flowers almost blinds me. It's completely unexpected.

"For me? But...I don't understand. It's not my birthday," I stammer.

"They reminded me of you. Now"—Cal changes the subject —"what can I do to help?"

I open and close my mouth several times before getting my head together. "Come on into the kitchen while I put these away. I'll give you the wine to open."

"Hopefully it's not that same crap you were drinking last night," Cal mutters.

"It's Iris's birthday. I sprang for a decent bottle," I reassure him.

"Thank God."

What can I do but laugh?

HOURS LATER, WE'VE DEVOURED THE MEAL, THE WINE, AND IRIS'S birthday cake. Sadly, our oven doesn't lend itself well to baking or I'd have made that as well. Sam and Iris are talking out on our minuscule porch while I finish clearing the table. "Please let that work," I whisper.

"Let what work?" Startled, I jump when Cal appears in the kitchen.

Laying a soapy, wet hand on my shirt, I gasp, "You scared me. I thought you were still in the bathroom."

He ignores me and advances. "Let what work?" he asks again.

Instead of giving him the verbal answer he wants, I nod toward the porch where Sam and Iris can just be made out. "They're perfect for each other. Both of them are so brilliant in different ways."

"So he's mentioned."

Turning to face the sink, I ask casually, "In all this time, do you realize neither Sam nor you ever fully explained how you became friends?"

"I was his professor last semester. It's not lost on you, your cousin's a brilliant guy. Taught me a thing or two," Cal says ruefully.

I grin because that sounds like Sam. "At least tell me he chose to educate you in private."

"If you have a towel, I'll dry," he offers, leaning a hip next to where I'm washing the dishes.

I shake my head. "You're a guest. Nonna would have me horse-whipped."

Cal gets close and whispers, "Your nonna's not here, and I'm not going to tell."

I lean forward until our foreheads are almost touching. "No, but Sam is, and he's often a tattletale to look better in her eyes. It never works though."

"Because you're a good girl?" His voice is lazy and seductive.

I don't know what's pounding more, my heart or the throbbing between my legs at the teasing. "I'll never tell. You have to figure it out for yourself."

A tension-filled silence descends between us. I've washed and set aside a few plates before I hear Cal say, "I'd like to."

I must have misheard him. "Excuse me?"

He reaches over and turns off the water. "I've wanted to get to know you better for a long time."

I turn the water back on and reach for a new dish. "Interesting way of showing it."

He takes the plate out of my hand and turns the water off again. "I'm being serious."

I turn the water on again. "So am I, Cal. I refuse to be a conquest in your bed. I'm worth more than that."

This time when he turns off the water, he turns me to face him. "I've never given flowers to a woman. I've never wanted to. I never looked at them and saw the essence of her in them. But when I was at the farmer's market this morning and saw you standing above them, they seemed to be reaching for you." He tucks a loose piece of hair behind my ear.

My breathing increases. "Why now?"

"Because I've lain awake for too many nights wondering what it would be like."

My head drops to the side. Cal leans in and whispers against my ear, "Take a chance before we run out of time."

Damn him. "All right. When?" If I'm doing this, I'm locking him into a date.

"Is tomorrow too soon?" My head flies back up, and my head almost collides with his. Everything I ever secretly longed for is on his face.

Including a smile.

"I told you I didn't want to wait," he murmurs just as his head lowers. But before he can kiss me, the slider opens as a happy-sounding Iris comes inside in front of Sam, who's grinning. Cal's forehead drops against mine. "Do you really like Sam, or can I just kill him? Because his timing sucks."

The mild annoyance combined with frustration in his words makes me laugh. "He is my favorite cousin. I might get upset if something happens to him."

"Fine," he grumbles. Kissing my forehead, he steps out of the kitchen. "Say six tomorrow?"

Leaving my spot at the sink, I enter the doorway between the two rooms. "I look forward to it, Cal."

"Me too. Sam, you ready?"

Sam groans. "Yeah." He grins at Iris, whose face just melts in pleasure. "Tomorrow night?"

"Absolutely," she agrees.

Well, well, well, I think smugly.

Cal's arm slides around my waist and squeezes. I tip my head back and smile. "Thank you for everything."

"Yeah, thanks, Libby," Sam chimes in before he ducks out the door.

With a quick squeeze, Cal follows him.

After the door closes, Iris and I give it to the count of ten before we both shriek, "I have a date!"

Then we shout, "You have a date?"

That's when we jump into each other's arms and hug the hell out of each other.

5

ELIZABETH

FIFTEEN YEARS AGO FROM PRESENT DAY

"I'm not sure if I agreed to go out on this date because Cal gave me sunflowers or because he smiled at me," I say to Iris.

"Calhoun Sullivan doesn't smile, Libs," she scoffs. "Despite your verbal confirmation of it."

"It's happened more than once." I stroke the petals of the blooms now sitting in a variety of bud vases we'd collected over the years in our off-campus rental. "It was…"

"What?" She leans her elbows on the island dividing us.

"Disarming. He comes off as this tough broody guy, completely not my type."

Iris snorts. "Not everyone is straight out of a fairy tale."

My fingers are flirting with the edges of the flower. "I didn't say they had to be. What I meant was I like someone who will talk with me. On the other hand, Cal doesn't strike me as the type to lay it all out there over a couple of beers. I mean, really, personal choice aside, is a first date the right time to announce you just got pierced?" I'm still bewildered by the conversation gambit of the blind date I went on last weekend.

Iris's laughter rings out. "You mean like…"

I nod furiously. "Oh, yes. Matt said something about too much grain in the punch at the Delta Sig party, and the next thing he knew, he woke up with a ladder." Over the screeching sounds being made, I try to retain my composure. "My question to him was, 'Are you drinking it now? Is this why you're telling me?'"

We're both past the point of no return laughing when there's a knock at our door. I'm still giggling as I cross the room toward it. "I mean, is this what I should expect when I go out tonight with...Cal." I breathe his name when I open the door.

"No, Libs, I don't think this is what you have to...umph!" I jam my elbow into Iris's stomach. "Oh, hey, Cal." She gives him a weak wave.

"Iris." Is it wrong that I love how he acknowledges my gorgeous best friend with only a nod all while his eyes never leave my face? "Hey, Libby. Busy?"

"We were just..." I step back to let him inside but find myself backing into my best friend.

"Doing absolutely nothing. In fact, we were doing so much nothing, I was thinking about studying for that poli-sci test you said we're going to have, Cal."

His dark eyes flick over to her for just a moment. "You mean the one you took Friday?" He arches a brow.

I want to smack my face into the palm of my hand at Iris's obvious behavior. I limit myself to just a small sigh that can either be interpreted as "You're a moron," "I can't believe he's here early!" or maybe, "What are you still doing here?"

Then again, it could be all three.

Iris quickly extracts herself from her mistake. "I think I bombed it. I'm going to hit the books again. Libs, call if you need me."

"Oh, I'll be sure to," I let all the love, humor, and irony fill my voice as she quickly escapes leaving me standing in the open doorway with Calhoun Sullivan. "Would you like to come in?"

"Sure." Cal seems to take up not just space but air as he comes into our living room. I have to keep telling myself he's just another guy when something is constantly pulling me toward him.

"I thought we said six?"

"You don't have a vase?"

"You came by to visit your flowers? I know they're not touching anymore, but they live close by. Think of them as graduating from high school sunflowers to college sunflowers; you have to let them live alone sometime," I sass.

Before I started talking, the darkly brooding look was back on his face, making me wonder if he wasn't getting ready to change his mind on our date. By the time I'm done, he's right in front of me. He tips my chin up just a bit before giving me that heart-stopping smile for the second time in one day. "What am I going to do with you, Libby?"

I look at him thoughtfully before answering, "Worry about laugh lines like the rest of us. If you keep losing that Zoolander look you have going on, you're going to get them."

Suddenly, I'm wrapped in Cal's arms as he barks out a rusty laugh. I snuggle in for just a moment because laughter is more special when you can feel it against someone.

"See? That wasn't so painful," I tease.

His twists in agony for just a moment. "This isn't the right time in my life for me to meet a girl like you," he flat out tells me.

"First, I'm a woman, not a girl. And second, what kind of woman is that?"

"The kind that touches my heart. The kind that makes me want to stay."

"What makes you have to go?" I wonder aloud. "We all have weeks before we have to leave."

He shakes his head, not answering me. Reaching up, he pushes a lock of hair behind my ear. Leaning down, he whispers his lips across my cheek, barely a caress. It's still enough to send me in a haze. His skin smells warm from being out in the quarter earlier mixed with the citrusy scent of his cologne and something else.

"We were talking about sunflowers," I whisper.

"I'll never be able to look at them again without thinking of this moment."

Pulling back, I close my eyes for just a moment. Opening them, I say flatly, "I appreciate your courtesy in coming by, but really all you had to do was call if you didn't want to go out on our date."

"The problem, sweet Libby, is I very much do. I just can't." He doesn't offer me any further explanation.

I don't see fit to give him any when I pull out of his arms to walk to the door, holding it open for him. "Thank you for coming by, Cal."

He walks straight to the door, only hesitating when he's aligned with me. "Libby, I'm a professor. I'm years older than you." As if those words are magically going to explain why I'm going to spend the night with a box of Kleenex and a tub of ice cream instead of him.

Instead I acknowledge, "I'm well aware of that."

He tries for patience. "I was in the military; I'm still part of the National Guard, and I got called up on assignment. I got the notice this morning after I went out for a run. I have seventy-two hours to report in."

His words cause a different kind of agony inside my chest because he's trying to take the time to reassure me asking me out was important to him.

"Was this important to you?" I wonder aloud.

And a moment later, the door is being wrenched away from my hand as Cal pulls me into his body. "It would be so much easier if it wasn't."

Our mouths are mere millimeters from each other as he bows his head. But I know if our lips touch now, there's no way he'll leave without branding me more than he already has.

I reach out and stroke his chest. "Keep in touch."

He hesitates a second before he steps back with a smile. "You email me. I'll write back when I can."

"Is that a promise?" I tease him. "Because maybe by the time you get back to Charleston, I'll need some new sunflowers."

He drags his fingers down my cheek. "I will. I promise. And I don't make them easily."

My eyes are unblinking on his. "You don't?"

"No, damnit, I don't." I don't move, afraid if I do, I'll break whatever spell is holding him bound to me instead of to whatever is trying to pull him away.

For long moments we're frozen, until Cal finally rasps, "God, my life? It's always about shitty timing," before he walks through the door, closing it softly behind him.

Leaning my head forward to rest on it, I whisper, "Yes, until the unexpected happens and someone brings you flowers. Then it's a matter of waiting until you get more."

Then with tears on my lashes, I duck into the bathroom before Iris converges on it to get ready for her date with Sam.

6

ELIZABETH

FIFTEEN YEARS AGO FROM PRESENT DAY

Dear Cal,

It's been a few months since graduation; I hope this finds you safe and well.

Sam came home briefly but has moved into an apartment closer to where his company is based. It's unusual not to have him just a few moments away. In fact, I can't remember the last time we spoke on the phone. When we last chatted, he said his training was going well, but it was consuming a lot of hours. I know he was planning on coming back for a family celebration we're planning on having soon.

Iris took a brief vacation, but I know she's at a specialized training facility to enhance her language studies. She hasn't said much, but it wouldn't surprise me if she ends up going to work for some major international corporation or the government. I'm so proud of her.

As for me? Well, my plans are slow but sure. I'm being very methodical. Too much is on the line for me to make mistakes. I'm in no major rush. I've been working for a small firm in Charleston and saving money by living at home. Trust me, that's no hardship. We're very close, and the location is convenient to town.

I don't know what I'm allowed to ask about your present situation, where you are, how things are. I'd love to be able to send you and the men and *women in your unit something, but I'm not certain what the rules are. Email me back to let me know.*

Know I can't walk past sunflowers in the farmer's market without thinking of you.

Stay safe and know you are missed.

Libby

Before pressing Send, I reread the first email I'm about to send off to Cal. I chew on my lower lip. I haven't heard from him, but I have no idea what it is that he's actually doing. I suppose I could ask Sam, but he's in training. Other than Nonna's birthday last month, I've barely heard from him either.

Oh, how I wish I could pick up the phone and call Iris, but according to the letter I just got in the mail, the intensive language program in Monterey has her "submerged deeper than I ever thought I would be, Libs. If you can believe it, I actually want to hear *just* an American accent."

While I was amused by her letter, I'm left in this odd space. My heart is lost trying to find its place between what was and what is while my mind is ready to forge ahead straight into the future.

Pressing Send, I give no more thought to the email as I answer the business line.

"Thank you for calling Salt Gallery. This is Elizabeth. How may I help you?"

7

ELIZABETH

FOURTEEN YEARS AGO FROM
PRESENT DAY

Hello Cal.

Iris came home today from her training in California. She was over the moon when she told me she'd taken a position with Alliance alongside Sam. I'm so excited the two of them will be working with each other. Honestly, I don't think there's anyone who quite understands my excitement the way you would.

I haven't heard back from you. Not once. Please don't take that as complaining; it's not. It's just one of my relatives mentioned you may have a military email address which—depending on where you're stationed—may be the only thing you can check. So, you may not be getting the emails I've been sending.

I just wish I knew for certain if you were well.

Things are changing here so fast! I took a <u>MAJOR</u> step toward accomplishing my dream last week. I haven't even told my family yet because they're going to flip. To be honest, I was going to tell Sam first, but he was out of the country again. Well, when he's back for more than a day, I'll let him know.

If you're getting these, send me a quick ping somehow to let me know you're okay. I've included all of my contact information at the bottom of the *email. I'm also going to be switching to a new business email soon. When I do, I'll be sure to let you know.*

All my best,

Libby

I finish typing in my new email contact information for Deja Vu. Even though the company paperwork has just been filed, I made certain I owned the email domain. Pushing away from my desk at Salt for the last time, a small, self-satisfied smile crosses my face.

I'm going to do it.

My phone rings. My heart begins to pound. Not so quickly after I just sent the message, surely... "Thank you for calling Salt Gallery. This is Elizabeth. How may I help you?" Even as I say the words, they seem odd rolling off my tongue.

I don't belong here anymore.

"Hey, Libs," Josh, my older brother by three and a half years, drawls. "Do you need an escort to the ball tonight? It would not be a hardship to have two beautiful women on my arm," he teases.

Since I'm well aware his wife, Bailey, will be on the other side, I merely roll my eyes and hold my tongue. Tonight is Nonna's annual charity ball. "I'll accept the arm to walk in with the heels I'm wearing, you dork. After that, I plan to enjoy myself all on my own. I'm a grown woman," I remind him.

"Stop reminding me. I'm getting sick of warning off all the idiots who work for us," he mutters.

"Then stop warning them off."

"Like that will ever happen."

"I'll see you at seven?" I check my personal email one last time, but it's empty. There's nothing in the inbox.

And, my heart is beginning to realize, there may never be.

So much for flowery promises, I think bitterly, as I close the lid of the laptop smartly.

"Just promise me you're not going to fall for some yahoo," Josh groans.

"I wouldn't bet the estate on it," I tease him breezily, before I hang up the phone in his ear. Gathering up my purse, I say goodbye to my boss, thank her again for the wonderful opportunity she gave me.

And then I leave to try to fall in love with my future.

8

ELIZABETH

THIRTEEN YEARS AGO FROM
PRESENT DAY

*C*alhoun,
    I overheard Iris and Sam discussing the fact you work with them at Alliance. This tells me everything I need to know.
I wish you nothing but the best in all of your future endeavors.
Respectfully,
Elizabeth

A few minutes go by before I get a ping in my email box. Startled, I open it. Somehow, I'm not surprised by the contents. The technical jargon just leads to a few simple words that solidify the unspoken message I was receiving since a month after I graduated from college.

[[Message returned to sender. Address Unknown]]

Very carefully, I file the message before I shut down my email program and head home.

There are people who actually care about me there. People who want to hear about what I've done today and every day over the last few years. People who understand I've finally bloomed into the woman I was always meant to be.

Strong, self-sufficient, and independent.

Even if that means alone.

9

PRESENT DAY

ELIZABETH

"How long was it before you saw Cal again?" Dr. Powell asks me.

Twisting my rings around my fingers absentmindedly, I answer, "Three years. Time enough for life to have dealt me with the kind of hardship and heartache that even if I didn't know what he went through personally, I grew up and understood the look Cal wore on his face wasn't because he was trying to attract all the women on campus," I say wryly. "It just had an added benefit."

Despite the chuckle, it doesn't stop Dr. Powell from asking me, "What do you mean?"

"In the years I knew Cal before, he rarely smiled. In the three years since I saw him, it was my time to learn what it took to cause someone to love like that. I understood why people saw the world through darkened eyes."

"That wasn't a good thing?" A question, not a statement.

"It's neither good nor bad. It just is. The problem is once your innocence is stripped away, it's impossible to return. Despite everything that's happened to me, to us, Cal says I manage to maintain mine." I shake my head with regret. "I don't see it when I look in the mirror anymore."

"What do you see?"

"Like many women, I see flaws. But when I look past the surface, I can see the scars of what happened and the time we lost because of it." Especially the lost time.

"What happened to make you lose that innocence?"

"The first sheen of it started to fade when I was engaged and cheated on. I know so many women who have gone through that, it's a disgrace. Respect your partner to end a relationship before starting a new one. It's just wrong and makes you doubt yourself in so many different ways." Coming off my high horse, I deflate. As much as I still hate what Kyle did, it led me to Cal. But nothing erases the ache in my heart over what happened next. "I lost more of it when my grandmother, Dahlia, passed on." Even now, I can't say the words without painful emotions surging through me. Fumbling, I reach for the box of tissues on the table next to me.

As I mop up the tears that begin to fall, Dr. Powell doesn't look away the one time I wish he would. "That would be Dahlia Akin, sole heir to Akin Timbers family fortune?"

I nod, because there's nothing else to do.

"I've heard she was quite eccentric," he comments diplomatically instead of asking me the typical question of what it was like to grow up on a plantation still considered enormous by modern-day standards.

I throw back my long hair and laugh. "Oh, Nonna would have said you can do much better than that, Doctor. She was a grande dame, a beautiful force, and made me long to go home every time I was away." There's an abundance of love in my voice that I imagine will still be there when I talk about her in my eighties.

"When I was going through the worst of my suffering, I imagined her by my side, the sass I learned at her knee flickering through my body letting me know I wasn't defeated though I may have been temporarily beaten. It was the gentle steel she forged in me that carried me through with the ability to come out the other side as I am."

A wide smile crosses the good doctor's face. "You'll have to indulge me a moment. Was it legend or truth that she had a room in her home dedicated to hats?"

Even though the memories are bittersweet, I smile through my tears. "Truth. It was decorated in rose-colored velvet. Each hat had a special stand crafted out of Akin wood. And all of her grandchildren —the boys as well as the girls—wore one of those ostentatious contraptions to her funeral."

Deep laughter comes from the man in the chair across from me. "I wish I knew that before I spoke to your cousin Sam the other day. I might have asked him which one he wore."

Perhaps my smile doesn't have the same kind of unguarded joy it would have shone with before everything happened, and so much happened between all of us. But the bonds have been repaired, so I do smile when I say, "It was hideous—a garish plum number with peonies and tiger lilies on the brim. If you do speak with him again, remind him that since he arrived late, he got stuck wearing it."

"Was Sam late for a reason?"

"Yes." I don't elaborate.

Dr. Powell raises his brow, waiting for me to continue, as if he has all the time in the world.

"Sam was asked to pick up someone who wanted to pay their respects to me—to the family," I correct myself automatically because back then, I truly had no idea what was in store when I saw Cal's dark hair gleaming in the sun across my grandmother's gravesite.

"I can only imagine your family's reaction to your cousin being late on that most important of days," he sympathizes.

"They were certain family members—one in particular—less than pleased to see his guest, but we all understood Sam was flying in. There was worry about how fast he would be driving. Since college, Sam had become somewhat of a speed demon." The panic and sadness on varying cousins' faces that day are etched in my mind. But those emotions paled when I told the family how Sam was part of the machinations that almost destroyed my life later. That's one thing Cal never grasped until that dark period in our lives and Sam forgot about the Akin family.

Don't dare cross us.

"Whatever shock they were feeling was nowhere near what I was when Calhoun Sullivan laid a bouquet of sunflowers at Nonna's gravesite," I admit. "Here he was after three years, with not one word to me in all that time. Yet, the darkest man I knew was bringing the sun on the saddest day of my life."

"What did you do?"

"I walked away. I had no choice." And at the time, I hadn't. Not that Cal held that against me.

He rarely held anything against me.

Nothing, that is, until I walked away from our marriage without giving him a chance to explain.

10

CALHOUN

TWELVE YEARS AGO FROM PRESENT DAY

A s we pull through the gates, I have to school my expression not to gawk at the overwhelming beauty I'm faced with. Sam slams his foot to the pedal, racing the rushing water to determine which one of us will get to our destination first. I have a feeling Sam's determined to win even though I have no idea why we're even here. "What the hell are we doing, Sam? Don't we have a funeral to go to?" I demand. I'm clenching the stems of the sunflowers in my hand so tightly, I'm afraid they're going to snap. It's the only thing betraying my nerves at seeing Libby again.

"We are. And I'm going to be royally fucked because I'm late."

"Dude, where the hell do you plan on putting someone else in this car? The trunk?" Sam picked me up in a silver Corvette after I finished my part of the debrief at Alliance. He was discharged hours earlier and went to get our ride. Not that I don't appreciate the sweet set of wheels, but with both of us being as tall as we are, the only thing that will fit into the tiny jump seat is a toddler.

Maybe. But it will still be a tight fit.

He doesn't say a word. When I hazard a look over, there's a ticking in his jaw. "We're not picking up anyone. Nonna's being buried here."

Sam drops the gear and presses the pedal again, whether to make up for time or his pent-up frustration, I don't know.

And I forget about it as the house comes into view. I can't hold back the "Holy crap" that escapes my mouth.

"And that's just the main house. Wait till you see the rest of the homes on the property." Sam slams on the brake, which flings us both forward, before sliding his car expertly into a reserved parking spot. If I didn't know any better, I'd swear we'd just pulled into a luxury-used-car lot because there isn't a single car here that doesn't cost less than my former military salary.

"Sam?" I start to ask, but before I can get the question out, a little girl comes running toward us wearing an adorable pink velvet hat on her head. In her hands, she's carrying the ugliest monstrosity of one I've ever seen.

"Sam! This is the last one left!" She flaps the hat at him. He scoops her up in his arms and twirls the pretty princess around in his arms for a moment, burying his head deep into her neck. "I told Nanny it wasn't your color."

"And what did she say to that?" He blows a raspberry into her neck, making her giggle.

I stand back, not wanting to intrude. She could have been Libby's child with her shining dark hair down the middle of her back.

"Nanny said you should have been here on time, and then you could have worn..." Suddenly, the little girl notices me. Scooching next to Sam, she says, "Hello."

Smoothing a hand over her head, Sam says, "Sydney, I want you to meet my friend Calhoun."

Instinctively, I squat down to her level and hold out a hand. "Hello, Sydney. My friends call me Cal."

Her green eyes, so like Libby's, widen. "You know my Aunt Libby too." She begins to edge forward.

Dropping my hand, I flick my eyes up to Sam, who shrugs. "I do."

She studies me a moment before coming to a stop next to me. Even though I don't want to intimidate the child, something tells me to stand. Neither of us say anything while I get an inspection that would have done Admiral Yarborough proud. Finally, Sydney does something I'm sure my many enemies would have loved to have done on many an occasion.

She stomps on my foot. Hard.

I yelp in surprise, almost dropping the sunflowers. Who knew such a tiny thing had such power?

"Sydney Elizabeth!" Sam yells. "What was that for?"

"Boys aren't supposed to make you cry. You taught me that, Sam." Stomping past him, she shoves the hat in his hand. "Here. We're in the back waiting on you."

After Sydney runs out of earshot, I turn to my partner and hiss, "Care to explain?"

He sighs before slipping the ridiculous hat on his head. "I honestly have no idea. But right now, I have to say goodbye to the woman who taught us all everything."

I nod. Even though I never had what Sam did growing up—a family, ties to keep me in one place, love—I appreciate the bonds that form over time when you're with people for extended periods of time. It's why I'm here to support him.

And maybe now that I'm stateside for a while, to see if Libby still needs some sunflowers.

Later as we're listening to the eulogy, I'm trying to control my shock. I never would have put together that Elizabeth and Sam are two of the many grandchildren of the legendary Dahlia Akin, American heiress. I've known Sam for years, and although I'm certain it came up in his security check, he's never lived above his Alliance salary.

As for Libby, all I can think about is my lips touching the rotgut wine she drank that night at the dark college bar.

It's just another shock on top of all of the others today.

Over the eyes of the casket, I take in her devastated face that's bravely trying to hold back tears while she comforts an older man who's crying into a handkerchief. A man who looks to be about my age has his arms wrapped around the infamous Sydney in his lap while a pretty blonde lays her head on his shoulder. His other arm is

43

curled around a tearful older woman. Next to them is Sam, proudly wearing the velvet hat and holding his mother's hand while his father's—Libby's uncle—head is bowed. I recognize them from the pictures Sam showed me on the flight back to the States.

And suddenly it makes sense. To Libby, to Sam, this woman wasn't Dahlia Akin. She was just Nonna.

The grief that permeates the air as a result is as strong as the scent of the flowers around the casket. And just as beautiful.

AKIN HILL, LOCATED ON A BLUFF RUNNING ALONGSIDE THE COOPER River, is a working plantation used not only for timber milling but for exquisitely handcrafted furniture sought after all over the world. It's here that Dahlia Akin, matriarch to the logging company that spans back generations, is now buried among relatives that fought in the Civil War. Or, as the preacher jokes, "The War of Northern Aggression," earning an equal amount of laughter and groans alike.

It's here in the graveyard that rests in the shade of the duck pond I walk up and lay the bouquet of sunflowers for a woman I never met but one I've heard about on many a dark night from Sam. She helped influence not only him, but the woman whose smile on a normal day is brighter than the flowers now resting at the base of her casket.

Libby, who's sitting in the front row with whom I assume are her parents, turns surprised, angry wet eyes on me when I stand back to my full height. I guess her young cousin didn't go running to her when she left me and Sam earlier.

After devouring my fair share of a low country boil, Sam slaps a slab of cake in front of me. I pry my eyes off Libby's demure beauty as she wanders between the tables amid the trees, greeting the family and friends who are celebrating in the way Dahlia Akin expressed she wanted to: with love, laughter, and "a good ole Southern picnic." Sam explained once we sat down at a table overflowing with seafood, boiled new potatoes, and corn, "Nonna didn't stand on ceremony with anyone. It's what made her so beloved. Most people spend their whole lives trying to be like her, and not because of this." He waved his hand that was holding a pimento cheese and ham sandwich to encompass the grand property we were standing on where everyone mingled while waiting for dinner to be served.

I take an enormous bite of the cake. "Jesus Christ, this is good."

Sam nods while shoving in his own forkful. "That's why I ran when they said dessert was ready. Libby made it. It was Nonna's specialty; no one can make it like either of them."

If I had any doubt before I was going to try to fight for the only person capable of bringing a smile to my heart with nothing but a thought, this cake sealed the deal—at least for my stomach. Shoving in another bite, the cream and pecans melt together on my tongue. "What's in this, exactly?"

"Butter."

Arching a brow, I mutter, "And now I know why you're not our cook when we're deployed."

"I'm not kidding, Cal. Nonna used to say her coconut pecan cake has a 'Southern amount of butter.'"

"How much is that exactly?"

"Don't ask. Just eat it and accept you'll work it off later."

Taking his advice, I shove in another bite and let out a small moan of pleasure. Then I ask a question I never would have under different circumstances. "What made you join us, Sam?"

I know we can't be overheard; there's too much laughter for that. Stories are being told on top of stories. A couple of people even pulled out a few instruments—shit, is that a banjo? —and a few people are dancing in the late-afternoon sun. I'm surrounded by people who have no idea of the darkness that lingers beyond their reach and the fact it's my job to protect them from it.

But it's the men who stand to brush their lips across Libby—trying to brand what I've instinctively claimed as mine—that causes my jaw to clench. I haven't failed at a mission yet, and the one to win Elizabeth Akin's heart may be the one I give everything in to. She's never going to know what hit her when I go after her with my charm, my mind, and what's left of my soul.

If I have a heart, well, it may be up to her to find it. I think she might be the only one who can.

I tune back into what Sam's saying. "I knew you were recruiting Iris," he admits.

I'm shocked. "You're kidding!" Iris Cunningham, Libby's best friend, is our linguistics specialist and is often sent in on undercover assignments. On top of which, she has earned herself an irreplaceable spot on the team as our "little sister."

All except for Sam, who's fallen irrevocably in love with her starting with that long-ago dinner on her birthday their senior year in college. Fortunately, the feeling's returned. Her heartbreak at not being able to be here for both her lover and her best friend is making her a crazy-ass bitch, I think. Not for the first time since I jumped on the flight yesterday am I glad we weren't on the same assignment when we got the news. Her handler said she's cursing everyone in the six languages she knows. "She's devastated, Cal. There's just no way to pull her out to be there without jeopardizing the mission."

"Keep her in," I ordered, cruelly. But I was the one who had to face a tearful Sam and break the news to him.

He understood; after all, they both knew what they were signing up for when they joined Alliance.

"Even though I wish she was here, I'm glad you are."

I get a little choked up. "Thanks, Sam." Before him, I can't say I really had a friend. Acquaintances, sure. But Sam might be my first friend. Of course, I wasn't leaving him to come back to this alone.

A small smile flirts with Sam's lips. "You know, Iris is so much like you it's scary. If it weren't for the fact you have a dick, I'm not sure which of you I'd have fallen for."

"You're such a douche," I laugh in his face. I take another bite of cake just as I hear behind me, "You're only just recognizing this? Tsk, tsk. And here I thought Sam presented those traits much earlier than now. Maybe around birth?" The voice is smooth as honey.

I don't have to guess the owner as only one woman's voice has ever caused chills to race down my spine. "Libby." I stand to face her.

No more than a foot separates us, but the distance on her face means it could be miles. "I'm so sorry for your loss." Now that I'm close enough to touch her, those words sound so lame in face of the devastation I can clearly read on her face. I reach out to touch her hand, and worry makes the delicious cake I ate curdle in my stomach when I feel how cold her skin is. "I'm here for anything you need. Anything." And I find myself meaning it. If Libby only wants to use my shoulder to cry out the emotions running through her like a virus, then I'll be there for every tear.

I don't understand what it is that makes me want to fix the world so she'll smile in it.

Stepping back so my hand drops, Libby's dead voice says, "Don't say something unless you mean it, Cal. I'm all too familiar with men saying pretty words and then not following up on them."

Her words are like a well-aimed kick when sparring. I feel like dropping to my knees and begging for forgiveness for breaking our date years ago. "Libby…" I start, but she turns toward Sam.

"Your parents are wondering if you plan on mingling with any of the family. Your friend is certainly welcome to join you." Without another word to either of us, Libby glides away. The black she's wearing makes her look pale and aloof, untouchable. There's no laughter in her face.

"I guess I wouldn't either if I'd just lost someone I love," I mutter aloud.

"What?" Sam asks. His face, filled with humor before, is much more solemn.

"Laugh. Libby looks…haunted."

Sam looks stunned for a moment before he shakes his head. "Cal, I don't know how to tell you this."

Frowning, I face him. "Tell me what?"

"That *is* Libby. Or I should say, Elizabeth. No one but her parents and Iris get away with calling her Libby anymore. Not even me. The girl you knew from college is long gone. Over the last few years, she's closed up." Sam sighs as I gape at the back of the cool, elegant woman greeting another table of people before moving on. "One time I was home in between missions. She wasn't supposed to tell me, but Iris said Mom and Aunt Natalie speculated if it was because of her engagement gone bad."

I almost fall back and land on my ass in the green grass. "She was engaged?"

Sam sneers, his lip curling. "Yes. For a few months. Her brother and I hated him from the minute we first met him. Turns out we had reason to."

I've never met the dick and I want to kill him. "What happened to him?'

Sam uses his fork to point to the man who's stopped Libby with his arm wrapped around another woman—one whose coloring is a lot like Sam's. "He works for Akin Timbers. And the woman he cheated on her with is a cousin. It's only at events like this she acknowledges either of them." He lets out a rough sigh.

Libby brushes by them without a word, but I can't help but notice the man's eyes admiring her ass. "Let me kill him," I hiss.

"If I thought it would bring our Libby back, I would. She's so closed up, the only person she ever really talked to about it all was Nonna." He shakes his head. "I thought I was closer to Libby than anyone—even Josh—but I haven't been able to figure it out. She's shut me out."

But in my mind's eye, I recall Libby's mini-me stomping on my foot in the driveway. *"Boys aren't supposed to make you cry."* Then there was the look on her face when I put the flowers on the grave out of respect. And intuitively, I know something about her metamorphosis has something to do with me

What could I have done? We never even had a first date. Quickly, I replay all of our interactions until my body gets tight. *"Maybe when you get back, I'll need some new sunflowers."*

And in three years, I never once made contact, nothing, despite the tangible connection between us. Not even a hello. I wanted to—God, how I wanted to—but it wasn't long after I left that I realized that Libby wasn't meant for the life I was leading. And I couldn't just go leaving her to constantly wonder and wait. So, I stayed away even though it just brought more darkness down around me. As for Libby?

Well, she probably thought she was a game, and with her tender heart, she barely decided to try again when she was betrayed. It was likely made worse every time Sam came home from a "business" trip, since he'd likely mentioned my name. Groaning aloud, I realize it likely would have been like salt poured into an open wound when Libby saw Iris. There's not a doubt in my mind Libby would have heard about the three of us working together at Alliance. Fuck.

"I think I know how to fix this." I hope.

Sam gapes at me like I've grown two heads. I'm not perturbed as I've seen the look numerous times during mission planning. "You do realize I've tried everything to break through to her, right? And that I love her more than I love my own sisters?" Then as an aside he mutters, "Shit, I need to be careful about saying crap like that here. Sure as hell, it will get back to them."

I'd laugh at his predicament if the one I was facing myself wasn't so damn dire. "I need to find time to talk with Libby."

Sam laughs. "Good luck with that. Every time your name's come up, she's…" Dawning realization crosses his face. "Son of a bitch, what did you do to hurt her?"

"Nothing. And that's the problem. I made a promise and then stupidly broke it."

"What kind of promise?" he asks suspiciously.

I let out a measured breath. "To talk to her. All she wanted me to do was talk to her."

Sam's about to say something when we hear a crying screech of "Aunt Libby!" Sydney goes running across the yard. Libby immediately drops to her knees, and Sydney crashes into her arms. The younger girl starts talking animatedly before pointing at her elbow, which clearly has a long scrape on it. Libby's face softens. She leans forward and kisses Sydney's wet cheek and then the hurt arm. Standing back up, she guides the little girl to the main house like a protective mother.

And in that moment, I realize how badly I fucked up because I just saw a vision of my future walk away from me.

I need to figure out a way to fix things between us and quickly.

49

11

PRESENT DAY

ELIZABETH

"How did he get you to talk with him?" Dr. Powell asks.

I shoot him a look. "This is Calhoun Sullivan we're talking about. The man doesn't understand the meaning of the word defeat, Doctor. Cal does what he does best: he planned a strategic attack and executed it."

We both laugh at my wry acceptance of my husband's skills. Still chuckling, he asks, "What do you mean?"

"Cal saw me go into the house with Sydney. He figured there would be few, if any, people inside. So—" I shake my head in bemusement at the memory. "—he followed me. What he didn't count on was what he found."

"Oh?"

I hesitate because it's difficult to explain. "I have always been Elizabeth Dahlia Akin. Nonna said I kept my emotions locked inside except for those people I cared about. Libby is who I'm comfortable becoming when people are allowed to get close to me. At college, I was different because I didn't have the chance to throw up those shields; Iris wouldn't let me." For just a moment, the reality of everything of those horrid months before the *Sea Force* comes rushing back: Cal, Iris, Sam. "So, Nonna knew I had the tendency to pull back

emotionally to protect myself, but my family—" I shake my head. "—
they'd just never witnessed it. Until my broken engagement. And
those years when Sam and Iris kept bringing up Cal's name. They had
no idea I was hurting because day after day I was waiting for a silly
little email."

"It isn't silly if it was a promise broken," Dr. Powell points out
logically.

"It seems silly now in light of everything else." We're both quiet for
a moment. I close my eyes for just a second before continuing. "Anyway, Cal followed me and Sydney into the kitchen."

"Then what happened?"

12

ELIZABETH

TWELVE YEARS AGO FROM PRESENT DAY

"Any better?" I've already cleaned and covered the scrape on Sydney's arm with three Band-Aids since three is her favorite number. Pressing a kiss to the wound, I meet eyes the same exact shade as my own. They're Nonna's eyes passed down to another female in our family. Mine fill with tears over my heartbreak knowing Sydney will never hear the stories Nonna shared with me as I grew from a girl her age with skinned knees as I tumbled over the roots of the trees running around the farm, like she did, to the comfort she offered me as a woman when a hopeful heart began to wither as day after day passed with nothing from a man who offered me flowers that seemed to promise me everything.

"Yes, Aunt Libby. Thank you." Sydney leans into me. "What about you?"

I hug her tightly. "Do you mean about Nonna?" At her nod, I go on. "It's going to hurt for a long time."

"Like it did about that man? Did he tell you I stomped on his foot?"

I pull back in surprise. "What do you mean?"

"I heard you talking to Nonna, Aunt Libby. When Sam introduced him, I stood up for you—the same way you're always standing up for me."

"Oh, Syd." I pull my brother's daughter against my heart again and let her love flow over me. "There was no need to do that."

"He made you cry." Her small little arms try to wrap around me. "I didn't mean to, but I heard you tell Nonna."

"I wish I'd known that, baby. I would have tried to explain." But what would I have said? That I didn't cry over Calhoun Sullivan? Because that would have been a lie. And I don't lie. Not ever.

I was the foolish girl who pinned happiness on nothing but mismanaged dreams. And as months passed without a word, I made excuses: he was busy, he wasn't settled. But when Iris came home talking about the business venture she was now involved in with Cal, I'd gone down to the river and sat as the water rippled past. I knew the last part of my girlish dreams were gone. There was something wrong with me.

Then I met Kyle. After the way that ended, I encased my heart in stone. Or so I thought. It was then I went to Nonna and cried.

Her words ring clearly through me. "Libby, there's more to the woman you are inside than falling in love with a man. There's a person deep in you that you haven't found yet. Find her, and then you won't be able to escape love—no matter how hard you try."

Sniffling into a hankie she'd handed me, I whispered, "Why do you think that?"

"Because watching you pretend you're okay is like watching myself all over again when I fell in love with your grandfather." Nonna's wrinkled hand cupped my cheek. "You already know who you are without him; now go find out who you are for yourself."

So, I have. I'm just not sure I'm used to it yet.

Opening up my design studio a year ago in downtown Charleston was a huge step for me. The first person I brought through the storefront was Nonna. She was railing at me all the way into town because I wouldn't take a dime from her. "Libby, I said find who you are, not to deny your heritage. Why on earth would you take a loan from a bank?"

"So I could say it's mine, Nonna. From the ground up, every square inch of it is mine. It's meant to be or it's not. No one can make the customers come in."

"Stubborn as a mule."

"I inherited that from you, as well." Pulling up to one of my reserved spots in the back, a miracle in downtown Charleston but something I negotiated when I bought the building, I gave her a blinding smile.

She blinked. "I take it back."

"What?"

"My objections. Whatever's beyond that door is worth whatever put your smile back on your face."

Leaning over, I brushed her soft cheek with mine. "That's you, Nonna. I'll be right around to help you out."

In my mind's eye, I can still picture the way her tiny hands brushed across each item at Deja Vu. I squeeze Sydney tighter. "Aunt Libby, you're squishing me," she complains.

"I'm sorry, bug. I was just having a moment of…"

"Déjà vu?" We both laugh at the double entendre. "Something exactly like that. Now, go find your Daddy and tell him everything's better."

"Can I stay over with you tonight?"

"I think your momma's going to need your sugars tonight, don't you?" I ask diplomatically because while I'd love nothing more than to have my niece cuddle with me, I know there's going to be a lot of sad memories tonight.

"You're right. But soon?"

"Anytime you want, baby." I kiss her head before lifting her off the counter. She scampers off the counter and runs full tilt out the back door. It slams behind her.

Alone at last. I brace my arms against the counter and let out the ragged sigh I've been holding in.

"Nonna, what would you have said knowing Cal laid sunflowers at the foot of your casket?"

"I don't know. What do you think she would have said?" My head whips up at the sound of his deep voice.

"This is our family home, Cal." My voice is polite. "Today, we're not receiving visitors."

"Cut the crap, Libby. I'm not just anyone. We've known each other for years." He advances to where I'm standing at the counter.

I quickly busy myself cleaning up the wrappers. "Actually, for all I really know you, you are just anyone." He opens his mouth to contradict me, but I shake my head. "What I know about you, Mr. Sullivan, I can enumerate on one hand." I drop the wrappers and begin. "One, you work with my cousin. Two, you're my best friend's boss. Three, for a short while, we spent some time together at the same university. Four, you were gracious enough to come to the funeral of someone who meant a great deal to us. That means you're...what? Considerate?" I wait a heartbeat before I lower my hand. "It must be something you've learned over the last few years." I start to walk past him to head out the back door.

He grabs my arm just as I'm about to pass him. "You have every right to be pissed."

Prying his fingers off of my arm, I nod. "I know I do. Didn't Sam warn you? We've been held to a standard of zero tolerance for lies our entire life. We've seen the effect they have on people's lives since family gambling and stealing almost bankrupted this family before our nonna and poppa saved our legacy with the timber mill. Then there were the lies from Poppa's sister, our great-aunt, who walked away from her family, leaving them without a mother. And Sam? He should know how I hate liars; after all, I lost a fiancé to being cheated on. Then again, maybe men don't talk about those kinds of things. But I'm tired of pretending to be something I'm not."

"Which is?" Cal asks.

"Me," I answer simply. "I'm Elizabeth Akin. I'm a smart, successful business owner. I'm a woman. And I'll be damned if I'll let any man make me a promise, then lie about keeping it." Calmly, I walk to the back door before I turn around. "Thank you for taking the time to come today for Sam, Cal. And I'm sure my grandmother would have appreciated the flowers."

"Is that what she really would have thought?" His voice is rough-edged. His dark eyes are boring into mine as if he can see through me.

"It's what she would have said," I tell him sincerely before I walk out the door and back out into the beautiful spring day.

IT'S DUSK. EVERYONE'S WHO'S SUPPOSED TO LEAVE HAS GONE. MOST OF the family is up at the main house, still laughing and telling stories about Nonna. I've put on a pair of jeans and a black T-shirt that says "Sunflowers stand tall on the darkest of days to find sunlight." It was a gift from Nonna after I opened Deja Vu.

Heading down to my favorite spot down by the river, I've got a blanket tucked under one arm. My hair, which has been twisted up all day, is flowing freely down my back. There's a part of me that will never grow tired of the view, the silence that's only broken by the rushing water, and the smell of the wood mixed with the grass and flowers. Spreading my blanket, I kick off my sneakers before I sink down. "It will always be home, Nonna, but it will never be the same."

"I never had a family or a home, so I don't know what you're feeling right now."

I jump at the sound of Cal's voice. "Sweet ladybug! What are you doing here? Shouldn't you be gone? Or, at the very least, with Sam?"

"I think I need to clear up some misconceptions. I was going to do that earlier, but it didn't quite seem like the time. You seem more yourself here." Before I can refute him, his sensual mouth curves. "Nice shirt."

"It was a gift from Nonna."

"An appropriate one. I still can't see them and not think of you."

And just like that, it all comes rushing back—the excitement, the disappointment, the anxiousness. And finally, the crushing pain. "I'll be sure to burn it, then," I lash out. "Now, do you mind leaving?" My hands are in fists at my side.

"I wasn't honest with you, Libby."

"Elizabeth," I correct him scathingly. "And no kidding, Cal. I figured you just weren't that into me when I didn't hear from you after I'd hear about how well you were doing over the last few years. I'd like to remain cordial, but I buried someone I was close to today."

"Jesus Christ, not that into you?" He stalks forward until his face is inches from mine. "I was so consumed by you, I stayed away for your own good."

The sound of my laughter is like glass shattering. "How kind of you."

"That's the goddamn truth. I can't give you all this." Cal's arm jerks behind him to indicate the estate. I'm about to toss him into the river behind me for thinking for a moment I gave a shit about money when he stuns me quiet. "I don't have a family to introduce you to. I don't have a 'Nonna' to learn from let alone cry over. I don't come from anything good. You abhor liars? I'm a consummate one. I've lied from the moment we met, letting you think I was good enough for you." He exhales roughly. "I just wanted you to know I always had you on my mind. There wasn't a day you didn't pass through it. After all, how do you forget the only person in the world who's ever made you smile?" Carefully, as if he's afraid I'm going to move, he reaches up and drags his fingers down my face.

The same way he did back at college.

Then he begins to walk away.

I struggle for enough time for my heart to beat twice before I call out, "I would have shared."

He stills. "What did you say?"

"If I'd thought you had cared, I would have been willing to share my family, Cal. We always have room for more."

He turns and faces me. "More...people?' he asks carefully.

I shake my head. "More hearts. The people you saw today were all loved."

His face twists. "What if I'm not good enough?"

"I can't answer that." There's a lengthy silence between us—two people who each ache for the other but can't escape the past enough to reach out.

Then we both do at the same time.

The tips of our fingers brush first. They slide against one another until our fingers are locked. Both of us are breathing hard as the distance is closed. I step off my oasis as Cal comes closer.

And we find the beginning of us somewhere in between as he takes me into his arms and just holds on.

"I'm sorry, Libby," he starts.

"Shh," I whisper. "Tell me later. Right now, just stand here with me."

For a long time, we do exactly that until the fear that this is a dream recedes with the sun. Then Cal guides me back onto my blanket and begins to ask me about Nonna.

As for a beginning, it was perfect—the dying heat of the day drying my tears at my front as Calhoun Sullivan supported my back. I could feel his smile against my hair when I told him something amusing. But the best was when I made him laugh. His whole body would shake along the back of mine as he held me cradled against his chest.

I don't remember how long we sat there talking. But by the time the stars lit the path back to the house, Cal was holding my hand and my heart was beating a little stronger in my chest.

13

CALHOUN

TWELVE YEARS AGO FROM PRESENT DAY

nowing I'm going to be working stateside for at least another six months is suddenly exhilarating. I stare at myself in the mirror as I slip the belt through the loops of the dark-wash jeans I paired with a black shirt to wear on my first official date with Libby. I'm meeting her at Deja Vu in a half an hour before we go out to dinner.

My phone pings with a text. Pulling it out of my pocket, I grin when I see it's from Libby. Then I frown when I read, *How close are you?*

I quickly type back, *My apartment is maybe a ten minute drive from the store why?*

Anytime you want to come get me would be great.

I quickly grab my wallet, shoving it into my pocket. Keeping my phone out, I race out of my apartment. *I'm on my way.*

See you soon.

This could just be that she's anticipating our date as much as I am, but every instinct is screaming at me to get to her.

It's been three weeks since her nonna's been laid to rest. I've spoken with or seen Libby every day. Whether that's because we've talked after she was finished with work—even though I've still been at the office—or we managed to meet up for a quick lunch, the pull between us that I acknowledged all those years ago is still there. It's just been dormant while I was a complete dumbass.

Sam and Iris have both cautioned me about being with Libby. "Don't start something with her unless you're going in for the long haul." Sam's still pissed at me for unintentionally hurting his precious cousin to begin with.

Iris, the damn pit bull, had her say in multiple languages. *"Vas tu foutre!"* she screamed.

"Calling your boss a fuck isn't the way to earn a good performance bonus," I replied calmly.

"I don't give a shit, Cal. She's my best friend, and you're part of reason she went from being...Libby to miserable. If I'd have known that, I'd..."

"What?" I demanded. "Shot me?"

"I'd have considered it," Iris retorted before slamming out of my office.

Slowly and way too cautiously, the light that shone from Libby before was emerging again. "I just hope she's all right," I mutter as I swing into my truck.

Backing out of my space, I manage to shave a few minutes off the time and swing into the reserved parking lot for Deja Vu in about eight minutes. Quickly, I make my way around to the front of the store. Entering, I hear Libby's voice say, "I don't give a shit, Kyle. And what the hell do you think your wife would say if I called her to tell her you're here?"

"Krysta isn't you, Elizabeth."

Libby's laughter is filled with bitterness. "That's not what you said when you decided to cheat on me with her. Now, get out of my store. And let me tell you, if you ever call my assistant and make an appointment under an alias again, I'll call the cops. As it is, you've got one minute before I call my family."

I'm going to kill him. The thought settles into my mind with such a comfortable ease. As I turn the corner, I prepare for anything. What I don't expect is to find Libby standing with her arms folded over her chest in a sexy as fuck black dress that hugs every curve and a pair of black high-heeled boots.

The man in question is practically on his knees when he pleads, "No, Elizabeth. Please don't call your family."

Libby snorts. "Like that's not happening." She uncrosses her arms and begins to dial.

Suddenly, Kyle whatever-his-name-is surges to his feet and grabs her wrist. "Elizabeth. Drop the phone. Let's talk this out."

Not. Happening. "Let her go," I growl, my hands fisting and unclenching at my side. Kyle immediately drops her wrist and steps back.

A flicker of relief crosses Libby's face. "Cal, I seem to have a bit of a situation."

"Want me to handle it for you?" I lean up against the jamb and cross one ankle over the other.

"Well, that all depends on Kyle…" But the man in question bolts past me out the front door. Libby shakes her head. "I didn't even get to knee him in the nuts like I wanted to," she says with a touch of mock despair.

"I could always go bring him back and hold him," I offer, but then we both hear the sound of a car squealing out of the parking lot.

"Sorry. I might have let you." Libby fiddles with her phone a moment before she picks up her work line. "Can you give me a moment?"

She's practically been assaulted in her office. I move closer to offer her what comfort I can. "Umm, sure?"

"Thanks." Quickly, she dials. "Josh? Hey, it's me. I'm sending you a file." She pauses for a moment. "You'll never believe who came to see me in the office." Another moment of silence. "Got it in one, brother. Oh, the usual—he wants me back, Krysta's a bitch, he's going to leave her." There's another moment of silence before a snort. "You might want to put in the headphones when you listen to it. I wasn't exactly ladylike in my responses. I don't want my niece mimicking this." She grins. "Now, Josh, I don't know what you mean, darlin'. I am not a bad influence on Syd. Yeah, hopefully, this will finally convince Krysta to divorce his ass." A long pause before a cryptic, "We can't help who we love, big brother. Okay, I've got a date I'm now officially late for." She rolls her eyes but smiles at me. "Yes, a date. I not only know how to spell it, I know how to vet them all on my own." She waits for her brother to comment before she laughs. And that laughter rips through me. "Love you, Joshua. Good night." Hanging up the phone, Libby grins. "Sorry, but if I need Krysta to wake up, I might need a witness."

"And here I thought you wanted me to beat the crap out of him." I let a note of despair enter my voice. And sadly, it's not faked. I want to pound out some frustration on that fucker.

Libby grabs her purse and walks straight to me on those awe-inspiring boots. "I learned a few things over the past few years, Cal," she explains.

"What's that?" Is that my voice that sounds so damn rough? I swallow hard when a catlike smile spreads across her face.

"The first is I'm worth a hell of a lot more than that," she sneers as she looks back at the chair, as if Kyle were still in it. "And the second is that I have to be able to take care of myself—most especially my heart."

"You're worth everything," I rasp. My arms slip around her waist of their own volition.

She steps back. "We'll see, won't we?"

Damn right we will. I extend my elbow to her. I owe her this date before I take her lips in a kiss neither of us will ever forget. "Shall we?"

"Indeed." Libby slips her fingers into the crook of my arm. "So, where are we going?"

"Do you like French food?"

"I do. I also like wine," she replies with good humor.

"Then I think you'll love the place I chose." Guiding her over to my truck, I turn her toward me after I open the door so I can help boost her in. I don't miss the puff of air that escapes. Sliding my hands over her slender legs, I ask, "All set?"

"Sure," she murmurs. Twisting in her seat, she reaches for her belt as I close the door.

"Well, I'm glad one of us is," I say aloud as I round the back to climb in.

Soon, we're ensconced in the car for a ride down Route 17 toward Mount Pleasant and a French restaurant Sam recommended as one of Libby's favorites.

❀

"You have to try a bite of this, Cal," Libby cajoles. She's holding up a bite of the cassoulet toward my lips. "It's my absolute favorite. The flavors are just layered on top of one another."

"It's going to be hard to top this duck," I argue. But the minute the cassoulet meets my lips, I understand why it's Libby's favorite. "Oh, God. I'll trade you."

Libby bursts out in laughter. "Not a chance." She dives in with renewed enthusiasm, but I'm frozen in place.

Her laughter is better than the wine we've shared, the tartare, and even the bite of heaven she just placed in my mouth. It's sunshine and happiness returning to my soul that's been missing for far too long.

And it's all my fault.

"I was an idiot," I blurt out.

Libby stills with her fork halfway to her mouth. Laying it down, she gives me her undivided attention. "I'm listening."

"I grew up an orphan, I told you that." It came up during the last few weeks when Libby asked about where my family was from.

Libby nods, so I continue. "I had nothing, Libby. Literally nothing of my own. I had to fight for everything I had including my education. I earned scholarships to go to college, and I worked the summers to pay for books."

"It made you appreciate what you have more," she says softly.

I'm grateful she sees it that way. "A man I worked for suggested I go into the military. I was discharged on a medical disability…"

Her hand shoots across the table. "Oh Cal, I'm so sorry. When did this happen?" The worry in her eyes guts me. I've been telling this lie for so long, it's become my life. But telling it to Libby is like cursing my own soul.

"Before I met you." I shove the worry aside. "I could still serve in some capacity."

Her hand slips away. "Yes. After you finished your last rotation is when you started working with Sam and Iris."

I've been approved to tell her this truth. "Libby, I've always worked for Alliance, even when I met you…" Her head snaps up. I continue. "I was recruiting future employees while I was teaching, and I got called up." The last part is a lie; Yarborough needed me on a top secret mission, but I can't share that.

Her interest isn't feigned. "What do you all do?"

I shake my head. "I can't tell you a lot about it since the work we do is classified."

Instead of being upset, she looks thoughtful. "I can appreciate that."

I'm flabbergasted. "You can?"

She shrugs. "Sure. My grandfather, Nonna's husband, was in the military. He took much of what he did to the grave. Can you answer general questions?"

If I ever thought Libby Akin was perfect for me before, now I know it for sure. "Some, yes." I pick up my fork and begin eating.

She does as well. "Do you still work in recruiting?"

I shake my head. "I work more hands-on with our customers establishing projects. Some are quick turnaround; some are longer and take me away weeks at a time."

She takes a drink of wine, swallows, before asking, "Are you able to have contact with people when you're on a project?"

"Why do you ask?"

"Because if I'm going to consider getting involved with a man who's potentially all over the US working on a contract…"

"The world," I correct her.

She accepts my correction with a nod. "I'd like to know I have some way of contacting him. Otherwise I'm going to feel like I'm involved with some black-ops guy who might disappear one day and no one will ever tell me why." Giving me a sharp look, she asks, "That's not going to happen, is it?"

I reassure her, "You'd be told if something odd ever happened to me." I make a mental note to have Libby's name listed to the people who need be notified in the event of an unfortunate event. Right now, only Sam's name is on that list, and I sure as hell don't want him to be the one to ever have to give her that news.

Not that I plan on that occurring.

She nods. Forking another bite of cassoulet, she chews before grinning. "Must suck for y'all. The government is riddled with paperwork. I imagine all your forms have to be completed in triplicate."

Suddenly, I'm the one laughing—something I haven't done in years. And I'm doing it with the only woman who's ever made me do it. "Yes. And let me assure you, it is a bitch."

She makes a tsking sound that makes me want to pull her up for a long kiss, something I promise myself I'm going to taste before the night's over.

Though I really don't want this night to end since I've waited for it for so many years.

14

ELIZABETH

TWELVE YEARS AGO FROM PRESENT DAY

"You can take me back to Deja Vu," I tell Cal once we're back in the car.

He frowns. "It's late, Libby. Let me just take you home and I'll pick you up in the morning."

I let out a low laugh. "Cal, Deja Vu is home." At his confused expression, I explain. "I own the whole building. My apartment is upstairs."

He grins, something I notice he never did even around Sam. A happy tingle flows through me. "Makes it an easy commute, I guess."

"You have no idea." An easy silence falls between us.

We're on the road a while before Cal reaches over, takes my hand, and squeezes. My heart thumps in my chest. I feel like tonight is one of those kinds of nights where life is spinning her wheel and anything can happen. Nothing will remain the same after.

I gently return the gesture.

"Deja Vu was what you were talking about in the bar that night," he suddenly says once we're back on Route 17 heading toward Charleston.

If anyone told me that all the walls I've built would fall away with one simple query, I'd have called them a damned liar. But Cal just managed to. "I can't believe you remember that."

We pass under a streetlamp just then. His jaw is clenched hard. "I probably remember more than you imagine I do."

"Like?" I challenge.

Suddenly, Cal's swung the car into the parking lot of Deja Vu. He's twisted in his seat until he's facing me. "When I'm out with colleagues having a drink, I remember what it was like to sit with you and drink bad wine. Every time I close my eyes, I can still hear your laughter. And I can't see a damn sunflower without missing you." His head lowers.

My lips part, my breath coming out heavy. "Three years," I moan. My tongue comes out to dampen my lips.

"And every minute of them, I've cursed myself a fool for not doing this." Cal leans forward and captures my lips with a hunger born of every moment we've been apart.

My lips part for him, my head tilting to the side. My arms snake around his shoulders, tugging him closer. I don't just hear the growl that comes out of his mouth, I taste it. It pulls an answering groan from my own. There's pure need communicating between the meeting of lips and tongues. It's pleasure and hunger.

And through it all, Cal's managing to ensure I'll never be able to resist him ever again.

All through one kiss.

Pulling back, Cal cups my chin, nuzzling my cheek. "Thank you."

I pull back confused. "You're thanking me?"

"No, I'm thanking whomever I have to for finally letting the timing be right," he says seriously before he lowers his head again.

Cal's tongue slips past before I have a chance to pull back in surprise. Giving myself over to it, I lose my reason and my senses. If a kiss is a stone meant to disturb the sheen of life's water, then the recovery of this one may wash me up on the shores.

Dragging me over the console, Cal arranges my legs so I'm straddling his lap. I rip my mouth away to whimper, "Oh, God."

Cal trails his lips down my neck. "Jesus, Libby, how did I ever walk away?" he groans.

And like ice water being dropped on me, I freeze up. Those words suddenly throw my shields back into place. This is a man who might walk away, and I'm not a woman to leave. "I don't know, but you did." Extracting myself from his lap, I climb back over the console. I lean down to pick up my purse from where I dropped it.

When I straighten, Cal's there. His lips capture mine again. After another devastating kiss that begins to melt the frost around my heart, he whispers, "I'm not walking away again. I promise you that. If anyone does any leaving, it's going to be you."

My lips quirk. "Do you mean for tonight or longer than that?"

Without hesitation, he says, "Both."

More of the frost melts. "Well, for tonight, I am going to say good night."

Cal nods before opening his door. "Don't move. I'll be right around," he warns.

Another shot of warmth steals through me. I wait patiently for him to open my door. Holding my hand, he escorts me to the back entrance of the building. "Do you have your keys?"

I pull them out. "Right here." I jingle them for good measure.

He holds out his hand. "For my peace of mind, let me do a quick walk-through?"

"Why?"

"Because of what happened earlier. For me? I need to know you're safe." His explanation is sweet, even if a little overprotective. I hand him my keys. Dropping a quick kiss on my nose, he whispers, "Stay here for just a second," before disappearing inside my apartment.

Within moments, he's back. "All clear."

"I didn't think he'd be that stupid." I start to move past him, but he hooks an arm around my waist. It reminds me of the way he stopped me all those years ago, and I stiffen.

"If a man has an opportunity to resurrect something he stupidly burned to the ground, he'll go to any length to do it," Cal rasps out. And I know he's not talking about Kyle.

He's talking about himself.

Unable to tear my eyes away, I don't avoid when he leans down and presses a gentle kiss against my lips before whispering, "Lock up behind me." Cal lets me go to stride to the door.

Suddenly, I can't help but ask, "Was tonight just about making up for our missed date?"

Cal freezes in place before turning around and facing me. We're feet apart, and yet the visual caress his eyes give me causes my nipples to tighten. "No."

"Then what was it?"

"It was just the beginning." Then he turns and walks out.

15
PRESENT DAY

ELIZABETH

"And it was?" Dr. Powell asks me.

"Yes," I sigh in remembrance of the early days of Cal's and my relationship. "Cal would randomly show up to drop off a coffee, lunch, or even randomly swoop in before work for a kiss. And the nights?" I let out a dreamy sigh.

"How would you describe it?"

I think about it hard. "Stirring? No, that's not quite strong enough of a word. Heady? Stimulating? The more I was with Cal, the more I felt like we were always meant to be. It's hard to describe the connection between us."

"Was it love?" Dr. Powell asks me.

I bite my lip and then answer, "I was in this odd place where I was falling in love with the ridiculous things about him that I never knew existed. Yes, for me it was, though I hadn't said so yet to Cal, nor he to me."

"Why hadn't you said it?"

"Self-preservation?" I respond dryly. After the laughter dies down, I answer seriously, "To be honest, I was terrified of letting Cal in. I'd already had one broken engagement, and frankly there was still so much I was afraid of."

"Like what?"

"Like giving up the part of me that knew how to stand on my own. I knew I could survive as Elizabeth Akin."

"But would you be happy?"

"Ahh, now you're asking me the questions I was asking myself." Another low chuckle that quickly subsides when I continue. "And the answer is simple. I'll never be truly happy without Cal in my life. Even when I left him, I knew that. After all, how can you be happy when your biggest heartache isn't dying but believing you have to let the person you love go to be with someone else?"

16

CALHOUN

TWELVE YEARS AGO FROM PRESENT DAY

"Big plans tonight, Cal?" Sam slams the door on his locker next to me. We just finished a ten-mile run after going over some intel that came in this morning. I was really hoping it didn't pan out to be anything and said as much to Sam a few minutes ago.

"Yeah." Reaching into my locker, I pull out my wallet and flip it open. Pulling out two tickets, I hand them over.

"How in the hell did you pull that off?" The awe in Sam's voice makes the amount I spent on those tickets worth it.

"It wasn't easy," I admit. "Tickets for Small Town Nights are next to impossible, but with Brendan Blake opening for them? I had to cash in a few favors."

"And sell your soul to the devil," Sam snickers.

"I did that a long time ago, buddy. But if it puts the kind of smile I suspect is going to be on Libby's face when we get to the arena, I'll do it twice." Instead of sliding into my normal dress slacks which I'd do before heading to pick up Libby, I tug on a pair of jeans with my dark dress shirt. Frowning, I growl at Sam, who looks like he's contemplating knocking me out to steal the tickets, "Hand 'em over."

"Iris is going to take my head off." Unfortunately for him, he's not wrong. What sucks for the rest of us is we'll all hear about it from the time Libby tells her best friend to the moment Iris forgives her boyfriend.

Sometimes the lack of a no-fraternization policy at Alliance has sucked over the years.

"Sounds like a personal problem," I tell him.

Sam doesn't hesitate to throw his middle finger up at me. "You're a dick," he informs me.

My lips twitch. It's still not a smile; the only one who can pull that from me is Libby, but since she's come into my life, even I notice I joke more with the team of people I work with.

Kind of helps to be in the good graces of the people who literally stand between your life and death.

Quickly, I run a comb through my wet hair and pull my socks and boots out of my locker before slamming it shut. "Hey." I get Sam's attention away from my wallet which is sitting on the bench next to me.

"What's up?"

"Can I get away with these boots at a country concert?" I lift my brown steel-toe boots. "You know I'm not going to be able to slip in any kind of weapon other than this." I hold up the tiny Swiss Army knife that dangles from the end of my key chain as more of a joke than anything.

Sam gives me a thorough perusal before throwing my words back at me. "Sounds like a personal problem. Why don't you think on it while I go try to find a florist to get some flowers for Iris to head off her eruption?" With that, he starts to saunter away, calling over his shoulder, "I hope Libby has a great time."

"That's the idea, you asshole!" I yell back. Contemplating my boots once more, I decide they'll have to do. I have to get to Libby. Lord only knows how much time she'll need to change when I tell her what our real plans for tonight are.

HOURS LATER, I AM POSITIVE I MADE A TACTICAL ERROR. I SHOULD HAVE just brought Libby to the show without telling her where we were going. Then maybe I could have enjoyed it without having to glare pair after pair of admiring eyes into submission over the way my woman sways to the music.

I sure as shit appreciated the way Libby's whole body thanked me, her long legs wrapped around my waist as she peppered my face with kisses. Even as her lips pressed against mine, they were smiling. Her cheeks were flushed with the kind of happiness I want to give her every day. I boosted her up so I could continue to stare at her, absorbing even more of her essence when she clasped her hands on either side of her face and screeched, "I can't go backstage looking like this. Goodness gracious, that would be so embarrassing!"

While I thought the jeans and T-shirt she had on were fine, what did I know? Libby squirmed in my arms, giving me a whole new set of ideas, before pleading, "Give me fifteen minutes. I know just what to wear."

Figuring it'll take her at least thirty, I meander into her kitchen to see if there's anything quick to chow down on. Even though we'll be grabbing something quick on our way to the North Charleston Coliseum & Performing Arts Center, I'd only managed to down a protein shake once I was done with my run. Frankly, I could have eaten half of the contents of her fridge, chow down on dinner, and still be hungry. Finding leftover fried chicken from dinner the other night, I yank out a leg and shove it in my mouth before closing the container and pulling my head out of Libby's fridge.

The chicken falls to the floor unheeded as I catch sight of my girlfriend.

Holy shit.

I about come just from the sight of her in a halter-top sundress that hugs every inch of her luscious curves that she paired with a pair of boots on her delicate feet. I almost swallow my tongue as I notice since her long hair is pulled over to one shoulder, her entire back, down to the waist, is bare.

"Fuck me," I whisper.

"If you're lucky," she teases. But I'm not kidding when I spin her around and press her body up against the entry to the kitchen. Backing her against the jamb, I drop my head down to her bare shoulder.

Libby lets out a sigh.

"Tonight's going to suck," I say tragically.

Her head jerks back in confusion. "What? Why?"

"Because I'm going to be too busy ready to kill every man there, and I won't have anything to do it with," I tell her truthfully.

Her sweet laugh smooths out the rough edges of my emotions. I trail my lips up her neck, then capture her lips in a quick kiss. "If we hurry, we can get a bite to eat before the show."

"Then let's go. You must be starved having come here directly from work."

Mournfully, I eye the chicken leg lying on the floor. Releasing Libby, I scoop it up and throw it in the trash. "You have no idea."

But as we stand in front of our seats close to the stage, even the energy of the concert can't eclipse that emanating from Libby. I grin as Libby sings along with every Brendan Blake song, like he's a megastar or something. It's not that he's not good—he is. He just may end up being another name people sit on their tailgates and go, "Oh, yeah. I remember that song." It happens to so many who toss their cowboy hat into the sound booth. Then again—my eyes narrow as he winks down at Libby singing his third song that hit number one on the country music charts—he did land the spot on the Small Town Nights tour.

I slide up behind Libby and slide my arms around her waist. I begin swaying back and forth with her as she's being serenaded from the stage. Whether it's because he saw his death on my face or just respects another woman's man, Blake tips his hat at me before strolling to the other side of the stage. "Having fun?" I yell into her ear.

Twisting back, she grins and tugs my head close. "I would have been happy just dancing with you to this at home." Rising up on her toes, she presses a quick kiss on my lips. But before her head turns away, she's already picked up singing the lyrics in time with the rest of the crowd.

And there, right there is the reason I used my connection to Wild-card Music—the label that represents Small Town Nights and Brendan Blake—to get the tickets and backstage passes. Because Libby doesn't expect it.

The only thing she wants is me.

It's a heady feeling.

Swaying with the music, all right in the world for this moment in time, I try to push aside the forty-five minutes of gratitude I endured from the president of Wildcard when I called to ask for the tickets. I tried to pay for them, insisted upon it. He refused to let me.

"Mr. Sullivan, you personally went in and grabbed my little girl out of a house of monsters. And you want concert tickets? Son, you could ask to follow them on tour."

"I'd feel more comfortable if I could pay, Mr. Wilde," I tried to insist.

"Do you know what my daughter's going to be doing next week?"

"No, sir."

"She'll be with her mother. Because of you." The warmth of pride at his words steals through me. "Now, tell me where to send you the tickets."

I rattled off the Alliance office address. "You'll have them tomorrow."

"I'm grateful, Mr. Wilde."

"No, it's I who is still grateful. I always will be," he said, right before he disconnected the phone.

I'm jostled out of my thoughts by Libby's jumping body as she and 11,000 other fans begin stomping their boots and their hands fly up in unison as Brendan Blake ends his set with his most famous song to date, "Broken Boots." His guitar is swung over the back of his shoulder, mic in hand as he crosses from one side of the stage to the other grabbing pens and posters to sign. Ripping off his cowboy hat, he signs it and makes a beeline for Libby.

"You've got to be fucking kidding me," I mutter as he puts it on top of her head. Libby beams up at him, almost causing the singer to miss a note.

Seriously, I should have brought her in jeans and a tee. But even as the thought again crosses my mind, I know it's not that. Blake's reacting to her the same way I do. This time, when I wrap my arms around her, there's no mistaking the violence in the look I shoot him.

God help us if he's backstage when we meet Small Town Nights.

Blake merely smiles broadly before saying, "Who's ready to turn Charleston into a small town for tonight?"

The crowd goes wild.

"Hmm, not sure if Shane and Amanda heard you. Who's ready for some Small Town Nights?"

The screaming response may be heard in Georgia.

"Thank you all for your warm welcome. My name is Brendan Blake; it's been a pleasure playing for y'all tonight. Keep an eye out for my second full-length album coming out next month..." He doesn't get to finish because the crowd goes insane. "Thank you, Charleston! Have a great night!"

The stage lights go off. Libby turns around, amazement on her face. "Can you believe that?"

"Incredible." I hope I manage to sound excited while I'm grinding my teeth.

"Cal, can you hold my purse just a second?" And without a word, Libby shoves it in my hand as she tears off through the pit. She's whipping the hat off her head.

"Shit! Libby, where..." But my voice dies away when I see her dash over to where the barrier between the pit and the seats begin. The kind of really crappy seats where you can't see the stage. The kind of tickets I easily could have bought and paid for if I hadn't made a call.

In them, two parents are holding hands with a little girl. She's strutting around dancing and singing. Libby walks up to them and says something. The little girl pauses. After a moment, they exchange hats. Soon, Libby is weaving her way back over to me.

And as she does, my heart realizes what it should have known years ago. I wasn't meant to know what love was until I met Libby

Akin. Now that I do, I realize it's a circle because she's the beginning and the end of it for me.

"You gave her your signed hat." I pull her toward me.

Libby shrugs like it's no big deal. "Nonna taught me to be grateful for the gifts I'm given and to share when I've got excess. Before I walked in the door tonight, I already had so much, Cal. So much. I had you."

I can't not kiss her after a comment like that. When I lift my head, I whisper, "If I had a choice between anything and you, Libby, you know I'd choose you, right?"

We're still kissing as the lights drop, announcing Small Town Nights' arrival on stage.

17

CALHOUN

TWELVE YEARS AGO FROM PRESENT DAY

We stumble into her apartment after the concert. I can't bear to lift my lips from hers long enough to let her turn off the alarm.

Libby reaches out a hand to slap at the panel and press a few buttons. I prove how grateful I am the alarm didn't go off by pressing her body up against the door. Sliding the dress she's wearing higher up her thighs, I pull one around my hip as I press deep against her.

She tears her mouth away to moan. "Cal—"

My lips brush under her jaw gently before I take a small nip. Using my other hand, I cup the fullness of her breast. "Libby, tell me you want me," I plead.

Her head jerks back as if she's been struck. Shit. Fuck. Did I push this too fast? I'm about to back away when all of a sudden, she wraps both arms around my neck and boosts herself up so both legs are hugging my back. Latching herself against my neck, Libby murmurs, "Make sure the door's locked."

Right.

Flipping the dead bolts, I turn, unable to believe I'm about to make love to the woman I've wanted for years but never dared hope I'd have the opportunity to touch. After all, how often can you touch the sun before you get burned?

I push her back against the door and drop my lips against hers. For long moments, I inhale the fragrant scent of her skin. As I grip the back of her neck, my mouth drops to the pulse throbbing in the base of her throat before I lift my head.

Libby licks her plump lips as if they've become dry in the few moments since I last had my mouth on them. "I want you, Cal." Her body shivers in my arms as if she's been imagining this moment.

She's not the only one.

Boosting her tighter against me, I feel her tight nipples press through her dress against my dress shirt. All it does is drive me mad to find out what they look like. Will they be light and pink, daring me to darken them with my teeth and tongue? Are they sweet berries? Or will they be taupe, wanting to turn toasty brown as I suckle them deep in my mouth?

I can't wait to find out.

Striding through her apartment, I make my way into her bedroom, hearing her moan against my ear as each movement of my legs rubs my cock against her thinly covered pussy. "I can't wait to find out how wet you are," I mutter. "To find out how slick your body's making itself for me. God, Libby, do you know how long I've wanted to sink my cock into you?" I barely manage to get the last word out when my knees bump against the side of her bed.

But it's her words that cause the lust to tear through my system. "Probably about as long as I've imagined you doing it," she admits. Reaching down, she unzips the hidden zipper along the side of her dress to almost midthigh. Reaching under her hair, she unties the knot holding the halter top up. Soon, there's nothing preventing me from getting to her luscious body but the pressure between us.

And it's unacceptable.

I drop her backward, gripping the edge of her dress as she falls. She lands softly, giggling as, in my haste, I manage to get her dress tangled up in her boots. "Laughing at me only delays me finding my way inside of you," I warn her with mock seriousness. But my lips are curving and my body's shaking as I try to untwist her dress before yanking off her first boot and letting it drop. The other goes sailing over my shoulder and lands with a crash that sends Libby into writhing hysterics on the bed. I can't help but join her.

Then part of my mind stills. Who would have ever thought to laugh at a time like this? Then again, why am I surprised? It's Libby. She brings laughter and light to every corner of my life.

Pulling my shirt over my head, I hop on one leg and quickly untie my boot before doing the same with the other. Libby lies on her back like a perfect offering, just waiting for me to take her. Finally, I shuck my jeans and join her on the bed clad in nothing but my black boxer briefs.

When our skin touches, it sends off sparks that I'd swear must be visible, but I can't see them in the dimly lit room. I drag my lips down her creamy, perfect skin to reach the light rose-colored nipples that are tightening even more as my mouth waters in anticipation.

I'm grateful for the dim light in the room as I can not only feel the heat of her arousal against my skin, I can see it as her skin flushes once my lips capture the first of the many treasures I intend on finding tonight. Flicking my tongue back and forth, I brace up on an elbow so my hand can tangle in her hair while my other hand cups her other breast, readying it for my lips, my tongue.

Libby is arching against me, her hands threaded in my hair, holding me tightly in place. "Cal, so good. So, so, good."

I release her nipple, to her dismay, but I surge upward and capture her moan with my lips. Her hands have slid out of my hair, and one slides down my back and into my shorts, pulling me flush against her body. The other wraps around my shoulders; her legs wrap around my hips, pressing her core into me. Imprinting herself on me. I grind my erection into her.

Her lips wrench away from mine on a gasp, and I know down to my core, neither one of us is coming out of tonight the same as the way we went in.

I cup Libby's other breast, holding it as my other hand drifts its way down to the joke of triangle silk she's been wearing beneath her dress. With a quick yank, I snap the strings obstructing me from getting to the heart of her. Cupping the heat, I let out a sound I'm not quite certain is human when I realize she's as wet as I am hard. I stroke my fingers through the thin curls covering her until they dance over her clit.

Libby moans. Her legs drop from my hips and begin to shift restlessly on the bed. "Oh, yes. More," she begs.

Pulling the scraps of silk out of the way, I return my hand to begin circling my thumb around and around her swollen clit that's so sensitive, Libby's practically levitating each time I touch it. Sliding down her body a bit, I situate myself so my head's in line with her breast. Just as I plunge two fingers into her tight, wet heat, I press against her clit and take the hardened nipple of her other breast into my mouth, sucking deep.

And Libby detonates, scoring her nails deep into my shoulders as she comes.

I let her down gently before I reach over the side of the bed for my jeans. Quickly sliding on a condom, I smooth my hands up her arms until our fingers are twined. Her eyes flutter open. I don't know what I expect to come out of her mouth, but it sure isn't "The gentlemanly thing would be to let me die in my perfect puddle of bliss."

I shake my head because the grin on her face belies her words. Releasing one of her hands, I lift her leg and press it back toward her chest. Nudging her opening with my cock, I raise a brow. "Want to try again?"

"Yes, please," she says immediately.

I pause, waiting for her to continue. When she doesn't say anything, I nudge myself in a tiny bit further. And hold.

"Oh, you mean you want me to say something to make you want to push that cock into my..."

Yeah, there's only so much I can take. I press my hips closer, gritting my teeth as her inner walls begin to clamp down. "Pussy," she whispers. "Push deep into my pussy, Cal. I want it. I want you so, so much."

And I push through the tiny muscles until I'm lodged deep into the woman I've only dreamed of having. After I release her leg, Libby promptly wraps both around me and reaches up to pull my head down to capture my lips in a brief kiss. Her lips keep moving around my face, touching down like a butterfly here and there.

I haven't even started to move, but already it's the best sex I've ever had as her nipples nestle themselves in my chest hair and her pussy clenches and releases all along my cock. God, if it's this amazing now, what's it going to feel like when I start to actually fuck her?

Libby grins. "I don't know, but anytime you want to get started, I'm on board with finding out." My head drops as I realize I spoke out loud.

I grin at her sass though. "Well, this time, I know a surefire way to deal with your mouth," I declare. Pulling out, I slam back in hard and deep. I'm rewarded by a long moan and her clenching down so tight, it's like nothing I've ever experienced.

And shock washes over me as my hips pull back and push in again. I know I never will.

Because it's Libby.

Push, pull, each time I do, Libby's hips rise and fall in cadence with me. Until finally, finally, she clenches and releases so hard, her orgasm is ripped from her a second time.

Burying myself inside of her, I come long and hard, whispering the only thing that matters.

Her name.

"Libby," I moan against the side of her neck.

Her hands smooth up and down my slick back even as shudders still rack her body.

Even as our heart rates return to normal, I know nothing is ever going to be the same.

Nothing.

Because I didn't just have sex with Libby. For the first time in my life—I made love. I just don't know if she realizes it.

WE SPEND ALL THE NEXT DAY IN BED BEFORE I HAD TO PREPARE TO HEAD to DC for a last-minute three-day jaunt the Admiral called me about late in the afternoon. I have to deliver a proposal to grant Alliance an exclusive contract with the Navy for intel in the Med and North African theater with him tomorrow afternoon. Since all I have to do is throw a few suits in a bag, I plan on staying with Libby as long as possible.

I was less than my normally unpleasant self on the phone—something Yarborough took great pleasure in pointing out—since I'd had less than twelve hours wrapped around the woman I'm quickly falling for before being jerked back into reality.

Libby did her best to soothe the bitterness away by joining me in her shower before I left. "Really, Cal, it's only three days. I'll be here when you get back," she told me as she rubbed the washcloth up and down over my chest. I withstood her slow torture for about three minutes before I boosted her against the wall and crushed my mouth against hers under the rain shower head.

Her brand of comfort helped but only insomuch as I can pluck out the memories while I sit in my room late at night and imagine her bright green eyes dilating before they drifted shut as I made her body writhe beneath mine.

I used to not care how long I was away. Now, I'm eager to get back. Then again, I never had anything as profound as Elizabeth Akin waiting for me.

Before I left, we spent the afternoon curled up at her apartment— just a football game and my woman. And damn, Libby smelled so damn delicious, she made me want to get down on my knees and ask her to call me out sick so I could spend the time eating all the things that would be good for me. While I was contemplating the merits of that, Libby shouted, "Oh, come on, Dawgs! You can play better than this!" amusing me to no end. "How the hell do you expect him to make a pass if he keeps getting sacked?"

Burying my head into her long hair, I burst out laughing. It sounded like a car backfiring.

Libby froze. "Every time you do that, I think I must be dreaming."

"What?" I brushed a kiss against the side of her neck I'd managed to expose. It'd been at least twenty minutes since I tasted her sweet skin. That's way too long when the only peace on this earth can be found in her arms.

"Laugh. You don't do it much, do you?"

I paused in trailing kisses down her neck. "I do with you," I told her honestly.

And just that quickly, the game was forgotten as she twisted in my arms. "Why?" Confusion was written all over her face.

I traced her lower lip with my thumb. "Maybe there's just something cute about the way you yell at the TV."

She rolled her eyes and turned around to watch the game.

Settling back, I pulled her tighter against me before answering her seriously. "You've become everything to me, Libby. I don't know how it happened, but I know for damned sure no one's ever been able to make me feel the things you do." Thoughtfully, I added, "I don't think anyone else ever can or ever will."

Her body stiffened before she turned carefully. Above the roar of a Georgia touchdown, she whispered, "I'm not sure if I understand what that means."

Looping my arms around her back, I tumbled her down to the cushions so she cradled me against the inside of her thighs. "I don't remember wanting to smile before you. I know for damn sure I didn't laugh."

Her eyes widened. "Ever?"

"What did I have to laugh about?" I scoffed. "I was a foster kid who knew I was only a paycheck until I was eighteen and was handed my walking papers. I grew up young and fast, honey. But one day, I heard this sound that startled me across the quad. It was pouring rain, and everyone around me was cursing about getting wet. But there you were laughing. You were just standing still with your head tilted back absorbing the moment. It's the first time I consciously remember smiling."

She was so still beneath me—no reaction whatsoever. I pressed on. "It was the first moment I felt something more for you."

"Why did you wait so long?" Libby asked in a very subdued voice.

"You were young, honey," I started to explain, but she cut me off.

"No. Why did you wait so long to come back into my life?" She fought to pull her arms out from where I had them trapped in between us. "God, Cal, why?"

"I don't know. Maybe because I unconsciously knew we'd end up right here and I was afraid..."

"Yes?" The edge of her voice was so lethal it could have been a weapon itself.

"I was afraid I wouldn't know what to do. I told you, I didn't know anything about relationships, Libby. Maybe some part of me thought I'd end up hurting you," I admitted. I didn't realize until the words came out, until she forced the truth from me, that's exactly what I was doing by not contacting her. But even as I held my breath, waiting for forgiveness for being a stupid ass and wasting precious time, Libby's eyes narrowed as she looked for the lie in my words.

"Promise me you won't lie to me about how you feel—about me, about anything."

"I promise."

"Good. Then you'll tell me what you're really thinking when I tell you the hat I swapped with the girl last night had Brendan Blake's phone number in it," Libby told me as calmly as if she was reciting a grocery list.

"What the hell?" I barked, the urge to find that singer and make him lose his vocal chords sounding more appealing.

Smirking, she cupped the side of my face. "I'm a big girl, Cal. And I know who I want. Remember that."

My heart was still pounding in a combination of fury and lust when I lowered my mouth to hers and said, "Yes, ma'am."

We didn't end up watching the rest of the game. I checked the score on the airport monitor.

Dawgs won.

Perfect day other than the fact I'm hundreds of miles away from Libby.

18

PRESENT DAY

ELIZABETH

We're both laughing as I recount my version of Cal's and my date to the Small Town Nights concert from the early days of Brendan Blake's career. "It was so much fun." I'm gasping for air.

"After everything that happened to you, Brendan reached out to you, correct?" Dr. Powell asks.

"I was truly shocked. I mean, he's *Brendan Blake* now." I emphasize Brendan's name because he's now country music's megastar. "I thought it was sweet."

"How did Cal react?"

The amused look I shoot him says it better than words can. There's more I could share about Cal's reaction, but I won't. Those memories are just between me and Cal. And they're delicious. My lips simply curve as I shake my head, refusing to answer.

Dr. Powell tries another tack. "So, other than the big dates, what kind of things did you do together?"

I cross my legs from one side to the other to get comfortable. "Everything and nothing."

"Do you mind elaborating?"

"Not at all. I grew up in the city, but I got to experience it again through Cal's eyes. Yes, we both lived there, but he never explored it. We'd wander the city checking out all of these must-do food places. I swear, for a man who grew up in the South, I was appalled he'd never had chicken and dumplings or fried green tomatoes! You'd have thought he was a Yankee with his eating habits."

"That seems almost criminal. Is now the wrong time to admit I've never had fried green tomatoes either?"

"It certainly is," I say with a touch of indignation. We both laugh again. I continue. "We went out to Fort Sumter and on the USS *Yorktown*, which is a must do. Then there were just the days when we'd drive and talk until our voices got hoarse. Those were my favorite days."

"The talking?"

"Any day I was with Cal, but especially those."

"Why?"

"I felt connected to him in ways that can never be replicated. I wasn't just learning about him in dribs and drabs; I was absorbing the information as if you'd dropped me into the Cooper River and I came out wet. I soaked it in. What we have now is different." What we have now was the result of tempering the edges of misunderstandings, loneliness, and fear and forging them into a love so strong that no foe in heaven or hell could break us.

Some of what I'm thinking must be reflected on my face. "Would you go back and change any of it?" Dr. Powell asks me gently.

"To change any of it is to change all of it. And I'm sitting before you because in my heart, I know this."

"According to my notes, after the incident on the *Sea Force*, you didn't reconcile immediately with your husband. Why is that?"

"Because accepting you can't live without someone and forgiving every lie they ever told are very different paths. And the first step begins with forgiving yourself for believing you're a fool when you have nothing to forgive."

"Very true, Libby." There are some papers shuffled before a smile breaks out. "I have a note here to ask you about the first time you told Cal you were in love with him."

I groan. "I felt like an idiot."

"Why? Did he not say it back?"

"No, because I screamed it. I never thought he heard me!"

"That makes no sense, Libby. You screamed it and you didn't think Cal heard your declaration of love?"

"I thought my face was going to kiss the ground, Doctor. Literally. I was screaming prayers and goodbyes at the same time."

"Dear Lord. Were you in a wreck?"

"No! He took me skydiving!" I'm still pissed as shit after all these years.

Dr. Powell drops his organized file of papers as all professionalism flies away. Kind of like the words out of my mouth the day Cal took me up in that plane.

19

ELIZABETH

TWELVE YEARS AGO FROM PRESENT DAY

I f I murder my boyfriend, will that get me sent to jail for the rest of my life? The thought tantalizes me as we're spending a perfectly beautiful Saturday preparing to die.

He just might die sooner if I think it will keep my feet on the ground.

As if he can sense my thoughts, Cal reaches over and squeezes my hand. "It will be fine. Now pay attention; they're telling you important information."

"It's important if you plan on doing this more than once," I hiss at him.

He just grins that smile only I ever get, and then he faces forward, the pressure on my hand urging me to do the same.

Cal got home from a two-week business trip just three days ago. Three remarkable days where I spent most of them in bed, making a few appearances at Deja Vu primarily to do payroll so my staff didn't up and quit on me. The rest of the time, I listened as Cal explained about missed connections, materials Iris complained she needed for the client that went up and missing, and lost luggage on the way home. I soothed him by saying, "It's over, you're here. That's all that matters."

He rolled into me, picking up one of the sunflowers he never fails to bring home after an extended business trip, and dragged it down my arm. "What did you do?"

Ache without you. It was on the tip of my tongue to say, but something was holding me back. When I went out to Akin Hill last weekend, I sat by Nonna's grave and admitted to her I was head over heels in love with Cal. "You'd love him too, Nonna. He complements and completes me." After explaining all of the ways I wasn't sure I could live without him if he wasn't a part of my life, I pushed to my feet and pressed my lips to the cold stone that has the biggest heart buried beneath it. "I just hope you can see everything. I wouldn't want you to miss the life I hope to build with him."

Instead, I told him, "I worked, went out to see the family, baked a little. Normal things, Cal."

He scowled. "You baked? What?"

Oh, my man wasn't going to be happy. "A coconut pecan cake."

Cal pushed up on his elbows. "Where is it?"

"Gone," I said nonchalantly. It happened to be waiting at Cal's in a cake carrier, but since he'd come here first, he hadn't seen it.

His mouth opened and closed like a fish. I don't even think he realized it. Finally, he was able to form words. "You couldn't even save me a piece?" He was so incredulous, I burst out laughing. Tears leaked from the corner of my eyes into the pillow beneath me. Then, there was something that tugged at my heart.

Hurt.

And my laughter dried up.

God, if there's a man who needs cake and smiles and laughter, it's Calhoun Sullivan. We hardly talk about it, but growing up without parents affected him. The way I nurture him feeds his soul. I touched his arm gently. The muscles bunched beneath. "Cal, honey, you know me better than that," I reminded him.

He relaxed imperceptibly. A rough smile crossed his face. "Then where's my slice?"

"Your cake," I emphasized. His lips parted as I continued. "Is waiting for you at your place. I thought you might stop there to get

91

your clothes. I didn't realize they'd lose your luggage and you'd come directly here, or I'd have kept it waiting for you."

Now, I'd like to smash the remains of the cake into his gorgeous face. This is some sadistic payback; I just know it.

Cal is patiently sitting through the beginner's skydiving course with me even though he's been a certified jumper for years. I'm sure that's because he knows if he doesn't, there's no way on this planet I'm staying, let alone going up in that plane. None. I lean over and whisper, "Aren't parachutes supposed to be for emergencies only?"

He coughs to hide a laugh.

"Okay, everyone." The instructor claps his hands together. "Let's practice what we learned."

Practice. Right.

Can I practice running away from the room screaming like a madwoman?

Cal stands with grace and pulls me from my chair. I groan. "I promise, Libs, it will be unlike any experience you've ever known. Trust me?" His dark eyes are shining down at me.

And another piece of Cal is handed to me. This isn't payback; this is something he truly enjoys that he wants to share with me. "Trusting you isn't the problem."

"Then what is?" he asks as we join the others in the practice room.

"My fear of only living long enough to see the earth come up to my face is," I grumble as I go over to the instructor, my partner for the tandem jump.

Cal leans against the wall while we move around in necessary training required for our certification for a while before he disappears. Good. Now I can't shoot daggers in his direction and can actually focus. We've practiced how we're going to be hooked up, how we're going to land, and everything in between. The only part we haven't practiced is my screaming, but I figure that's something I don't need to work on.

Finally, the moment I'm dreading arrives. "Who's ready to fly?" Bruce, the instructor and the man who's going to hurl me to the earth for my final moments living, calls out.

The entire room—save me—erupts in cheers.

"Then let's go!" Bruce leads the way. Cal and I are somewhere in the middle. Cal's got a pack on his shoulder he didn't have before.

"What's that?" I ask.

"My chute." It takes me a second before I realize Cal's already got his harness in place. He slips on a pair of dark shades, but even without being able to see his eyes, his entire demeanor is relaxed.

It's just another reason to hate him right now.

"Libby!" Bruce calls out to me. "Come on over so I can get you in your harness."

"You're not getting a blow job for a month. Don't imagine my mouth on your dick because it isn't happening." I grit my teeth in a semblance of a smile at Cal before turning on my heel to stalk away.

He barks out a laugh right as I take the first step. Reaching out, he snags the back of my shirt to halt me. "One thing, Libs?"

"Yeah?"

"I'll bet your mouth will be wrapped around my cock by the end of tonight. You have no idea, baby, but the rush..." Instead of finishing his sentence with words, Cal chooses then to kiss me, leaving me incapable of telling him the million and a half ways he's wrong.

Instead, I'm left light-headed by the feel of Cal's hands on my hips drawing me close against his body so I can feel his arousal. Knowing this may be the last time I feel these lips on mine, my arms twine around his neck as I give in unconditionally. His head slants and draws me deeper into the kiss, his tongue stroking against mine over and over. The passion is driving me dizzy, crazy, in a world that's suddenly gone upside down. The only thing to hold on to is Cal, so I do.

Slowly, our lips part. His are fuller and glossy from where my tongue has gone over them, my teeth nipped them. "Go to Bruce, baby. It's time to fly."

This time, there's no sass when I reply, "But I just did." Still, I turn and head over to the instructor, who has a knowing smirk on his face.

I don't care. I can officially die happy since the man I love just kissed me goodbye.

20

ELIZABETH

TWELVE YEARS AGO FROM PRESENT DAY

"A re you ready?" Bruce yells to another tandem team. They give him a hand slap/fist bump thing before easing to the open doorway. Each one. Is it some kind of come-back-alive ritual of the crazy helmet people?

"I'm surrounded by lunatics," I whisper.

"What's that?" Cal yells as he adjusts his goggles. He looks cocky and so damn hot I want to jump him in the back of the plane—not strap myself to Bruce and go out the front of it.

"Nothing," I yell back.

"Are you ready?"

I look away, nauseated. "Sure. I'm just fine."

Cal opens his mouth, but whatever he's about to say is interrupted by Bruce yelling over the wind whipping through the open door. "Elizabeth! Let's hook up."

I give him a thumbs-up. I just hope I'm the only one of the four of us still left on this tin bird—including the pilot—who can tell it's shaking life a leaf. Standing in front of Bruce, I'm outwardly calm as he attaches the D-rings to the fittings on the back of my harness under Cal's watchful eye. Cal reaches over and jerks the harness a few times. Hard.

"Ready to fly, baby?" Cal yells.

"Sure." But the rolling pitch to my stomach has other ideas as Bruce frog-marches me to the door.

"Remember, step as far onto the platform as you can, Elizabeth," Bruce yells.

"Libby. If I'm going to die, call me Libby." His rough beard rubs against my face as he chuckles.

"You'll be fine, Libby. In fact, let's celebrate. You're about to be my 12,000th jump."

"Can we make it to 12,001?" I'm practically begging.

"It's going to be fine. Cal's going to hop out right behind us," he tries to assure me when it does nothing of the sort. Why do I want him telling me the man I love is about to do something so monumentally asinine as jump out of a plane after me? "Shouldn't he go first so we can, I don't know, save him or something?" Didn't I see that in a movie once?

My foot begins to edge out onto the platform, and the wind is whipping through the jumpsuit I'm wearing. Yeah, there's no need to hide how hard I'm shaking now because I'm clutching the oh-shit bar at the edge of the plane door like someone's declared it's a winning lottery ticket.

"Libby, you can do this! I promise. Nothing's going to happen."

Sure. After all, what could happen when you're 14,000 feet up in the air being held up by a harness that's been worn by umpteen number of people before me? These are the questions I should have been asking in class instead of sassing Cal. Now, as Bruce gently rubs my fingers, I may never have the chance.

"It's the only way down?" I'm going to cry soon if we don't do this; I just know it.

"It's the best way," Bruce says.

"Then do it. Just do it."

"Okay. On three. Let me signal Cal." He tosses a two-finger salute to my boyfriend. I lift one hand from my death grip to do the same. *Courage, Libby,* I mentally tell myself.

Instead of letting me put it back, Bruce snags my fingers and places them around my waist, holding them snugly. "You call it."

"One," I call shakily.

"Two..." The next thing you know our bodies are pitching forward. "I love you, Cal!" I scream with all my might, my eyes so tightly shut they might as well be fused together, figuring there's no way anyone can hear me.

We tumble. I feel my entire being forced open and backward into Bruce's. I'm waving my hands in every direction. I come into contact with something, I just hope it isn't something like the cutaway thingy. We're spinning, twisting, turning. "Oh, sweet Jesus, deliver me safely," I chant. Not that anyone can hear me. Except, I pray, God.

The devil who holds my life literally in his hands is laughing. I can't hear it, but I feel his big body vibrating. I just hope like hell it's not separating the harness that holds the two of us together.

I begin to pray in earnest.

"I never got to tell Cal I love him before I die! Holy God. Sweet Lord. I swear, I meant to tell him."

My arms are swinging. I have no concept of where we are, how far we've fallen.

All I know is I have no center.

"God in heaven, forgive me for taking your name in vain."

I feel a tap on the front of my shoulder as Bruce and I are floating, and I scream, not that anyone can hear above the wind. I'm struggling against Bruce when he forces us back into position. It's only due to my need for oxygen my eyes pop open, and there he is. All I see is the beauty of Cal's face. There's something different about it. Maybe it's the covering of his helmet softening his normally taciturn features but...

I'm about to reach out for him, to be brave enough to touch him midair, when Bruce suddenly yanks the rip cord to our chute and we're jerked up feet away from Cal, who's still falling in the sky.

We float along gently for a few moments. As we get lower in altitude and I figure my chances of not succumbing to my death are better, I have to admit this part's not bad. So, I decide to unwedge my big-girl panties from my throat and redeem myself by asking, "How fast were we going when we jumped?"

"Us or the plane?"

"Us? You know when we were, um, free-falling?"

"At a guess? Somewhere between 120-140 miles per hour."

"I don't even drive that fast! Forget being in love with him. I'm killing him the minute we hit the ground," I declare.

"Are you always this fun because if you are, I might see if Cal wants to sign you up to get certified."

"There is no way you're getting me back in that damn plane," I announce to Bruce haughtily.

"Well, if this is going to be your only jump, let's make it a good ending. Landing procedures. Remember, lift your legs, Libby. I control the landing. When we glide in, I'll try to land on my feet depending on the wind. Check?"

"Check." I'm seriously paying attention.

"My feet will hit first. You'll feel the impact through your body. If you do, put yours down. You'll be standing, and I'll capture the chute. Otherwise, you'll end up between my legs and I'll cushion you. Check?"

"Check." I want to land much more gracefully than I took off. Then, I want to set fire to this rig, steal Cal's keys, and go home and eat the rest of the coconut pecan cake on my own.

I see another canopy below us. Pointing to it, I ask, "Is that Cal?"

"Yep. We're circling to let him land first."

Gee, more time in the air. I'll be sure to thank him later. I can't give it much thought because the ground is fast approaching. I feel Bruce's legs lift, giving me a silent cue to lift mine. I do. Then, miracle of miracles, his feet grab hold. I drop my legs, and we both stumble forward. "Holy crap. We made it! Get me out of this thing so I can kiss your face."

"I think someone might have a problem with that, though I appreciate the offer." Bruce unhooks us, but just as I'm about to turn around to thank him for saving me from certain death, my body is hauled against Cal's.

His hair is tousled, like after I run my fingers through it. His eyes are dilated, as if he's in shock. Immediately, my anger is wiped away out of concern. What could have happened? He's been on the ground maybe a minute more than Bruce and me. "Honey? What's wrong?"

"Not a damn thing." Cal yanks me into his arms. One hand cups my cheek while the other bands tightly around my waist. It's so tight, I can feel it through the rig, the jumpsuit, and my clothes I'm wearing underneath in the beautiful November South Carolina day. "I just thought you should know I love you too."

"Oh, my God. You heard me? How?" I blush to the roots of my hair.

"Does it matter? Or does it matter that I'll love you every night you close your eyes and every day you open them."

"No matter what?" I say shakily, not entirely certain if that's due to Cal's declaration or the fact I'm alive to hear it.

"I love you, Libby. I will always be yours."

"Good. Then you'll still love me when I forgive you for making me jump out of that tin can." Shoving my way past Cal without even a kiss, I storm back toward the training facility. I don't care that I'm likely being laughed at.

Never again. I will not experience that hell ever again.

21

CALHOUN

TWELVE YEARS AGO FROM PRESENT DAY

I'm grinning like a fool as Libby's strides eat up the distance quicker than I've ever seen her move. Even pissed as hell, she didn't deny loving me. And I love her so much, I'm consumed with it. I can't make it without her anymore.

God, I don't know what I did, but help me keep doing it.

Just as the thought passes through my mind, Bruce tosses an arm over my shoulder. "I didn't realize it was Libby until she told me to call her by that name right before the jump. Wait till I tell Dawn." Both Bruce and his wife, Dawn, were team members of Alliance when I was in college. After they retired a few years ago, they opened Sunrise Skydive. While it's open to the public on the weekends, it serves as a training facility for teams like ours during the week. Even though they retired a few years ago, they still keep their nose in the game, just in a different way.

During their transition out, they got to know Sam and Iris well, helping them understand the nuances of the job the way only another agent of Alliance can. Oftentimes, our jobs are as simple as gathering intel and providing it to the right agency for them to act upon. Since we have no capability to arrest any suspects, we're limited on what we can do. Then there are others where we're the ones sent in, my specialty being kidnap and rescues, and our very lives depend on each other not only for the intel, but the backup.

As teams often do, when the adrenaline high is done and we're waiting to go home, we share. For Sam and Iris, Libby was a frequent topic of conversation. Hell, she still is. At least with me. But when Bruce and Dawn were on the team, I would sit nearby absorbing any news about her I could. I should have recognized then what she meant to me, but I needed her to show me what it was.

Love. The kind that will never end.

"That's Libby," I confirm.

"You're a lucky son of a bitch, Cal."

"Of that, I'm aware."

My lips quirk as Bruce ticks off a small list about Libby that doesn't delve into the depth that I would describe her. "She's gorgeous, feisty, smart from all accounts, and despite being a terrible diver, she has a direct line to God, 'cause she apparently works miracles. Look at you."

I glance down, seeing my own custom rig, and raise a brow in question.

He goes on. "I've never seen you smile until today, let alone laugh. And she tolerates you trotting around the world trying to save it?" Bruce shakes his head.

I squirm a bit at the last. "She knows I work for a contractor named Alliance, but she doesn't know the extent of what we do. All she knows is it involves security and it's classified."

Bruce's arm drops from my back, making me feel like I've lost something precious that I never had before. Acceptance.

"You have to tell her, Cal."

"I have to do what I think is right for her." I stop moving and face my longtime friend. "I have to protect her. That's my constant mission. You saw her up there." I jerk my thumb up to the cloudless blue sky above us. "What do you think she would do if she knew I had to do that on occasion?" *Walk away.* The painful thought whispers through my mind.

He opens his mouth and shuts it. "Basing your love on a lie is going to come back and bite you in the ass."

"I'm not lying to her," I insist.

"If you're not lying to her, you're lying to yourself. What you're keeping from her is a large part of who you are."

"What I'm keeping from her is what we keep hidden from any number of people," I retort.

"She's not just anyone."

"No, she's precious to me. All I want is for her to just be as happy as she is today for the rest of her life."

Bruce looks at me pityingly. "Then keep lying." He holds up his hand as I start to protest. "Because in the long run, it won't work. She either accepts you—all of you—or your love is going to wash up on the rocks. She may have trepidation, but your job as someone who loves her is to get her past her fear. Hell, Cal. You could have taken her on that jump today. Why didn't you?"

A tick in my jaw betrays me. I don't say a word.

Bruce continues. "A woman as unique as Libby Akin has been made out to be doesn't strike me as the type to waste her time on someone who won her heart through lies. If all the stories I've heard about her over the years are even partially true, a woman who has a heart that enormous?" Bruce steps back. "Then it's you who's in trouble. Just be honest with her and you'll never have to wonder if today will be the day she walks away and you can protect her from the world you're so afraid of hurting her." With those last parting words, Bruce gathers his parachute in his arms and starts to walk away.

I stand stock-still for a few moments. I can't lose the light that Libby has brought to my life. Now that I know I have her love, I'll do anything to protect it.

Anything.

Even if that means hiding the parts of me I know will send her running away.

22

ELIZABETH

TWELVE YEARS AGO FROM PRESENT DAY

I 'm excited Cal will be back from his trip tomorrow. Thank goodness this one was only a few days. I giggle to myself as I type a few notes into my computer. "You'd think he's taking over some third-world country."

"Did you say something, Libby?" One of my interns pops his head in. "Need anything?"

"No, Leland. Thanks for asking, honey."

"Of course. Saw you managed to sell the grandfather clock today?" There's awe in his voice. "How many more days until that beast is moved?"

Quickly pulling up the schedule, I announce, "Two weeks." Leaning back in my chair, I casually toss out, "How would you like to help me rearrange the display?"

His jaw slackens. "Me?"

"What? Did you think I brought you on only for your ability to charm the customers?" I tease gently. I stand, working the kinks out of my back from too much time behind my desk. "You have a flair with accessorizing. I'd also love to get your input on my sketches for the holiday." Even though it's only June, I have to start placing subtle items throughout the store soon so by the time fall comes around, I'm not completely shutting down for the transformation.

"I'd be honored, Libby."

"Then let's plan on that once we get rid of Big Ben." I smirk over the nickname we gave the monstrous clock.

Leland gives me a charming smile. "You've got it. If there's nothing else, I'm going to go home. You headin' out soon?"

I groan. "I should probably catch up on paperwork."

Leland frowns. "But I thought you always left on time when Cal got home from a business trip?"

"That's why I'll be out early tomorrow," I tell him.

"Hmm."

"What is it?"

"I wonder how his truck got here is all. I went to help my last customer with... Libby?"

But I'm already racing past him to the back of the building. Throwing open the door, my heart flips in happiness because Leland is right. Cal's truck is sitting in its usual parking spot.

"I guess you didn't know?" Leland comes up behind me.

I shake my head. "No! I've got to go shut down."

But Leland just smiles. Handing me my purse and an envelope, he leans down to hug me before saying, "I've got it. Have an amazing night, Libby." Turning, he strolls down the hall toward my office while I clutch the envelope in one hand, my purse in the other.

Quickly shifting the bag to my shoulder, I use my nail to slit the edge of the envelope open. I slide out the card and gasp. The paper is as fine as any I've ever touched. It's almost fragile beneath my finger, but it's what's on the cover that makes my heart pound before I even open it.

It's a sunflower.

With trembling hands, I open the card. *"There is no way..."* I read aloud. I flip the card over. I peek into the envelope.

Nothing.

"Cal, honey. I think you forgot the rest of the message," I murmur as I pull out my keys to my apartment upstairs. Unlocking the door, I slide through, close and lock it behind me. Turning, I freeze in place before my breath whooshes out. "Oh, my God."

Every other step has a card on it, and the ones that don't have candles on them. "What is this?" I wonder aloud. Dropping my bag and keys, I move over to the first step and pick up the card. It's a different feel than the first one, which I haven't let go of. I open the envelope and find another card of sunflowers, this time it's a photograph of a field of them. *"For you to understand..."*

I climb the next two steps and pick up the card. *"The depth of my love for you."* My heart sighs. Anxiously, I go up the next two stairs. *"I don't just want..."*

"Today with you."

"I want your tomorrows as well."

"My heart will always be yours, Elizabeth."

My heart is pounding as I pick up the last card. With shaking hands, I open it and read it aloud like I have all the others. *"Open the door, honey."* Clutching the cards to my chest, I reach for the knob to my apartment.

Then, they all fall from my hands as my arms drop to my side in shock. "C-C-Cal?" I stammer out as I look down on him.

Down.

Because he's on his knees in front of me in a room filled with sunflowers and candlelight.

"Oh, my God." My hands fly to my mouth.

His full lips curve in that sexy smile that I know is all mine. "I want to start over one more time with you, Libby." Cal reaches into his pocket and pulls out a small velvet box.

"Yes." The word is out of my mouth before his long fingers can manipulate the hinged top.

"Honey, I think you're supposed to wait for me to ask the question," he teases, but the love in his eyes warms me from my head to my toes and all the places he makes me tingle in between.

I drop to my knees and scoot forward until I'm within touching distance of him. "Yes," I repeat huskily.

"Elizabeth Akin, I should have known when you healed all the cracks of my heart with your smile and your laughter, infusing them with so much joy that I found my own, it had to be love. I'm sorry it took me so long to find my way back to you." He pauses.

I want to strangle him and kiss him. Knowing I'll have the chance for the rest of my life to do both is the only thing preventing me from doing either. Trembling, I sit back on my heels.

"I never want us to end, but it's time to begin the last part of our lives together." Pulling open the box, Cal removes a yellow diamond set in a yellow-gold band. Lifting my shaking hand, he kisses the back of it before he slides the ring on. "It reminded me of sunflowers. It reminds me of you."

"God, Cal," I plead. I don't know how much longer I'm going to be able to hold off crying, and I don't want to. I want to memorize every moment of this with clear eyes.

"I love you, Libby. Always. Please marry me?" His deep voice, which normally carries a note of both seductiveness and command, is pleading. "I didn't know how to love until I found a woman who taught me what it meant. You make me feel everything."

Without delay, I give him the word I said to him ever since I stood in the door and found him on his knees.

"Yes."

Cal grabs me into his arms and, standing, lifts me into his arms. He kisses me long and deep, devouring me as he moves us over to the couch. "The bedroom's not far," I murmur, knowing Cal's penchant for taking me more than once.

He kisses me. "I want you next to the flowers that fade beneath your light, Libby." Reaching behind me for the zipper to my dress, he falls silent for a moment before a breath hisses out between his teeth when he spies the strapless bra, thong, and garters I'm wearing. "Damn."

It's nice to know that on a night where Cal's made my heart explode, I still managed to surprise him.

23

PRESENT DAY

ELIZABETH

"How long did it take for Cal to talk with you about who he was?"

Lifting my wrist, I glance down. "How long have we been talking?"

We both laugh. Dr. Powell shakes his head at my sass. "All joking aside, you'd known each other for years, had been dating a while. He knew your family—some would say fairly well. When did he open up?"

The light dawns. "You mean about his past. About how he grew up." Fury begins to crawl across my skin like I've just stepped in a nest of fire ants.

"Yes." But it's said warily as if he realizes he's unleashed something he can't control.

"Isn't it ironic that a man whose life has been so picked apart in so many ways has given his whole damn life to protect the very people who have the freedom to hurl insults at him about our marriage? About his honor? I'm the one wearing his rings; it's between me, Cal, and God to determine what's right and wrong!" I shout.

Dr. Powell holds up his folder as if that's going to protect himself.

It takes me a moment to realize I've picked up the juice at my side. "Oops. Sorry." I take a moment to calm my temper down.

"I was afraid I was about to be bathed in apple juice," he jokes.

"It's not as sticky as orange," I return.

"You're an expert on this?"

I flush hotly. "Well…"

No longer afraid of flying juice bottles, Dr. Powell leans forward. I acquiesce. "It was actually the morning after Cal and I got engaged. We were talking about kids."

"You both wanted them?"

"I did. Cal didn't."

"And that angered you?"

"No, what angered me was the reason why." I hesitate. "This isn't really part of our story."

"But it ultimately affected it," Dr. Powell counters.

True. And it's not like this information isn't public knowledge by now. "I'd been dating Cal for roughly six months, yet he deflected any mention of his birth parents. He'd mentioned being a foster child on occasion. And I knew the man I fell in love with enough to know when to push and when to bring issues to me on his own time."

"And that happened that morning."

"Yes. When he mentioned he declared he never wanted to have a child carry on his name."

"His full name?"

I shake my head. "No, his name at all. He didn't want a child to carry the Sullivan name. Frankly, he didn't want me to carry a child of his at all." Smoothing a hand over my bulging stomach, I mentally reassure our soon-to-be blessing that's not the case now.

"Why on earth not?" Clearly, I've shocked Dr. Powell.

"Because deep down, Cal was ashamed by his past. He was always so self-assured, I assumed he had moved past it. I was wrong. But it took us having it out that morning to prove differently."

"How?"

Shifting to get more comfortable, I lay my hand over my baby bump. "Cal surprised me with breakfast in bed," I begin.

24

ELIZABETH

TWELVE YEARS AGO FROM PRESENT DAY

Sunlight streams through the windows, only tempered by the sheers protecting my bedroom from any potential eyes that might try to peek in from the street. It's not enough to stop the light from catching the facets of the ring that's such a new yet beloved weight on my hand and sending little rainbows dancing all around the walls of the room.

"I can't believe it." My voice still holds all the heartfelt amazement when I said a version of those words last night as Cal slipped the ring on my hand.

The clatter of dishes startles me away from my bliss. "Believe it, Libs. This is it. You and me, forever." A shirtless Cal crosses the threshold of my room carrying a tray of coffee, mugs, and pastries.

I mock pass out against the fluffy pillows behind me. "I must've died last night. There's no way I managed to get the guy and breakfast in bed. Things like this just don't happen." Using the heel of my hand, I jostle the side of my head as if to knock everything back to rights.

Quirking a brow as he sets the tray on the bed, Cal asks, "Did this"—he runs a hand up the inside of my leg. I shiver in response —"scramble your brains?"

Dreamily, I arch into his gentle touch. We both moan when I reach out and trail my fingers up and down the rigid length rising up behind his jeans. "You're wearing too many clothes," I complain. I shift the leg his hand isn't on against the tousled sheets in invitation. My other hand smooths the place in the bed where he lay next to me in between long bouts of lovemaking all night long.

Quickly, he shifts my hand before shucking his jeans. They fall to the floor with a thunk. Moving the tray from the side of my bed to the nightstand, he crawls on top of me. "The coffee will keep."

"This won't," I agree, just as the hair on his chest brushes against my sensitive nipples. A surge of warmth builds below, waiting for Cal to release it.

He pushes my tangled hair away from my face before he runs the tip of his nose against mine. "Did you sleep well, my beautiful fiancée?"

I sink my hands into his hair, positioning him just where I want to kiss him. "Never better," I assure him. "You?"

He shakes his head.

My brow furrows. "Why not?"

"I spent the night holding you, marveling at how everything's changed since we met." His lips touch mine, too briefly in my opinion. "To be honest, if I could be awake every moment we're together, I'd sleep through the parts of life where you're not by my side."

My fingers tighten against his as he deepens our kiss. It's worshipping and reverent at the same time. His tongue plays against my own, driving thoughts of anything but this out of my head.

This is all I need is my last coherent thought, before Cal drives us to a place where only the two of us exist.

"Do you think the coffee is still good?" I murmur much later as I'm curled against Cal's perfect body.

He bursts out laughing. I snuggle deeper. "Forget I asked. I don't need anything but the sound of your laugh to start my day perfectly."

Combing his fingers through my hair, he asks, "Why's that?"

Reluctantly lifting my head, I adjust myself so my eyes meet his. "Because it makes my heart brighter," I say simply.

His smile turns tender. "Saying things like that isn't going to get you coffee. It's going to make you exhausted."

I adjust myself so I'm curled against his chest. "I don't care."

"Nor will it give you the opportunity to call your parents to tell them about the wedding."

I make a dismissive sound. "When I decide to emerge from my cocoon of bliss, they'll still be there."

His body's shaking against me. "A cocoon of bliss?"

"Happy wife, happy life, buddy. Better get used to it."

A light tap lands on my rear for that bit of sass. "Hmm, if that's the case, then I need to figure out when I'm going to move in." He drops that bomb so matter-of-factly, I start coughing as I choke on my own breath.

"What?" I manage to wheeze out. I've never lived with anyone but Iris or my family. Even when I was engaged to Kyle, as brief as that was, we never lived together.

Rolling over so he's lightly pinning me, Cal's smile fades. "This—you and me—we're forever, Libby. Through the laughter, the pain, the good and bad." How is it my heart can pound so hard when it's dissolving in my chest.

Eyes burning, I nod, because I want this too. I just didn't realize how much.

"We don't have to wait to start to have our future, Libby."

Gripping his biceps, I give in. Kind of. "Honey, I have no problem with you moving in, but it's going to be a problem with you running back to your place each day to change for work. There is no, and I mean no room for your clothes. So, instead of you moving here, why don't we figure out where we want to buy a home together? Maybe a place where maybe your clothes can take up residence? And—" My demeanor changes from teasing even as Cal tries control his uproarious laughter. "—we can get a few extra bedrooms for extending our family later."

His face closes up. "Children?"

"Well, yes." Why this comes as a surprise to him, I don't know. "Cal, you've met my family. It shouldn't come as a surprise I'd want children." I bite my lip.

"With how I grew up, I hadn't given them much thought. Until I met your family, I didn't see the beauty in children, I saw the burden," he admits.

"Surely your foster parents…"

He shakes his head. "They were just there, Libby. They didn't hurt me, but love?" His voice holds a note of disbelief. "I knew brotherhood from my time in the military, and I recognized familial love from you and Sam."

"But parental love?"

"Never. Not until I came to Akin Hill and sat on the fringes of a woman's funeral and realized the stories being told about her—from the pastor down to her great-grandchildren—were spoken with despair and tragedy in their voices and smiles and tears on their faces." He brushes my hair back from my face. "It was your nonna who made me realize what I had growing up wasn't normal."

"What we had wasn't standard either, Cal," I feel compelled to point out.

"The estate, no. The love? Adults and children demonstrating not only respect out of duty but out of uncontrollable emotion? You'd have had that because of the people you are." He rubs his thumb over the apple of my cheek. "I finally had a name for the emotions you made me feel," he whispers. "I didn't know what it was before because no one ever said it to me. But all day, I saw it. I felt it, and it wasn't about me. It was a woman I'm damn sorry I'll never get to know."

Me too, but I don't say it aloud. As I rub my hand up and down his arm, I catch sight of the diamond gleaming on my finger. It holds nothing on the facets of this incredible man.

"What is it about children that concerns you?"

"That I could pass on to them whatever I came from," he says bluntly.

"Cal," I try to speak, but he shakes his head.

"Libby, my time in foster care..." he begins. "It was cold. It was harsh. If that's my example, what do I do?"

"You trust in your family."

His head pulls back. "My family?"

"Mine," I remind him simply. Because over the last six months, Cal's managed to win over my parents, Josh, and even Sydney, who—as Cal put it—was determined to maim him the first time they met. Despite the fact Cal claims he has no idea what a family's supposed to be, he's seamlessly blended into mine.

He goes on. "I was left on the doorstep of a garage in Calhoun, Georgia. Sullivan's garage, to be exact, before I was taken in by the Bauers. I only have a name because it was pieced together. I don't want to taint the beauty of you by asking you to take my name, let alone pass that along to a child."

"Will you abandon me?" I stop him before he can continue. "Will you disgrace our family, whatever it ends up being? Will you betray me?"

"Never!" The vow is spoken roughly.

I curl up and grip his face. "Then I will take your name. If we're blessed with them, our children will carry your name. With the man you are, how could you not think I wouldn't want them, or that they wouldn't be proud of their father when I'm going to be proud to be his wife?"

The vulnerability on his face undoes me. "What kind of man is that?"

"Strong. Loving. Committed. And all of those things made me fall in love with you, Calhoun. More importantly, they're what made me say yes."

Cal's words rush out. "I want us to have the same kind of life you did, Libby. I want there to be love." He takes in my room. "You have that here."

I sweep my fingers over his cheek. "And we'll recreate it somewhere else. Love isn't a place, Cal. It's each other. And we'll always have that."

Pulling my hand to his lips, he kisses right above the diamond he slid on the night before. "Yeah, we will."

We talk about the big and little decisions over the rest of the day and well into the night, leaving the bed only for food and to use the bathroom. Otherwise, we're wrapped around each other, planning for our future together as husband and wife.

Mr. and Mrs. Sullivan. When I take my vows to love, honor, and cherish this man above all others, I will become Elizabeth Sullivan.

And in the dark, I feel like I won a major war when he whispers, "Elizabeth Akin Sullivan," just before he slips inside me again, his hands memorizing every inch of my skin in the moonlight.

25

CALHOUN

TWELVE YEARS AGO FROM PRESENT DAY

An overwhelming sense of pride washes over me as the FBI reunites the missing child with her parents.

"Nice work on the intel," an unexpected voice comes from next to me. A masked member of the private firm used to locate the daughter of the wealthy Connecticut family murmurs, "If you're ever looking for a job, look us up."

"Not that I need a job, but aren't you making that kinda hard?" I flick my finger to indicate the ski mask he's wearing. "No clue who you are, man."

Amusement sparks in eyes as green as Libby's. "Not really. You're good at what you do. If you want to, you'll find us." And with that, he turns away and pulls a hoodie up before dislodging the cover that's permitted us both to observe the reunion between Charlotte Collins and her family from an unused hospital room across the hall.

Shaking my head at the arrogance, I catch sight of the clock. "Shit." I have twenty minutes to be downstairs so I can get the helo out of Danbury to La Guardia. Then, it's a straight shot home to Libby.

I hope she's not too sleepy. I grin at one of the pretty nurses as I make my way down the hall.

I feel an all-night celebration coming on.

26

PRESENT DAY

ELIZABETH

"Seeing Cal with a gun didn't set off any alarms over the years?"

I actually laugh. "My family—all of them—grew up on 3,500 acres which border water, Dr. Powell. Guns were necessary on Akin Hill to keep away wildlife and venomous snakes." I lean forward. "I understand they are not something everyone understands. But in an environment where scaring off a wild boar could prevent injury, you learn to respect them." I sit back against the couch.

"You weren't surprised when you saw Cal had guns at home, then."

"No. Not at all. Listen, it wasn't like we were in a competition where we were going tit-for-tat in a fight to finish where I had to have more shoes than he had guns." That earns me a deep chuckle. "He had, at the time, a few handguns and a rifle. It was less than my brother and father each kept at their homes on the estate."

"So, linking them with his military background never crossed your mind?"

"Not at all. I remember weekends where we'd load up the truck, head out to Akin Hill, and he'd go out on the ATVs with Sam, Josh, and Dad. All of them were prepared in case they 'ran into problems.'" I laugh. "Mom used to call it their playtime. Aunt Lukie would call it their male-insecurity bonding time." I smirk.

"And what would you be doing while the men would be 'bonding'?" Now, even Dr. Powell can't say the word without laughter in his voice.

"Four women and a wedding, Doctor," I drawl. "There wasn't a weekend we were at the estate when I didn't have my wedding binder in my hand. I was coordinating schedules to try on dresses, interview photographers, tastings, printers; you name it, I was calling the shots."

"Cal wasn't involved in planning?"

I purse my lips. "I wouldn't go so far as to say that. I knew what he didn't want, and he had a few absolutes. Plus, he was in charge of my bouquet. Beyond that, there were only a few things he really wanted to be involved with."

"Like what?"

"The food." But even as I say it, a remembered twinge runs through me.

"What is it?"

"Nothing." I try to push the memory aside.

But Dr. Powell won't let me. "It's something," he probes gently.

"It's just...it's silly." I wave my hand to move past it.

"Libby, tell me," he encourages me.

Knowing he won't let me out of it, my lips twist. "Cal had been away until the day of his birthday on a business trip," I begin.

27

CALHOUN

TWELVE YEARS AGO FROM PRESENT DAY

"Hey, baby," I call Libby from the plane that's about to land at Joint Base Charleston.

"Happy Birthday, my love. Did you decide where you want to go for dinner tonight?"

"To tell you the truth, Libs, I'm exhausted. Do you mind if we celebrate at home—just the two of us?"

There's a purr in her voice when she responds. "That sounds wonderful. I'll pick up something on my way home from the studio. I'm wiped from dealing with the caterer anyway."

A shaft of guilt slides through me. It hurts more than the knife that nicked me in the alley in Belgrade last week. Fortunately, that particular cut looks like I sliced it open on a plastic chair, which is exactly what I told my fiancée when I video chatted with her.

Libby's taken on so much of our wedding planning. Even for a "family and friends" event, she's still wearing herself to the nub. But she thinks I'm trying to wrap a major business deal when in reality, I'm trying to put the nail in the coffin of a small but persistent group of arms dealers in time to take my wife on a romantic getaway. "How about we head out to the estate this weekend?" I suggest, knowing she'll appreciate the help of her family with planning a wedding I'm all too eager to attend but know I have no business planning at this late stage.

There's silence on the other end of the line. "Actually, I was hoping we'd have some time alone."

My voice drops, uncaring who on the flight can hear what I'm saying over the noise of the transport. Fortunately, the specialized filter on the phone makes it sound to Libby like I'm in a regular office. "You know that sounds better than perfect to me, baby."

"Good." She lets out a breath of air I immediately pick up on.

"Why do you sound relieved?" I ask suspiciously.

"Get home and you'll find out," she teases. "What time will you be done at the office?"

We're circling in preparation for landing. "I figure a few hours," I say, praying our debrief doesn't take long enough to make me a liar. Again.

"Okay. Text me when you're ready to eat," she says happily. "I love you."

"I love you, Libby. Always." Hearing the phone click in my ear, I hold on to it for a second more before stowing it in my cargo pants. When I glance up, both Sam and Iris are glaring at me. "What?" I ask.

"You need to tell her, Cal," Iris tells me, not for the first time.

"Why? So she can worry every time I walk out the door?"

"No, because we're all lying to her!" she cries. "You're marrying her, for the love of God. She's not a security risk. We should be able to—"

"No." I cut her off. My eyes shift to Sam, who's remained quiet throughout the exchange. "You agree with Iris."

"You've been together for a year, Cal—since Nonna died. If you can't trust her with this part of who you are, what kind of marriage are you going to have?" His words eerily remind me of what Bruce said to me the day Libby and I went jumping.

"It's not that easy," I grate out as our transport touches down. The team stands to gather their gear before making their way down the back of the plane. Nothing more is said until we're all off the scalding tarmac and back in the outbuilding waiting to load up in the van to head back to Alliance. "I just want to protect her. I remember everything you said to me about her smile dying, Sam. Do either of you want to see it go away again because she's afraid?" I admit softly.

Sam cringes even as Iris turns her face into his shoulder. I nod. "Yeah, that's what I thought." Turning to the other members of our eight-member team, I call out, "Load up. Debrief in one hour, and let's make this one short, boys and girls. I want to get home tonight."

A chorus of "Yes, sir" comes from the men and women I've served with since I was recruited for Alliance in college. In a lot of ways, I wish I could openly invite them to my wedding. I gave myself a pat on the back when I suggested to my future wife we hire security due to the press's renewed interest in her family since our wedding announcement appeared in the papers. Libby had seen more than one member of the press lingering outside of Deja Vu, her brother reporting the same at the estate. With this being the first big family event since Dahlia Akin passed, she agreed.

Now, by paying an exorbitant fee, my team will get to see me bind my life to the woman I love.

I don't care what it costs. I just want everything perfect that day.

SEVEN HOURS LATER, I CRINGE AS I INSERT THE KEY INTO THE LOCK AT our home in West Ashley and know I'm royally fucked. It's just before midnight, and the house is dark save for the porch light burning.

Libby pissed I can deal with; Libby hurt is not a good thing. Even as I'm trying to figure out how to fix this, I get caught up in a web of something that immediately makes me wish I was armed. "Fuck," I hiss out.

"Cal?" I hear a sleepy voice from the couch. I flick on the light on the hall table to illuminate the room enough to find my future bride dressed in what might be the sexiest nightie I've ever seen her wear. The butter yellow sets off her summer tan and dark hair.

Forget dinner—suddenly after two weeks away, I'm hungry for something different.

"Hey, baby. I'm sorry things went late." I drop my bags and head in her direction before I realize I'm still twisted in whatever trap was set by the diabolically pissed-off woman now sitting on the couch with her arms crossed under her breasts.

Quickly, I set about untangling myself when one of the strings pulls something down to hit me in the head. It's a Mylar balloon. Snarling, I whip it away from my face before my anger dies away.

Happy Birthday, Cal! is embossed on it.

"Oh, fuck. Libby..." I don't care if I drag all the balloons with me, I need to hold her.

But not being hampered by a dozen balloons, she quickly darts away. "I know you don't make a big deal of it. It was stupid, really. I'll see you in bed when you come up." And before I can say another word, she races up the stairs.

But not before I miss the tears in her eyes.

I pry my shoe off with the intent of leaving the guardian-like balloons behind when I freeze in place. Slowly, as if in a trance, I make my way to the dining room table where there are the kind of silver domed plate covers you only see in restaurants. Lifting it as if it's going to bite, I realize it's much worse because the thought that went into this is going to leave a hole in my chest like the one I inadvertently caused by not calling to tell Libby I'd be late.

It's a preview of our wedding dinner: lobster, green beans, and mashed potatoes. And like the night, it's completely ruined. Libby didn't just want to give me a birthday surprise—she wanted to give me her excitement over what's supposed to be the most special day of our lives.

"Fuck," I whisper to no one in the empty room. All this sweet, beautiful woman has ever wanted was to love me, and I somehow keep fucking it up at every turn.

Not wanting Libby to have to deal with this the next day, I begin to clear the table while trying to figure out how to make it up to her because I never again want to see the light dim in her eyes.

28

PRESENT DAY

ELIZABETH

"How did Cal make up for that?" Dr. Powell asks me.

I frown thoughtfully. "It wasn't so much making up for a broken date or a missed birthday. I even said that to him the next day. I felt like he wasn't putting me, us, above his business. And I said if that was the case, maybe we shouldn't get married if he was having second thoughts."

Dr. Powell gapes at me. "How has this never come up before?"

"Was it pertinent?" I ask back. God, it feels good to be the one asking a question versus answering them. "Cal understood what I would and wouldn't tolerate. I was fine with his intensity toward his job; after all, he was determined to make something of the nothing he had growing up. In fact, wasn't that what I had essentially done with my own business?"

"True," Dr. Powell concedes. "And you were happy?"

I nod. "By the time our wedding came around, yes. I believe we were both deliriously so. We were human, Dr. Powell. We fought about things like sorting laundry, and electric bills, and savings—everyday things."

"But you never knew?"

Closing my eyes, I wait for the pain, but I'm surprised when it doesn't come. Maybe five years is long enough for the time to ease this particular wound. "You mean I never knew that my husband was lying to me with every word out of his mouth? That he had a whole life outside of the one with me? No, I never did."

"How did you find out?" His voice doesn't change, for which I am grateful.

"Oh, it would be years. Six from the day we got married, to be exact."

"Six years?" Now, the incredulousness.

And as much as I've forgiven Cal for the deceit, I can't quite help the bitterness that enters my voice at how naive I was. "Astonishing, isn't it? In the early days, I used to wonder if everyone thought I was just stupid."

"I doubt they thought that, Libby."

Thoughtfully, I nod. "True. Each of them was trained to lie. But the truth of what happened comes later. Cal and I did get married. It was a fairy-tale wedding. And I have to say, I've never felt Nonna's presence at any other time more strongly until I was on the *Sea Force*."

29

ELIZABETH

WEDDING DAY – ELEVEN YEARS AGO
FROM PRESENT DAY

I love my dress, but it's my veil that has me motionless as it's attached to my head and then pulled forward over my updo, covering my perfectly applied makeup.

"Libby, you're breathtaking," my mom whispers.

"Simply stunning, sweetheart," Aunt Lukie swears.

"If Cal doesn't cry the minute he gets a load of you, then he really is a robot," Iris declares. This makes my lips twitch into a smirk as I've heard more than once from my best friend and maid-of-honor what a pain in the ass my future husband is to work for.

With Nonna's veil finally on, I'm ready to walk down the aisle. "Can we do a final check?" I ask.

"Something old," Mom says.

My fingers trail over the fragile lace edging of Nonna's veil. "Check."

"Something new," Aunt Lukie says next.

My fingers touch the yellow diamond earrings that were delivered to my suite earlier that perfectly match my engagement ring. "Cal took care of that."

"With a note that almost ruined your makeup," Iris gripes. I glance around me, but from the pedestal I'm standing on, I can't reach anything that won't damage either her aubergine bridesmaid dress or my wedding gown. I settle for sticking my tongue out at her.

She laughs. "Save that for the altar." Which sets us all groaning.

"Next," I call out.

"Something borrowed." Iris grins.

I hold out my wrist to show off Aunt Nancy's gold bracelet that has flowers on it. "It's on."

"Something blue," Mom says.

When she does, Iris and I exchange glances. "Yeah, Momma Nat. We got that one covered."

"Absolutely," I assure my mother.

"I don't want to know," Mom tells my aunt.

"Neither do I." Aunt Lukie covers her face.

"Remember your makeup!" I cry out.

"Right. What about the sixpence?" Aunt Lukie asks about the last of the tradition.

Wiggling my foot in my wedges, I feel the small coin that was used at Mom's wedding to Dad lodge against my heel. "Got it."

"I swear, the last one is the grossest one," Iris declares. "I mean, who wants a sweaty penny in their shoe for luck?"

"I don't know," I say with a touch of exasperation. "But if you think I'm bucking tradition when I'm marrying Cal, you're a crazy bitch."

"Libby, language," Mom scolds me. Then she turns to Iris. "But she's right, Iris."

We're all cracking up when Dad walks in the room. Then the air seems to disappear. "Libby, you're breathtaking."

"Daddy, do not get me started crying," I warn him as I fan my face.

"Here." Iris shoves a wad of tissues in my hand. I reach beneath the veil to dab gently at the corners of my eyes.

My father approaches me with his arm held out. "I think Cal's going to lose his mind if he has to wait much longer. Even though I'm not ready to let you go, are you ready to meet your husband at the end of the aisle?"

Pausing only long enough for Iris to get behind me to help lift my dress, I step off the pedestal and take my father's arm. "This is the beginning of the rest of my life," I say simply.

His face contorts with a flash of pain before it smooths out. "Then let's get it started." He holds me while Mom hands me my bouquet and squeezes the top of my hand tightly. She then follows Aunt Lukie out of the room. Sam and Josh are waiting for them at the base of the stairs to escort them to their seats, but it will be Sam who stands up for Cal.

Iris carefully holds up my dress behind me while I hold her bouquet as we three descend down the steps of Nonna's old home. All I wanted was to get married here so Nonna could see my joy where she once held me during my sorrow. And in just a few moments, it will all come true.

I'll become Elizabeth Akin Sullivan, Cal's wife. A shiver courses through my body at the thought as Iris arranges my dress around me before she steps in front of me.

"I love how happy he makes you," she whispers.

"Me too," I whisper back. We're both pretending my father can't hear us.

"If he ever makes you unhappy, I'm probably going to kill him."

"Since I can't imagine that ever happening, I think you're off the hook for that one," I joke.

My heart flops in my chest when Iris just squeezes my hands. "It's love, Libs. I imagine it's bound to hurt at some point," she says philo-sophically.

"But not today," I state emphatically.

"No, not today." Letting me go, she peeks around the corner and murmurs to Josh. Soon, the music changes and I know he's escorting my mother to her seat.

My breath catches as Iris disappears around the corner of the house, the long curls we left out of her updo being picked up in the breeze.

Dad and I move forward. "All this for a trip to Grand Cayman? Sure it's worth it?" he jokes.

"It's nice to see where I get my sense of humor," I jibe back.

"Well, Josh is just like your mother, so it makes sense," he muses.

I tip my head toward him and grin. "Plan on embarrassing me during the speech?"

"Maybe. Is it enough to get you to change your mind—maybe stay my little girl for another twenty years or so?"

"Daddy." The tightening of my arm brings me closer to his side. "I'll always be your little girl."

We turn the corner of the house just as the music changes. "No, sweetheart," he begins. The crowd gasps, but it's Cal I search for. His jaw is unhinged and working up and down. As my father begins walking me up the silk-covered aisle, Cal finally regains some of his aplomb. "It's time for you to become Cal's."

I feel like my skin is being electrocuted with little shocks by the way he's looking at me. It's a heady combination of love, awe, and possessiveness I'll never forget.

When we get to the end of the aisle, Dad places my hand in Cal's and says, "Her mother and I do," in response to the minister's question about who's giving me away, before lifting my veil long enough to kiss me on the cheek.

But that moment is all I need to glance at Cal. When I do, I'm shocked to see the veil hid the fact his eyes are swimming in tears that have yet to fall.

Nerves settled, I squeeze his fingers and turn my face to the daylight as my heart blooms with happiness.

CALHOUN

WEDDING DAY - ELEVEN YEARS AGO
FROM PRESENT DAY

"I, Elizabeth Dahlia Akin, take you, Calhoun Sullivan, to be my lawfully wedded husband..." Libby repeats the vows she said earlier in my ear as we slow dance to yet another song under the string of lights at the estate. "I think those might be some of my favorite words ever."

Twisting my head, I capture her lips in a long thorough kiss. "And that's just a preview. I can't wait to drag your sweet ass out of here to do much more."

"Promises, promises."

"I'll give you promises," I whisper against her neck.

"Will you?" Her voice has a heartbreaking ache to it that pulls at my gut. Dragging my lips up the column of her exposed neck, I brush her lips with mine.

"Will I what?"

"Will you give me a promise?"

"Anything you want, Libby. You don't even have to ask."

"Promise me this is forever." She bites down on her lower lip.

My thumb eases it out of the way before I soothe it with my tongue. "I promise you, Libby. Here, now, in front of the people who love you, love us, I will always be yours. After all, I've been yours for the last four years."

Her brow furrows. "But we've only been a couple for just over one."

Just by opening myself up, I give her a wedding present that far surpasses the diamonds glinting at her ears. "Baby, from the minute I asked you out, I've been yours. All of this was just a formality."

Libby stops moving in the middle of the dance floor. Couples are jostling us from either side, but neither of us are moving. I slide my hands up the tight-fitting bodice of her wedding gown until my thumbs rest just under her breasts. Reassuring myself she's still breathing, I whisper, "Libby?"

Shaking herself, she whispers, "I will always be yours," right before someone leans on the breaker that plunges us all into darkness. Women begin shrieking in high-pitched voices while men try to calm them down.

But my Libby? She just laughs, pulls me close, and says, "I'll take that as Nonna's sign to make out with my husband."

Even as I'm kissing the hell out of my wife, I realize the promise Libby asked for is more sacred than that.

It's a solemn vow.

With those few words, my wife gave me the things I never dreamed of—the things that men go to war and live for. I have love, a home, and a family. Her words are scratched so deeply on my soul that I know if she's ever taken away, a part of me will be plunged into a darkness even deeper than the one that has people scrambling to turn the lights back on at our wedding.

31

ELIZABETH

HONEYMOON – ELEVEN YEARS AGO FROM
PRESENT DAY

S ugar sand is just beyond our balcony doors. I wonder if I'm going to have the chance to sink my toes into it at least once during the week we're here. Then as Cal's hand smooths from my hip up to my breast from behind and begins to tweak the nipple hardening under his tender ministrations, I begin to realize I don't care. There's sand back home in South Carolina.

Rolling to my back, I stretch my arms above my head. "Good morning, husband."

Swooping in for a kiss laden with wild passion, my tongue gets tangled up with Cal's for long moments before he pulls back. "Good morning, wife. How about we start every morning like this?" It's said wistfully as we both know reality's going to intrude rudely once we fly home in a few days.

Ignoring that, I wrap my arms around his neck and declare, "That sounds perfect to me."

Dropping his head down, he strokes his tongue along the seam of mine, demanding admittance. After another short, mind-reeling kiss, he declares, "Good."

I run my tongue over my lips, trying to capture the taste of Cal on my lips for those mornings when I know work will keep him away.

His eyes follow my movement. Lowering his head again, he peppers quick kisses on the corner of my mouth before he smiles.

All I need is this: Cal smiling at me in the morning. Keep fame and fortune—all I want for the rest of my life is the man I can't live without smiling at me like he can't bear to exist without me either. My arms curve around his neck; I want to taste that smile.

After I've done so thoroughly, I realize Cal's hand has slid from my rear to cup my breast again. The tips of his fingers are feathering my nipple lightly. Arching into his hand, I moan as all the nerves in my body twitch in pleasure.

Cal rolls on top of me, the length of his cock pressing against my damp curls. "Yes, please," I plead. We've long since dispensed with condoms since I got on the pill. Right now, I want to feel the hard length of it pressing into me. Reaching down, I wrap my hand around the length. Giving it a strong tug, I quickly find myself being rolled onto my stomach.

"I love when you touch me, honey. Fucking love it," Cal growls next to my ear, sending a shiver down my whole body as he crawls over the back of me. "But right now, I want to touch you, taste you, then I want to feel you ripple along the length of my cock as I'm buried so deep, you forget where you end and I begin."

Panting, I push up on my elbows just enough to turn my head and nod. The next thing I know, one of Cal's hands has slid beneath my breast, cupping it at the same time his mouth devours the curve of my neck. The other plays with my lower lip.

Unable to resist, I close my teeth over it, nibbling and sucking at it before he slides it out to start thumbing my other nipple. I moan, "Yes, more."

"Jesus Christ, Libby." Cal's voice is shaken. The sex between us has always been off the charts, but right now, we have a hunger for each other we've never experienced.

And I love it.

Cal slides down my body, dragging his chest hair over my sensitized skin. He reaches out and snags a pillow to slide it beneath me before smoothing a hand over the curve of my ass. Taking a small bite of it, he then smooths the sting with his tongue, before telling me, "Lift."

I comply immediately.

He flips over onto his back, resting his head on the pillow. Pulling my hips down, he slides his fingers in just before my clit comes in contact with his waiting mouth.

Yes. Oh, God. "Oh, more," I whimper.

Tearing his mouth away, Cal kisses the inside of my thigh. "Ride my face and fingers. Catch fire for me, my beautiful wife. Then, I want to take you on your knees all wet and open for me."

My hips buck in answer. It's a good thing they manage to talk for me, because I can't find words. My head has dropped into my hands as Cal's mouth begins to suck on my clit as his fingers press deeper. He twists them, curling them inside of me, never letting up on the sweet sucking of my clit until I jerk as I cry out coming.

As I float back down to reality, I wonder aloud, "Who knew married life would be like this?"

Then I feel my legs being spread. A quiver races down my spine when I feel one hand trail over each vertebrae until it finds purchase on my hip. The other begins stroking the skin of my ass. Then I feel that hand slide around and begin caressing me between my legs, working me in tight little circles until my head falls back against him.

"God, Cal, I can't..."

"You can. You will," he demands as he curls his back over mine. His hand slips away long enough for him to guide his cock inside of me. And just like every time since the first time, I feel like I'm whole because we're connected in the most elemental way possible.

Cal begins thrusting, driving into me in short, quick strokes. His free hand not gripping my hip is alternately tweaking my nipples or circling my clit. I keep grinding back against him. My head is on his shoulder.

Bracing myself on one hand, I wrap the other around his neck. Cal, taking that as a sign, swoops my other out from beneath me. I cry out. "Cal?"

But his thrusts don't miss a beat. Now, with both hands free, one glides up over my ribs to cup my breast, and the other notches itself between my legs, putting pressure firmly against the spot where we're joined, the heel of his hand rolling firmly against my clit. His wicked mouth works my neck, and soon I'm chanting, "More, Cal. Yes, yes, God!" And driving down, I come again, this time around his cock.

"I'm coming, Libs. Just like that. Stay..." Cal's voice breaks as he surges up into me, and his body jerks as he spurts deep inside of me.

Still joined, we collapse back against the sun-warmed sheets of the bed. "I love you. Of course I'll stay," I whisper in the quiet of the room.

I get a tight squeeze as a response.

My eyes start to drift shut. Just before I find sleep, I hear Cal whisper, "I love you, Libby. Always."

Knowing that, I realize I really don't partially care if we leave the hotel room for the duration of our honeymoon. The water looks just perfect from our room without us frolicking around in it to mess up the perfect ripples.

There's time enough to do that at home.

PRESENT DAY

ELIZABETH

"I thought I knew what it was like to make love to Cal. Until my wedding night when I knew we were an irrevocable us, I had no idea."

"There was a difference?" Dr. Powell asks, unperturbed.

I blush a fiery red. "Cal's guard was completely down during our honeymoon—maybe for the first and only time during our marriage before the events on the *Sea Force*."

"So, it was a significant change?"

Crossing my legs in front of me, I wish I'd made us later than we were because the memories flashing through my mind are stirring my pregnant body up. "The difference of Cal before our honeymoon and during are like comparing a springtime shower to a hurricane. Or like when someone jumps in a swimming pool and you get splashed versus a tsunami." I laugh softly. "We like to say we went to Grand Cayman for our honeymoon, but the reality is we could have been at the Super 8 off of I-95 for all we saw of the island."

Dr. Powell smiles. "It sounds…"

I interrupt. "Like paradise. It was absolutely everything I ever wanted from the man I dreamed of."

"So, what changed? When did you start to notice the cracks in your marriage?"

I feel the bite of my nails in my hands as I hold back my initial response. "I really don't know how to answer that."

"Try."

"I didn't notice any problems other than Cal working unusual hours. Occasionally, that would happen, so I didn't think anything of it. That is, until…" My voice drifts off.

"Until you left."

"Wouldn't you?" I finally snap. "If you found yourself in the same situation I was in, would you not have walked away?"

He opens and closes his mouth. I'm waiting for the typical platitudes I receive from the number of people of his type over the years, so I'm floored when he answers, "Yes. Presented with the same evidence, I likely would have."

I sag into myself. "Throughout the time I was filing for divorce, I was dying inside. Because I had a secret I still had yet to share with anyone. By the time I boarded the *Sea Force*, I was ill with the ramifications of it."

"Are you ready to talk about them?"

At that moment, the child growing inside of me rolls, reminding me that what happened on that boat wasn't my fault. I'm nodding even as I answer, "Yes."

33

ELIZABETH

YEAR ONE - TEN YEARS AGO FROM
PRESENT DAY

W ith every trip that Cal takes, more and more conflicting emotions arise. I'm so proud of him for building the company he works for to a force to be reckoned with, but at the same time, I've only been married for six months and I've seen my husband for maybe half of them. There are nights when we're talking on the phone—my only connection when he's trying to sell work—that I feel like I only have part of his attention.

And I mourn because I was supposed to have all of his heart.

With the way he seared my soul to his, I don't feel like it's just him who walks out the door every time he leaves; he's taking more and more of me with him. Where before I was strong enough to be on my own, accepted it. I let him in past my defenses. Now, I just exist in the moments in between.

I'm supposed to be stronger for love, but I'm weaker, and deep down I know this isn't the way it's supposed to be.

Tonight, I stayed late at Deja Vu to write up some invoices and do payroll. It's after eleven and I haven't eaten much today. Since I almost paid one of my employees $25,000 instead of their normal $2,500 salary, I know it's time to head out for the night. "I'm sure Jackie would have loved that."

It's easier to spend the long nights working late instead of at home. Here, I can reach some sort of fulfillment. What do I have there to sustain me but longing? Closing down my laptop, I lock everything away until I come back tomorrow. Grabbing the bank bag I need to deposit on the way home, I toss it in my purse before I slip out the back door. After locking up, I slide my keys in my pocket before crossing the lot to head in the direction of my car.

Unlocking it, I start the car and head onto the main road. Since I can't have what I really want—which is for Cal to be waiting for me when I get home—I debate swinging by my favorite sub shop. "If Cal keeps these trips up, he's going to come home to two wives instead of the one he left," I mutter, knowing I haven't cooked a decent meal in weeks.

Accelerating through the light on Meeting Street, I turn on North Market when I hear a screech of tires.

Then there's only black.

I DON'T KNOW HOW LONG I'M IN THE DARK. WHEN I WAKE UP, IT'S LIKE being in a different world. Everything is in such contrast to what happened. I try to shift, but I let out a painful moan.

"Marcus? She's awake. Thank heavens." My mother lifts her head from the side of my bed where it's been resting next to my hand. She squeezes mine so hard it hurts. I try, but I barely manage to exert enough pressure to reassure myself I'm alive.

Darting my eyes around, it penetrates I'm hooked up to tubes and monitors. "Hospital?" I manage to ask.

"Yes. Do you remember anything that happened?" My father steps up to run his hand over my hair.

I immediately start to shake my head, but when I feel the pain shooting through my neck, it all comes back: locking up, driving, the crash. "Yes," I get out.

"You scared us, baby," my mother whimpers.

I swallow with a throat that's too dry. "Water?"

Dad shakes his head. "Only ice chips."

It sounds miraculous. He reaches over for the container and puts a chip on a spoon. I eagerly take it from him. Rolling it around my mouth, I can taste the lingering effect of dryness start to ease. "How bad?"

Mom winces and looks away. Dad's hand, which had resumed stroking my hair, stills. "We can talk about it later, honey."

"Tell me." It's taking all my effort to ask.

"Why don't we wait for the doctor to come in?" Mom suggests.

Just then, the door pushes open. A tall blonde woman with a wedge haircut wearing a long white coat appears. She's making notes on a tablet before her attention focuses on us. "Wonderful. You must be Mrs. Sullivan. I'm Dr. Devin. I've been monitoring you since you came in."

I just nod, too overwhelmed by what's she's saying to speak. Then the memory of burning pain from the car wreck returns, and I gasp.

"If you're feeling any pain, Mrs. Sullivan, all you need to do is push this button here." Dr. Devin hands me a small black button. "This is your pain medicine. Don't worry, you can't push it too many times," she teases gently. "It's set to only release so much per hour."

Dr. Devin's head tilts toward Mom and Dad. "Mrs. Sullivan, when your parents came in, they had a copy of your medical power of attorney. Your husband was listed first, but from what I understand, he's unavailable. Now that you're awake, I'd like to confirm I can speak freely in front of them."

Ignoring the wrenching ache her words cause not my head but my heart, I murmur, "Yes," so she continues.

"The police are going to want to speak with you when you're a little more lucid."

"Wanted dinner," I mumble, still reeling over the fact Cal's not at my side. I have no concept of time, but shouldn't he be here?

"I imagine you're quite hungry. We can't allow you solid foods just yet. Maybe not for a few more days," Dr. Devin informs me.

I inhale sharply, which was an error in judgment. I groan in pain. "Why not?" But Dr. Devin can't answer what I really want to know.

Where is my husband?

"You're in the intensive care unit."

That still doesn't answer my questions. Helplessly, I reach for my father's hand, but I can't quite manage it. He reaches down and takes it. I try not to resent the fact it should be Cal's, but bitterness is beginning to seep into my veins.

Dr. Devin continues. "You've been unconscious for almost twenty hours. We took scans to make sure there wasn't a hematoma. We've been constantly monitoring the amount of brain swelling to ensure it was dissipating so we didn't need to help facilitate it further."

"What does that mean?"

"By draining it, Libby," Mom says as she squeezes my foot. "They were concerned there was too much pressure on your brain. It's one of the options they discussed with your father and I. Dr. Devin was concerned her team might need to drain the fluid around your brain, but you turned a corner, honey."

"Your responses to stimuli improved remarkably around hour eight. We decided after the second set of scans to let nature work its course." Dr. Devin picks up my left hand. "Your husband is out of the country?"

I nod, wincing. Then beseechingly, "Cal?" It's a question for my parents.

"We're trying to reach him, sweetheart. I'm sure it's just the time change," Mom assures me.

"I'm betting he's already on the plane on the way home. At least he better be." Dad mutters the last to himself.

"When you speak with him, there's nothing for him to be worried about long term. However, I'm very concerned about Mrs. Sullivan's short-term situation. I will not release her to her own care."

I swallow hard. "I can't go home?" I want the comfort of Cal surrounding me even if he isn't there—his scent, our home, our bed. Despite how much knowing that stings.

Dr. Devin squeezes my hand again. "Mrs. Sullivan…"

"Elizabeth, please."

"Elizabeth, if you continue to improve, we hope that you'll be moved from the ICU by tomorrow, down to a regular room to be monitored for one day before discharge. It's my professional recommendation you're not to be left alone for the next seven days."

"Work…"

"You are prohibited from any sort of computer work for the next month, Elizabeth." At the words of protest forming on my lips, Dr. Devin's smile firms. "That's nonnegotiable."

My mother jumps in. "I can help."

"If I want my employees to get paid, no you won't." Then hoping my words didn't hurt her, I murmur, "I'll need you in other ways, Mom. Maybe Josh can help me with payroll?"

"Anything, Libby. We just need to get you well."

The pain ricocheting in my chest hurts as much as that in my head. "And my husband can't be reached?"

"No, honey. But we're trying." Mom's voice is strained.

"Then it might be best for me to go home with you," I manage to get out.

Dr. Devin squeezes my hand. "That sounds like a sound decision. Why don't you rest, Elizabeth; it's the best thing for you now."

"Isn't that what I've been doing?" But I can't deny the pull of my eyelids drooping.

"The more you rest, the quicker you'll heal," I'm reminded.

No one has to tell me twice. I want to go back to the darkness where reality didn't intrude to hurt so much. Closing my eyes, I shut out all of their faces and voices before I absorb any more pity than I already have. As if to reiterate my point, I press the button on the pain machine again and again. And again.

Sweet relief begins to flood through my veins. I begin pressing the pain medicine button in earnest. The drugs are kicking in; I can feel them slithering through my veins.

There's silence in the room as I start to go under. A door opens and closes. Then just before I lose consciousness, I hear my mother hiss at my father, "Call Cal again."

"He should be answering," my father growls.

No, Dad. He should be here. And an unnoticed tear leaks out of my eye before I go back into the void.

34

CALHOUN

YEAR ONE - TEN YEARS AGO FROM PRESENT DAY

"Nice driving, Cal," Sam says laconically. "Next time, why don't you hand out barf bags."

Iris, who's been puking in her boot for the last fifteen minutes, gives her nonverbal agreement of her husband's assessment.

"Listen, it wasn't my fault you literally got caught with your pants down and the situation went from hot to inferno in about two minutes."

"Yeah, but we got the intel," Sam smirks. "And the location of the weapons warehouse."

Since I can't disagree with him, I focus on driving because one false move and none of us are making it home. We're barreling down the Italian Alps in a stolen Humvee trying to escape the carload of Spanish tangoes on our ass. The team split up. Even though it's the other team that has the intel, they want Iris and Sam for playing them to get it.

"Fuck me," I curse as my phone pings with an incoming voicemail just as I'm taking another hairpin turn. "Whose fucking idea was it to try to take this route to the rendezvous point?"

"Yours," Iris manages in between bouts of nausea that I'm beginning to suspect have little to do with my driving. "And I hate you for it."

Sam and I both chuckle. "Hey, Sam?"

"Yeah, man?"

"Check my voicemail to make sure nothing's changed. It's been pinging nonstop since we crossed over from Germany. If we're not meeting up with the team in Meiringen, we need to know that stat."

"On it." Sam leans over the seat and snags my phone out of the holder. Flipping to the voicemail app, he frowns. "Cal, these are all from the family. And there's..." He begins to count under his breath. "Seventeen of them since last night."

"What about your phone? Iris's? Anything?"

Sam whips his phone out of his pocket and begins to curse roundly. "Mine's been on silent. There's at least ten."

Something's wrong. There has to be. Panic begins to whip through my veins. "We can't call them back. Not until we reach base," I snarl. "We're not safe."

"Can we listen to the messages?" Sam growls at me.

I calculate the risk. "Are the messages already downloaded from the secure number?"

"Yes."

"Then yes. Find out what the hell is going on!"

A minute passes. Not a sound from the back seat other than the consistent heaving. "Jesus, Sam. What the fuck is going on?" I scream.

"Just get us to base as fast as you can, Cal. Get us home." The note of joviality in Sam's voice that lives there even despite his own wife being ill is suddenly missing.

"I swear to God, I'm going to turn around and punch you. Then you can worry about your wife ending up over the side of this damn cliff," I threaten. "What the fuck is wrong?"

"It's Libby. She's been taken to the hospital."

I don't give a thought for Iris's retching in the back. She could stink up the vehicle with the noxious fumes, and all it's going to do is cause me to drive faster. All I hope is that they have their life insurance paid up as I take hairpin turns at a speed that should topple all of us off the side of the cliff yawning below us.

I don't care that when I pull up to the base, I pull up with an envoy of official cars trailing us—likely salivating to ticket me—instead of the ones who were determined to capture us. All I care about is managing to shave fifty-seven minutes off our drive so I can call my wife's family.

All of whom proceed to rightfully blister my ears but refuse to let me talk to the woman I love before I board the transport to take me home.

Her father's words ring through my brain over and over. "You should've returned my calls, Cal. Maybe then Libby wouldn't feel like she's going through this alone," he snapped out, right before he slammed the phone down in my ear.

Going through what?

The thought haunts me on our flight back to Charleston where I don't bother to debrief my team or Yarborough. Instead, I head straight to the hospital after changing into a rumpled business suit. I fiddle with my wedding ring, the weight of which I'm still not used to since I haven't had it on in the last few weeks. I pray with all my might I'll find my Libby safe and sound.

35

ELIZABETH

YEAR ONE – TEN YEARS AGO FROM
PRESENT DAY

I want to be left alone so I can drown in my pain, but in a hospital, that's next to impossible.

Cal's still not here. I do know he finally called; then again, half the hospital might know that—Dad was shouting so hard.

I'm ready to leave the smells of sanitization, the constant people wandering in and out of my room, and the lack of privacy. Josh has already been by Deja Vu with his spare set of keys and grabbed my laptop. At least my employees will be paid next week.

It's after one in the morning. The cheerful nursing staff turned off the lights in the majority of the room, but there's one lit so they can come in to check my vitals. Every time they do, I want to lash out and ask them, "Why bother? What does it matter if you find out if I'm breathing when I don't feel like I'm alive?"

My heart's somewhere on a business trip and too busy to come home.

My wedding rings are on my rolling tray table, taunting me. Where is he? Not by my side, that's for damn sure. It's been forty-eight of the worst hours of my life since I opened my eyes in the ICU. I've awoken to a severe concussion, the knowledge of being hit head-on by a drunk driver, and the not-so-gentle reminder my husband

144

considers his job more important than his marriage. My mother or father has been constantly by my side when they're not running errands for me to move back to the estate because I'm not able to stay alone when I leave the hospital, because there's no one at home to take care of me. Like a husband. I still don't know where Cal is. Then again, I've also stopped asking.

In sickness and in health...what part of this doesn't qualify? The door behind me opens and closes quietly. Dully, I ask, "Blood work or blood pressure?"

"Neither. I didn't know if you were awake. I just got here and needed to get to you as fast as I could. I didn't even change." Cal's voice wafts over me from the door.

I hate there's a part of my heart that leaps in joy because I'm about to shatter it. "Why bother now? You should have gone home to get some sleep; you must be exhausted." I keep my back turned.

"Libby." My name is wrenched from him.

I close my eyes as his footsteps approach the bed, but his presence still overwhelms me. He smells of airplanes and everything I've been craving since my eyes opened. I don't trust myself not to cry in relief and anger, and right now that's the last thing my head needs.

I wish I still had the IV pain pump so I could just click it and Cal would disappear—just like all the other pain I've endured. But I've been awake for almost two days; I know my schedule by heart since I've spent more time awake praying each time the door opened, the man who's hovering behind me would come through it. Now that he's here, I feel like I'm trapped into talking to him.

Why would tonight be the night I sent Mom home to get some rest? Oh, yeah, that's right, because I love her. I debate pressing the nurse's button; I know they'd come in. I just want someone to run interference when I tell my husband to go away—just for a little while.

Pain is supposed to hurt like this, not love.

"I didn't get the messages; I swear it, Libby."

"Go home, Cal. Come back tomorrow when we've both got some rest." Inwardly, I acknowledge the fact I won't sleep at all, but at least the next round of pain meds will take off the edge of hell happening right now.

"You have every right to be furious with me, but I need to see your eyes. Just let me know you're okay." Cal's voice is pleading with me to turn around and face him, to forgive him. But this isn't something as simple as coming home and screwing up a birthday surprise.

I could have died.

And the cruel realization I come in second to the man who's supposed to place me first is worse than the accident.

It might be I want to inflict some pain of my own, but bitterness gives me the fortitude to move my hand away from the call button and to the one to raise the head of my bed. "Stand back, please. I need to do this carefully. The last thing I need is more pain."

I slowly raise the bed the way Dr. Devin told me to, taking deep breaths along the way as the room spins. Finally, when I'm fully sitting up, I slowly rotate my head from the left to face my husband. The pillow that was cushioning the injured side of my face falls to my lap when I do. *Great*, I think bitterly, *another thing to resent Cal for.* "I see you, but do you see me?" I hiss.

Cal's face is paper white. "What happened to you?"

"I'm not reliving this nightmare when I'm supposed to be resting. You got what you wanted, now give me what I want. Go. There's the door."

"Libby, the bruises..."

"I'm well aware." The side of my face is swollen and bruised.

"Why didn't anyone say..."

"Maybe you should have called back, say two days ago?"

"I couldn't be reached." He doesn't volunteer any more information, and it just leaves me exhausted.

"Fine. I'm done, Cal. I need my rest. Can you just come back in the morning?" Since I'm curled on my right side with my head elevated, my left hand flicks in the direction of the partially closed door.

Cal, of course, misses nothing. "Where are your rings?"

"On the tray behind me." I'm too heartsick to care about his reaction.

"You took them off?" There's torment in his voice. I recognize it because I've been living it since the minute my eyes opened and he wasn't there.

"They took them off when I was first admitted *three days ago.*" I emphasize the words. "They were given back to me just a few hours ago."

He moves to go get them but pauses when he hears my voice. "No. Not another inch. I'm so hurt, it's physically causing me pain."

"Let me get your nurse." Cal moves to my headboard to press the button to call my nurse when my words stop him.

"I don't want you to. I don't want anything from you right now except for you to fucking leave!" I clutch my head as my yelling sends new shafts of pain through it. "Isn't that what you're good for? Leaving me alone? In the last two days, I've realized I've spent more time alone than together since we met. All I'm asking, just this once, is do it when I ask you to." I can't stop the sob that comes from my chest.

"Libby, please let me hold you," Cal begs.

I can't shake my head no, nor can I speak. Fortunately, someone walks in who can.

"Cal, you need to go home. They're trying to spring her from here tomorrow. They can't do that if she can't pass the tests she needs to." Josh's voice comes from the door.

I want to ask how he knew to come, but I can't. All I can do is draw my knees up to my chest and press my aching head against them. "Just go." My voice is muffled through the blankets, but it's clear.

"I…" Cal starts to say something, but then he must change his mind. "What time do visiting hours start in the morning?"

"Seven a.m. Not long at all," Josh tells him.

Unfortunately, Cal's next words do nothing to reassure me. "I'll be back at 7:01, Libby. That's a promise."

I don't reply because right now, I can't rely on promises. In sickness and in health—it seemed like the ultimate promise. And I've been waiting for the person on the other side of that vow for days.

It shouldn't be that way. And before I slide those rings back on my finger, we're going to have a conversation about it.

I hear Cal's retreat. Josh firmly closes the door behind him before he comes directly to me. "Okay, sister, how do I get you to rest?"

"Call the nurses." I can't lift my head at this point, the throbbing is too intense. "I don't know what time it is, but maybe it's time for my medicine."

"Or maybe if they see your present condition, they'll call Dr. Devin," Josh mutters, not reassuring me that I'll be leaving. I need to leave. I need to be able to go home. And I don't mean to the house I share with Cal; I mean to Akin Hill. While the thought originally appalled me, as each hour passed with no word from him, the appeal increased. There, I wouldn't be tempted to work, I would have love surrounding me, and maybe I'll heal.

And if Cal gives half a damn, he can come to me.

"Hello, Elizabeth. What's... Oh dear. What's wrong?" Chantay, my night nurse, strides over to my bed. "Let's get you lying back down, first. Then you can tell me what's wrong."

Everything. Everything's wrong when it should have been perfect. As Chantay begins to ease me back against the bed, I catch the glimmer of my rings out of the corner of my eye. I refuse to admit it's the sight of them that causes the tears to fall harder as the bed's being lowered.

Under Chantay's gentle care and Josh's protective regard, I calm down enough to make it the additional fifteen minutes until my next pain dose. But this time, I accept the IV pain meds instead of the oral ones. I'm not ashamed to admit I want to feel the drugs running through my veins instead of the toxicity of my thoughts. It will be the last night I'll be given such a haven as I know Cal will be back.

It doesn't take long between the medicine and Josh stroking my hand that I'm soon dozing with that last comforting and painful thought.

36

CALHOUN

YEAR ONE - TEN YEARS AGO FROM PRESENT DAY

I t's the fifth day I've driven out to Akin Hill. And maybe it's just me, but every time I make the drive, the days seem to be getting shorter.

The light I've come to rely upon is fading.

I can't unsee Libby curled up in her hospital bed, bruised and battered. Now that I've been told the whole story, I'm sick to my stomach knowing if her car was hit just a few feet in a different direction, her accident could have been fatal.

I could have lost her.

After I went back to the hospital the next morning, I understood why I was being forced to endure the censure from my wife and her family after Marcus dragged me out of the room to explain.

I wasn't there when Libby needed me.

It doesn't matter the lives I may have saved halfway around the world. What matters is my world might have ended.

My cell rings. I answer it with one hand. "Sullivan," I bite off.

"Cal, how's your wife?" Yarborough asks, concern in his voice.

"Resting. Healing. It's going to take time." Even to my own ears, I sound like I'm convincing myself.

"That's good to hear. Sam did a little research earlier," he begins.

"Sir, I want to remind you we're not on a secure line," I caution him. The last thing we need is for him to announce Sam hacked some poor schmuck's database and is about to spend time in the big house because we didn't have a warrant.

"I'm well aware of that, Sullivan," he snaps.

"Sorry, sir. Continue."

"There's going to be some additional people visiting your wife today. Maybe after their update, she'll be able to rest easier," he tells me cryptically.

I take this to mean they arraigned the fucker who hurt Libby. "Would it be possible for me to pay their new distinguished guest a personal visit?" I'm really asking to visit the asshole who hit Libby for ten minutes. He'll be dead, and I'll feel much better.

"Negative. That will not be happening, Cal."

"You're no fun, sir."

"Your only job is to take care of your wife. You are officially on leave until she comes home. Do you understand?" my boss declares.

You mean if she comes home, I think wearily. Every day I go to see her, the chasm between us just grows. A quick glance at the box in my passenger seat gives me a small measure of hope.

Small, but not much.

"Cal, do you understand? No calls, no coming to the office, no trips," he enunciates.

"I'll have to train or I'll lose what's left of my mind, sir. Things... they're not good."

"I thought her health was improving?"

"I meant between us. I fucked up, Rick." Now I'm not talking to my boss, but to my friend. "I should have been able to have received those calls in Germany. The fact they didn't come in..."

"Was a massive FUBAR. We know it. We'll work it out before you get back. Work on your marriage. Consider it an extended honeymoon." He hangs up in my ear.

"This one sure as shit isn't like the last," I mutter. Turning down the private road that leads to Akin Hill, my heart begins to pound. I pull up to the call box at the end of the driveway. Dialing the number for Libby's parents' house, I wince when I hear Marcus's hostile "Yes?"

"It's Cal."

He hangs up without a word. But the gates swing inward. "Okay, here we go." Slowly, I accelerate my truck through the long drive so I can visit with my wife.

Hopefully today I can find the words I need to get her to talk with me.

Maybe she'll feel more open after the police leave.

Pulling up in her parents' driveway, I walk around the front of the car and slide out the heavy package. I jostle it in my arms while I lock my truck. Not that dropping it can make it much worse. I just want Libby to see it in one piece.

"WE APPRECIATE YOU COMING OUT ALL THIS WAY, LIEUTENANT BRIGGS." My father-in-law shakes hands with the department representative they sent to convey the news that the person who hit Libby will remain a guest of the county for some time. "I'm sure that will help all of us sleep a bit more soundly tonight, won't it, Nat?" Marcus's arm tightens around his wife.

"I know I will, but what's most important is you, Libby. How do you feel, honey?" Natalie turns to my wife. Libby's bruises are beginning to change color, but the biggest transformation is the lack of smile. My chest spasms in agony, realizing I may be the cause of it never appearing again.

"I appreciate the visit, yes" is her response. Her face is pale and filled with shadows, but how much of that is due to what happened versus what I did to her?

"Why don't we walk you out, Lieutenant. Cal, can you stay with Libby for just a moment?" God, I want to hug my mother-in-law right now.

Marcus obviously feels differently but holds his tongue. Instead he walks over to the bed and kisses Libby on the forehead. "We'll be just a few moments, honey."

"That's fine, Dad. I need a few moments of peace to process this," she replies.

The three make their way out. I hear Natalie exclaim, "Libby, it looks like Cal brought you a gift!"

My wife raises a brow in my direction. "Oh? More sunflowers."

I flush. There are vases of them around the room, none of them near the bed. "No, not those."

Libby turns her head to stare out the window, seemingly indifferent to my presence.

"I…" The expression on her face isn't giving me any hope. Then again—I shore myself up internally—she isn't shoving me away. "I baked you a cake. Coconut pecan—your favorite."

Libby's eyes bug out before she turns it back toward me. "I'm sorry. Can you repeat that? Maybe there was hearing issues as a result of the injury," she asks with a little of her old sass.

"I had a little trouble, but I made it through the whole recipe."

"You've got to be kidding me. That cake takes me hours, Cal. I hand shuck the damn pecans."

"Shit, you're supposed to shuck the pecans?"

Her hand flies to her mouth to hold back the giggle. "Oh, sweet heaven, have mercy. Where is it?"

"In my defense…" I leave the room and quickly come back with the box. "I followed the recipe."

"So, I know it's going to be dry because that doesn't include the extra butter, but go on." She nods. Her eyes are beginning to dance. It sparks something inside of me I didn't realize I'd lost.

Hope.

And I bask in the glow of that tiny light emanating from Libby. I decide to keep telling her about the disaster she's about to open. "By the way, where do you keep the measuring cups?"

"Did you borrow some?"

"I improvised," I tell her proudly.

"Improvised? With what?" Libby practically screeches before a soft moan makes her remember her head.

I don't hold back. "Our wedding mug. I figured it was an eighteen-ounce mug. I estimated."

"Heaven help me, I have to see this cake." Libby tilts her head back. I can't tell if her head's hurting or if she's praying. I figure if it's the first she'll tell me. Certainly, she's let me know that more than once in the last few days.

"Well, if you're sure." I wait for her to lift her head before sending her a smile, one she cautiously returns. I place the box in her lap. I vaguely hear her "Umph!" as the weight of the disaster I baked weighs down her thighs.

"Cal, what on earth is in that box?" Libby demands. "It weighs a ton!"

Leaning over her, I absorb the light floral scent she wears. It's obvious someone's helped her clean up, but up close, I can still see the bruises that go well into her hairline. "God, I'm so sorry, baby. So, so sorry."

Hesitantly, she raises a hand to touch my cheek. "Okay," she whispers.

"Okay?" What does that mean? I pull back so I can see her face.

"It means we have my recovery to figure out where we go from here, Cal. Because I need you to remember you made a choice when you married me. We planned to be together forever. We did, Cal, not you and your job. I won't go through something like this alone again."

"You won't." It's a vow.

Searching my eyes, Libby finally nods. And it's like benediction has been granted. "Now, how do I open this?"

"Are you sure you want to?"

She pauses. "Is it really that bad?"

"Probably worse," I admit.

"Then I definitely want to see it. I want to be able to bask in glory when I make you one in the future."

"I just don't want you going into a coma at the sight," I mutter, pulling back so I can lift the top off the box.

I'm not sure if it's my words or the cake itself that makes Libby laugh hysterically. "What…is that…Cal, you weren't kidding about the nuts!" Her laugh is the balm my heart needs. "I don't want to imagine what the kitchen looks like."

"I'm bringing in a professional to clean it," I joke.

She grins before poking at the cake with a brave finger. Then to my surprise, she calls out, "Daddy, come see how Cal mutilated Nonna's cake just for me."

"I hope you bought life insurance for us if you expect us to eat that," Marcus mutters as he steps into his daughter's room. His eyes the cake askance. "Son, you need to go down to the kitchen with Natalie for a while to learn how to make something edible. Otherwise, you'll either die of starvation or have a hell of a commute to work while Libby's recovering." It's as close to an invitation to stay as I'm going to get.

"Well, since I have the next month off to take care of my wife, I'm certain I can learn how to crack an egg between now and then," I state calmly.

But it isn't the reaction to the time off that garners the most attention.

"You didn't crack the egg," Marcus says slowly.

"The recipe didn't say to," I say defensively.

"Oh, boy," Libby mutters. "Hey, Dad? Can you get a picture of me with the cake?"

I beam with pride—for about two seconds until Libby says, "Because there's no way in hell I'm eating it."

"You got it, honey." Marcus goes off in search of Libby's cell phone.

"No way in hell?" I demand of my wife.

"Cal, if I made this for you, what would you have done?"

"Um." She has me there. "Kissed you, said thank you, and politely handed it to someone to dispose of."

"Sounds like a plan." She crooks her finger at me. I lean down. Libby's lips linger just a moment longer this time. "Thank you. Dad, are you ready to take that photo?"

"I can't find your phone. We'll use mine."

"That works." Marcus takes a picture of Libby holding the cake. "Now take this—somewhere—and bring me some of Nonna's bread pudding, please?"

"You got it, honey." Marcus shakes his head as he carries my ice breaker out of sight.

Libby watches as it goes, a bemused expression on her face. "Now, tell me what happened to your phone that no one could reach you?"

As I begin to tell my wife what went wrong, I notice her expression is a lot less tense even though the fierce determination is still there. I haven't won, but I haven't lost because of the vows that we made—vows that will cause Libby to run if she feels they're broken.

And now I know it.

PRESENT DAY

ELIZABETH

"W as that the first real fight in your marriage?" Dr. Powell
asks me.

"It was more than a fight. A fight is when you want
to buy a new couch and you disagree on the color or whether or not
to get leather. I questioned who Cal was at his very core. And that
scared me."

"How?"

"Such a simple question with a million answers, Doctor." I lean on
the arm of the couch with my chin in my hand. "I was supposed to still
be living in a honeymoon phase. Do you know where the term derives
from? I looked it up while I was recovering." I hold up a hand. "Yes, I
know. I wasn't supposed to look at computers."

"I believe it means the term, not the act, relates to period following
marriage meaning love and happiness. Some say the first month, some
say the first year. And I'm glad I don't have to scold you for breaking
doctor's orders." There's a sternness to Dr. Powell's voice.

"Let me guess, you're a parent?"

"A grandparent, actually."

I grin. "Well, rest assured. My mother did when she caught me. But
here's my point: if people dating back to the Renaissance understood

the significance of that delicate period of two lives merging together by documenting it when so few things were in that era of history, how could my own husband not understand the vows we took had significance?"

"You didn't feel Cal took your vows seriously?"

"Not then, I didn't. For the record, now, I do. But immediately after the crash? I questioned whether our love was going to make it out of the state of ecstasy and denial we'd been living in. I knew what I wanted out of marriage; I thought he was on the same page." I let out a sigh.

"It wasn't the same?"

"It wasn't the same timing, something I would have understood if we'd talked about it."

"Would you have delayed marrying your husband?"

Hmm, an interesting question. One I've never been asked before.

I think about it before responding. "No, but maybe I would have spent more time at home? I would have accommodated Cal's schedule more knowing each moment we had together was precious instead of wasting any of it fighting."

"And would that have been honoring your marriage? The marriage Cal wanted you to have?"

I laugh. "I guess not. In the end, we all have to be content with who we are, and our partners have to accept us for who that is."

"What was life like in the years between your separation?"

"Busy! Deja Vu built a strong clientele not just in Charleston, but up to Charlotte and all the way to Atlanta. I expanded my own business when I saw Cal's wasn't letting up any."

"And that didn't bother you? The fact his work wasn't slowing down?"

"After the first year, after the scare of our marriage being in such trouble, I understood it more. Cal got me read on—a vernacular for being able to hear certain types of information—to a certain extent, so I learned a little about the business."

"What did you think it involved?"

"Computers. I knew from an early age my cousin was a huge

hacker, so I presumed Cal was as well. Back then, I kind of pictured Alliance as this big think tank. It's so much more than that." An evil smirk crosses my face. "But I will state with one hundred percent no guilt whatsoever that Cal likely suffered every time I called him with a problem about my work network—something Sam designed for me."

"Live tech support?"

My lips twitch. "I think he bought himself the T-shirt that says, 'I won't be your technical support.' After the accident, I insisted on being able to contact him at all times. That was nonnegotiable. Cal agreed and that's when he hired Rebecca. She was—and still is—a godsend. I mean that in every way. I went from having a husband who'd work fourteen-hour days in the office to a husband who worked normal hours at least three days a week when he was home. She organized him and basically became his drill sergeant."

"And you met her when you toured the Alliance office?" Dr. Powell asks me.

"Yes." God, thinking back, I was so nervous that day. How far we've all come since then.

"What was it like?

"I can't really talk too much about that." Now that I've been fully briefed on everything Alliance did, and what Cal does now, I know what I can say and what I can't. "Let me just say there was a formal office in addition to the training facilities. After my first visit, I was given unrestricted access to the office space."

"What did it make you feel to see that part of your husband's life?"

"Proud," I say immediately. "My husband was doing an important job that helped people; I understood that even if he couldn't talk about it."

"What can you tell me about your first visit to Alliance?"

"I was greeted in the lobby by Cal. He was wearing a suit that was pressed for once." Then I begin to share about my first visit to Alliance and what it was like to enter this part of my husband's life for the first time.

38

ELIZABETH

YEAR TWO – NINE YEARS AGO FROM PRESENT DAY

Hmm, the building looks fairly ordinary from the outside. About six, seven floors, I wonder if the reflective glass is tempered enough to keep Cal's office cool.

Following the protocol Cal reminded me of over breakfast this morning, I pull up to the gate. I roll down my window and offer a hesitant smile. "Hello. I'm Elizabeth Sullivan. I have an appointment to see my husband, Calhoun."

"Yes, ma'am. May we see some ID please?"

"Certainly." I reach in my bag for my wallet. Sliding out my driver's license, I hand it to the somber-faced individual.

He enters it into the computer before holding it up. His eyes flicker back and forth. "Here you go, ma'am. I'll just do a quick walk around to get your tag and you'll be all set."

Anxiously, I wait for him to come back. "All set, Mrs. Sullivan. Do you know where you're going?"

I nod. Then because the butterflies in my stomach get the best of me, I blurt out, "Does Cal have to do this every morning he comes to work?"

Leaning down with an arm braced on my window, the guard answers, "Employees access through a different entrance, ma'am."

"Well, it explains why he leaves so early," I mutter as I shift my car back into gear. "Thank you."

"Thank you, Mrs. Sullivan. Have a nice day." He raps the roof of my car as the gates in front of me warning me of persistent video surveillance open.

"Nice. Right. Not exactly the word I'd use." I wave as I drive off.

I can hear Cal's voice in my head saying, "Drive to the front of the building. There will be signs for visitor parking. Any of the spots there are fine."

I navigate to a spot close to the building. Taking a quick moment to check out my gloss in the mirror, I debate whether I need to send the manufacturer a letter of thanks since it's still perfectly in place. "It's just an office, Libby. Stop being so nervous." With that mental shove, I open the door and swing my legs out.

It takes only a few minutes in the warm South Carolina air for me to reach the lobby door. Before I can reach for it, it's being swung outward. I almost stumble back on my heels. "Excuse me," I say automatically. I grab onto the handle to hold it open for whomever is exiting.

"I didn't mean to startle you, Libs." Cal's deep voice sends ripples of awareness through me.

Relief flows through me. "Hey. I thought I'd have to wait. Didn't you say they'd have to call you?"

He smirks and it makes me want to push him against a wall to lay my brand on him here where no one has ever seen it before. He holds out his left hand. The glint of gold beckons to me like nothing else other than the love in his eyes. "They did. From the gate. Let's get you a badge, and then I'll give you the tour."

I take his hand. "Sounds wonderful."

Cal tugs me toward him and brushes his lips against mine. "That's you. This will be fun." He turns and holds me close to his side, and we walk as one unit to the front desk. "Karl, this is my wife, Libby. She needs a visitor pass for today, but I know the Admiral has requested a long-term pass for her."

"I received the request from Yarborough this morning, Cal. You know that takes seventy-two hours."

"Not a problem. Libby, this is Karl. He handles all access into and out of the facility."

I hold out a hand. "A pleasure, Karl."

He smiles. "You as well, ma'am. Here's your badge for today. As long as you're escorted, you're fine to go anywhere in the building except…"

Cal cuts him off. "I'll give her the full rundown; there's no need to go through everything."

"You got it, Cal." With a jaunty smile, Karl turns back to his computer.

Cal slips the red visitor badge over my head. "Remember what we talked about?"

"Yep." I lift my new accessory. "This doesn't come off until you take it off me."

Behind us, Karl coughs hard. Cal just shakes his head. "Then, let's go." Cal takes my hand to lead me to a bank of elevators. There's no up or down button, only a badge reader. He uses his own badge and taps it. "When you have your permanent visitor pass, you'll be able to do this," he tells me.

Okay, I knew Cal was into some high-tech toys, but this is ridiculous. But there's a nagging thought riding through my head. "Cal? You work for an admiral? I thought you weren't in the military anymore."

"He's retired, Libs. Still doesn't mean the man didn't earn his rank."

"Right. Got it. So, will I meet him?" As the elevator is climbing, so are the numbers—five, six. We get off at seven, though I note there's a R, likely leading to the roof.

Cal waits for me to step off the elevator before saying, "Where do you think we're going to first? To say the man is still torqued with me for not receiving an invitation to our wedding is an understatement."

"Oh, my goodness! You can't drop that kind of news of me and expect me to handle this! I need days—mainly to kick your ass."

Cal grins. "Libs, don't worry. I told him it was mainly a family affair."

I'm going to pass out right in the elevator lobby. "We had close to two hundred people there," I retort.

"And if you think back to your nonna's funeral, it was mostly family. Come on." He tugs on my arm as I dig in my heels. "I promise, it's going to be fine."

"That's what Josh said after we snuck out of the house for a Hootie concert," I mutter. "I was grounded for six months."

Cal bursts into laughter as we walk into an enormous office. The man behind the desk has close-cropped salt-and-pepper hair and is dressed in a suit that must have been tailored for his broad shoulders. "And of course, he's every woman's dream of what their men will age like," I say to myself.

Or so I think.

The man bellows out a laugh and comes around his desk. "Rick Yarborough, US Navy retired." He holds out his hand. "It's an absolute pleasure to finally get to meet you."

Now that he's standing near me, I kind of want to curtsey. Instead, I take his hand in a firm grip. "A pleasure, Admiral."

He wings a brow in Cal's direction, who just shrugs. "Libby—may I call you Libby?"

"Of course," I stammer. "Did I do something wrong?" *Already*, is what I want to add to that sentence.

"Now, why would you think that?

"Maybe because my husband told me in the elevator you wanted to come to our wedding?" I blurt out.

The Admiral shoots my husband a look so frigid it should take a week to thaw him out. "You don't say shit like that to a wife."

"You'd know. You've had three," Cal drawls. He comes up behind me and wraps his arms around my waist.

"Three," I squawk.

Yarborough waives his hand in the air. "Was too young the first time; we're still close friends. I set her up with her husband. Second one was just a mistake. Piece of work, that one. Third one—couldn't live without my Molly. Been with her going on twenty years now."

"Wait. Hold on." I lift a hand to my head. "How can you have been married three times when you're like what? Fifty? Did you overlap them or something?"

Cal roars with laughter while Yarborough grins. "She might be good for you, but she's better for my ego."

I'm hugged closer as Cal says, "Don't I know it," before turning me to face him. "Honey, the Admiral actually just turned seventy this year."

I whip around so fast my hair smacks Cal in the face. "No. Way. That is not possible."

"I didn't retire until I earned my second star, Libby. Twenty-four hard years I spent serving after I graduated the academy. And you know what? It took less than six months before I realized I was going to go stark raving mad out of boredom. That's when I decided to open Alliance's doors."

"That's extraordinary," I tell him. "You're a true patriot, sir."

Cal's boss beams at me like I passed some kind of test before extending his arm. "Mrs. Sullivan, it would be my honor if you'd let me escort you for a few moments around Alliance."

Breaking away from Cal, I tuck my hand in his arm. "It's my pleasure to let you."

"I'll just follow behind," Cal sighs.

"Good. Listen and you might learn something," Yarborough retorts. "So, as I was saying, Libby, I started Alliance with the concept of being able to provide the data here"—he taps the side of his head —"back to the government. For a small fee, of course."

"I imagine the institutional knowledge you have is something others would pay top dollar for, sir," I agree.

"Indeed. And of course, I was right."

"Here we go," Cal gripes.

"Why don't you go wander off and play with a computer or something?"

"Because if I do, you'll have sold your brilliance to George Washington just to impress Libby. Stick to the facts, old man."

"I'll get him for the old crack," the Admiral mutters.

I pat his arm. "If you don't, I will."

So, I get a very brief history about Alliance—the redacted version according to Admiral Yarborough since much of it is "Classified. I wish I could tell you, Libby, but I just can't." But, even then, I still enjoy it because I finally feel like I've been let into that inner sanctum of Cal's other life.

Finally.

"I CAN'T BELIEVE YARBOROUGH ESCORTED YOU THROUGH THE FACILITY himself," Cal grumbles as we sit in his office having lunch that his assistant, Rebecca, brought in for us.

I take a bite of my pasta salad and chew. "So, what? I'm sure he does that with more important people than me."

"Libby, I've never seen him do that since I worked here—even with clients. More often than not, people are trying to kiss his ass."

I frown thoughtfully. "I wonder why that is."

"Well, he's a former admiral," Cal says as if I just don't get it.

"No, what I mean is, when I bid on work, I'm the one who's essentially playing to the client needs. He must know he has a product so special it can't be replicated by any other company or he'd be kissing ass to get work, just like the rest of us," I point out.

Cal's face is thunderstruck. "I never thought of it like that."

I shrug. "You don't own your own company, hon. I do."

"Honestly, Libby, do you worry about that a lot? You've always said business is strong." Cal takes a bite of his own lunch, watching me while he does.

I pause before I fork another bite in. I don't know where Rebecca got this, but I'm going to have to ask. It's delicious. "My business is solid, but that's because I work to make it that way. I study the market, I make adjustments, and I continuously train my people." I put my container on the coffee table in between us. "I can't sit back and relax; I have people depending on me."

"But it's what you want?"

"There's nothing I've wanted more next to you," I tell him honestly.

Cal's fork clatters to the table. Leaning forward, he nabs the back of my neck. Our lips come together in a kiss that's rife with love. "There's nothing more important to me in this world than you, Libby."

"Same here. I love you, Cal."

"I love you too. Let's finish up so you can get a chance to talk with Rebecca some more. I need the woman who controls my heart to be comfortable with the person who has access to me while I'm away."

Since I vehemently agree, I pick up my pasta and grin. "We're going to have you so twisted up, you won't know which one of us is really controlling your life."

"Listen, if I get more time with you out of it, I'll take it."

We both grin before we resume eating.

39

CALHOUN

YEAR TWO - NINE YEARS AGO FROM PRESENT DAY

"I don't think there's a more perfect woman for you in the world, Cal," Yarborough says to me later as we share a drink together in his office. A new contract has just come in, and we're celebrating with a quick glass of bourbon—the Admiral's choice.

It has been since I started working for him years ago. I just used to watch quietly from the sidelines instead of being invited in to join him.

He rolls the heavy crystal glass of amber liquid back and forth in his hand. "There's something I want to talk with you about."

"What's that?" I take a sip of my drink

"Buying into Alliance."

The coughing isn't due to the alcohol; it's due to the fact I can't breathe. "What did you just say?" I manage to wheeze out. I'm also using my tie to wipe my face as I spit my drink out.

"I'm not getting any younger, Cal. And who do I have to leave this to? Meeting your Libby, it made me think about the future. The future of all of you."

"Then it goes to Molly," I declare.

"Who wants nothing to do with this. She'd rather be at the house ready to blister my hide for being late so she has an excuse for burning dinner since she can't cook. No, what I need is a plan." Finishing his drink, he stands. "And I want you to think of one."

"Me? Why me?"

"Because, you know the business side as well as the mission. You know who to bring in to assess it for a fair and reasonable value."

"Rick, this could take months—possibly years with the amount of balls we have up in the air. And with the type of balls, I don't want just anyone getting the chance to fondle them," I caution him.

"Agreed. Do the due diligence. In the meanwhile, I'll make some provisions, just in case." Plunking down his glass, he walks behind his desk.

"You promise, you'd tell me if you were sick?" Somehow, I'm haunted by this lack of knowledge.

My boss, my mentor, and now the man I call a friend merely smiles at me. "Cal, according to you, too much knowledge can potentially be dangerous to those you care about. It can cause them too much stress and worry. That's not for you to be concerned with. All I need are some numbers."

Finishing my own drink, I set the glass down carefully. I see his play. Now that he's met Libby, he's pissed—just like Sam and Iris are—that she's being kept in the dark about the nature of our work. "Okay. I'll work on that."

"Good. Be safe going home. Give my best to Libby." That's a new add-on to the end of our celebratory conversation, but not that surprising considering how taken with her he was.

"I'll be sure to let her know. My best to Molly."

Yarborough pauses in the doorway. "In all the years we've worked together, that's the first time you've said that too. Libby truly does bring out the light in you, Cal. Don't fuck it up." And with advice that's as delicate as a two-by-four upside the head, he saunters out the door, leaving me to wonder if the things that haunt me in the middle of the night are fears that Libby will be in danger.

Or are they my fears that she walks away because of the lies I've told despite the love that encompasses every decision I make for her, for us?

Either way, I've got a lot of thinking to do.

40

CALHOUN

YEAR TWO - NINE YEARS AGO FROM PRESENT DAY

"I could stay just like this forever," I tell my wife honestly. I trail my fingers over the smooth curve of her hip that's been exposed during our lovemaking. With a grin, I ask, "We can have food delivered to our bed, right? That can be considered special instructions on our to-go order."

Libby rolls onto her back as she laughs hysterically. Even though I love I evoked my favorite sound in the world from her, right now she's too far away. "C'mere." I pull her back so her curves are nestled against my body and her head lies against my heart. "You realize everyone thinks we're on a tropical island somewhere," I begin.

Libby rolls onto her stomach and pushes up on an elbow. "That's because we couldn't decide on time for you to give work enough notice. I would have been happy with that small island off the coast of Africa."

Yeah, if I wanted to worry the whole time about the intel that crossed my desk about two months ago. Without an ounce of remorse, I smooth my hand over her ass before giving it a smack to distract from an argument I thought we'd already buried.

"Hey!" Libby cries out indignantly, reaching back to rub the stinging spot.

"I was just letting you feel what it would have been like to have received all the shots you would have needed for that trip." I slip on an innocent look that my wife scoffs at.

"As much as I hate to admit it"—a smile tugs at the edges of my mouth as Libby speaks—"I love the idea that everyone thinks we just decided to go back to the Caymans. At least this way we can stay here and still answer the barrage of questions about what we did."

"If they know us half as well as they claim they do, they should assume we're doing exactly what we're about to do," I mutter.

"Which is?" Libby flutters her lashes coquettishly at me.

"This." Right before I roll her onto her back and proceed to demonstrate how years into our marriage, she still sets my blood on fire.

HOURS LATER, OUR STOMACHS CAN'T BE IGNORED. I FINALLY REQUESTED for an order of subs to be delivered to the house from a place that normally doesn't do it—paying an enormous sum for the delivery when I explain I also need them to go by their floral department along the way. We're still in the bathroom after our very enjoyable shower when the bell rings. "I'll get it," I say quickly. Drawing up a pair of basketball shorts over my legs, I drop a kiss on Libby's lips and race for the front door. Fortunately, she's in the middle of pulling up one side of her long hair, so I know I have about twenty minutes before she's ready to join me.

I make it to the door in record time, snagging my wallet along the way. When I open it, the patiently waiting delivery kid is holding not only a bag overflowing with subs—which Libby claimed she was craving—but a bouquet of sunflowers.

Perfect.

"Thanks so much for doing this." I wanted a surprise for Libby even though we agreed on no gifts since we just bought a new house. But flowers don't count, right? I want today to be about her and me, not about any mistakes.

Especially the ones she has no idea I make day after day.

"Not a problem at all, Mr. Sullivan." I'm handed the bag, then the enormous vase of sunflowers the store put together.

Cradling the blue vase carefully, I slip a few twenties out of my wallet and hand them to the surprised teen. "I don't have any change, sir."

I shake my head. "That's for you. You have no idea about how happy you're about to make my wife. Thanks again."

"No, thank you, sir." The kid practically leaps down our front steps toward a beat-up Honda. I don't spend too much time remembering I used to drive a car almost exactly like that when I was first in college. Instead, I hurry back inside and begin setting the dining room table, placing the sunflowers in the center with lit candles on either side.

When Libby comes down about fifteen minutes later, our subs are laid out on our wedding china, flutes of champagne poured, and the lights dimmed. Yet, it's me who's struck dumb when I see my wife in a black, deep V-neck, all-lace nightie that barely covers the parts of her I want to devour more than the meal I ordered. Her hair is mostly dry and twisted up, exposing her creamy shoulders. "God, you're beautiful," I rasp.

Libby blushes. "I know we said no gifts, but I couldn't resist."

"Turn around." The command is guttural, but my lovely wife complies. The back of that scrap of temptation drops down to the base of her spine. And the straps are so insubstantial that one good tug and the entire thing will be a pool at her feet.

I can't wait to test it later, but right now, I have to make certain Libby's taken care of.

"First I have to feed you. Then, well, I wouldn't expect to be wearing that for too long."

"You don't like it?" Libby's feigned innocence is in direct contrast to the fire flicking in her eyes as they roam my face, my chest, and below. She knows what she's doing to me, the minx.

Slipping an arm around her, I tug her against me so she can feel exactly the reaction she caused. "You know damn good and well I love it. I just think it might be time for you to make up for all that sass you've been throwing at me," I drawl, trying to get the upper hand.

I utterly fail as Libby's face lights up like a Christmas tree. "Really?"

I groan as I press my head into the side of her neck before letting myself taste her. It's a shock that even as my lips make contact, she stiffens in my arms.

"Cal? What's all this?"

Ah, she threw me so off balance, I forgot about my surprise. Loosening my arms, but not entirely letting her go, I pull her in front of me. Lowering my head, I whisper, "Happy anniversary, honey. I know we said no gifts, but I couldn't let today pass without showing you how much I love you." Feeling her body start to shake in my arms, I tighten my arms. "Always, Libby. Always."

"You got me sunflowers," she says wonderingly. At my nod, she asks, "How?"

"I'll never tell."

"You always manage to make me feel more special than I deserve." Her voice is filled with joy. "You're the most honest, caring, handsome man in the world. There are so many days I just count my blessings for you."

The shaft of rightful guilt I feel doesn't belong here. Not today. "I'm the one who's lucky, Libs. Every second I know you love me, it's a gift I never imagined I'd ever have."

Turning back to face me, my wife blows me away when she says, "The feelings I have for you don't have a name yet; they're that enormous."

And that's how I ended up making my bride of two years wait even longer for her dinner as I pulled her down to the area rug beneath our dining room table and made sweet love to her with only the bouquet of sunflowers as witnesses.

41

PRESENT DAY

ELIZABETH

"So, the sex hadn't changed in your marriage?" Dr. Powell asks.

I shake my head. "I still couldn't say Cal's name without the shivers." A brief smile flits at my lips. "Kind of the way it is now."

"Taking us out of the timeline for a few minutes, do you realize how extraordinary it is with everything you've been through you both have managed to hold on?"

"My heart isn't complete without his beating close by," I sigh.

"There are some who might say you're weak for that."

"Admitting my heart hurts without his has nothing to do with my being a strong, capable woman. It has to do with the fact that there's a cadence to the way a heart is supposed to beat, and mine's wrong without Cal's." My eyes close for a moment in anguish while I admit a truth. "Underwater, you don't hear your heartbeat in your chest. You hear it inside your head. It pounds in between your ears so hard and strong. If the beat's off, it's just a constant reminder that everything is wrong. Just wrong. Wrong." Opening my eyes, Dr. Powell's compassion is almost my undoing.

"We're all individuals for a reason. Each of us is unique. What works for my life and my marriage won't work for you or for the person who greeted me when I came into the building. What works is as individualistic as wild and terrifying as the love we're supposed to have, the families we raise, and the lives we lead. Why should I be considered weak because I fought through hell for my version of that?"

"You shouldn't," Dr. Powell assures me. "Do you think your marriage would be as strong now if you hadn't lived through what you did?"

"It would be different. But as to whether or not it would be stronger, I can't answer that. There would have been trials by life in some form or fashion. Of that, I'm certain."

"What makes you say that?"

"Because we all start our marriage with the intent of being perfect, but none of us are. And frankly, none of us would get married if we could see the trials life intended to throw at us," I say simply. "We'd all be afraid of the reward if we knew the risk."

Dr. Powell nods slowly and makes a quick note. "You got married young, Libby."

"I was twenty-five. Not terribly young."

"Did you have a plan for how you wanted your relationship to progress?" At my confused look, Dr. Powell clarifies. "Married, get the business established, start to have babies, that kind of thing."

Ah. "I think I know where you're going with this."

He lifts his ankle to rest on his other knee. "I thought you might." His eyes flicker down to my thickening waistline.

"Sam and Iris are excellent parents. They love their children a great deal," I say quietly.

"Would you like to hear what Sam said about you when I asked him about it?"

I chortle. "This should be interesting. I wonder if I should have warned him his answers would affect his Christmas gift from me."

Dr. Powell laughs. "He said, 'Libby was nothing but supportive when Iris announced she was pregnant with our first child. There was never a time my wife ever felt like she wasn't being showered with love. It's one of the many reasons why Libby and Cal are Rachel's godmother and godfather, respectively.' How does that make you feel?"

"Like I did an excellent job of hiding my own emotions."

"Which were?"

"That I was hurting because I felt like I was never going to have children because my husband was never home," I admit.

Dr. Powell blinks as if what I said shocked him. "Really?"

I nod. "I was over the moon for Sam and Iris and defeated because my husband had no idea how much I was deflecting."

"Deflecting what?"

"How resigned I was to being second fiddle in my marriage to his job." I then tell Dr. Powell about the days around Iris's big news.

42

ELIZABETH

YEAR THREE - EIGHT YEARS AGO FROM PRESENT DAY

"Hey, babe." I'm juggling a cup of coffee and my laptop bag as I unlock my office inside Deja Vu. "What's up?"

"I just came from the doctor." Iris's voice is faint. "Libs..."

The phone bobbles in my hand as the shock in hers resonates through me. "Iris, what is it?"

"I've been sitting here for thirty minutes trying to figure out who to call first. I...I don't know what to do."

"What's wrong?" I don't care I'm yelling so loud it's likely the customers working with my assistant Amy on the showroom floor can likely hear me. "Spit it out!"

After a moment's pause, she whispers, "I'm pregnant, Libs. Sam and I are having a baby."

It takes a moment for the shock to fully penetrate. My cousin and my best friend got married less than six months after Cal and me after dating exclusively since college. Yet, with the way the two of them travel—as much as my husband—I never imagined I'd be hearing this coming from my best friend's mouth. Meanwhile, I have to say something. This is the sister of my heart. "Are you happy?" I ask cautiously.

"I...Libs, I never thought about it. I always assumed you'd be the one with a houseful of kids, not me."

Yeah. Me too. But I keep the thought to myself while I help my best friend edge away from panic and realize this is a moment to be celebrated. "Iris, maybe the time isn't what you were prepared for, but you and Sam? You were made to raise a child."

Her sniff comes through the line. "You think?"

Shoving aside everything I'm feeling, I assure her, "Absolutely. And think of the amazing support system you have backing you up."

"Aunt Libby," her watery voice rasps. "I'm going to have a baby. And it's going to be able to call you that."

Locking away the anguish her words are causing, I say, "Damn straight they will. How are you going to tell Sam?"

"Oh, God. I didn't even think about it."

Sitting down behind my desk, I lean back in my chair. "What made you think you were pregnant?"

"I didn't. I thought I got some bug from the crap I ate in Germany."

My ears pick up. Germany? "You were on the last trip with Cal," I say flatly.

"Well, yeah. It's a part of my job, Libby."

I don't say anything in reply. The silence expands between us.

I can't help the overwhelming rush of resentment washing over me. There are days like these where it feels like love just doesn't feel like it's enough—where I'm pushed out of a major part of my husband's life despite doing everything possible to be a part of it. Despite the efforts Cal has made to keep more in the loop, what I've ended up building is a lovely relationship with his assistant, not a greater intimacy in my marriage.

And I'm not sure how to breach it.

But I know I have to be the one to pick up the pieces; otherwise I'll just be pushed aside.

"Well, you'll have to let me know what you end up deciding," I say lightly.

"Libby," Iris starts, but she stops. After all, what is there to say.

Nothing. That's what. My husband is her boss. And without his go-ahead, she can't tell me a damn thing.

"I'm going to have to fight Aunt Lukie overthrowing your shower, aren't I?"

She lets out a relieved laugh. "Oh, undoubtedly. The first grandchild on her side of the family? If the estate wasn't thirty minutes away and we didn't spend so much time out of the country, it wouldn't surprise me to find out she's was poking holes in Sam's condoms."

While I'd normally laugh at her impossibly funny truth about my aunt, the reminder that she, my cousin, and my husband spend more time out of the country than in it sends the coffee I've already drank churning in my stomach. "Honey, I hate to cut this short, but I have a call with a client in just a few." It's in an hour, but I need the time to compose myself.

"Oh, I didn't realize." Disappointment laces her voice.

"We'll have to make plans to talk more when there's more time."

"Well." Her voice is hesitant. "We're wheels up in a few hours. That's why I wanted you to know."

An incoming beep tells me I have a call. After Iris's last comment, I can just bet who that is. I ignore Cal's incoming call and focus on wrapping up my conversation. "Is it safe for you to travel?"

"For now. We'll discuss it again at my next appointment."

"Well, you be safe anyway. That's my future niece or nephew you're carrying." Another beep in my ear tells me my husband is becoming impatient.

He can just wait. After all, I'm going to have to wait an indeterminate amount of time to see him again, won't I?

"Absolutely. I'll call you when we're home. Have a good call, Libs. Kick some design ass."

"Always do." My lips tip up. "Take care of you."

"Always do." She hangs up.

Seconds after Iris disconnects, Cal's ring sounds. I let it go on for a moment before I answer, "How long will you be gone this time?"

"Hi, Cal, how's your morning?" he drawls sarcastically.

"Hello, Cal." But I don't apologize. I'm exhausted and it's only 8:45 in the morning.

"Why didn't you pick up? Is everything okay? I tried a few times." His voice is concerned.

"I was on the other line." I decide not to tell Cal about Iris's call. If my husband was going to be home tonight, I'd likely end up sharing that news as it will make its way through the family by then. But since they're headed out for parts unknown, who knows when she'll begin to share it with the people she works with? A kernel of warmth flickers inside of me that she called me to share before she left. As for Cal, well, he can find out Iris and Sam's news once she decides to share.

"Something wrong?" he asks.

"No." I don't elaborate. I just wait for him to continue.

Which he does. "We just got a call about a job, Libby. I'm leaving in a few hours. I should be home in a few weeks, tops."

By now, my computer's booted up. As I scroll through the calendar, one item jumps out at me—the Akin black-tie family benefit we put on annually. I put a note to let my mother know she doesn't need to account for Sam, Iris, or my husband. "Please let me know when you land," I ask him quietly. I'm too used to the last-minute trips now, and despite the fact each one is slowly draining a little bit of my happiness from me, I knew what I was getting into when I married Cal.

Didn't I?

Shaking my head, I tune back in to what he's saying. "...really don't think it will take two weeks. I hope to be back before the ball."

Sighing, I say boldly, "Cal, if past trips are anything to go by, you're going to miss it. I'll let Mom know."

"Libby, it's not like I want to," he says carefully.

"You never want to."

Silence arcs between us. I break it. "Listen, I have a call soon."

"New client?"

"Yes. Have a safe trip. I assume Rebecca will call me with any information I should have."

"Of course. I love you, Libby. Always."

"I love you too. Safe flight." As the phone disconnects in my ear, I think about my words.

I do love Cal with my heart and soul. His long absences are just becoming more and more draining on our marriage.

No, it's never the love that's in question. On days like this, it's just harder. That's what make the days when it's effortless even more precious.

Pushing the crappy start of this day out of my mind, I pull up the estimate file for the client in Charlotte. It was Amy's idea to do some advertising in the vast metropolitan region just a few short hours away. And besides, with Cal gone as much as he is, I need something to fill my time. My business is taking off in that region.

I just haven't had a chance to tell my husband that yet.

The call comes in. My assistant puts it through. After we get through discussing the mockups I sent up, I'm asked to fly up for the initial consultation. After a second of hesitation, I say, "Of course, Mr. and Mrs. Stiles. I'd love to come up. We can finalize the drawings and spend a few days confirming our choices."

"When can we look forward to seeing you?" Larry Stiles booms through the phone.

Since all of my nights just opened up, I say, "Is next week too soon?"

"Not at all, Mrs. Sullivan. I'm so excited to get started," Tia Stiles gushes excitedly.

"As am I. I'll confirm my travel arrangements, and we can determine the best time to meet at the design center," I tell them warmly. After ending the call, I lean back in my chair. I catch a copy of Cal's and my wedding photo on the corner of my desk.

If I can't have Cal at home, maybe a little travel of my own will do the trick. Maybe it will fill the void that's missing inside of me that's being left empty every time my husband goes away.

43

CALHOUN

YEAR THREE - EIGHT YEARS AGO FROM PRESENT DAY

W alking into the first ballroom at Akin Hill, two weeks later, I'm astounded as I have been the last two years I've attended the charity event to raise money for the Lowcountry Food Bank. Dahlia and Bernard Akin started the tradition over forty years ago when they realized that despite their healthy wages, much of the monies of their employees were going to help their loved ones be fed over the holiday season.

Not for the first time do I wish I'd had the chance to meet Libby and Sam's grandmother. The woman was an indomitable force; she might have given Admiral Yarborough a run for his money, I think ruefully as I scan the room for my wife, who I've missed desperately.

I wonder if Iris told her the big news before we were sent off to gather intel on a potential resurgence of the Basque Separatists in Spain. It turns out it was a concrete threat which we passed off to our friends at the agency, who will do what they need to in order to squash it. But we had some downtime in Spain while we waited to see if we were going to be spun up again. Since Iris didn't indulge in the Coke and red wine with the rest of us, she gave up her news.

The entire Alliance team is elated to have a "...future team member to train. Do they make earwigs in baby size?" Pete, our site logistics specialist, teased Iris.

She punched him in the arm before Sam wrapped his arms around her and said, "You have to knock that shit off, babe. Someone's going to hit back, and then I'm going to have to ask someone to kill them."

"Just think," I mused, as I lifted the glass I just toasted her with to my lips. "We have a designated driver for the next however many months."

We all lost it laughing. I even join in, as Iris used both fingers to flip me the bird.

Picking up a glass of champagne from a passing waiter, I salute Marcus and Natalie, who appear to be surprised to see me. Mentally shrugging, I assume Libby didn't get my updated itinerary from Rebecca. I left a message for my assistant to tell my wife I'd meet her here at the party.

Wandering from the first ballroom into the second, the vibe changes from genteel mingling to an almost electronic symphonic beat. Couples are paired off performing the tango with an avid crowd cheering them on. If I could find my wife, we could show them a thing or two. I frown, scanning the fringes of the crowd for the dress I remember Libby had originally planned on wearing tonight: a fitted white lace dress that would look fabulous against her lightly tanned skin.

I almost choke on my drink when I catch sight of her on the dance floor with a man I've never seen before.

Libby's dark hair is pulled away from her face in long glorious curls. In an emerald-green halter-style gown with delicate pleating that crisscrosses low over her breasts, her body is fluid and her movements are electrifying. The tailored bodice flows into panels revealing a hidden slit. Each time she lifts her leg, it rises to her thigh, flashing glimpses of her slender leg as her partner twists and twirls her so fast.

And there's a rapturous smile on her face.

Knowing how to blend into a crowd so I'm not seen, I continue to watch the captivating couple as they make their way forward and back, always in motion, not staying in one place for more than a heartbeat. They're two bodies moving as one, in tune in a way I don't think I've ever seen before. I quickly take a gulp of the champagne that burns in my stomach like battery acid.

Who is he? Did Libby bring a date to this party since she thought I would be out of town? I'm choking on rage.

When the song ends, Libby is draped down his side like a glorious bolt of satin down his muscular arm. I'm just about to shove past the applauding crowd until my wife is pulled straight up and she gives her partner a high five. Another man steps into the circle to join them. He lays his lips on the forehead of the first and holds out an arm to escort my wife off the dance floor.

It jerks me out of my delusion.

What was I thinking? I berate myself silently. Libby loves me. She'd no more cheat on me than I would on her. But for a moment, I questioned her.

Why?

Making my way around the circle of dancers to where the trio is standing, chatting lively, the only conclusion I come to is because I've missed her desperately. I've been gone too much lately. Maybe now that Iris has declared she's going to be slowing down, I'll talk to Libby about what Yarborough wanted me to almost a year ago, potentially buying into Alliance. Maybe that will give me the opportunity to be in town doing the behind-the-scenes operations the Admiral partakes in. It's not that I want to be on the go all the time; I just want to feel like I'm using my skills. On the other hand, pulling back means I can spend more time with my wife. Even as the options fly through my head, I pause just behind Libby, absorbing her presence. One of the two men drawls, "Elizabeth, it appears you have an admirer."

"It's a good thing I'm married, then, Chase."

Yes, it really is. Wrapping my arms around her from behind, I feel her body lock before I whisper in her ear, "Surprise, baby. I made it home."

Maybe it's my imagination, but her body seems to tense a little bit more. But there's nothing but pleasure on her face when she turns slightly to press a kiss to my cheek. "Welcome home, Cal."

Not exactly the effusive greeting I was expecting. Then again, it's the Akin ball; Libby's likely to be more restrained in front of other people. I'll save the greeting I normally receive for later when we're alone.

"That was one hell of a show," I tell her. Libby blushes to the roots of her hair. I grin before holding out my hand to her dance partner. "Cal Sullivan, Libby's husband."

"Chase Corbett. A pleasure to meet the man who captured Elizabeth's heart. My partner, Bryce." He tips his head with a loving smile to the man who danced so beautifully with Libby.

Keeping my arm around her waist, I shake both men's hands while explaining how Libby snared my interest. "It was more the other way around—almost from the moment I saw her."

Libby rolls her eyes. "Oh, please," her honeyed voice teases. "I'm at best a close second to your work, Cal. But that's okay. I knew the man I was marrying."

My mind recoils in shock. How can she not understand her importance in my life's priorities? That my heart doesn't exist without her? *Or maybe,* a little voice taunts me, *it's because there's a part of her that's right? That Libby will always come in second to your work?* Disabusing that notion and stifling the concern, I shake my head. "That's just not true."

Libby pats my chest a bit condescendingly, in my opinion, and she turns back to the other men and continues chatting. In the course of their conversation, I learn they're a client of my wife's as well as Akin Timbers as they own several exclusive mountain retreats in the Biltmore area.

When did my wife expand her business into North Carolina? I'm disturbed I didn't know but keep quiet as the conversation flows around me.

"I'm so thrilled the design I provided worked for your image of the space," Libby says as she accepts a glass of champagne from a passing waiter. Snagging another one for myself, I include myself in the soft clink of glasses with the others.

"Brilliantly," Bryce says enthusiastically. "It's one of the main compliments we receive from the guests."

Libby's smile widens with satisfaction. I'm so proud of her, I can't hold it in. I lean down and brush my lips against her cheek. "Your talent is amazing," I tell her.

She shrugs her delicate shoulders to offset the compliment, but Chase's voice jumps in. "I concur. It's rare for someone to be able to walk into a space and not overdesign it. We were still able to add unobtrusive touches of us without it ruining the overall impact."

"That's my job," she protests.

"No, that's your gift," I correct.

She blushes a delicate pink that draws my attention down to the low V-neck of her dress. Unable to stop myself, I take the champagne glass and run it along her bare back.

And am floored when she steps forward out of reach.

"Libby!" We all turn our heads. Josh is waving her over to a crowd of people. "Come over here for a moment?"

With a helpless shrug, Libby says, "Duty calls. If you'll excuse me?"

"Of course, my dear," Chase says gallantly as he steps back to make way for her.

"Save me another dance later, Elizabeth," Bryce chirps.

Before she can step away, I catch her wrist in my fingers. "I'll be around." Lifting her hand to mine, I brush a kiss along the knuckles.

She smiles before walking toward her brother.

Maybe it's a trick of the light or her makeup, but I could swear the smile never made it to her eyes.

"So, tell us Cal, what do you do?" Chase asks.

And I begin to explain the outsider's knowledge of what Alliance does for the US federal government.

"Sounds...stimulating," Bryce says, with a delicate pat to his mouth to hide his yawn. "Excuse me. Must be too much champagne."

Thinking back to our most recent fact-finding mission in Spain, I sip the dredges of my champagne from the glass to hide my smirk. "You have no idea."

Then again, no one really does.

44

ELIZABETH

YEAR THREE - EIGHT YEARS AGO FROM PRESENT DAY

I'm sitting on the edge of the grass skipping rocks into the water, watching as each rock ripples into the river. Each skips over like a hit-and-run—a perfect analogy of my life with Cal.

The morning after the party, I'm still trying to get my bearings after my husband came in. And the peace I normally find on this one place on the property isn't meant to be found.

Dragging my knees upward, the handful of rocks in my hand fall heedlessly next to me. "What's happening to us?" I whisper aloud.

"I don't know." I jump, not only because of the fact I'm not alone but because Cal continues on and what he says seems to lay the blame of us entirely at my feet. "Who was that woman last night? She was a revelation." Cal drops down next to me.

I shift uncomfortably. "What do you mean?"

"A business expansion? A dress that could bring a man back from the dead? The way you wrangled money out of all those donors?" Cal shakes his head. "I didn't recognize you, Libs."

I choose my words carefully. "I don't know why this is such a surprise."

"The woman from last night dazzled me." I feel the warm blush of that compliment for the duration of time it takes Cal to open his mouth, leading us into dangerous territory. "She sure as hell isn't the same woman I'm sitting on the edge of the grass skipping rocks into the water with."

"How would you know? You're never home" is snapped before I can stop myself.

"Whoa. Libby, honey. That's not what I meant." Cal holds up his hands.

"Then what did you mean, Cal?" I demand.

"Just…I don't know. I guess we would be considering other things."

It comes to me then he knows about Iris and Sam's news. "I guess when you work with your spouse, there's better odds for the kind of miracle Iris and Sam are expecting. Then again, it'd be nice to not only have my husband around to make our child but to help raise him or her." Pushing to my feet, I start to move away.

Cal grabs my hand before I can shift more than a foot. "Libby, I didn't come here to fight." His voice sounds so tired. For a moment, I waver, realizing if he flew in yesterday, he likely is exhausted. But then I remember the nights I spend with half of my bed, my life, my heart aching, and I turn my head aside.

"I work so I don't feel the loss of my dreams anymore, Cal. If I've changed, it's because I understand that now." Removing my hand from his, I ignore his pleas to stop as I make my way down the grassy knoll back to the house.

Because I can't let him see me cry. I do too much of that while he's away and I'm alone.

HOURS LATER WHEN I GET BACK TO OUR HOME, I DRAG MY WEEKENDER and dress bag into the house. The smell of food cooking surprises me. After our fight, I was certain Cal would have headed into the office. "Hello?" I call out as I drop my bags at the base of the stairs.

And then the lights dim. The candles I didn't notice before sitting at the base of each sunflower that is in its own individual vase pop out throughout the room.

"Oh, Cal," I whisper. My heart melts and aches because the sweetness behind the gesture means everything to my heart and nothing to our lives.

Footsteps behind me precede arms wrapping around my waist. His voice is warm next to my ear. "You were right; I have no idea what it's like for you. But I want you to know that if your dreams have changed, hon—" Cal gently turns me in his arms. "—then all that matters is I'm a part of them."

My head collides with his chest as I wrap my arms around him. Maybe I can't change our marriage, but maybe we can.

It certainly appears as if Cal wants to try.

Lifting my head up, I slide my arms around him and hug him tightly. "I love you."

"I love you, Libby. Always."

I don't know how long I stand there holding on to him. All I know is that once again we're suffering because of another consequence of a job I only understand on the surface.

Even as Cal lowers his lips to take mine in a kiss rife with apology and filled with love, I just know I can't go on living the way I have been.

I have to be the woman I've always meant to be. I just thought I'd have a husband by my side to do it.

45

CALHOUN

YEAR THREE - EIGHT YEARS AGO FROM PRESENT DAY

"What do you think?" A few weeks after the Akin ball, Libby and I are home. Yarborough and I finally got the results of the three independent reports and have come to an agreement. It will drain all but one of my offshore accounts to do it, but I want to take the gamble. I want the roots to here, to Charleston, to Libby.

There's a fire roaring while we talk about the deal Yarborough agreed to last week where he retains 50 percent of Allied and allows me to buy 25, Karl the other quarter with a first option for Karl, Sam —once he gets the capital—or me to buy in more at a later date or in the event of the Admiral's demise. Of course, that's not what I tell my wife. Still, even though they're a fraction of the actual purchase price, the numbers I gave to Libby to buy into Alliance had her face paling.

"I know we can afford that, but…"

"But what?" I pressure her.

She shakes her head, stubbornly not saying anything. But I want her words. I want to know what she's thinking.

"I…I don't know what to say." Libby shifts under the throw to get more comfortable.

Twisting so I'm facing her more directly, I ask, "What has you concerned?"

"Two things come immediately to mind." But Libby doesn't continue.

Leaning forward, I capture her chin in my hand. "Honey, talk it out. I know this seems like it came out of nowhere..."

Libby snorts. "You can say that again."

I continue, but I file her reaction away. "But it took a while to get the necessary industry research. We were waiting on three independent assessments of the business value, which can't be done overnight..."

"So, why am I just hearing about this now?" Libby demands.

"Is that one of your concerns?" At her emphatic nod, I rein in my temper. "We've been married long enough for you to understand I can't talk about my work, Libby." My tone of voice is one I use on clients who just don't understand we're not mercenaries for hire. They normally don't appreciate it.

And apparently neither does my wife.

"I understand that, Calhoun," Libby informs me icily, stressing my full name to impress upon me her full displeasure at being talked down to. "However, my concerns also extend to barely getting to spend time with you as it is! Do you really think adding 'owner' to whatever it is you do for that company will have you sleeping in our bed more?"

My temper slips when I snap back, "It hasn't changed the number of times you've been gone from it recently."

Libby freezes. "I'm surprised you noticed considering you're never around when I'm missing from it." Pushing to her feet, she tosses the blanket down on the couch between us—a line not to be crossed.

Making her way over to the door, she calls over her shoulder, "I know you want this, Cal. Do what you think is best."

It's the last time I see my wife before I climb into bed because she never comes down for dinner despite my ordering her favorite subs. I even bribed them to bring her sunflowers just like I did on our anniversary last year.

190

But Libby's so hurt because of my callous comments, not even bringing one to bed and trailing it down her arm while whispering, "I'm sorry," gets a rise out of her.

And the next morning, I'm treated to a shell of my wife whose eyes don't sparkle.

I did that and I have no idea how to fix it.

WEEKS LATER, LONG AFTER I'VE SIGNED THE PAPERS WITH YARBOROUGH, I finally call Iris into my office. Steeping my fingers together, I tell her the story of what happened.

Iris gives me a pitying look. "You never learn do you. Tell her, Cal. For God's sake, just tell her."

"You heard her reaction, Iris. What will knowing get her?"

Standing up out of my chair, my wife's best friend glares at me. "I don't know. Maybe something we all demand in our marriages: the simple truth," Iris snipes, before she stomps out of my office, slamming the door behind her.

Turning to face the windows, I contemplate Iris's words. No, I can't tell Libby everything. If I do, it will crush her. But now that I've taken on partial ownership, I can damn well try to be home more.

With that in mind, I push away from my desk and head toward Yarborough's office to flesh out our new roles more thoroughly.

46

ELIZABETH

YEAR FOUR - SEVEN YEARS AGO FROM PRESENT DAY

"Elizabeth Sullivan," I answer my phone absentmindedly. "That couch belongs on the opposite wall," I call out.

"Yes, Ms. Sullivan," Frank, the lead of my Atlanta moving team, responds. "Be careful, boys. Those floors were just refinished." His team makes noises of assent as they lift the large sofa that was misplaced.

I speak into the phone as I observe the new placement of the largest piece of furniture in the recently redesigned living room. "I apologize for the delay. This is Elizabeth," I repeat.

"Hey, Libs." It's my brother. "What'cha up to?"

"Just loading in the furniture for the Harrison house. You?"

"Calling to pick a bone with you."

"Oh?" Seeing a minor catastrophe in the making, I say, "Hold on, Josh. Benny, no. That goes into the son's bedroom. This is the guest bedroom."

"Sorry, Ms. Sullivan." Benny grins sheepishly.

I look at the complicated picture pattern he hung up. "Not a problem. Nice job on laying out the pattern. If you can replicate that, we'll be golden."

He gives me an enormous smile and an unexpected compliment. "That's why we like you, Ms. Sullivan."

Taken aback, I ask curiously, "Why?"

"Because you could just yell. Instead you always find a way to make us feel good about ourselves." Benny begins to peel off the delicate nonstick template I'd had made so hanging the art would be easier. "I'll just go get this hung in the right room."

Forgetting for a moment Josh is on the line, I bask in the genuine compliment. Then I lift the phone back to my ear. "After that, you can peck at my carcass, Josh. I just got the loveliest compliment."

"I heard. And it's well deserved, Libs. You remind me more and more of Nonna each day with the way you inspire the people around you."

"Damn you," I curse him. "Of all the things you could possibly say to get the waterworks started." I begin to sniffle. Patting my dress slacks, I realize I don't have a tissue. I slide the back of my hand under my eyes.

"It's the truth. So is the fact I'm going to enjoy making you repaint Sydney's bedroom walls because she decided to color them with the pack of Sharpies you gave her."

I try to stifle the giggle that image evokes, but I can't. "I tried to tell you she wasn't interested in horses."

"Next time, how about giving her paper?" he says exasperatedly.

"I did." Pursing my lips, it comes to me. "Mom said last week her antique Waterford vase was filled to the brim with perfectly round circles of construction paper. Do you think your little darling used the hole punch to fill it up?"

"How long did it take her to calm down?"

"From laughing?"

Josh groans in my ear. "Jesus. It's like living with you all over again."

"Except you can't go telling on Mom about her because she's all yours," I singsong. Leaving the guest bedroom, I receive a ping. "Hold on a moment, okay?"

"Sure."

Pulling up my texts, I see there's one from Rebecca, which I'll read later. I'm sure it's just another extension of Cal's trip—which has already gone two weeks past due. I haven't seen my husband in over a month. There's a new one from Quincy Harrison, the divorced single dad who owns the home I'm redecorating. Quickly reading it, I mutter, "Fuck," before calling out, "Everyone, the homeowner wants to be in with his son *this weekend*. There's a bonus for everyone if we can get the home complete before he stops by at 5:00." It's now 10:30. "Think we can do it?"

Frank calls back, "Step it up, boys and girls. We all know what kind of bonuses Libby offers. That's cash plus a cake, in case you don't remember." There's a cheer from everyone in hearing distance. "No more mistakes," he says firmly. To me he assures me, "No problem."

I shoot a quick text to Quincy, letting him know to drop by after work, before resuming my call with Josh. "Listen, we just hit a major deadline. The homeowner wants delivery tonight."

"And this is where I let you go. You're not planning on driving home after working all day though?" The care and concern I feel from my brother both warms and pains me.

It should be what I receive from my husband, but he's too busy halfway around the world chasing his own dreams to hear about mine anymore. I shake my head. "No, I have the hotel through the weekend, but if we do finish tonight, I'll drive back in the morning."

"Good. How about bringing your painting arm this weekend?"

I laugh, as intended. "Goodbye, Josh." Pressing End, I begin to find a room where I can focus on the details that make this a design that gives you the sense of déjà vu—the feeling like you've lived here before.

Which is exactly why I'm hired.

QUINCY HOLDS UP A GLASS OF WINE AND TAPS IT AGAINST MINE. "THANK you, Elizabeth. EJ and I are going to be very happy there. It's like…"

I smother the smile trying to bloom. "Like you've always lived there?" I ask innocently.

"Exactly that. After everything he's been through in this custody battle, that's all I could hope for."

We chat for a few moments about his young son, how he's adapting to his new school, when my phone rings—out loud. I frown because there's only two numbers who can get through when I set it for privacy mode: my mother and Cal. Concerned, I say, "Excuse me, that's home."

Quincy waves his hand. "By all means."

My hand is already reaching in my purse pocket for my phone, and I'm stepping away from the table. "Hello?"

"Where are you?" It's Cal.

"I'm working. Where are you?" I'm confused.

"Standing in our house wondering why our home looks like it hasn't been inhabited."

"Probably because I've been on a job for the last three weeks," I say caustically. "When did you get home?"

"A few hours ago. I thought you might be at the office until about thirty minutes ago. When I called, they said you weren't there. Where's your client? Do you want to meet for dinner?"

"I'm already out to dinner. With my client," I clarify.

Behind me, the hostess answers the phone, "Thank you for calling the Peaches Preserve. Please hold."

There's a pregnant pause before Cal asks, "Where are you, Libby?" His voice is quiet.

"I'm in Atlanta. I just wrapped up the job I was working on this afternoon. I'll be home in the morning."

"You didn't get Rebecca's text?" Cal sounds angry.

"I saw she texted, but I didn't have the chance to check it as I was finishing *my* job which required completing a house in less than ten hours. I thought I had through the weekend to complete it," I bite back. "Besides, I thought it was just going to tell me you were going to be delayed. Again."

"I wasn't. I was coming home. To you."

195

"And tomorrow, I'll be back. All that's left is receiving the final payment, sleeping, and driving home," I say firmly. "I'm happy you're home safely. I love you, but I'm at dinner with the client right now."

"I'm not sure how I feel about this," Cal mutters.

Welcome to my world. I was so certain I thought it until I hear Cal's sharply indrawn breath. Shoving past it, I whisper, "I do love you, Cal. I have to go now. I'll call you from my hotel."

"I love you too, Libby." I hear the phone click in my ear. And suddenly the success of today has drained from my body, leaving me feeling hollow.

Turning, I head back to my table to wrap up my meal with Quincy. Wincing, he mutters, "Uh-oh, I recognize that look. I've seen it in the mirror too many times. Do you want to talk it out, or are you in the thinking stage?"

Since I don't want to know what the look on my face says, I lift my wine to my lips and avoid the question entirely. "Is there anything you'd change about the house? Better let me know. I leave in—" I glance at my watch. "—in ten hours."

Quincy launches into a detailed approval of every room, expounding of how much he loves it.

I'm glad because right now I need someone to love something I've done since I don't much love anything about my life.

47

CALHOUN

YEAR FOUR - SEVEN YEARS AGO FROM PRESENT DAY

"Where's Libby?" Iris asks the minute I toss my phone onto the kitchen counter. She and Sam decided to stay over as a surprise for Libby since we'd been gone for so long. Sam takes a long pull of the beer that was one of the few edible items in our fridge.

I guess I understand why now. "She won't be back until tomorrow. She's wrapping up a client dinner in Atlanta." Snagging my beer, I take a drink. "I guess we're on our own another night."

Sam frowns. "Did she not get the message..."

"Apparently, Libby's so accustomed to Rebecca calling her with news that our trips have been extended that she didn't bother to check." I flick the cap of the beer into the sink, uncaring if it scratches the stainless steel.

Iris gives Sam a concerned look before she slides off the barstool and wraps an arm around my waist. I loop mine over her shoulder. "Listen, Cal, she's not entirely wrong."

I pull away, our arms falling in between us, fingers brushing. "I don't want to hear this."

"That's the problem—you don't!" she throws back hotly. "You're pissed your wife isn't here, but what was she supposed to do? Walk off her own job?"

I open and close my mouth a few times because anything I say at this moment would come out sounding like an asshole. Iris gets back in my space and pokes me in the chest. "You're gone as much as you're here, Cal. You have to expect her to fill her life while you're gone."

Sam scoffs. "It could be worse. Instead of building an empire, she could have left your sorry ass like Pete's wife did. I mean, look at what he came home to after our last trip."

"That's not funny." My heart begins tripping in my chest at the very idea of Libby sliding out of my life because of the job. "I'd sooner give up Alliance than I would my wife."

It's Iris's turn to laugh. "You say that, yet your every action says otherwise, Cal." Finishing her drink, she puts the empty bottle into the sink. "Let's go home to Rachel, Sam. I spend enough time with Cal as it is. If Libby's not here, there's no reason to stay."

Iris's words strike me hard in the chest. She's right. Without Libby around, there's no happiness. So, what reason is there to stay? Putting my beer on the counter, I walk them to the back door. "Good trip, guys." Even to my own ears, my words sound lackluster.

"Yeah, buddy. It was." Sam slaps me on the back.

Iris squeezes my arm as she passes in front of me. "She'll be home tomorrow, you said?"

I nod, my throat too tight to speak.

"Then maybe we'll drop by then." Iris bounds down the steps.

"Call first," I yell after her.

She waves at me as she walks to the car. I stand at the door and wait while she and Sam pull out until I can no longer see their head-lights down our street.

Closing the door, I snag my beer and move into the living room. Dropping down onto the sofa, I say to the framed picture of Libby and me taken on our wedding day, "Is it really the effects of the job causing these problems? Or is it that I was never meant to have you in my life? I don't know if you know it, honey, but it's thoughts of your smile that keeps the darkness at bay on the days I'm not with you. It's the only way I can keep doing the job." I reach over and plop my beer on the table next to me.

Tipping my head back, I only intend on closing my eyes for just a moment. This last trip was a bitch. What we found once we rescued the computer mogul's niece was beyond words. There were piles of bodies in that pit...I shudder as the images flash into my mind. Pulling Libby's favorite throw off the back of the couch, I wrap myself in the scent of her instead of the lye. "Never should have happened," I mumble as sleep threatens. "Right under their noses."

But instead of Libby's sweet arms to hold the nightmares of the first night at bay, I'm assaulted by the memories of the girl chained up. Then my heart trips in my sleep as I recall being given authorization to go in and get her once we provided the intel that assured us all she wouldn't be set free. Then the issuance of the secondary mission of leading the joint task force back to the camp to begin to identify the decomposing bodies. "Nooo," I groan.

"Shh. It's just a nightmare, Cal," Libby's honeyed voice whispers. Her delicate hand runs over my unruly hair. I jerk up, almost slamming my head into hers. A quick scan around the room shows me the bleakness of the dark outside.

"It's not morning," I accuse. I press the heels of my hands against my eyes as I try to force my heartbeat to some semblance of normal.

"I couldn't leave things the way they were after we talked," Libby admits quietly. "When I was done with my business dinner, I went back to my hotel, packed, and checked out. I just got home."

"What time is it?" I manage to croak out.

"A little after one. Come on, we'll deal with it the morning. Let's get you to bed." She shifts away in preparation to stand, but I don't let her. Instead, I tumble her down on top of me. Rolling her so she's braced against the back of the couch, I search her face. She looks exhausted—as if she hasn't slept well in weeks. And suddenly, I'm humbled and ashamed. "I'm sorry." The words are out of my mouth before I realize they were on my lips. "I was a jackass," I admit.

Libby rubs her hand over the scruff on my cheek. "I have to do something to distract myself or go mad."

199

"I get it." And I really do. This is why I've never told her the extent of what we do; I don't want her worrying while I'm gone.

"Okay." There's a long pause where we do nothing but take a moment to learn each other after so much time away. It seems like we have to do that a lot because the other person keeps changing and becomes just a touch more unfamiliar each time I come home.

Or maybe it's just me who thinks that? I shake my head. Rolling away from Libby, I push to my feet. Offering my hands down to my beautiful wife, I pull her up into my arms and into a hug—one I desperately need to reassure myself that the flash of pain I glimpsed on her face when I held her was only temporary.

48

PRESENT DAY

ELIZABETH

"So, Cal began to resent your job?" Dr. Powell asks incredulously.

"It seems impossible, doesn't it? But as Deja Vu became more and more successful, it seemed like I was arguing more and more about not being at home. Expansion meant more business, and more business meant more trips." I shrug.

"As you turned thirty, you were on top of your professional game. Tell me about it."

"I worked hard in the seven years since I started my business. I had a staff of eight full-time designers by that point, was turning over two million dollars of profit, and was featured in local magazines as well as a few national ones. Deja Vu was absorbing the energy my husband wasn't around to receive."

"Nor did you have a child to direct it to either," Dr. Powell concedes.

"Exactly. But it turned out to be a good thing for Deja Vu. Being a business owner takes focus. Elon Musk once said being an entrepreneur is like staring into the abyss of death." I shake my head. "I have a greater appreciation for that, and yet it still holds true. You don't own your own business without being willing to give it everything."

"And you did?"

"Where else was I supposed to direct my feelings?" I ask with a shrug.

"To your family some would say," Dr. Powell challenges me.

I pause before responding, knowing my words hold significant impact. "We all get tired of trying to fight a battle where there appears to be no recourse. In my case, I was fighting against broken promises. When Cal bought into Alliance, he swore he'd make more time for us. That was long past. At what point was I supposed to stop waiting and start living? Because before long, I feared there wasn't going to be much left for me to hold on to."

"What do you mean?" Dr. Powell probes.

"I feel needy when I talk about this." I shake my head.

"People who are in a loving, committed relationship should have certain expectations."

"Fair enough. Cal had to go out of the country before my thirtieth birthday," I begin.

49

CALHOUN

YEAR FIVE - SIX YEARS AGO FROM
PRESENT DAY

"Y ou're packing again?" Libby walks into our bedroom just as I'm zipping the top of my black travel duffle.

"Yes. I just got a call from Sam a few moments ago. Something's come up with one of our clients in Europe." I hasten to add, "It should only take a few days. We'll all be back in time for your birthday."

I cringe on the inside as Libby shrugs. "If you can't make it, just have Rebecca send me a message so I can cancel the reservation." God, I really don't want to miss this; it's Libby's thirtieth birthday. We're all supposed to go out for a night on the town to celebrate, the same way we did for Iris's.

"We'll be back, Libby," I say firmly.

"All right." Her voice is understanding even as it's bracing for defeat.

I don't want her to prepare for anything. I want to be with my wife. "Only a few days, Libs."

"Cal, it's your job. I've lived it for how many years? Just let me know." Turning, she slips out of the doorway, and I want to call her back. I want to make her understand if it wasn't for the most dire of needs, I wouldn't leave her side. But the boy in me who was left alone to grow up on my own can't bear to imagine a child out there crying for parents who want their children back.

Grabbing my bag, I heft it from the bed. Making my way down the stairs, I stop by Libby's office where she's focused on something on her screen.

I wonder what it is. I didn't used to have to; I used to know exactly what clients she had, what she was doing, who she worked with. Now, in so many ways, my wife is a beautiful stranger I'm dying to get to know again.

"All set?" Is her voice overly bright, or is that my imagination?

"Yeah. I have just a few minutes before Sam arrives to pick me up."

Libby stands up and comes around her desk. Smoothing her hands over the lapels of my topcoat, she tips her head back. "Safe travels. Call me when you're able to. I'll let Rebecca know of any changes in my schedule." She brushes a soft kiss against my cheek before starting to slide out of my arms.

And I realize if I let her go, I'll be letting everything go. I tighten my embrace. "Libs?"

Her body naturally conforms to mine. "Yes?"

"You know how much I love you, right?"

I hear a tiny sigh escape her lips before she nods. "Of course." Even though it's a Saturday, Libby's in heels. I frown. Come to think of it, she's fully dressed for work.

"I didn't know you were heading in today?" Why does my voice sound so accusatory? After all, I'm the one who's about to leave for an indeterminate amount of time.

Libby just shrugs. "I got a call late yesterday to meet with a client for about an hour. Since it's a new line of business, I agreed to meet with them."

"What kind of..." My question is interrupted by the tooting of Sam's horn outside. I give her a crooked smile. "We'll finish this up when I call later."

Her lips hitch. "Right. I'm sure we will." Just when I'm about to ask her what that means, Sam honks for a second time. I turn my head to begin cursing at the window when Libby's fingers slide over my jaw, bringing it forward again. She rises on the balls of her feet. Brushing her lips against mine once, twice, I don't have to be invited a third time to deepen the kiss.

Unfortunately, as Sam lays on the horn, I have to tear my mouth away just as it was getting interesting. "I'm going to kill him," I announce.

Libby's smile thaws, which is what I need right now. "Just travel safely, okay?"

Giving her a final kiss, I make my way out of her office and throw open the front door. Holding up a finger to ask Sam for one more minute, I wrap my arm around Libby, who trailed me there. "Consider this an early gift for the birthday girl," I say, before I crush my mouth down on hers.

Long moments later, I lift my head. "You light up my world, Libby."

Her countenance softens. "Cal…"

"I'll be back to celebrate with you in just a few short days. I love you."

"I love you too." And my last image of my wife smiling for quite a while is her leaning against the door as I jump in the car so Sam can get the three of us to the airfield to make our transport to Finland to be briefed before we head to find our target in the Ural Mountains.

FIVE DAYS LATER, I'M CALLING HOME TO WISH MY WIFE A HAPPY birthday on a secure SAT phone because I didn't make it back. My mind isn't surprised when she doesn't answer.

My heart is devastated.

I disconnect, hold the phone to my chest, and whisper, "What's happening to us?" before stepping back inside the tent I'm sharing with Sam and Iris so we can get close enough to the camp where the twin children of the United States ambassador of Sweden are being held for ransom.

I haven't completed the mission, have my boss up my ass, and I broke another promise to Libby.

What's happening to my life?

50

ELIZABETH

YEAR FIVE - SIX YEARS AGO FROM PRESENT DAY

H is dark hair is hanging over his ears since he didn't have a chance to get a trim before we left for dinner.

At thirty-six, Cal's more devastating to look at than when I first met him. I could sit for hours and study the candlelight highlights the lean planes of his features. Absentmindedly, I reach for my wineglass on my right. Swirling it around, I listen to Cal finish ordering the extravagant dinner he thinks I need.

What I need is to scream in agony over the overwhelming politeness that's beginning to exist in my marriage. *When did I lose my lover and gain a roommate?* I think hatefully. With a flick of my wrist, the red wine I ordered is sent swirling.

"I don't remember you drinking red," Cal remarks.

There's a lot you'd notice if you were home to see it. Instead of lashing out when Cal's trying, I simply answer, "On one of my trips to Atlanta, a client suggested this."

"Business seems to be going well." He lifts his own glass and takes a drink.

What, are we on our first date? The urge to throw back a scathing reply is on the tip of my tongue. Until the candlelight catches my wedding rings, sending a twinkle in my eye. I let it go. "It is. There's a possibility of being featured in a few magazines." I shrug it off as if the news is nothing major even though when the news came in, I sobbed because I wanted to share it with my husband.

But he was away. Again.

"That's incredible, Libs." He lifts his glass. I click mine against it. "We have more than just your birthday to celebrate tonight."

"I suppose so."

Cal pushes back from his chair. Coming around the table, he slips his fingers into his pocket of his suit jacket. Pulling out a solitaire choke chain, he clasps it around my neck before brushing his lips against the back of it.

Shivers I can't control race through my body. "Cal, there was no need. All I want is you." It's the God's honest truth. I just want to find that spark that's been missing from my marriage.

"You have me, honey. I will always be yours. I just thought you deserved this. The way it lights up reminded me of you." Another kiss to the curve of my shoulder, which I lean into.

"Thank you," I tell him sincerely. And I mean it. I truly do. No matter what ripples our marriage might have to endure, this is the man I love.

My fingers play with the unfamiliar weight as he makes his way back to his seat. Gone is the solicitous husband; in his place is the sexy man I've never been able to resist. "I can't wait to see you wearing just that later."

And I can't help but tease him, "If you're lucky."

He winks just as our appetizers arrive.

LATER THAT NIGHT, CAL IS SLEEPING NEXT TO ME AFTER THOROUGHLY making love to me. True to his promise, I'm left wearing nothing but the gift he gave me as a belated birthday present.

I don't know what makes me do it. Grabbing my cell phone, I pull up our joint credit card account. I just want to be wrong. Please.

But my stomach pitches when I see the purchase from earlier

today. It's to the infamous jeweler whose distinctive blue box Cal left in our closet so he could appear romantic when he slipped the choker around my neck.

He didn't even get my gift until today. All this talk before he left was just that—talk. He had no plans. All of this was just an afterthought, just like I am.

Closing my phone and setting it to the side, I carefully unhook the delicate chain and lay it on my end table before extracting myself from Cal's embrace and settling down onto my side of the bed the way I normally do.

Curled up and alone.

51

PRESENT DAY

ELIZABETH

Dr. Powell flips over another page of notes. "You're telling your story with a different perspective now which is understandable. Put yourself in the you of when you first got married. Was Cal right that you couldn't have handled the day-to-day details of what his job entailed?"

"Unequivocally, no," I say flatly.

"That's certain."

"Trust is supposed to be absolute. It's the cornerstone of a marriage. Secrets do nothing but erode it." I press my hand into my mouth because the emotions grip me so hard. "I had so much to forgive..."

"Do you think the attack escalated your forgiveness?"

"I wouldn't say it escalated forgiving Cal. I will say my priorities shifted. When your life is on the precipice of ending, you never perceive it in the same way. The injustices that seemed to matter so much still matter, but their significance is reduced. I don't know if I'm making sense." I'm frustrated.

I always am when I get this question.

"Talk it out," he encourages.

"The emotional weight of what I'd been through on the *Sea Force* didn't allow for me to handle what happened in my marriage. The lines that were crossed by Cal? Well, he had to deal with them as much as I did."

"And he obviously did."

I nod. "Yes. Eventually." I rub my hand back and forth over our child knowing this miracle under my heart wouldn't exist if he hadn't.

"Would you attribute the lies as the single thing that almost broke your marriage?"

I think carefully before answering. "It's more complicated than just lies. Cal's lies led to a lack of communication which grew as the years passed. We went from being almost obsessively in love with each other—it was like I bloomed when I saw him—to having a best friend that I lived with and occasionally had sex with. The extraordinary was missing. I thought about ways to get it back while Cal would be away because I realized I was lonely."

"When did it all start to fall apart?" Dr. Powell asks quietly.

"'Seek and ye shall find,' Doctor. Or in my case, seek and it shall destroy." My lips twist in bemused irony. "One day, one moment, and my world collapsed."

"You mentioned earlier you thought your marriage was over."

"Oh, I was certain it was. After all, when you walk in on your husband kissing another woman, it's a pretty good indicator. Isn't it?" I murmur, "Because seeing is always believing, right?"

"So they say."

"The problem is when you don't know the truth—ah, yes, back to those pesky little lies—it's hard to believe the truth when someone you love finally wants to tell it to you."

"How hard was that for you?"

How hard was it for me to believe my best friend and my husband were having an affair? "It was like a tidal wave crashed over me and sucked me out into the darkest water."

"Can you talk about it?"

"Due to a lot of intense therapy, I can." I start from the afternoon of my sixth wedding anniversary, when one call changed our lives.

Irrevocably.

52

ELIZABETH

YEAR SIX - FIVE YEARS AGO FROM PRESENT DAY

"Sullivan." I wake up to Cal's inked back as he rolls over to grab his cell on the second ring. Instead of wasting the glorious vision in front of me, I decide it's time to indulge myself in my husband's body.

After all, it's not every day you get to celebrate six years of marriage. It hasn't been easy, but we've made it. And right now, we're on a good stretch where I don't feel like we're so far apart emotionally. My heart sighs happily as I curl an arm around his waist. Snuggling up against him, I begin to run my tongue delicately along the lines between his shoulders.

Even though he shudders, it doesn't distract him from his call. He's all "Yes sir," and "Of course."

I decide to up my game.

Sliding beneath the duvet, I trail my mouth down over the dimple over his ass cheek before I get tough with him by rolling him onto his back. He instantly complies, though still manages to say, "I understand, completely." But when I glance up at him from where I'm curled next to his hip, Cal's eyes are on fire. His nostrils are flaring, and the muscles of his stomach are tense.

I don't go for the head of his cock like I'm sure he expects me to.

Instead, I scoot down lower and gently take one of his balls into my mouth, licking and sucking. The other, I roll tenderly in my other hand. My nose against inhales the musky scent of us still lingering on him.

When I hear him say goodbye, I release his tender skin and lift myself slightly to take the head of his shaft into my mouth, but I'm thwarted.

"Have to make this quick, baby." He rolls and tucks me under him.

Before Cal can kiss me senseless, I slam a palm against his chest. "Why?" I ask suspiciously.

A look of pain crosses his face before he admits, "I have to be on a plane in…"

"It's our anniversary, Cal!" I yell.

His head drops until it's touching mine. "I know. If it wasn't for the fact this deal could blow up at any moment, there's nothing that could pull me away from you."

I sigh, knowing it's useless to argue. There are just days I wish he would see he's already achieved so much. I thought it was all going to slow down once he bought into Alliance. When are we going to get a chance to enjoy it, each other?

Suddenly, an idea pops in my head. "I could come with you," I offer.

A flash of shock crosses his face before he falls back on the bed laughing. "Sweetheart, I'm going to be gone at least two weeks. There's no way you can be ready to go in less than three hours."

"I bet I can." I start to move from the bed, but Cal catches me around the waist.

"You won't have the energy. Not when I'm done with you." Lowering his head, he kisses all thought out of my head. "But I love you for wanting to come with me. I'll miss you."

"I always miss you," I tell him truthfully before Cal's lips capture mine.

And while I'm lying in bed after as he's throwing clothes in a bag later, an idea starts to formulate.

I don't know why I never thought of it before. It's so simple, it's perfect.

And I'm doing it.

🍥

FOUR HOURS LATER, WHEELING A WEEKENDER BAG BEHIND ME, I WALK off the elevator toward Cal's office and enter his outer office. Rebecca should be here; she said she'd meet me out front.

I perk up a bit when I hear the low murmurs of voices coming from the direction of his inner sanctum.

Oh, thank goodness. I bet Cal left something in his office and Rebecca is having to search for it; it's not the first time it's happened. Approaching the office, the voices become clearer.

And a moment later, I wish they hadn't.

"I can't believe we have to go today of all days." A voice strangely familiar to me comes out of my husband's office. "Not that I'm not excited, it's just…"

"I know." Cal's voice comes through the open door. "The timing sucks."

"I'm so happy, Cal. So excited."

"You and me both, Iris." I can't hear their lowered voices, but I'm close enough now that through the crack of his office door, I see my husband lean down and kiss my best friend's lips. Then, as if that weren't enough, he does something that tells me the truth about their feelings for one another.

He gives her my smile. The smile he said long ago I brought into his life with my laughter and love. The smile he took from our bed this morning and is directing in the eyes of another woman.

I think I might die right here if it weren't for the distant ping of the elevator.

Nonna said she didn't help raise weak women. I wasn't going to prove to be her exception. Quickly making my way over to Rebecca's desk, I grab a piece of stationery to hastily scribble a note. I've finished writing it and am folding it on my way out the door when I run into my husband's harried assistant.

"Mrs. Sullivan." She anxiously throws a glance at my husband's partially closed door, telling me everything I need to know.

The wife is always the last one to find out.

"I'm sorry, Rebecca. I received an emergency call. Will you be sure to read this message to Cal once he reaches his destination? I know he's already in flight." The look of relief that flashes across her face makes me want to slap her.

But I'm Dahlia Akin's granddaughter, and no matter what, they'll never break me.

No one will.

"Of course, Mrs. Sullivan. I hope everything will be all right."

"In the end, I'm sure it will be best for everyone." Leaving her to puzzle that out, I nod before making my way toward the elevator.

I have no way of realizing the choice I made in that very moment would change everything in the next few months.

Everything.

53

CALHOUN

YEAR SIX - FIVE YEARS AGO FROM PRESENT DAY

"Yeah," I answer the phone with a snap. With Rebecca's name having come up on the screen, I don't engage the filter to hide the noise of the transport carrying us to Berlin, then to catch a flight to North Africa.

"Boss." Rebecca's so quiet, I can barely hear her.

"Becks, you're going to have to speak up. I can barely hear you over the engines."

There's a slight pause before, "I said, Libby left you a message. I was told not to read it to you until you made it to your destination, but I couldn't wait. And you slipped out the back before I could hand it to you."

My heart, wondering what the hell I'm going to do to make this up to my wife, lightens a little. Maybe she's not quite as hurt as I thought at me shooting down her idea of coming along with me. "What did she say?"

There's dead air on the other side. So much that I pull the phone away from my ear to make sure I'm still connected. I bark out, "Becks?"

"I...I can't read it, Cal." I realize Becks hasn't hung up. She's gasping for air.

I lurch forward, as much as the five-point harness holding me strapped in will let me. "What happened to Libby? Becks?" Sam and Iris's heads snap in my direction. They're both frowning. I shake my head and shrug to indicate I have no clue yet.

"She's not hurt." I let out a rush of air—too soon, it appears, when Becks tacks on, "Physically. Oh, Cal. I was going to stop her outside, but I missed her in the elevator."

A ball of dread forms in the pit of my stomach. "What does the message say?"

"I..."

"Fucking read me the message!" I roar. Other than the plane, not a sound is being made.

Rebecca begins to cry. "It says, 'I wonder now if it's irises or sunflowers that really make you smile. Does it matter when you kiss both of them? Don't race home; I won't be here when you get back. I guess our 'always' is over.'"

My mind whirls. What the hell is Libby... No. Immediately, my eyes drift across to where Sam and Iris are clutching each other, likely flashing back to the last time we received an emergency call about Libby. Worry is etched on their faces. My mind is spinning. If Rebecca didn't manage to stop Libby from coming up the elevator, then Libby...

"No! Fuck no! She misunderstood what she saw!" I'm screaming at Rebecca. There's not a single member of my team not listening in.

"Whatever she saw, Cal, I'm sure she did. We all know you love Libby. She's your everything." Rebecca is openly sobbing.

"She misunderstood." I feel the dampness on my own face and swipe at it angrily. "I'll call her as soon as I can. That will give her plenty of time to calm down."

"I figured you'd do that. So, I tried to contact her."

Bless Rebecca. I sag back in my seat. "And?"

"And her number is going directly to voicemail. Cal, it says, 'If this is my lying, cheating, son-of-a-bitch husband, I only want to hear from your attorney.' Then it disconnects."

217

I don't say another word. All I do is press End before saying three words to Iris and Sam.

"You were right."

Then I hurl my phone to the floor with such force it should shatter into a million pieces. The only thing protecting it is the ridiculous case surrounding it. I just wish I had something like that over my heart. Because I break down, not giving a damn who sees.

Libby used to tease me that I'd never remember our wedding anniversary. After today, knowing I've lost it all, how could I ever forget it?

54

ELIZABETH

YEAR SIX - FIVE YEARS AGO FROM
PRESENT DAY

"What are you doing here, Cal?" I want to smack the pleading look off his handsome face. "I believe you were told by my attorneys I have absolutely no desire to see you. Ever." My words are succinct in case my point wasn't made clear enough by the utter disgust in my voice.

"You left," he says as if he's still shocked by the fact I would walk out on our marriage after catching him in the arms of another woman.

"You're a smart man, Cal." I push to my feet behind my desk, but I don't walk around it. I need the barrier between us so I can hold up this cold facade and not use my nails to tear out his fucking wounded eyes as I unleash holy hell on him.

"How long has this been going on, Cal?" I ask mockingly. "Months? Years?"

He remains stubbornly silent in front of me, but each word I say is riling him.

Too fucking bad.

"I hope you were made aware part of our divorce mandates you being tested for AIDS and STDs."

His jaw begins to tick. "I never slept with Iris."

"It's a pity I can't believe you, now isn't it?" I drawl. Fury over what I saw unfurls through me. "How could you do this to me? To Sam?" I hiss.

"There are things you don't understand…"

"Do I need to recommend Sam gets a paternity test for Rachel?" The words are out of my mouth before I can stop them, but God, seeing the pain they inflict on Cal makes it worth the further wounds I just caused to my own heart.

"How can you stand there and believe the crap spilling out of your mouth?" He's yelling now, and somehow it settles me.

Because Cal being the injured party is a damn joke. "What would you do if you came home and found me wrapped in a man's arms, Calhoun? If his lips had just lifted from mine? If there was an intimacy there you could sense?"

"I'd talk to you," he calmly says.

"You're so full of shit. Unless, of course, you wanted to talk with me about an open marriage?" His jaw falls open at my query. "So, what's yours is yours, but what's supposed to be mine is leasable? Fuck that. And fuck you."

"Libby." Cal moves forward, but I hold up a hand. "Please, talk to me, honey," he pleads. "There are reasons for what you saw."

"There's nothing to say." I'm firm on that.

"Please. Give me five minutes."

I'm astounded he thinks he deserves five minutes of my time. There's a small part of my heart that wants to hear what web of lies he wants to spin, but the large part that held out hope he'd call me after he got my message from Rebecca holds it back. Just the sight of him is making me more nauseous than I had anticipated at seeing him for the first time—though I had prepared myself for it being at the arbitrator's office, not my design studio.

"I can barely stand the sight of you," I spit out.

He winces, but it's the God's honest truth.

I gave him forty-eight hours to get my message. Two days of nonstop crying where despite the vitriol I left as my voicemail, I was checking it to see if he cared enough to call. Instead, I was getting updates from Rebecca that, "Cal was out of touch and he would call me when he could."

After receiving that debasing message, I called my brother and had what may be the most humiliating conversation of my life that ended with Josh saying, "Pack a bag. We'll get the rest later," my brother came to get me to drive me to Akin Estates. It took me a week at home and a few days with the help of my mother, my brother, and my sister-in-law to move out of the home I shared with Cal, taking only the things that were mine—nothing of ours.

Cal still hadn't called. But Rebecca did still—business as usual—leaving me messages as if I gave a damn about how much longer it was going to be until Cal was going to be home because it wasn't a home anymore.

Three weeks after my nightmare started, six weeks after my sixth wedding anniversary, I was living in the house I inherited from Nonna before Cal made this attempt to bridge the gap between us. But now, it's way too late. I've already engaged attorneys, removed my wedding rings, and systematically started closing the doors on my heart that had anything to do with Calhoun Sullivan.

Just like I'm about to do now.

"You must think I'm a bigger idiot than I thought if you think I give a damn about you and your reasons. Take them, and Iris, and go find somewhere to fuck them both." I find the inner fortitude to storm around the desk. "Now, get out of my office before I call building security to have you escorted out." Reaching my door, I fling it open. My hand is so tight around the knob, I'm certain it's going to break off in my hand.

Cal moves toward me slowly. There's a wretched look of pain on his face I can't look at anymore, as if his heart is suffering. "Don't do this to us, Libby," he beseeches.

"I didn't, Cal. You did. Remember that." Just as he crosses the threshold, I slam the door with all my might. Then I lock it.

I can't care how Cal feels. I'm dying inside every minute I'm alive knowing the heart I believed was mine belongs to someone else. I'm the one who lies in bed night after night crying, my body reaching for him—intuitively—even though he's spent more time out of our bed than in it. God, was he sleeping with Iris on all of these trips? What about Sam?

He betrayed me, but what's scarier is I never knew it. For however long, I lay beside him, loving him with my entire soul, and he may have been thinking about someone else.

Just the thought sends me racing for the bathroom attached to my office so I can retch into the toilet. It isn't the first time I've felt this way since I realized our forever was his for right now.

I can't see him.

I can't listen to him.

I won't be lied to by him again.

The only way I can get through this it is to ensure all communication is through our attorneys.

With that decision, I rinse my mouth out with mouthwash before getting a glimpse at the pale, sallow version of myself in the mirror. With a disgusted sigh, I close off the lights on more than just my reflection.

I turn them off to my soul.

55

ELIZABETH

YEAR SIX - FIVE YEARS AGO FROM
PRESENT DAY

"Libby," I hear Iris call out to me. I ignore her. Much as I have the same way every time she, or her husband, has tried to call me or speak to me in the last week since they all returned from their little getaway. I have nothing to say to the woman who's been having an affair with my husband—well, my soon-to-be ex-husband.

I've never asked my family to use my Nonna's money, not to start up my business, not for my wedding, not for a single damn thing. But when I went to them and told them about Cal and Iris, I didn't have to. Mom, Dad, Josh, many of my cousins including Krysta—which surprised the hell out of me but shouldn't in light of the fact she's trying to divorce Kyle—all volunteered to go with me to the board of trustees to release some of my trust for lawyers.

Everyone, that is, except Sam.

He refuses to believe his wife and his best friend are having an affair. He refuses to listen to reason when my parents called him to have a family meeting. Even when he found out my lawyers shoved a subpoena at Alliance and demanded the travel records for Iris Cunningham Akin and Calhoun Sullivan. He's been adamant about trying to reach me to convince me I'm the one who's wrong. And despite my refusal to listen, he's remained nothing but persistent and determined to show everyone, including our family, he stands behind his wife. So far as I know, he's still living with her even though his parents are threatening to go to court to sue for full custody of Rachel since she spends more time with her grandparents than she does her biological parents.

I know the feeling. When I looked back on my computer the other night, I realized that Cal and I actually spent only 40 percent of our married life in the same state. If you count work hours, that number drops even lower.

Sam won't listen to me. His only agenda is to convince me "...what you saw wasn't what it was. Please, Libby, stop being so stubborn and talk with Cal. For all our sakes."

"For all your sakes? You have a stake in this, Sam? Beyond the fact your wife was kissing my husband?" I yelled. Before he could answer, I did. "No. You're supposed to be my family, my protector, someone who loves me unconditionally."

"That's supposed to be your husband," he countered.

"Well, look how well that turned out. He ended up with your wife. Must be a side effect of loving me," I drawled sarcastically, before I hit End to the call.

I haven't spoken to my cousin since. I certainly haven't spoke to the woman who was involved in the triangle that ended my marriage.

But until I hear her calling at me wildly across Harris Teeter, it didn't dawn on me how much I lost. My heartache hasn't abated because it wasn't just one part that was damaged; it was all of it. I didn't just lose my husband on the day I walked in on him and Iris; I also lost the woman I believed to be the sister of my heart, my best friend since college. And then there's Sam—a man I'd been raised with since I was a child, someone I was closer to than my own brother.

My hands grip the top of the shopping cart as she races up to me breathlessly. "Can we talk?"

Ignoring her, I reach for a plastic bag. Gala apples are on sale. Cal loves...damn. I throw them down and push my cart ahead until I reach the strawberries I know the bastard detests because the seeds get caught in between his perfect teeth.

A whimper of a sound is emitted behind me.

I ignore it.

An amused voice I don't recognize says my name. "Libby, is that you?" My head swivels quickly before my lips twitch into a fond smile.

"Murphy," I say warmly. I hold out both hands, which he accepts. He leans down to brush his lips against my cheek. "It's been longer than forever."

"Since Nonna's funeral," he agrees.

"How have you been?" we both say simultaneously. And then we laugh.

Murphy Rogan and I dated in high school. He was sweet, charming, and if I remember correctly, very married. "How's your wife? Kids?" I let go of his hands to reach for the strawberries I'm now determined to buy.

"Kids are doing wonderful. Growing like weeds. Here." He whips out his phone.

"Oh, Murph, they are too precious." This is another thing Cal took away from me. Not intentionally, but his "trips" kept pushing off us having kids. A rush of hot bitterness races through me. Maybe he wants them; maybe it just wasn't with me. A pang hits the region of my heart that this is another facet of life I'll never get to know.

With a smile, he takes his phone back. "I know. As for Trisha—" He shrugs. "—she lives her life. I live mine."

My eyes narrow. "What the hell does that mean?"

He takes a step back at the ferocious bite to my voice. "Libby, did you not know I was divorced?"

"What?" I'm startled. "When did this happen?"

He waves his hand. "A ways back. It's better this way, mostly for the kids. What about you? I know you got married."

My smile fades as I hold up my ringless hand. "Not for much longer."

He winces. "Ouch."

"You don't know the half of it." I can feel Iris still in the store disapproving of my conversation with Murphy the way she used to hate the guys I'd date in college.

But, so what? She's fucking my damn husband.

Murphy looks thoughtful for a moment. "I'm not seeing anyone."

I sass him. "Are women finally becoming immune to your charms? Such a shame."

He grins, and the dimple that would flirt with me back in high school makes an appearance. "One of the many things I always loved about you, Libby Akin."

"What's that?"

"Your mouth." Judging from the way his eyes cast down to it, he's remembering more than just the way I didn't put up with his posturing.

I laugh. For the first time in a month, I laugh. And it feels so good.

"What's your number?" he asks.

I rattle it off to him, and he programs it in. My phone rings a moment later. Murphy grins. "Be sure to add me to your favorites."

"There's only so many spaces, Murphy." Then I tease him. "You have to earn that spot."

"You know I'll try awfully hard, Libby." Now there's a glint to his eye I haven't seen since...

Since my wedding anniversary. I shut down inside. "I... Give me some time, Murph, okay? It's not going to be easy."

"It wasn't for me either. But use my number, Libby." At my hesitancy to respond, he smiles understandingly. "It helps to have a friend who's been there."

And this is why Murphy Rogan is one of the good guys. "I just might do that."

He reaches over and squeezes my hand. "It was really good to see you, Libby."

"You too, Murph." And soon, I'm left remembering football games and homecoming dances intermingled with despair.

Then comes the anger when I feel a hand on my arm. "Libby," Iris says quietly.

"I look at you and I used to see my best friend, someone who I'd die for," I begin.

Iris starts to speak, but I cut her off. "Now, I question everything about who you were, about who I am. Did I know you were fucking my husband and deep down I didn't want to face it?"

"It's not like—" Iris begins to protest.

And it's one time too many. I can't hear from this woman, this person who was supposed to be my best friend, a sister not of my blood, more lies.

My right hand flies out and backhands her across the face. She stumbles back more out of shock than pain, much to my regret.

"Lies! Everything you've hid from me is a damned lie. Everything you did is a broken vow. All of it coming to light—would either of you have said anything if I didn't walk in on it?"

Despite her hand pressing against her right cheek, she imperceptibly shakes her head.

And I deflate.

Finally, the truth. I just had no idea how much it would hurt or how exhausted I would feel after.

Iris looks so beautiful even right now. Her long black hair has wisps of curls around her ears and neck. Her hazel eyes are fathomless. "I loved you," I whisper.

"Libby, please just let me talk."

I shake my head. "I loved you because there was kindness that lived in your heart, daring that lived in your soul, and warmth in your hugs. You were the sister I never had and always wanted. I opened my heart and my home to you. My mistake was in believing the bonds of family I extended to you were returned."

"Stop. God, Libby, you're killing me."

"You mean the way you already did me?" We're drawing a small crowd, but I don't care. I can see the manager making his way forward. Someone probably reported me for assaulting another customer. *One more thing to call the lawyers for,* I think sardonically. But I'm going to get all of this toxicity out before I'm eaten alive by it.

I can already feel it crawling through my gut.

"I would believe a weak man could cheat and lie, but a sister? I never would believe that of someone who claimed to love not only me but my family, who watched the horror I went through after I was cheated on by my fiancé the first time. And yet, you touched my husband?" A murmur goes up in the crowd.

I ignore it.

"So, no Iris. I don't need to listen to you. I was your best friend. I was your family. And I was the godmother to your child. Now? All I am is the woman telling you to go right to hell where you deserve. And I don't care if you're hurting—you deserve to be." Leaving my cart exactly where it is, I push through the gaggle of people, some of whom are applauding at this point to make my way toward the exit with my head held high.

I may be crumbling on the inside, but she will never see it. No one will.

56

CALHOUN

YEAR SIX - FIVE YEARS AGO FROM PRESENT DAY

Themon room while I am arguing with my attorney on the phone.

"I don't want anything from the house." I listen to my attorney while I pace. "I don't expect Libby to give me any of her inheritance."

I stop dead. "No, I don't even want the fucking divorce, Lewis! Get that through your damn head! I want to talk with my wife. I refuse to sign a damn thing until I can talk with her." At my yell, the noise from teams surrounding me drops dramatically.

"Cal," my lawyer tries to placate me. "Libby could come after your piece of Alliance."

"If it means I get the chance to talk to her, then let her try," I snarl before I hang up the phone. I'm just about to hurl it across the room when Sam snags it out of my hand.

"Calm down, Cal."

I turn and glare at him. "Why won't she talk with me?"

Suddenly my phone rings. I snag it back from Sam, answering it without checking the Caller ID. "What?" I bark.

"Hello, Cal," my brother-in-law, Josh, says somberly. "If this is the way you've been trying to reach my sister, it's no wonder she won't speak with you."

Crap. I shove my hand through hair that must already be standing on end. "Josh." When I say his name, Sam's eyes bug out. "I thought it was my attorney calling me back," I admit.

"I always thought of you as a man of honor, Cal."

"Josh, it's not—"

"What I think? What Libby *saw*? Jesus Christ, man, are you calling my sister a liar? Were you not kissing Sam's wife in your own damn office?"

God, hearing these words come out of Josh's mouth makes it seem so sordid when it was anything but. "You don't understand," I choke out brokenly. My legs crumble beneath me. I end up with my ass to my heels. "Sam..."

"Does Sam know?"

I turn wet eyes up to my best friend and whisper, "Yes."

"And what does he have to say about it?" Josh demands.

I shake my head. Then realizing Josh can't hear me, I say, "Nothing."

"Nothing. I see. So, here's what I understand. While my baby sister's life is crumbling in front of me, the three of you have some kind of arrangement?"

I don't say anything. I can't make my mouth work like it wants to, like it needs to. It opens and closes, but no sound comes out.

Josh takes my silence as his answer. "I just want to know why you can't leave her in peace, Cal. Just...stay away and leave us all in peace."

I'm still crouched down, my head bowed, when I feel a hand touch my shoulder. My head snaps up into the weathering face of Admiral Yarborough. "Come on, son. Let's get a plan of attack together."

My brows lower in confusion. "All I wanted was to protect her. To protect all of us. Was the only way to stop it by not falling in love with her?"

Yarborough leans down, his voice weary. "Cal, the truth is we can't help falling in love. And to be honest, I don't think you'd be the man you are if you were able to." Pushing up, he holds out a hand. "Now, come on. You can't do this alone; you've screwed up too much already." Shooting a filthy look over at Sam and Iris, he says, "All of you, my office. I need to know everything about how to approach your family. God only knows, with my luck, they'll shoot first and ask questions later."

"You're probably right, sir." Sam nods.

I swipe my fingers under my eyes. "If I'd just have told her…"

"You can't wish for what you should have done, so stop wishing and start doing. Otherwise nothing is going to change. Not your life and certainly not your marriage." With that sage piece of advice, Yarborough strides away, expecting us all to follow.

I scramble to my feet, following after him as quickly as I can. I know I love Libby with everything I am. But with all the half-truths I've told, the omissions, the flat-out lies, and all the pain, will the love I have be enough to light the shadows I've created in our marriage?

57

CALHOUN

YEAR SIX - FIVE YEARS AGO FROM PRESENT DAY

M y leg is jumping up and down. I reach for the cup of coffee that was set down in front of me and realize my hands are shaking. Am I so jaded to what I've become that this is what adrenaline tastes like? Is it the raw fear of knowing there may be no going back to the life I had with Libby? That the last smile I ever exchanged was with the wrong woman?

I can't manage to find that center of calm that comes so easily to me. I puzzle that for a moment while I wait for the person I'm meeting to slide across from me. Every time I've boarded a flight to leave Libby, I've done so with confidence because I know she was always waiting for me at the end. She's my center, my touchstone, my heart.

"I fucked up," I whisper aloud.

Just then, a man slides across the booth from me in the diner not far from the estate. Even if I hadn't known Josh for years, I'd recognize him being related to Libby. They look too much alike. "The question is how much." His voice is hard, giving me no quarter.

I don't insult him by holding out a hand, but I do greet him. "Josh."

"Cal. Now, tell me what the fuck you have to say so I can go back to my life and you to yours."

I don't show any reaction to the pure disgust in his voice. I'm certain that no matter what I tell him, there's going to be plenty of that before we're done. "Do you mind if I bring a few people over to help explain?"

He tips his head in acceptance. "I assume you mean Sam and Iris. And though I want to see them about as much as I want to see you..."

"Please, Josh." I lean forward. Lowering my voice, I add, "We have authorization to tell you enough so you'll understand."

His brow arches when the word "authorization" comes out. "Fine." But the hostility on his face isn't easing.

I turn away from my brother-in-law and nod to the two people in the corner. They put down the papers they were reading. Iris, in a disguise her own mother wouldn't recognize her in, slides into the booth next to Josh. Snuggling up next to him, she says in her own voice, "Hey, cousin."

Sam plops himself down next to me, a ball cap and wig disguising his features enough that it takes Josh a moment to realize it's him. "What the hell?" Josh manages to get out.

It's Sam who answers. "Right or wrong, the lies he told her all these years was his stupid-ass attempt to protect her. He never cheated on her, Josh."

Iris snorts. "As if Cal's ever looked at another woman since he set eyes on your sister. Every mission we've been on for years—"

Josh interrupts her. "Mission?"

I take a deep breath. "Alliance isn't just a government contractor." Before I can say any more, Josh scrubs his hands up and down his face. When he's done, the anger has drained out, and what's left is the fatigue.

"I think all of you better start from the beginning." Pinning me with a glare that would do Admiral Yarborough proud, he orders, "Starting with you."

Over the next few hours, with Sam and Iris's help, we loop Josh in as much as we can. We're only interrupted as the waitress refills our coffee at sporadic intervals.

At the end, Josh looks worse than he did when he came in.

I have even less hope when he says, "God, Cal, all you needed to do was tell her the truth. All she asked from you was your honesty and your love. You wouldn't have had to change for her to still love you, but this?" Shaking his head, his next words include Sam and Iris. "While I'm proud of you, all of you, for what you've done, do you understand that in the end you sacrificed Libby's dignity to do it? Is what any of you did better than what Kyle and Krysta did to her?" Just hearing Josh compare us to the asshole who cheated on my wife all those years ago makes my stomach churn up all the coffee I've drank. He continues. "You have no idea of how you devastated her. It's been weeks since this all happened. And in that time, she's just finally—finally—realized she won't be crushed again." Tapping a tearful Iris on the shoulder, he motions for her to slide out of the booth.

Tossing down a couple of bills, Josh leaves us with this. "You may not be able to change her mind, Cal, but you will always have her heart. She may try to love you less every day, but that's impossible for her. The effect you have on her is too great. But she needs time."

Just as he's about to turn to go, Sam calls out, "Josh?" The other man stills. Sam presses, "Will you help us?"

He shakes his head, and my heart withers in my chest. "But I'll help her."

Sam slumps in relief. Iris begins crying in earnest.

And me? I think the beating of my heart may indicate I'm having a heart attack because maybe I'll have another chance to hold my wife in my arms and bring her flowers for no reason. I'll get to tease her about her sass, while she rolls her eyes at me. And God, maybe I'll get to touch her sweet lips with mine.

"There's still a chance, Cal," Iris whispers. Sam murmurs his agreement as he reaches for her hand.

I nod, because I can't speak. I just know as long as there's breath in both our bodies, there's always a chance. It's then I press the heels of my hands into my burning eyes to release some of the pent-up emotion by letting my tears flow with two people who are feeling my pain right alongside of me.

58

ELIZABETH

YEAR SIX - FIVE YEARS AGO FROM PRESENT DAY

"**W**hat the hell is that?" I know damn well what the squirming ball of fur in Josh's arms is, but the inane question escapes my lips anyway.

"It's another gift from Cal." Josh shrugs.

My lips part in shock. "You're kidding me."

"Listen, the thing has peed on me twice—there's no way I'm kidding. Cal is just asking for an ass whooping with this one."

A small smile breaks through the mask of stoicism I've worn for the last two months. "Why would he get me a puppy? I mean, first of all, the obvious. We're getting a divorce."

"Which he's been fighting at every step," Josh interjects. "Like the cards, the flowers"—he gestures to the bouquets of sunflowers over my shoulder—"and the gifts"—he nods at the album I'd been looking through right before he arrived—"isn't an indicator of him trying to win you back."

I give him the point. "True. That doesn't mean I can just forget." And just like that, the image of him and Iris slides into my head, which hardens my heart. "Give him to Sydney," I say firmly, turning my back on the whimpering ball of fur I want to reach out to with all my might.

"No."

I whirl on him. "I can't keep it!"

"Why? Because he's from Cal?"

Hesitating, I sit back down on the couch before I reach for the puppy. Stroking its silky fur, I admit, "If I accept the puppy, I'll weaken more. I'm already feeling pressure to hear him out. And Josh, God. I don't know if I can sit there and listen to all the reasons why I'm at fault for our marriage not being enough—why he sought out another woman."

"After all this, you still don't believe him?" I shake my head no. Josh sighs. "Then tell me, why do you think he's going to say it was your fault? Why do you think you weren't enough?"

Still holding another of Cal's peace offerings, I wander to the window. "He was my world, and I think I was only his distraction. The last few months have forced me to replay nearly seven years of memories, reliving every moment. And the tragedy is we spent more time apart than together in those years."

"That doesn't bode well for any marriage," Josh agrees.

"No." I admit something I haven't said out loud to anyone. "I replayed our wedding ceremony the other day. Talk about an act of pure torture." Josh just shakes his head at me. I shrug and continue. "He never promised me fidelity. So, was Iris the first or only the one I caught him with? How am I supposed to trust him again?" I laugh bitterly.

Josh is silent as I release some of my pain. "If I told you I talked with Sam and I have a better idea of what's going on, how upset would you be?"

"At you?" He nods. "Not very. In the end, it's not going to matter. My life with Cal has been nothing but a lie. While a single event may be what pulled the thread, what is there to hold our lives from completely unraveling? What happened kicked my ass and broke me, but it opened my eyes to the fact that I have a life based on very little substance. I need to find where the core of that is and build off of that."

Josh goes to open his mouth to speak, but I stall him with a hand.

"Since you know more than I do right now, would you be able to forgive your spouse with pretty words?"

"No, but maybe those words lead to some very necessary ones," he retorts.

I cede the point. "I'll make you a deal."

"What's that?"

Looking down at the sleeping ball of golden fuzz in my arms, I say, "I'll have my lawyer hold off sending the next round of papers. I'll agree to sit down and talk with Cal when I get back from my vacation if you agree to potty train this gift. I'm leaving the country in three days; I can't handle all of this beforehand. So, it's either going back to Cal or you train it."

"Deal. I'll train it," he agrees immediately, surprising me. Moving next to me, Josh whispers, "Do you want to save your marriage, Libby?"

I've asked myself this question a million times. "How do I save a marriage based on lies?" I ask him simply. "All I can do is try to save what's left of my heart."

He nods, neither judging nor berating. "Do you still love him?"

Leaning against my brother, I vocalize something I've only admitted to myself—well, and to Nonna when I've visited her grave. "I don't think there will ever be a breath I take where I don't love Calhoun Sullivan. But loving someone and losing them over and over to a fight you never knew you were in? Well, I'm not sure if I can do that anymore."

I move to shift away, but he stops me. "I don't think you've lost, Libby. I think you won without even trying."

"But what did I win, Josh?" I face the window again.

Josh comes to stand next to me. "Do you remember when we'd skip rocks across the water?"

A light laugh escapes. "You'd skip rocks. Mine would just plunk down into the water and cause ripples to happen."

He grins. "You always did suck at it."

I nudge him with my shoulder. "Thanks a lot."

"But your lack of throwing skills isn't why I brought it up."

"Why did you, then?"

"Because eventually you learned to drop your rock with perfect timing. Right after I skipped my rock. You always said the ripple effect of your rock changed the path of mine." Josh turns, takes my shoulders in his hands, and says seriously, "You were right."

"What's your point?" Frustration is evident in my voice. The puppy in my arms begins to stir. I soothe it gently.

Josh waits until I'm done before he says, "It's up to Cal to explain, but let's just say, you've caused a shock wave to his path."

I scoff. "Right. If I was so important, then explain to me how…"

Josh shakes his head. "I don't know. I just know that you have to talk with him. You can't make a decision this absolute without speaking with him first. You have to know, Libby. And isn't knowing better than wondering?"

I bow my head. It's answer enough.

"Don't underestimate the effects of what your love means to that man."

With sad eyes, I hand the yet unnamed dog to my brother before leaning up to kiss him on the cheek. The tiny thing whimpers and tries to curl up in his strong arms. "The truth would have cost him nothing. But lies seem to have cost him everything. He's told so many, and I deserved none of them. The worst one is the one he's told to himself—that I wouldn't question the words 'I love you' that he said over and over." I start to walk from the room.

"But you'll keep your promise," Josh calls out.

I stop in place. "Unlike my husband, I don't lie. I'll meet with him when I'm safely home. Even if it's to wish him the best with his new life."

I'm halfway up the stairs, intending on finishing packing, when Josh calls from the bottom, "Why are you so determined to walk away?"

"Why are you suddenly on his side?" I snap back, answering his question with one of my own.

"Maybe because I don't want my sister to be living with regret for the rest of her life."

"Was it my decision that caused this?" I ask quietly.

"No, of course not." He looks abashed. "Cal started this."

I climb down the stairs until we're eye level with each other. "Yes. And if I can figure out a way to erase the pain of those images, it would be a hell of a lot easier."

He pushes a lock of my hair behind my ear. "I understand."

I cup his cheek. "You don't." He opens his mouth to protest, but I lay a finger on his lips. "You don't, Josh, and I hope you never do."

"Yeah." His sighed word brushes warm air against my finger, making my nose wrinkle in distaste. "I just wish I could see you smile again."

"Maybe someday." Looking down, my eyes get big. "Josh…" I try to warn him, but I'm too late. Cal's gift has leaked again on his shirt.

Josh curses roundly. "Shit. This is the third one today."

I can't prevent the giggle that escapes. Josh's head snaps up at the sound. "Damn, Libby, if he"—he nods at the puppy, who's now trying to lick his face—"makes you laugh, maybe I won't potty train him."

I shake my head, the first smile in months flirting with my mouth. "You know the deal, brother." Leaning over, I scratch Cal's gift under the chin. "I think I'll call you Darcy," I croon.

"Darcy?"

"From *Pride and Prejudice*. He lies to Elizabeth in the book, if you remember."

Josh opens and closes his mouth. "A more appropriate name could not be given to you, young Darcy." Leaning forward, he almost crushes the puppy between us. "Safe travels, Libby."

"It's just two weeks," I say gently.

"Two weeks where I'm going to have to deal with Syd bemoaning you not being around. Be careful and come home in one piece, yeah?"

I laugh even as he makes his way to the door. "I'm going to learn a lot about myself," I remind my older brother.

"Who said you needed to?" He gives me a wink before disappearing.

After the door closes, the house feels strangely empty. I climb upstairs to finish packing. Part of me wants to reach out to Cal to thank him for the gift, but there's another part of me that can't. I need to figure out who I am again without being wrapped in both lies and love because both are killing me.

"The effects of this are going to remain with me for a long time," I say aloud as I close the lid on another suitcase. A quick check of the time makes me realize I should get something to eat. Leaving my bedroom, I meander downstairs to the kitchen to find something to munch on.

Maybe the open sea air will make me hungry.

And I need to do this. If I'm honest, I've lived for Cal for so long, I need to know what it's like to live for me. I need to discover a new love for myself because maybe then I'll find the strength to go on by myself.

I need to know I'm worth loving and I always was.

59

PRESENT DAY

ELIZABETH

"Darcy?" Dr. Powell's voice holds a note of amusement.

"Let me assure you, our dog is a flirty pain in the ass," I tell him. There's a roar of laughter. "If Cal intended to get me a guard dog, Darcy sucks. I don't care if it is part German shepherd, those traits are obviously suppressed by the golden retriever."

More chuckles. I continue. "Thank God for Josh. By the time I did come home, Darcy was fully housebroken though. And saddle broken," I add on.

"Saddle broken?" Dr. Powell's voice is strangled.

I nod. "Sydney was having her baby dolls ride him like he was their own mini personal pony. I swear, it was like she was training him. I have no doubt once this one is big enough, it will be Darcy who is trying to get him or her up on his back." I touch my stomach gently.

"Do you know what you're having yet?"

I shake my head. "I don't want to know. I want to be able to memorize the look on Cal's face when the doctor tells us for the first time." There are so many other horrible memories I want to subdue with good ones.

"How long before your time aboard the *Sea Force* did you find out you were pregnant?"

I open my mouth and close it. This is hard for me to admit. "I suspected it for a few weeks after Cal confronted me in my office. But I was so certain it was stress." I reach for my juice and take another small sip, needing the emotional break.

Dr. Powell quietly states, "But it wasn't."

My heart aches in ways that years later I know I'll never recover from. "No. I faced the music the day after I received Darcy from Cal. I went to my gynecologist and found out for sure." Tears fill my eyes. "I felt the need to keep this super quiet until I got back."

"Yet you told your brother?"

I nod, tears falling openly. "I did. Cal did so much traveling. I remember him saying someone should always know all of your itinerary and medical conditions. For me, since Cal was out of my life at that point, that person became Josh."

"What was his reaction?" Dr. Powell sets his papers aside, reaches for a bottle of water. Just the sight of it makes my stomach queasy.

Waiting for the nausea to pass, I admit, "He freaked out. He told me I should call Cal immediately, but I wanted the time to determine if I thought we could move on from what happened." Lowering my head, I whisper, "I put myself first."

"There's nothing shameful in that, Libby."

"If I had spoken to Cal, there's no way I would have been on the *Sea Force*. Maybe our child would still be alive." The guilt of this has lived with me for more than five years. It's almost cleansing for me to say it out loud.

"And maybe something else would have happened. Have you thought about things from that perspective?"

"I have so much guilt from that time in my life, it's hard to separate it all."

"Then maybe you need to hear what Cal has to say about it," he declares.

My head snaps up. Then calm, even footsteps sound behind me. I'd know that walk anywhere. As he gets closer, I smell the cologne he sprayed on before we left the hotel this morning. And everything in my heart settles.

Cal.

I twist around as he approaches the couch I'm sitting on. "What..." I start to ask.

"You didn't think I was going to let you go through this alone, did you?" Cal's breath whispers over my lips before they take mine in far too brief of a caress.

"Thank you for joining us, Cal."

"I appreciate the invitation, Dr. Powell."

"Your wife and I were just discussing her guilt over your lost child." Cal's hand squeezes mine so hard, I risk a glance over at him.

God, if love could heal wounds, then everything in the world would be fixed by the emotion on Cal's face. "Baby, it wasn't your fault."

I choke up while I try to explain. "If I'd just picked up the phone..."

"Libby, nobody has the power to predict what would have happened if you did. What if you had? What if we agreed to meet and"—he knocks on the wood table next to him—"there was another wreck? We could have just as easily lost Angel that way."

Dr. Powell interrupts us. "You named the baby Angel?"

We were so lost in each other, neither of us realize what Cal said. It's me who admits, "Since it was his or her soul who saved mine, it seemed only fitting."

He nods. "I want to go back to the phone call. What phone call are you talking about?"

"Cal called the morning I left for Malaga. And there was a part of me that wanted to pick up the phone."

"What stopped you?"

What did stop me? I give myself a few moments to think before I explain.

ELIZABETH

YEAR SIX - FIVE YEARS AGO FROM
PRESENT DAY – OCTOBER 17

My bags are packed, my carry-on with my passport and my boarding pass for both the plane and the ship is waiting by the door, and I'm just waiting for the car to pick me up to take me to the airport.

Wandering over to the window seat, I pick up a pillow and hold it against my stomach, remembering last night when I called Josh to come up for a quick chat before I left. The shock on my brother's face, followed by wonder, when I told him I'm barely two months pregnant is seared on my brain.

Squeezing the pillow tight, I wonder if that's how Cal will react when I tell him. Because divorce or not, my husband has a right to know.

Leaning back against the window frame, I think about my explanation to Josh about why I wasn't telling Cal until I got back from my cruise. "I'm tired, Josh. Every day is a strain. All I do is wake up and wonder what happened to my life, and I go to bed missing my last kiss. Every. Single. Day. I need something else to think about for just a little while before I wrap my mind around the fact I'm never going to be able to get Calhoun Sullivan out of my life—that I'm going to have to live with this pain day in and day out for the rest of my life."

Josh opened his mouth to speak and then shut it without saying a word. He simply opened his arms. I walked into them, letting the warmth of his hug seep into my body. He pressed a kiss on top of my head and rocked me back and forth for a long time before whispering, "I'm going to love your baby, Libby."

"I already do."

And it's true. Shifting the pillow to the side, I rub my hand up and down. "You'll always be the piece of your father that I'll cherish, little one. You have no idea how much you'll be loved. Just knowing you're a part of me is already giving me the strength I need. I know so many people would be questioning Fate right now, but I'm giving thanks for you in ways you can't understand." I'm about to say more when I hear my cell phone ring.

Sliding from where I'm sitting, I walk over to the entranceway and grab it. Cal Calling. For the first time since our anniversary, I debate picking it up. There's an urge to share this news with him, but a wry curve twists my lips. Somehow, he'd yank me off that plane, and I wouldn't get the time I need on the open ocean to get my head together.

Biting my lip, I don't decline the call. I let it go to voicemail. Maybe later, I'll actually listen to it instead of deleting it. But even though my attorney would tell me I'm about to weaken my position, he doesn't know what I do. And the life of our child supersedes my bitterness. I don't care if it kills me, I won't let this precious child know an ounce of hatred between its father and me.

I pull up my text app and quickly type out, *I'm sorry I missed your call. I'm on my way out of town.*

Cal's response is instantaneous. *That's okay. If I'd known, I would have waited on your gift.*

It's fine. I left him with Josh for him to begin house training. I add a swirling emoji at the end and press Send.

Cal types, *LOL. I'm sure he appreciates that.*

My thumbs hesitate. *It was sweet, Cal. Thank you. I always wanted a dog.*

I know. We should have got one before now. There's a pause before, *I miss you, Libs. Every moment of every day.* My eyes close in pain when I read the words.

I miss everything, I admit. I continue to type, *But I also can't forget.*

Libby, there's so much you need to know.

Josh indicated as much.

Can we talk. Please?

I'll be gone a few weeks. I need to go. There's too much here clogging my head. Wetness stings my eyes as I press Send.

Just promise me you'll hear me out. Please. That's all I'm asking.

I hear the toot of the horn outside. The car's here to drive me to the airport. Realizing my time's up, that I need to leave this here for now, I type, *When I come back. I have to go.* Because I know Cal and I have a great deal to discuss.

And not just about what happened to end our life together, but about the life we managed to start without intending to.

I slip my phone in my pocket just as the doorbell rings. I open it. "Yes?"

"Mrs. Sullivan?"

"Yes?" I repeat.

"I'm Andrew with McNeal's Transportation. I'm here to take you to the airport." He does a courtly little nod of his head. "I'll be happy to talk your bags."

I open the door wider. "Just the two large ones, please. I'll get my carry-on."

"Yes, ma'am." The tip of his head again. I ignore the buzzing in my pocket while Andrew carries my bags outside. I ignore it while I get settled into the back of the black town car. I finally can't ignore it when he puts the car in gear as we pull out of the drive.

Please be careful.

Tell me you left your itinerary with someone?

You're precious to me, baby.

I will always be yours, Libby. Just yours.

I send a quick text to my brother to remind him of my email with my trip information. Then I close down my phone and let the tears I swore I wouldn't allow to come. With a hand pressed to my stomach, I attribute it to hormones which I'm sure will be flaring up quite a bit over the next few weeks.

"Why did this happen this way?" I whisper aloud.

"Excuse me, Mrs. Sullivan? Did you say something?" Andrew asks.

"Sorry, nothing." At least nothing that I haven't asked myself in the last few days a million times.

61

ELIZABETH

YEAR SIX - FIVE YEARS AGO FROM PRESENT DAY – OCTOBER 19 1400 HOURS GMT

After a seventeen-hour flight, multiple layovers, and where I briefly debated driving from Madrid to Malaga, I'm finally being escorted on board the *Sea Force*. My legs are trembling. I attribute it to the combination of getting my sea legs as well as the overwhelming beauty of my home away from home for the next two weeks.

An older, dashing man with an Italian accent captures my hand. "Welcome aboard, Signora Sullivan. It is our pleasure to have you aboard the *Sea Force*. I am Alessio, your cabin steward. Please allow me to escort you to your suite." He holds out a courtly elbow, which I slip my fingers into.

"Thank you so much," I say. "The ship is magnificent." My head keeps swiveling from side to side. I gasp aloud as Alessio walks us through the gallery. Sparkling gems glint under carefully lit glass cases. Well-recognized paintings are arranged beautifully on the walls. "Oh, my goodness. What do you look at first?" I wonder aloud as I turn to take it all in.

Alessio gives a rough laugh. "The most priceless object in the room, of course." When I spin to see which of the many items he's referring to, I end up blushing hotly.

His dark eyes are fascinated on me hungrily.

I'm uncomfortable beneath his direct perusal. Not only am I finally at a point where I might be willing to listen to my husband's explanations, our child rests under my heart. Even if I were interested, which I'm not, my own honor would demand I firmly put Cal in the past before I bring anyone or anything into my present.

And Cal is too firmly locked in my present.

Making my way toward the exit, I offer a vague smile while wondering if it's possible to get a different cabin steward. "I'm still adjusting to the time zone changes." Not a lie since my pregnancy decided to drain my energy this morning when we landed. "Is there time for me to lie down before we depart?"

Alessio nods slowly, understanding my unspoken rebuff. Holding out his arm, an arm I really have the urge to ignore but courtesy demands I take, he says, "Of course, signora. I'm terribly sorry. Let us not delay further in getting you to your suite."

Unspoken between us, the word *alone* hovers, but no mention of it is made. Instead, Alessio continues to give me a preliminary tour of the ship on the way to my suite.

All I need are a few moments of blissful peace to just forget in the ripples of the sea. I'm not sure which it will be.

MANY HOURS LATER, AFTER WE'VE SET SAIL AND PARTICIPATED IN THE mandatory evacuation drill, I've showered and changed into a sleeveless plum-colored wrap dress. My long hair is pulled back from my face to keep it out of my eyes as I walk along the deck admiring the setting sun.

I texted Josh earlier to let him know I got on board. He told me that Darcy had already peed twice on his floor and Syd had trampled through it while "helping me clean it up. You owe me more than you know."

My response back was a bunch of laughing emojis. But just before I turned off my phone, I flipped to my text messages with Cal from the day before. The last two lines make me want to howl in pain while at the same time wish he was standing next to me.

You're precious to me, baby.

I will always be yours, Libby. Just yours.

Now that I have our little one to think of, am I thinking more clearly? Or is it that time and distance is starting to cause the immediate anguish to fade. I start to send him a picture from the boat when I realize I can't bring Cal here. I need this time to make sense of what remains of my heart. And I refuse to apologize for taking the steps I needed to for protecting myself. No one said heartbreak was fair. I found that out as my heart lay in pieces and I had to walk on them out the door.

What Cal hasn't realized is that it wasn't just his world that was upended when I asked for the divorce; mine was affected more. Because in the little that remains in the aftermath of all the betrayals, some of which I suspect I haven't even learned of yet, I have to find the courage to love myself again.

And I fear that will never happen.

DINNER IS TRADITIONAL SPANISH FARE. WHILE I LONG TO TASTE THE bounty of seafood, I wisely stay away and stick with the firewood chicken that is reminiscent of that cooked at Casa Botín according to our waiter. Its smoky, rich succulence falls off the bone and practically melts on my tongue. "Delicious," I pronounce at first bite.

I do indulge in a few bites of the traditional family-style paella served. Avoiding the seafood itself, I concentrate on the rice that is, quite simply, like taking a bite of the sea. "I don't know about the rest of you, but I've never had better," I say to the McCallisters sitting to my left—an older couple from Texas celebrating their twenty-fifth wedding anniversary.

Camille, the wife, agrees. "I normally don't get the chance to dine out like this. It's divine."

I take another bite and swallow, before responding. "Are there not many restaurants like this near where you live?"

Her husband, Linc, guffaws. "Honey, if it doesn't involve steak, I normally don't eat it. But Cam wanted to do a trip like this her whole life." He lifts her hand to her lips. "Who was I to refuse?"

Ignoring the pang around my heart, I tell Camille, "You have a keeper."

Conversation flows back and forth around the table easily. Much of the talk is about Funchal, our first port that we'll reach in two days.

"Do you have any plans in port, Elizabeth?" Camille asks.

Swallowing a bite of crème caramel, I reply, "I plan on exploring the Worker's Market and the Sacred Art Museum. I own a design firm at home, so I'm fascinated by art. I'd love to be able to find local pieces to bring back to incorporate for my clients."

A gentleman, David, who's traveling with his husband sitting across the table, asks, "Where's home for you?" His British accent is absolutely droolworthy.

I smile. "Charleston, South Carolina."

The two men look at each other and smile. "My sister used a firm there when she and her husband were redecorating their home in Atlanta. His company transferred them there, what was it, Matthew? Two years ago?" I shake my head. It would be too much of a coincidence if the lovely couple I took the job for ended up being related to the people across from me. "Diana said the firm did a fabulous job. Perhaps you've heard of them—Deja Vu?" He turns to his husband while I blush to the roots of my hair. "I always thought the name was clever. It's memorable."

I finally find my voice. "Thank you. My grandmother used to say she'd always have these moments of déjà vu, whether it was running into someone she felt like she knew or living an experience she'd already had. She said listening to those moments was how she knew to be successful in business. So, I chose the name in her honor."

The two men gape at me. "It's your firm," David reiterates.

I nod.

He laughs. "Then if you weren't taken through the antiquities room when you came on board, you must check it out. There's plenty of items to tempt a designer of your caliber. But hands off the art nouveau vanity mirror. I have my eye on it."

"I can't promise anything. I haven't seen it yet since I was taken through the jewels room." My lip curls slightly.

Everyone laughs, especially Camille, who asks, "Baubles aren't your thing, Elizabeth?"

My left hand, which has been resting in my lap, clenches. "Not really, no. Just a few cherished pieces that were given to me over the years." *Like the wedding rings I haven't worn in two months*, I think to myself.

"Well, if you don't find anything to tempt you in that room, it's highly unlikely you'll ever be the kind of woman who will," she proclaims.

Linc mutters, "Can you teach that? If you can, maybe you'll be a good influence for Camille on this trip and we can manage to put our children through college."

To change the focus off me, I ask, "How much is college these days?"

Well, that sends Linc and the rest of our tablemates on a rant. Even I gasp when I hear that $30,000 is not unusual for a private college tuition. Per year. "That's outrageous."

Linc gives me a look of sheer torment. "And we have four."

Camille hits him. "You enjoyed making them well enough."

I begin to choke on my dessert. But in the back of my mind are a million questions like, how did you make it this far? Did you ever want to give up?

Did you ever doubt your love was strong enough to make it?

I, of course, don't ask them. Instead, when dinner is finished, I wander up on deck for a bit. I stare at the stars for a few. I wander around the deck chairs that I'm certain will be filled with bodies trying to bask in the rays of the sun. And finally, I stand at the rail near the front of the ship and watch as the boat breaks through the waves of the water, uncaring of the ripples it leaves in its wake.

It's forging a new path, just like I need to.

With that, I head down to my suite as exhaustion overtakes me.

ELIZABETH

YEAR SIX - FIVE YEARS AGO FROM
PRESENT DAY – OCTOBER 22 1549
HOURS GMT

I 've taken so many pictures at the Sacred Art Museum, I think my finger might be permanently crooked. But there's a wide smile on my face as I board the *Sea Force*. I'm so inspired by the Flemish art section, the size and composition of which I've never seen before, as well as the vast collection of sculptures, mainly from Mechelen and Antwerp.

In my mind, my sketchbook is already in my hand as I show my sea pass and identification to gain access to the ship. I think the tile work would look astounding in the bathroom display, I muse to myself as I slide my bag onto the conveyor belt to be x-rayed. Then if I... I slam into someone in front of me. "Oh, excuse me. I'm so sorry!" My eyes widen when I meet Alessio's amused eyes.

"Ah, Signora Sullivan. You have daydreams in your eyes. It's quite lovely," he muses. Stepping aside, he allows me to precede him through the security scanner.

I'm so flustered, I don't realize he must be right behind me because as soon as I pick up my first bag, he's already handing me my second. "Here you are."

"Thank you." Why on earth does this man disconcert me so greatly?

He shrugs before giving me a smile that displays his dimples but doesn't seem to reach those bottomless eyes. I turn away. "I'm sorry, I don't know much about life at sea. Was today your day off? Did you have time to enjoy the city?" I drag out Nonna's reminders to be polite no matter what the circumstance—you never know when it will come back to benefit you.

He rubs his thumb against his lower lip. "You are unique, signora. Are you aware of that?"

I step back. "Excuse me?"

"There are not many in your elevated position as a guest on a vessel such as this who would ask a question about a crew member. Even as we stand here, you see how many I serve who don't acknowledge me."

I shrug, growing more uncomfortable by the minute but feeling trapped into saying something. "I can't speak for them, only myself."

He nods, as if making a decision before answering. "I did have a few hours of shore leave. I had just enough time to run a few errands."

"Well, I hope your day worked out as planned, then."

I start to make my way to the elevator bank when I hear him say behind me, "It was. It may just need a few small adjustments."

Why I feel like I need a sweater or a warm drink as a result of the chill that races through me after that comment, I don't know. I just offer Alessio a polite smile as I step into the elevator, anxious to get back to the sanctity of my room.

When I do, I toss my bags onto my bed. I grab my sketchbook and head out onto my balcony. Slowly, I sit in the lounge chair to relax. I flip to the last page and lay the tip of my pencil to the paper. As I take in the terra-cotta roofs of Funchal, my hand begins to capture vignettes of the details and scale of the artwork I saw today. I make notes in the margins of the colors and textures that grabbed my focus.

After an hour of doing this, I flip the page. Deliberately, I open the door to all of the pain. I draw a man with his head lowered to a beautiful woman with curly hair. His face has just lifted from hers, and there's a smile on his face.

My heart aches when I study the image I drew. There's a closeness between them, something indescribable I never picked up on before that moment. As the familiar pang begins battering my heart again, I drop my hand to my stomach. We're forever linked now. I have to deal with what I saw and process it. Forcing myself to look down, I study the image of Cal and Iris I drew. What else was hiding right before my eyes all these years we were married?

The pain of realizing I was lied to prevents me from listening with an open heart to Cal now. But if I'm honest, it's not just because of this; Cal and I never had the level of open communications we should have. If there was something that needed to be said, we said it. We never held back when it came to all of the important things, but maybe, and this makes my chest want to explode, Iris could get him to say the little nothings, the things he needed to say but didn't know how.

And right now, I need to let him know I'll always love him regardless of if he loves someone else. Because he doesn't know it yet, while I want to be his everything—because that's what he is to me—I need him to be able to give his child more.

So, I turn on my phone. I take a picture of what I just drew. Opening up my text message, I type the greatest truth when it comes to love and the greatest lie when it comes to my happiness.

If Iris can make you this happy, then I wouldn't be the woman who loves you if I didn't step aside. We'll talk when I get home, but I hurt because I heard your heart beneath mine for so long and I didn't listen to the fact it wasn't beating for me. I'll always love you for what you gave to me, Cal.

I press Send before I can stop myself. Then I shut down the phone to get ready for dinner. I need to figure out what to wear since it's formal night. Even though I'm not hungry at all, I figure I'll manage to swallow down enough to satisfy what I need to for our baby. It will all taste like sawdust to me anyway.

63
PRESENT DAY

ELIZABETH

"What was your reaction when you got that text, Cal?" Dr. Powell asks my husband.

"If I knew where she was, I would have figured out some way to get to her," Cal growls. His hand holding mine is almost white with tension. "There I was sitting on my hands waiting for her to come home to tell her the truth, and here she was trying to tell me it was okay if I didn't love her anymore." Cal glares down at me.

"I didn't know," I say helplessly.

"Was I still breathing?" he counters.

"Yes."

"There's your answer, Libs. If I'm breathing, then it's because my heart's still pounding. And it only beats for you." Cal lifts our entwined fingers and rubs his lips over my knuckles.

I'm lost in the sensation until there's a discreet cough. Dr. Powell's smile has faded. "I hate to move on."

Cal stiffens next to me. I lay my head against his shoulder. "It's okay," I whisper.

A low rumble starts deep in his throat.

Dr. Powell holds up his hands in surrender. "It's difficult to discuss," he begins.

"You're not the one who will catch her staring out windows, remembering. I should have protected her. I'm the one who will gladly hold her through any nightmares this might induce. But every time, I want to slam my fist into the people who want to dissect what happened from start to finish. This is our life." Cal's frightfully calm. "What right do you have to more of it?"

"Cal." I lean into him and lay my head on his heart. His lips come down and kiss the top of my head.

"Why don't you start, Cal?" Dr. Powell says quietly. "Pick up from where Libby left off."

He holds me tight against his chest. "I'd just received her text and called Sam and Iris into my office to discuss it."

64

CALHOUN

YEAR SIX – FIVE YEARS AGO FROM PRESENT DAY – OCTOBER 22 1349 HOURS EST

I'm still clutching my phone in my hand when Iris and Sam close the door to my office. Without a word, I hand my phone to them. Until this moment, there was never an all-consuming panic I might not get my wife back.

Until now.

She loves me enough to let me go. I don't know whether that kind of love is so selfless I should feel honored or pissed. I think it's a bit of both. Then I hear Iris crying behind me, and I whirl around to find her in Sam's arms. "That's so beautiful." She's crying so hard the words are next to impossible to make out.

Sam shoots me a helpless look as he strokes his wife's back. "Babe, she's letting him go," he points out gently.

"Because she loves him. God, are men that stupid? Libby loves Cal so deeply, she won't accept less than all of him. Since she figures she doesn't have it, not that it's true, she's setting him free so she can hold on to the memories." Lifting my phone again, her face contorts. "And she's giving her blessing to your happiness, no matter what that is." Iris's face buries deep into Sam's neck.

I would give my life to be with her right now, to explain everything so she doesn't harden her mind against me in the ten more days she has on her vacation. "I don't care what anyone says, I will be waiting for my wife when she gets home. She's not going one more day without understanding it all."

Sam's head, which had been bent over Iris's, snaps in my direction. "Everything?" he asks with a note of hope in his voice.

"Everything." With or without anyone's intervention, I'm going after my wife.

"She figures you're already looking for the next possibility," Iris warns me. "Even with explanations, winning her back isn't going to be easy."

"Don't you understand? Without Libby, life has no possibility. I don't love her because she's willing to walk away; I love her because she may be willing to stay." Sinking into my chair, I put my head in my hands while my friends stare at me agape.

HOURS LATER, I'M REREADING THE TEXTS BETWEEN ME AND LIBBY OVER the last few days while sitting in the corner of the common room when everyone goes static. "We interrupt this broadcast to bring a special news bulletin…" Standing, I make my way closer to the TV. "Shut it, everyone!" I call out. "Let's see if we're going anywhere."

The volume of the television goes up as the yapping from the people goes down to a low-level buzz. The news announcer says in a shaky voice, "The *Sea Force*, a luxury yacht that originated from Malaga, Spain, four days ago, stopped in Funchal, Portugal, for a day of excursions. Less than twelve hours after it departed the small island, an emergency distress signal was picked up by the USS *Lassen*, a Arleigh Burke class destroyer on maneuvers out of their homeport of Mayport, Florida. Only fifteen miles away, they quickly headed in the direction of the ship. Approximately five miles out, they received a communication. The *Sea Force* has been hijacked. Approximately two hundred people are yet to be accounted for."

My jaw clenches. "There's a reason they targeted that ship."

And as if she can hear me, the announcer continues. "The luxury liner has a jewelry and antique exhibit on board valued at close to a hundred million dollars. Although all passengers were subject to additional screening, it's suspected, though not yet confirmed, one or more members of the crew are in league with the pirates."

She takes a shaky breath. "Before making this announcement, all emergency points of contact for all persons on board the *Sea Force* have been notified."

Suddenly my phone begins vibrating in my hand. It's Josh. A sick feeling begins crawling up from the bottom of my stomach. I push the button to answer. "Yeah?"

"Are you watching the emergency news broadcast?" His voice is raw as if he's been screaming, crying. Or both.

"About the *Sea Force*?"

"Yes."

"What about it?" But, instinctively, I already know what he's about to say. Breaking away from the team, I start sprinting down the hall that leads to Yarborough's office. I get there just as he hangs up the phone. Yarborough's head swivels toward me. His face is horrified for a second before it's wiped of all emotion.

And in my ear, Josh confirms everything when he chokes out, "Libby's on that ship, Cal. Can...is it possible to get her home?"

Slamming open the door so hard it ricochets back at me, I answer the only way my heart will allow. "Yes. We'll do everything we can to get her back. I swear it, Josh. We'll bring Libby home."

"Thank you. I...Cal..."

I cut him off before he can apologize for not interceding with Libby. Jesus, if it wasn't for me, none of this would be happening. "I'll call you back as soon as I know what's happening."

Facing the man who gave me the skills I need to save my wife, I state flatly, "Don't try to keep me out. You'll regret it."

"I just got a request to send in a team to help with tech. Do you honestly think you can lock it down enough to make the decisions to save not just her, but to help rescue the 112 passengers and 95 crew we have yet to account for? Because if you can't—" He braces his aging arms on the massive desk that once intimated me sixteen years ago.

Now, all it does is offer me reassurance. "If you can't, your wife might die. You have to decide now."

"Would you trust anyone else if it was one of us?" Our lives are the closest things I can equate to Yarborough on the significance of being a part of this team.

"No. I'd demand to be there—to be a part of this. Which is why I'm giving you the choice." He collapses down into his chair. "Pick your team, Cal. Anyone. Get them ready to fly out to the *Lassen* within the next two hours."

I nod. Moving out of his office, I choke down my fear. I'm unlocking my phone to call Josh back.

He answers on the first ring. "Cal?" His voice is shaking.

Not giving in to allow mine to do the same, I tell him, "I'm taking Sam, Iris, and a team out to the *Lassen*. We're going to go bring her home."

He's sobbing on the other end of the line. I tip my head, the increase in my breathing the only thing betraying my true emotions. "When this is done, if she still ends up wanting to walk away, I'll let her."

"Cal…" But I have to get the words out.

"Beyond every part of me that knows I can't live without her, I need her to be happy, Josh. She had every right to demand that from me. Now, I'm going to make sure she lives so she can have it—however she wants it. I'll call you with updates." I hang up while he's protesting.

Striding back into the common room, I'm swiping a hand across my face. "Sam, Iris. I need you both for ten minutes. The rest of you are on standby." I have to break the news to them to see if they can handle this mission.

Just because there's no way I'm being kept off that helo doesn't mean I won't give them the choice.

65

ELIZABETH

YEAR SIX - FIVE YEARS AGO FROM
PRESENT DAY – OCTOBER 22 2048 GMT

By the time dessert and coffee is being served, most of the passengers at my table have a greenish tinge to their features. I haven't experienced nausea yet in this pregnancy, but as David, then his husband, Matthew, excuse themselves repeatedly, each time coming back perspiring harder and harder, I become slightly queasy.

That mild feeling starts to turn into a full revolt as the man from the table behind me shoves his chair back so hard as he races from the dining room, it jolts me forward, practically landing me face-first in my fresh vanilla bean ice cream.

I lean toward Linc, the only other person not ill at our table. "Do you get seasick?"

He frowns. "The seas are a little turbulent tonight, but nothing that should be causing this kind of reaction. Camille has been on boats plenty of times, Elizabeth." Just then, Camille stands and grabs her napkin. She races on stilettos for the exit. "See? If she's able to run in those shoes… If you'll excuse me, my dear."

"Of course. Go," I urge him.

David sits again, his face pale but resigned. "What did you have for dinner?"

Since none of the specialties contained anything but fish, I went for something from the standard menu. "The filet and fresh vegetables."

"Then I fear you may be one of the few of us who won't be dealing with this tonight," he says bluntly. "I suspect we all have a form of food poisoning. Darn swordfish must have been bad."

"I never thought it could come on that suddenly," I question as David starts to look a little green again.

"I don't remember it happening this fast the last time, but it's entirely possible."

"Do you think we should call the medic?" Concern laces my voice.

David shrugs before he grips his stomach tightly. "If it is, we're all going to get the same advice. The symptoms might range from diarrhea to nausea, stomach cramps, and vomiting. There could also be fever and chills. Stick to our cabins, don't bother the other passengers. If it's worse, call the ship's clinic." He groans. "If you'll excuse me, love." David shoves away from the table.

A few minutes pass before Linc returns. "David thinks it's food poisoning," I blurt out.

His face grim, he nods his agreement. "Don't go outside for a walk tonight. Half the passengers are unable to make it back to their rooms, so they're availing themselves of the open deck to relieve their nausea."

My nose scrunches. "What did Camille have for dinner?" I ask curiously.

"The chef's special. Mussels." At my frown, Linc asks, "Why?"

"That's not what David and Matthew had." I bite down on my lower lip.

"Maybe their refrigeration system went bad." Linc gives a disgusted look at the creamer sitting next to his coffee. "If that's the case, then neither of us is going to be immune for long."

"True. And on that pleasant thought, maybe I'll head back to my cabin for the night."

"Do me a favor, Elizabeth?" Linc stands with me. "Check in with us in the morning? You're traveling alone, and I don't like the idea of you being ill."

A warmth steals across my heart. I reach for his hand and give it a quick squeeze. "Go take care of Camille. I'm sure things will be fine by morning."

But just as we're about to leave, the ship's alarm goes off. "All passengers, make your way to your muster stations. This is not a dri—"

The last word is eliminated by a gunshot followed by a scream before all sound is cut off from the PA system.

Linc grabs my arm. I feel the fine tremor in his fingers. "Come with me, Elizabeth. We have to go find Camille."

I nod, too scared to say anything. Together, we race toward the entrance of the dining room to find something beyond horrifying.

It's blood, copious amounts of blood. Only it's not due to any gun; it's from the passengers as they continue to heave their dinners.

I bury my head against Linc's arm. "Oh, God."

"What the hell kind of food poisoning does this?" Linc wonders aloud.

We both hear footsteps behind us. Turning in unison, neither of us expect what happens next.

Two men approach. Simultaneously, one uses the butt of a gun to clip Linc in the jaw while the other delivers a slap across my face that makes what I gave to Iris in the grocery store a mere love tap. It knocks me backward in my gray silk heels, dropping me in my short, silver sequined dress to the floor.

Linc drops to his knees to check on me when there's a cocking of weapons. We freeze amid the waste being expunged by our fellow passengers.

"It really would have been so much easier for both of you if you'd just had one of the recommended specials for dinner. Now? Well, your fate depends on whether or not you decide to please me. And you haven't had much success at that so far, have you, Signora Sullivan?"

I know that voice.

Lifting my head, fear takes over my overwhelming concern for my fellow passengers as Alessio approaches, his malevolent smile in direct contracts to the blood splattered shirt he's wearing.

And the gun in his hand.

66

PRESENT DAY

CALHOUN

"Who was still alive at that point, Libby?" Dr. Powell asks her gently.

"That I knew of?" Libby reaches for a tissue, but I hand her one. "Thank you."

I just shake my head and pull her tighter against my side. Dropping a kiss down on top of her head, I mutter, "Babe."

She wipes her eyes before answering. "The captain and the bridge crew; I recognized them from the videos on the television in my room. So, the five of them." Inhaling sharply, her breathing accelerates. I'm about to call for a break as she struggles to recall who else was moved into the bar located directly above the bridge where she was held captive for thirty-four of the worst hours of her life. "Linc, who I swear kept me sane." I squeeze her tighter, if that's even possible at this point. God, if it hadn't been for Linc McCallister, I don't know how my wife would still be sitting here as emotionally stable as she is right now. I owe the man a lifelong debt of gratitude.

Libby couldn't be closer unless she were sitting right on top of my lap, and if that's where she needs to be, then so be it. I shift her so she is, and she shoots me a grateful smile before turning back to Dr.

Powell. "There were a few members of the crew alive who weren't involved in Alessio's scheme, but..." Her voice drifts off.

"But?" Dr. Powell probes Libby gently.

Her voice catches. "Alessio used most of them as examples. Their deaths were so brutal."

"In what way?"

Libby flings the details at him like bullets firing from a gun. Then, like a gun that clicks when it's empty, her words start to stumble. "In the way of stripping them and then allowing all of his men to shoot them? Allowing their bodies to fall over the rail..."

I shake my head, salty wetness flying everywhere. I don't care. Hearing this, however many times, guts me.

"Go on, Libby," Powell urges, making me want to coldcock him.

"Don't make her, Doctor. Not now." I place my hand protectively over our child. Twisting so her face is accessible, I murmur, "You don't have to do this."

She grabs the back of my neck so hard, it hurts. I'd let her pull out all of my hair a chunk at a time if it would help. "I have your love. I can do anything."

"You can, but you don't have to," I argue.

Leaning my head against hers, the tears that flow between us spark more memories. Of being on board the *Lassen*. Being helpless to do more than listen and advise while knowing my wife was being tortured on board the *Sea Force*. I tune in as I realize she's started talking about what happened.

Shit.

"...being dragged from the bar down two flights of stairs to the pool deck—afraid to scream, afraid not to. Praying someone was finally coming to save us. Praying to die before if they weren't."

God, Libby.

"The moments of 'worst' began to bleed together. Food and water deprivation—not that I'd eat or drink anything after the way they'd slaughtered everyone. Then there was the sensory overload. We'd be blindfolded; then they'd take it off. Light and dark. The beatings we endured were terrifying. The thing is? It was nothing in comparison to what was in my mind."

"And what was in your mind?"

"All my regrets. And giving up on my marriage was the biggest one. Over and over in the dark, I prayed Cal would find happiness one day."

And I'm done. I bury my head into the curve of my wife's neck, feeling her courageous heart. But somehow, I manage to get out, "That never would have happened without you."

67

CALHOUN

YEAR SIX - FIVE YEARS AGO FROM
PRESENT DAY OCTOBER 23 0023
HOURS GMT

There's barely enough light from the red glow in the transport carrying us to rendezvous with the destroyer in the Atlantic to make out the shapes of the bodies of the other people on my team. Some are doing a final check of their gear; some are sitting with their heads tipped back in the zone. All of them are probably thinking I shouldn't be on this helo, that I'm a damn risk to each and every one of them. But there's no way I'm going to sit on my ass waiting for information about Libby.

Between my time in the Navy and my time working for Alliance, I've been on hundreds of missions with some of the men and women in this bird. Not a single one holds the importance this one does because I failed at being a husband long ago.

Holding up my hand, I finally realize the moment for what it is— my truth serum. Even though I never was susceptible to that shit in my training, I understand now how others can be. The way your heart starts pumping into overdrive; the urgency to talk to anyone about anything because if you don't, your mind is going to go crazy.

The most important uniform I've ever worn is the band on the third finger of my left hand. The most critical vows are those I spoke in front of my friends and family tying my life to my wife's. And the most treasured promise is the one that came along with telling Libby I love her.

The tragedy is having to fly a thousand miles in the middle of a nightmare to admit everything everyone's been saying to me about her is right. I mistook Libby, soft and sweet, as someone who needed to be sheltered and coddled. She needed my protection, my strength.

The reality is just because her core of steel is hidden beneath a blanket of softness makes it no less strong. I should know. How many times since the day the papers ending my marriage were served to me have I tried to talk to her? Most notably, when I tried to corner her at Deja Vu where Libby stood in front of me calmly telling me she didn't "give a damn about me and my reasons. Take them, and Iris, and go find somewhere to fuck them both," right before she slammed the door to her office in my face.

How did I not realize she had to be as strong as me to withstand a "businessman" who'd take off for parts of the world unknown for indeterminate amounts of time. And not once, until she wanted to surprise me on our anniversary, did her faith in me waver. Libby's love was steadfast until she was certain mine wasn't. My surprise shouldn't be that she filed for divorce, but that she didn't want a damn thing from me.

Then again—my hands clench into fists in the dark, my wedding ring pinching beneath the glove on my left hand for the first time—I know why she didn't. Anything she asked for would require her to be bound to me.

Memories of the week I was served my divorce papers two months ago bombard me as the *whomp-whomp-whomp* of the blades take us closer to our destination.

"Don't take this the wrong way, Cal, but you're a fucking idiot if you don't find a way to fight this," Sam told me.

I shoved off the couch in the common room and yelled, "Don't you think I know that? For God's sake, Sam, she's the best part of my life."

Iris regarded me coolly. "We've all heard that, Cal, but you never let her in. And you had plenty of time to."

I shook my head. "She can't handle this kind of life," I protested. "Just because I'm protecting her doesn't mean I don't love her."

"It means you're a damned fool," she growled at me. "The Elizabeth Sullivan who I just encountered isn't weak; she's a woman. And women in love are the strongest and most dangerous creatures on the planet. We'll do anything to nurture those we love, and we'll do anything to harm those who threaten them." Iris rubbed her cheek.

I still can't believe my wife took a swing at her. "I apologize again..." But Iris cut me off.

"Do you have any idea what I'd do if I thought Sam was screwing around on me? If she ever forgives any of us for this, I'm going to have to teach her to hit though; she hurt herself in the process." Iris glared at me like this is my fault, not the imagination of my wife. My ex-wife if she gets her way.

Which she won't.

"We're bound by an oath..." I started to say, but before I got another word out, my partner and his wife were laughing in my face.

"And you could have got her cleared, Cal." Sam's face sobered up. "Don't take this the wrong way," he began.

"Is there going to be a right way?" I interjected.

"Probably not," he admitted. "But you liked having the extra excitement of the dual life. It kept your adrenaline up when the missions were over."

"That's a damned lie!" I shouted.

"Then tell me why you've been married for six years and your wife still has no fucking clue what it is we do?" Sam shouted back. "Businessmen? What the fuck do we sell?"

Swiping up the bottle on the table, I drank from it long and well before answering, "Ourselves. So people like my wife can have their dreams and never realize this country is constantly in danger."

Sam exhaled harshly before turning his back to me. "Yeah."

Iris wasn't quite done though. "The woman who's my daughter's godmother just told me to go to hell, Cal. And that's entirely on you. If you'd told her—"

"Then what? Every time I'd have left, Libby would have panicked!"

"But at least she'd still be in your bed and not being hit on over the strawberries because she's not wearing her wedding rings anymore." With that final blow, Iris stormed out of the room.

The emotional pain that tore through me was worse than the physical wound I suffered when I'd had to dive for cover when we were taking fire during an extraction and my ACL got jacked.

I'd told Libby I was playing a pickup game of basketball with my coworkers.

Her gentle teasing of "Cal, honey, you need to stop thinking you're in your late twenties. One of these days, time isn't going to be on your side." All while she baked blueberry cheesecake, something that made everyone at Alliance practically weep in pleasure when I brought the leftovers in a few days later.

Back then, I scoffed at the idea time was passing by. Now, I'd give anything to live in my memories instead of the present.

Because in about an hour, the helo I'm in is about to land to go assist in a hijacking being broadcast around the world.

One which involves my wife.

68

CALHOUN

YEAR SIX - FIVE YEARS AGO FROM
PRESENT DAY OCTOBER 23 0800
HOURS GMT

Tensions are high on the *Lassen*. And it's a safe guess that mine probably account for 50 percent of them in the conference room we're all crowded in despite the SEAL team taking their fair share of space.

Lieutenant Parker Thornton, SEAL team leader, slams his fist down on the table. "We have no eyes and no ears. What the hell are we going into?"

I shove off the wall. Flicking my thumb at Sam, I growl, "That's why we're here, Lieutenant. There isn't anything Akin can't hack into, including the *Sea Force*. He'll get you the eyes and ears you need. We're not waiting on permission."

His eyes narrow before he says, "Jurisdiction?"

"We have it."

"When did it come in?" His voice holds a note of disbelief. International jurisdiction is a bitch, and right now, there's a battle happening in Washington over it.

"It came in from the moment I found out my fucking wife is on that boat." Thornton's jaw tightens. I slam my open palm down on the conference table. "We've never worked under the same rules you boys have. We'll get you the evidence you need for orders. You just spend the time in between polishing up your knives and guns to be ready to move the minute the brass gives you your go orders."

Pointing a finger at me, Thornton accuses, "Jesus, you're trying to get us all court-marshaled with that attitude, Sullivan. We can't just do a snatch and grab of your wife; there's two hundred lives we need to account for. We need to know who we're fighting against. Fuck, we're FUBARed before we go in if this is the kind of support you're planning on providing."

Leaning in close, I bite out, "We've covered your ass more times than you care to admit, Thorn. I know what the damn mission is. We're not going to let you down now." Especially not now.

"It's not your team I'm worried about," he insinuates.

Yeah, well, I have to give him that one. It's not my team I'm worried about either. I just continue to hold his stare until he scrubs his hand up and down over his face. "Don't give me a reason to have you pulled, Cal."

With a tight nod, I turn away. "Just lead us to the bridge. We'll get everyone eyes and ears within the next few hours."

"Right." Turning to the captain of the *Lassen*, who's been letting our pissing match go back and forth without a word, Thorn gives his approval. "Alliance is on the bridge. My men will use the HUMINT provided to plan and strategize against the hijackers. We'll spin up possible attack options against the *Sea Force* while preventing the hijackers' escape."

I interject at this point. "Remember, our goal is to take out the bogey with the least amount of lives lost. Taking the hijackers alive is the secondary objective."

Thorn says matter-of-factly, "To you. But it is a mission objective to be considered." Around the table, his team agrees silently by nodding.

"Not at the cost of the civilian lives," I shout. My team pushes off the wall.

The captain stands. "In this case, let's wait for the intel to point us in the direction we need to be going, men. Alliance, follow me. Let's get you up on the bridge." As he turns away, I hear him mutter, "Before any blood is spilled on my own damn ship."

Silently, every member of my team follows the captain out of the room. I'm the last to cross over the hatch when I hear Thorn call out, "Cal?"

I pause with my back to him. "Yeah?"

"We know what's at stake. This is a potential disaster. You need to be prepared for it." The words are brutal, but I still turn around to face Thorn.

"Do you think anything could prepare me for what's happening, whether I was sitting at home or here?"

"No. But right now, bury your emotions, Cal."

I give him a humorless smile. "Don't you know, Thorn? That's what got me into this mess in the first place." Quickly, I move out of sight and nod to the patiently waiting captain. "Let's do this."

69

ELIZABETH

YEAR SIX - FIVE YEARS AGO FROM PRESENT DAY OCTOBER 23 1000 HOURS GMT

Every time someone leaves the room, they don't come back. If I used my fingers and toes, I could count all of us. At least all that I can see. And meanwhile I cling to Linc's hand whenever I can. I'd do it more frequently if I wasn't terrified they'd rip him away from me too.

We're bound with our hands behind our backs, ankles tied, and forced to sit blindfolded in the center of the room. I only knew how many people we started with because I heard them say *"Ventitré."*

When I murmured that to Linc, he told me quietly, "That's Italian for twenty-three. God, Elizabeth, if that's all that's left..."

That was the first time he grabbed my fingers with such a sharp pain, I almost gasped aloud. Because it meant the chance that his wife was likely not among the survivors. My tears were absorbed by my blindfold as I whispered back, "Libby. Everyone who cares about me calls me Libby."

"Silenzio!" was shouted at us.

So, we stayed quiet. Waiting.

"Captain." Alessio's dark voice comes out of the dark. Both Linc and I tense. "If you would come with me, please."

"No," the captain bites back.

"I see. A pity." Suddenly, there's a strangled sound from where, I don't know. The blindfold has distorted my sense of direction. "Give us a moment, Diego, then remove the blindfolds of our guests."

"Of course, Alessio." Another name, another voice. And soon, I'll be able to put a face to it.

Not that it will do me any good.

Long moments go by. I reach behind me and squeeze Linc's fingers as boots approach. I let them go just in time as my blindfold is ripped from my head. Tears immediately appear as the sunlight streams into my face. "Daylight," I whisper.

"*Silenzio!*" Diego barks down at me. Tipping my head back hurts from the hit I took earlier, but I do. I recognize the man with the gun as the one who hit Linc. "Quiet! No talking!" I nod and quickly look down so I become more adjusted to the light.

A few minutes later, I hear shrieking screams. I begin to pant heavily. "You turn. You look!" Diego shouts.

Now, as much as the dark hampered me, I almost wish for it back. The blindfold would have saved me from watching as the captain is shoved in front of Alessio and the enormous glass window by one of the kitchen staff who danced around the first night waving his napkin.

Alessio knocks on the window with his gun. "Come, Diego. It is time to show our prisoners what happens when they don't obey orders!" His muffled voice sounds cheerful.

Diego lets out a bark of laughter. "You all watch. Watch or same happens."

We do. Those of us who are left watch as the naked, bloodied captain begs for his life. He begs, he pleads, he rescinds his offer not to help.

And they still shoot him.

Before kicking him over the side of the deck.

My stomach roils. Bile comes up in my mouth. I heave a little, but Linc hisses—just before Diego stalks back into the Titan Bar, with an almost cheerful look on his face—"Swallow it down, Libby. Don't make them take you next. I wouldn't be able to stand it. Do. You. Hear. Me?"

I give an imperceptible nod. I swallow the acidic taste down, apologizing profusely to my precious child for the horror it is suffering.

And I'm praying with all my might that Cal understood my last message; I hope he understood I want him to be happy and that I love him in the event I never get to tell him.

70

CALHOUN

YEAR SIX - FIVE YEARS AGO FROM
PRESENT DAY OCTOBER 23 1100
HOURS GMT

The first mission after Libby and I moved in together involved intelligence gathering in a savagely brutalized village in an African country. After witnessing the atrocities done to the women by not only the men of the village but by their male children, I came home practically homicidal. I couldn't go straight back to Libby's and my home. For days, I lay in my bunk in the training barracks staring into nothing as teams were deployed to God only knows where, afraid of what would happen if I went home and touched the woman I loved.

If I think back, it was likely that first mission after we were an "us" that solidified when I realized I could never, would never tell her that I wasn't just working for just a government contractor now. I knew I would have to compartmentalize my life and keep my work away from my soul. I needed to keep Libby's perception of the world as untouched as the sunflowers I compared her smile to. And yet it was my duty to never let her know mine was hiding the filth they grew in.

But now, as I stand on deck with a pair of binoculars focused on the yacht holding my wife captive in the distance, I wonder if I should have gone home? If I should have let her know who exactly the man was she was going to be married to. Was it worth saving her from worry? Was it worth the hell we're both going through right now?

Because even though she thinks she doesn't know me anymore, I know her. While Libby might be sporting a few lines of worry and maybe some gray hairs, she'd still have her smile.

What she wouldn't be doing is suffering at the hands of captors.

She'd be at home safe. And I'd be free from the horror that's choking me with every breath I take.

ELIZABETH

YEAR SIX - FIVE YEARS AGO FROM PRESENT DAY OCTOBER 23 1700 HOURS GMT

I didn't understand the true meaning of pain until hours passed staring at the sunlight reflecting off the ocean, reliving each moment of my life. Instead of unlimited moments to pretend I'll be okay, life is whittling down to regrets. My hope is dwindling as fast as the sun begins to set on the horizon. Devastatingly fast and yet not fast enough.

It's all just a matter of time.

I pull my knees up as close as I can to my chest, despite the burn it causes in my shoulders. My hair falls forward, giving me a shield for just a moment. I know it won't last long; I'll likely pay for it, but I need it. I sneak a peek to make sure Linc is still breathing.

By the grace of God or the Devil, he is.

He's curled in the corner, bruised and bleeding. What they did to him...I shudder. I can see the purplish outline of where Alessio's boots kicked him repeatedly because the master-at-arms wouldn't turn over the codes to the ship's safe. I both admire and hate the ship's officer because he wouldn't. I overheard the conversation; they want access to that impenetrable safe where the jewels for the auction are. And the officer is using it to barter for his life.

Of the few of us who are left, I think we all wish we had something that valuable.

I've been praying for the life nestled deep inside of me. In the depth of my heart, I've already forgiven Cal. And I forgave myself. Why did it take something as catastrophic as this for me to realize the man I love wouldn't have tried so hard to make me listen if he truly didn't have an explanation?

He wouldn't have. He has more honor than that. But while it doesn't resolve the wear and tear on our marriage, I pray with all my heart he interprets my last message to be happy.

I may never get to tell him that myself. I hear a savage groan from Linc that echoes the truth of my fears.

Emotional pain can't kill you though it might feel like it. It's easier to strike out with actions than to listen. If I think about it, I've been slowly dying for two months. I've suffered by my own hand, due to my own lack of sight, by planting myself stubbornly in one location and not moving. I just wish the people in this room could be spared the mirror of my heart's lesson.

I've thought a lot about Nonna, both in the last few months and since I was dragged up here last night. I can't escape the tremor that racks through my body knowing I'll be with her soon. All those moments with her from learning how to cook and listening to her stories about falling in love flash through my mind. Memories of words of wisdom about being a gracious woman as well as a tiger of a business owner while sipping cocoa, then wine by her fireplace, warming a body racked with chills. And learning from her that only love would cause the ripples in my life to alter its course.

"You might not have thought of this situation," I whisper quietly enough, I'm sure I can't be heard.

But I'm wrong.

Dark boots stop in front of me. "What did you say, signora?" Alessio sneers.

I rub my lips together in an attempt to bring moisture them. They're so dry and cracked from the lack of fluid. "I was talking to my grandmother."

Alessio grips my face hard. I can't control the sound that escapes. "Unh!" My cheek is swollen and tender from...was it just yesterday?

"Your grandmother? Is she here?" Jerking my head back and forth, my neck is whipping every which way. I don't answer. "No? Then what must we do to shut this pretty little mouth of yours?"

I bite my inner cheek.

Jerking my head forward and back, he screams, "Answer me, damn you!"

"I'll...I'll be good. I swear."

With a cruel smile, he stands. Hauling me to feet which have no feeling, I stumble against him. "If you want to live, you'll be better than good." Shoving me backward, I fall awkwardly on my arms. Shooting pain rips up both shoulders.

But it's nothing like the pain that causes me to curl into myself when I feel his boot land right below my ribs.

"Before, you didn't want me to touch you. Now, if it means your death, will you beg for me to touch you, Signora Sullivan?"

Twisting my head, my eyes are staring right into the sun. Tears leak out the sides. I whisper, "No."

I feel a different boot in my back as Alessio crouches down. "Oh, I think you will. Diego, show our guest what happens to women who misbehave, would you? We haven't made an example of one yet."

My mind's in too much shock to register the lash of the leather. At first there's a sharp pain, but then the burn. I scream, "No! Stop!" I try to curl my legs up to protect my baby—Cal's baby—but other hands hold my legs down.

"Again," Alessio demands.

This time, my mind hears the hiss before the lash. My bare legs jolt.

"Libby!" Linc weakly calls out.

"Ah, is that your name? Libby? So precious," Alessio murmurs just as his foot kicks me in the side.

And I turn my head and retch.

72

CALHOUN

YEAR SIX - FIVE YEARS AGO FROM PRESENT DAY OCTOBER 23 1730 HOURS GMT

Y hands are trembling as I rip the headphones off my ears. Listening to Libby's cry of pain sent me from fearful to murderous. "God help her," I whisper aloud.

"Cal, are you going to be able..." Pete starts to ask me again. One of my own crew? I'm out of my chair, my hands wrapped around his throat before he can even finish his sentence.

"Ask me again if I should be here when it's my fault she's even over there." Exerting the slightest pressure, I enjoy the way his face reddens before I let him go. Sam lays his hand on my shoulder, but I shake it off. "I'm fine," I snap.

"You're about as fine as she is," he tells me. "Lock it down, Cal. Libby needs you more than ever, and she doesn't even know it." Along with the encouragement, I hear the undertone in his voice. "The ship's captain, Thorn, neither will think twice about throwing you in the brig." I get it. We're here because they need the help only Alliance can provide. But I'm quite possibly the largest liability next to the hijackers themselves; I'm a man with too much to lose if we fail. Because if we do, I'll never forgive myself.

They might as well bury me alongside Libby.

"It's locked," I bite out as I return to my station. I slap on the headset just in time to hear Libby grunt before what sounds like her body hits the floor.

Then there's only the muted sounds of her sobbing while the bastards talk animatedly.

"Iris, what the fuck are they saying?" I shout.

She holds up a finger. I'm just grateful it's not the middle one. "They're arguing with each other, Cal." A pause. "One keeps saying the only reason he kept her alive is because she's so beautiful." She swallows hard. "But now she's unclean. He's cursing at her, saying she ruined his plans. Oh, God. She's screaming! There's a gun on her!" Iris shrieks.

I turn my focus back to praying while I listen for either the sound that's going to make me reach for my own weapon or her precious voice. "Come on, baby. Come on!"

And then my life is given another reprieve—I hear her faint voice amid the men. "I have money." Libby's slurred voice is giving me a moment of grace from the yawning jaws of hell just waiting to accept me.

Iris slams her fist repeatedly on the console. "Broadcast this!" she yells.

The room is silent as we all listen to my wife barter for her life. "How much, Libby?" the same voice that my wife identified as Alessio questions. "Enough to stop my men from putting a bullet through the front of your dirty little face?" He slaps her again.

God, I wish I could be the one to personally put a bullet in that motherfucker. Then I hear Libby's voice rasp, "Does twenty million work?"

"Ah, sweet Libby, how do I know you have that kind of money?" Alessio taunts her.

She coughs and then spits. Likely blood, I think grimly. "Because I'm one of the heirs to Akin Timbers. That's what's available today at my present age if I can convince the board of trustees to release the amount one lump sum." She wheezes, then coughs again before continuing. "Somehow, I don't think they'll have a problem, though they'll want to know I'm alive."

"For twenty million US dollars, I think we can keep you alive a little longer. That doesn't mean you won't enjoy some more of our hospitality until we're ready for you." Alessio slaps her so hard, we all hear her head clunk to the floor.

"Find out if she's telling the truth. If she is, then keep her alive," Alessio orders. "Diego, go. Validate her identity with the members of the crew on the bridge. Find out from Lorenzo if she lies."

Iris is translating as fast as the asshole is talking. Everyone on the *Lassen* is scrambling. Phones are being picked up. Thorn stands stock-still waiting for confirmation this is a valid play before he passes it down to his team.

I begin shouting, "I'll call the Akins! Libby's parents can contact the lawyers on the board of directors. They can demand a proof of life for the release of funds. They'll need to make this look good!" I'm running out of the room already dialing Josh's number.

He answers on the first ring. "Is she safe?"

And it guts me to have to answer, "Not by a long shot. Here's what's going down." I begin to tell Josh what happened. And when he starts crying, I understand why. "It will be okay. We'll get her back," I vow.

"But will she be the same?" he chokes out hoarsely. Then he tells me something that no one knows but him—not even Libby's parents.

But by the end of the call, I'm the one who's curled up against a wall rocking silently. Iris and Sam find me there with my head resting against my secure SAT phone. "Cal, what's wrong? What did my family say?" Sam leans down, bracing an arm above me.

I shudder. "They're in. Tell Thorn to make contact with the Akins." I can't say the rest—not to them, not to anyone. Even though the fault lies with me, Libby would never want them to know what I just learned. "I need to see the ship's doctor immediately." Shoving to my feet, I shove past them and stalk down the passageway.

"Cal?" Iris calls out. I freeze and turn around. "We'll get her through this. We're going to get her out of this alive."

I nod without saying a word but immediately turn away in order to locate the doctor. Because if what Josh told me is accurate, then I'm more concerned about rescuing Libby alive more than ever since the beating the terrorists just inflicted upon her may have caused her to abort our child.

A child she conceived on the day she believes I betrayed our marriage.

A child, who if it did die, may have just saved its mother's soul by giving up its own.

As I cross over the bulkhead into the sick bay, I can't stop the hot tears streaming down my face. *Please, God, forgive me.* If I could go back and tell Libby everything, I would. But since I can't, help her realize how much I love her.

And I always will. Because if she dies, I won't live much longer than she does.

73

PRESENT DAY

CALHOUN

"You couldn't have prevented what happened, Cal," Libby reassures me. She turns to Dr. Powell. "It wasn't his fault. If there's any blame to be had, it's…"

"If you say yours, I swear to God, Libby, I'm cutting off your chocolate supply," I threaten.

My wife's head snaps toward mine. Her eyes, which were desolate just a moment ago, are full of fire. "You wouldn't dare." Libby is at the point in her pregnancy where she is craving food, and everything she wants involves chocolate as a side item. Even when she wants pickles —which is seriously gross. I power through and give it to her though. She could ask me to eat it for her, and I would. But I hold firm on this.

"All the 3 Musketeers, the Hershey's, and if you think I won't eat your hidden stash of Milky Way Dark…" my voice threatens.

She pouts. "That's just wrong. You're supposed to be pampering me."

"I'm not taking away your peanut butter and milk," I remind her. Next to the chocolate, she's been living on Jif and skim milk. She can take and leave most other food—all but those three things.

"We'd be headed back for divorce court if you even thought it," she grumbles.

Dr. Powell grins. I just shake my head. "As you can see, we don't let each other cast blame," I start.

Libby joins in. "And if we start to think the other one is, well, we know how to find the right way to bring each other back."

"So, taking away chocolate works with you?" Dr. Powell asks.

"Actually, Cal goes out of his way to make sure I have everything I need. We're just teasing." She looks up at me like I hung the moon and the stars. My chest compresses because for so long, I received that look when I didn't deserve it. Now, I never take it for granted. "He'd never take away anything from me." She shifts against me restlessly.

"Are you okay?" I ask, concerned.

"Fine. Just getting more comfortable."

"We can take a break if you two need one," Dr. Powell offers.

"I'd rather not," Libby says.

"Are you sure?" My hand releases hers to cup her face. I check for unusual signs of distress. Instead, I find wrenching sadness and determined resolution.

"I'm certain." Her hand reaches up to grip my wrist as she begins to wrap up the story. "My family confirmed my identity by going public with a press conference," she starts.

CALHOUN

YEAR SIX - FIVE YEARS AGO FROM PRESENT DAY OCTOBER 23 2300 HOURS GMT

"We interrupt your broadcast to take you to Charleston, South Carolina, where the family of Elizabeth Akin Sullivan is holding a press conference."

My arms are crossed over my chest while my eyes are glued to the screen hanging in the center of the bridge. Josh steps up to the microphones amid the clicks of what must be hundreds of cameras in front of the gates outside the entrance of the estate, which almost drown out his voice. "On behalf of the Akin family, as well as everyone who works for Akin Timbers, I would like to confirm my sister, Elizabeth, is among the individuals presently being held for ransom on board the *Sea Force*. We have received a formal request for her ransom."

A flurry of questions immediately hit Josh in the face, including the one we all prepared him for. "How do you know she's still alive?"

"Do you know who else is still alive?"

"Is anyone else confirmed dead?" That question causes a hush to whip through the crowd.

Josh turns a face haunted by fear toward the voice though it's unlikely he can see it amid the flashing bulbs. "At the advice of federal law enforcement and legal counsel, I am not at liberty to discuss how I am aware my sister is still alive. Suffice it to say, we're confident she is. We will do whatever is necessary to bring her home safely. On her behalf, and on behalf of those on board the *Sea Force*, please pray for those still on board the ship." His composure almost breaks on those last words before local law enforcement guides him off the platform and safely behind the gate.

Thorn steps up next to me. "He handled it well."

"Yes." Much better than I would have. I likely would have shoved my way through the reporters to wring each and every one of their damned necks.

Thorn stands silently next to me for a moment before saying, "Sam read me in."

My jaw clenches. "It's my fault..."

Thorn steps in front of me. "Cal, you can't say that."

I let out a bitter laugh. "Sure, I can. She thinks I'm having an affair with her cousin's wife, who happens to be her best friend." I scrub my hand over my face. "I can't do this now. Not if you want me to keep it locked in."

"You've done a hell of a job." Coming from this man who I've known for more than a decade, that's the kind of compliment I'd normally revel in. Right now, I couldn't care less. I turn my attention back toward the TV news anchor, who's giving a play-by-play of the press conference.

"They made sure it was broadcast on every major news network worldwide," he advises me quietly.

I just nod; I can't speak. Fortunately, Thorn doesn't require me to. His hand just clamps down on my shoulder, whether in support or in acknowledgment I'm holding up to my end of our bargain, I don't care.

Out of the corner of my eye, Sam's still trying to hack into the *Sea Force*'s bridge while Iris has her ears on the bar where the captives we know are alive are being kept. We're all waiting for the reaction to the broadcast on the ship so close we can see it out the glass window.

The red clock above the TV turns over to 28:00:00. Twenty-eight hours. My mind starts to wonder if they've given her water? Food?

Beyond the hell we've been able to hear, what else is she being forced to endure?

And will she recover from it?

"Until Libby changed the game, there's no way I would have said this was a K and R mission," Thorn murmurs.

My body tightens. "What do you mean?"

"Look at the profiles of everyone on that boat, Cal. By no means is Libby the wealthiest. What does that tell you?"

My mind works rapidly. "It's a subterfuge for something else."

"Exactly. Now that they opened up the table for negotiation, Cap's going to try to make contact. See if we can get a count on survivors."

I understand Thorn's reasoning. "When?"

"Thirty minutes. Be ready," he warns me before turning away.

I remain where I am mainly because I'm frozen in place by what the news outlet just flashed up on the screen. A picture of me holding Libby on our wedding day. My face is buried in her neck, but hers is incandescent with joy.

When did that look start to fade? I'm in a place between enchantment and despair, tuning out everything around me for the long moments, until my name is called. "Cal! Check this out! We just got eyes into their bridge."

Shoving away my emotions, I stalk over to where Sam's standing with a Navy ensign. "Let me see," I order. Sam has been working nonstop to hack in, only to be met with this firewall or another back door. "Took you long enough."

"Would have been easier if we could have just forced the issue." At my sharp look, the Navy officer quirks a small smile. "Don't get me started on international law. Bane of my existence."

"I just bet." Watching over Sam's shoulder, I can see two of the *Sea Force* crew members being held at gunpoint by a single man. "Is there any way to get them any kind of word without getting them killed?" I demand. The captain comes up quietly behind me.

"I can try, but I can't leave it up long," Sam warns. Dropping back into his own chair, he clicks a few keys on the small device he plugged into the more powerful Navy mainframe. Within seconds, the screens around the room are replaced with computer language. "Come on, you little bastard, let me...no. That's not the one I want. Not that console. I don't want it near the reflection. What's the other fucking console number?" He types quickly for a few moments before keystrokes fly so quickly on the screen, I can barely make out words on every third line. "US NAVY" "FRIENDLY" "TURN SHIPS CAMERAS ON." Sam presses a button and suddenly, we watch as the screen he was working on disappears and the bridge camera comes back up. "Come on, come on, do your checks," Sam mutters.

"Why did you ask him to do that, Sam?" the captain asks.

"Because while I can hack into most of the locations, it's going to take too much time. If he gets the balls to help me out, then we'll have eyes everywhere," Sam says grimly. "It's our best chance to be able to plan the attack."

"You don't think they'll notice?" I ask, disturbed that anything could risk the survivors' lives.

"I think if they would, they'd have their own guys in the chair, not the crew," Sam replies.

"Look!" Thorn calls out.

All of our heads snap forward as the defeated first officer sits up a little straighter. His eyes narrow at the man holding the gun in front of his console before he announces, "We need to cycle some water before we overheat and we become a target." It's a trumped-up excuse.

We all hold our collective breath.

"Then do it!" the man screams. "Just do it!"

"Aye, aye, sir." Without a glance at the monitor in front of him, his fingers begin flying across the keyboard.

Sam yells, "We're getting eyes!" Then, "Oh, God. No." Sam's shocked face flies to mine.

My stomach falls. What is it?

"Throw them up on screen," the captain barks.

"Sir..." Sam's voice is choked.

"What are you waiting for, Sam. Just do it," he orders.

"Yes, sir," comes his weak reply. Within seconds, we see the reason for his hesitation.

"Oh, sweet God. Have mercy on their souls," I whisper.

"I…I need to call this in. How many…?"

"Everyone," Thorn says grimly. "Anyone we can't see in the bar or on the bridge is dead."

We wanted to know how bad it was, and now we know. It's worse than we could imagine, and it still isn't over yet.

75

CALHOUN

YEAR SIX - FIVE YEARS AGO FROM PRESENT DAY OCTOBER 23 2340 HOURS GMT

"How many do you think..." Iris can't even get the question out.

I shake my head. Turning to Thorn, I ask, "What does this do for your plan?"

"I never expected..." Even Thorn is at a loss for words as the cameras display a virtual bloodbath. "This has gone right to hell. We've got to call this into SecNav so the president can be briefed, sir," he addresses the captain respectfully, all of his military training still in check even at a moment when his face is finally demonstrating the horror that's been on mine ever since I learned Libby's on the *Sea Force*.

"I'll worry about that; your only concern is how to get the remaining people off that ship. Alive," the captain adds firmly. "Using whatever means possible." Everyone in the room understands what's being left unsaid; we no longer care about taking the hijackers alive. Not since we have the visual proof they've just become terrorists of not just our nation, but of those of any of the dead passengers and crew.

Thorn claps his hands together. "Let's get to work. We have to assume the hostages have been without food and water for at least thirty hours…"

As if his words release all of us from the wretched images on the screens, which look like someone took a snapshot of a house of horrors and has it playing over and over on a loop, we jump back into action.

Making my way over to Sam, I ask simply, "What do you need?"

"Unfettered access to every mainframe I want, when I ask for it. Get those motherfuckers on the line, Cal, and tell them to stop dicking me around." His fingers pause for the briefest moment. "Every moment I spend arguing with someone, we're risking…there's a chance…" He swallows hard to check his emotions. "Just get me what I need."

I'm already pulling my phone out to call Yarborough before Sam finishes, and step out of sight. He answers before the line can ring on my side. "How bad is it?" His voice is the Admiral that any man on this ship would cower under.

Except me. Beneath it, I hear the worry for my wife, for me, for Sam and Iris. Because Rick knows none of us are coming out of this mission the same as when we went in it, no matter the outcome.

"It's worse than anything we could have ever imagined, and that's without Libby being on board." I don't measure my words. The luxury of doing that flew out the window the minute we saw the true state of the ship. "Rick, we have eyes, and it's worse than anything I've ever seen. It's worse than anything *you've* ever seen. Even Thorn's in shock," I tack on, knowing he'll get the full magnitude of what we're facing without my going into explicit details.

"Dear God. What do you need, son?" Shaking off the shock, he becomes exactly what I need in this moment.

The former Admiral who's ready to knock heads together.

"Sam needs unfettered access to assist Thorn. There's no plan without it."

"You'll have it within the hour," Yarborough assures me.

"Make it thirty." I punch the Off button on the SAT phone and go back onto the bridge to wait.

Twenty minutes later, I get a call back. "Tell Sam to call this number." Yarborough rattles off a string of numbers to me which I immediately memorize. "The president made a call."

Not giving myself time to react, I turn to Sam and give him the information. "I'm heading down to see what Thorn needs."

"Copy," Sam mutters as he dials. I hear him declare, "This is the USS *Lassen*. I have eyes on the *Sea Force*. I need access, now," just as I turn the corner and head down the ladder to the floor below me to see what kind of party Thorn's planning.

"You're going to what?" The disbelief in my voice can't be hidden.

"We're going to move the ship close enough so we can swim it," Thorn assures me.

"How?" I yell.

"We're going to have the captain call over with hostage requests from the families of all the passengers," Thorn replies calmly. "We're going to demand they bring all the hostages out for a visual inspection on deck."

I hate the fact it might just work.

"Then what?"

He rolls his eyes. "That's where your boy comes in. We're going to shut off all power to the *Sea Force* but our eyes before we board the craft."

Christ. I turn away, scrubbing my hands up and down my face until I grip my hair so tightly, I might be yanking it out by the roots. "You're sure this is the best way?" I finally ask. "They could decide it's not worth it and kill them all."

"Yes. They could." My back stiffens at his words. "But Cal, it's the best plan we have to get all the hostages in one place, keep our forces together, and get them out."

My breath whooshes out. "Right." Around the room, my team's scattered amid the Navy task force and SEALs we've been working with—except Sam and Iris. They're holding one another, giving each other a moment of comfort before we go to war.

I catch Sam's eye. So much of this lies on his shoulders. "Can you do this?" Holding up a hand before he responds, I tack on, "Be one hundred percent certain, Sam. Yes or no?"

"Yes. I'm positive."

Thorn's fist hits the table in front of him. "We're wasting time," he declares.

"No, we're not. If Sam says he can do it, then let's get it done." I lift my chin at my best friend.

"Operation Mermaid is a go," Thorn declares. "Team, gear up and stand by for my command." The SEALs surge to their feet and move to the door.

"Sam, team, back to the bridge," I order.

We have a limited time until we hold the lives of a few sole survivors in our hands.

"This is the captain of the USS *Lassen*. Please acknowledge this transmission."

We all hold our breath and wait.

And wait.

Finally, long moments later, we hear, "What do you want?" from a hostile voice with an Italian accent.

And we let out a breath as the first hurdle has been breached.

We're in play.

ELIZABETH

YEAR SIX - FIVE YEARS AGO FROM PRESENT DAY OCTOBER 24 0500 HOURS GMT

"**A**lessio! Come quickly to the bridge!"
The high-pitched yell from Diego snaps me from my pain-riddled lethargy against the wall. What's happening now?

Alessio takes no mind as he stomps on my bare feet as he races past me to get to the door. I don't even cry out as it's just another ache in my overly abused body. For just a moment, I tip my head back and close my eyes against the bright sun that's blinding me. Or maybe it's guiding me?

Inside the Titan Bar, all sounds have ceased. The quiet of yesterday has become more deadly—as if that's even possible. I can hear the electric humming of the air-conditioning, but it still doesn't prevent the sweat dampening my skin or dry the tears from my eyes. Hazarding a glance at Linc—who managed to land near me after his last run with Diego—I see his breathing is shallow. Risking another round with the sadist myself, I barely breathe the word, "Ribs?"

Without acknowledging he heard me, his head bobs up and down. Then he risks more by saying, "Escape if you can."

"What?" I'm so dehydrated I must be borderline delirious.

"Help..." He coughs before turning his head to the side and spitting. God, I hope it's not blood. Linc goes on. "GPS not moving. They'll come."

With dawning hope and horror, I realize that must be why Alessio was called to the bridge. And I whisper, "We'll both make it."

Linc shakes his head. "Cam..."

And I get it. I just haven't said it aloud. Without Cal, without his baby that I'm certain is gone, what do I have to go back to that's worth fighting for?

"Promise me, Libby," Linc coughs again.

And I do, because I can't imagine we'll have the chance where escape will be a possibility. Besides, I'm too weak. "I will."

With a sigh, his body rests against mine for just a moment before we hear thunderous footsteps approaching. "I will too."

Alessio bursts back into the room, a wild look on his face.

"I hope you all can walk. Everyone will be moving down to the pool bar on deck two in less than an hour. And you'd better smile pretty; your lives depend upon it." Alessio stands in front of me and Linc. "Especially both of you. Libby, dear, for shame." My head is turned sideways with the casual crack of his hand against my cheek. "You didn't mention all of the money your family would be willing to pay to get you back." The bastard chuckles as he moves away. "One hour! Diego, begin to untie their legs. Get them on their feet." Then he tacks on, "Shoot them if they run."

"Of course." Diego fires a shot into the ceiling just for fun. We all cower. "Now, who wants to be next?"

Unsurprisingly, no one volunteers. Diego just laughs.

It's then I realize it's either Alessio or me who's leaving the *Sea Force* alive, but it isn't going to be both of us. There's no way that could happen.

It's almost a calming thought to know it will all be over soon—one way or another.

AN HOUR LATER, WE'RE FROG-MARCHED DOWN FOUR FLIGHTS OF STAIRS.

At one point, I have to slam my body back to prevent Linc from tumbling headfirst. Alessio frowns darkly but doesn't reprimand me with word or fist.

I guess we're both too valuable.

From the stairwell, we're led out into the sunlight. I blink repeatedly to try to adjust my eyes, but it's next to impossible. Even though I've been staring at the light for days, I didn't realize the bar windows were tinted until just now.

I'm so delirious between the blood loss, the lack of food, and the bright light I wonder if the shape in front of me is really a ship in the distance or just my desperate imagination. As I walk past Diego, he shoots his gun off at nothing, for no reason. I can't take the chance.

I promised Linc, and this may be my only opportunity.

They line us up in a straight line. It could be because of the gray blur I see in the distance or because they finally plan on picking us off one by one. I have to go on the assumption the gunshots were a precursor to what's to be my fate. After all, if someone was coming to rescue us, why haven't they done anything by now?

It has to be a ruse.

While there's frantic screaming in a language I don't understand, I run. A shot whizzes by my head before I roll my body over the rail. And for the first time since this nightmare began, for a small immeasurable moment between the boat and the water with the air racing over my skin, I'm free.

Maybe not my body, but my soul is.

There's no more pain of remembering as I smash against the high waves causing the water caps to ripple out. There's nothing aching in my body as my body is sucked beneath the cold.

Death doesn't frighten me because I've realized I won't hurt anymore. And if I die, at least I did so because I made the decision to try to save myself, not because people on a boat somewhere were listening to our hell and needed to plot and plan. If I die, it will be by choking on the water I tried to use to escape from the loss of love.

Being in love is like the waves of the ocean against a boat adrift at sea. It can be peaceful, lulling you into a sense of tranquility. Other times it's like a tidal wave—a force of destruction so powerful, you're going under no matter how you try to protect yourself.

Either way you're at the mercy of the waves.

Today, I would gladly drown for having experienced it at all again with a man like Cal. And yet, even under the onslaught of pain racking my body, I don't have regrets.

I want my last memory to be the fierceness of his eyes from the first moment I saw him to the last when he was begging me to listen and all the moments in between when he talked about the love he had for his job, his colleagues—and now that I've had nothing to do but think about where we went wrong, for me.

The freezing water drags me under ceaselessly since I don't have the use of my arms. The silver dress, which I was so desperate to hang on to in the Titan Bar, now makes me wish I could strip it off. Even if it's a millisecond more, it might help me to survive.

I just want another moment to live so I can apologize for my mistakes. Even if it's only in my heart, I pray my words are heard.

I wish I was stronger, but I feel so exhausted.

I stop fighting the current, and I use the last bit of my strength to conjure the image of Cal I've been carrying in my mind, knowing it's the last time I'll see him.

Too bad he's yelling at me to fight. A weak tip of my lips lets in salt water I don't bother to spit out.

I know despite everything, I will always be Cal's. Oh, how I wish I'd have picked up that call before I boarded that plane for Spain. I content myself as I drift downward with recalling his voice the first time he told me, "I will always be yours."

Now, as my heart is ready to burst, or maybe that's my lungs, I send up one final prayer. *I love you, Cal. Be happy. Whether that's with Iris or with someone else. Find your forever.*

My eyes flutter shut just as Cal appears in front of me. Magnificent. But I know I can't be headed to heaven; God wouldn't be so cruel as to remind me for eternity of the beauty I threw away because I wouldn't listen.

My last conscious thought before the black engulfs me is *I will always be yours.*

❀

I WAKE UP FEELING LIKE I'M CHOKING ON SALT WATER AND BLOOD. I expect the whiz of the bullets to whiz by my head.

Did I dream it all? My hand twitches against my bare leg. I feel an icy wetness. No, my plunge into the Atlantic happened.

I'm just reaching out to feel something attached to my arm when I hear the unexpected.

An American voice.

"Mrs. Sullivan, my name is Jessica Fields. I'm the ship's doctor on the USS *Lassen*. Can you hear me?"

I try to speak, but my voice is shredded from the lack of moisture and the screams. All I can manage is a hoarse "Yes."

Is it possible I'm not dreaming? Tears start to well. I know if they fall and it's a dream, I'll soon be ripped from my mind to pay for them.

A comforting hand squeezes the one that's just only bruised and maybe not broken. "Cry, Elizabeth. It's safe to cry now."

So I do, for a long time. There are other people in the room—men, women, I don't know which and I don't care. I focus solely on her gentle hand holding mine and ignore everything else, which includes cutting off the shredded silver sequined dress I've been wearing—has it been days?—still on my body. My plunge into the water washed away the foulest of the stenches, but I'm still wiped down with anti-septic cloths before a gentle, but necessary, physical exam is conducted. Dr. Fields reassures me throughout, keeping me calm with a low conversation that ends up with me in some more tears.

"I think I knew the exact moment when it happened," I whisper. I can't see her as she slips off her gloves, but I hear the snap. Dr. Fields is at my side instantly.

"You were aware you were pregnant?" she asks me quietly.

I nod, even knowing I can now set Cal free—truly free. I wanted this part of him to love forever. And knowing that last part of our love was killed for what? For greed? I dissolve in another round of tears.

"I have to get more fluid into you, Mrs. Sullivan. Can you drink anything?" Feeling my shudder, she squeezes my hand before making some quick notes on her chart. "Are you allergic to any anesthetics?"

I shake my head, but— "I won't be knocked out. Not after…" I shudder as vivid images of what I just lived through flash through my mind.

"We can numb you using twilight…" Dr. Fields begins, but I adamantly shake my head.

"No."

"Eliza—"

"Libby. Please call me Libby," I plead.

She nods. "Libby. I can't guarantee you won't feel both physical and emotional pain," she warns me.

My breathing accelerates. "What's what I lived through but that?"

Her eyes close in acknowledgment. "By now your family has been made aware you've been rescued. Do you want to contact them first?"

"Only my brother knew I was pregnant. I…I need this moment between me and my child before I call them."

Her hand lies gently on my shoulder. For just a moment, we're not victim to doctor. We're woman to woman, and she's trying to absorb some of my pain. Oh, how I wish I could let her bear some of it.

"Relax. As soon as I feel comfortable you're hydrated a bit more, we'll begin." Her head snaps to one of the other women in the small room. "No visitors. Not now."

"Yes, ma'am." The woman steps out.

"Just relax, Libby. Someone will be in here with you at all times." She starts to leave before I call out hoarsely.

"Wait!"

Dr. Fields turns around.

"Linc? The others?" my scratchy voice manages.

And her lips curve into a smile. "Rest, Libby. Everyone who was still alive, including Mr. McCallister, was safely rescued from the *Sea*

Force. What you did…" She shakes her head. "Let's just say it gave the SEAL team the distraction they needed to do their job."

I let out an enormous sigh. And while I only understand about 10 percent of what she said, I heard the most important thing. Linc's alive.

Now, all I want is to be left alone to be free to let all my emotions loose.

HOURS LATER, AFTER THE D&C IS FINISHED, THERE'S AN UPROAR outside the medical suite.

Everyone's heads turn.

Not mine.

Because my eyes are wide at the roaring of "I don't give a shit if you throw me in the brig. Let me in to see my fucking wife, God damnit!"

It can't be.

I begin to shake as the door flies open, and suddenly Cal's filling the entrance. "Libs?" His voice breaks.

Until that moment, I wasn't sure if I had any strength left in my body, not with a litany of physical injuries a mile long let alone the medical procedure I was recovering from. But the wounds to my heart start repairing themselves seeing the gold band on the third finger of his left hand gleaming starkly against the all-black ensemble he's wearing. I stumble on weak, bruised legs to the arms of man I love.

"Ca…" I try to say his name, but I can only mouth it. My voice has disappeared.

He lowers his head on mine and whispers, "I'm right here. I love you. I swear it. I will always be yours." The wetness of his tears mix with mine as they freely drip down his face. "Thank God you're alive." He buries his head against my neck, his shoulders shaking.

There's still so much to understand: How is he here? What

happened? But in comparison to what I endured, it can wait. I have time to figure it all out.

Cal once said I was his everything and more. As he lifts me in unsteady arms to carry me back to the sick bay bed, I can't reconcile the man who said that with one who deserted our marriage.

And that's when I really begin to sob. Because it's safe to mourn not picking up a telephone when in your heart you really wanted to.

"Shh, Libby, I've got you. You're safe."

77

PRESENT DAY

ELIZABETH

"I know you've been asked how you don't have fully developed PTSD after this, Libby. How did you manage to move on with your life?"

I think about this question because the answer is a very personal one. "I was told to feel the emotions and not to bottle them up."

"Who gave you that advice?" Dr. Powell asks. "Not that I think it's incorrect. In fact, it's probably what I would have recommended."

"One of the SEALs. I was up on the flight deck on the *Lassen,* heavily guarded, a few days after I was rescued. It was before Cal, the Alliance team, and I were being flown back to the States. I could see the *Sea Force* in the distance. I was shivering." I start to shake now in memory. "He began to talk with me."

Cal's warmth seeps through me as he hugs me closer. It gives me enough strength to continue. "Coming face-to-face with a living funeral pyre that I, myself, almost died on, it left more than the physical marks on me. I was afraid to go to sleep, afraid to wake up—I was just afraid."

"I think that would be understandable," Dr. Powell says gently.

"But the biggest emotions I felt were desolation and shame," I admit.

"Survivor's guilt." He nods.

"It was more than that. I lived, yes, but our child hadn't. To have that confirmed may have been more awful than anything I endured on the *Sea Force*. Then there was the loss of time. I was damning myself for being stubborn and walking away when I took a vow to Cal that I wouldn't."

"Your heart was suffering," he concludes.

"Very much so. And when I couldn't hold it in anymore, that individual was there. He recommended I talk to a specialized Navy trauma psychologist."

"So, you're aware there's a difference between a doctor like me and a trauma-informed care specialist?"

I nod. "Very. It was explained to me during my first phone call with my doctor. I think he best explained them as guiding principles."

"And you felt comfortable talking to a man after everything that happened?"

That question startles me. "I was with men who were just as traumatized as I was, Dr. Powell. Possibly more so. It wasn't due to my sex that I was harmed; it was because I was *there*." I place an emphasis on the last word. "Dr. Rhumed helped me identify what my ultimate goals were."

"And those were?"

Without hesitation, I answer. "To be able to let my emotions run their course. To grieve the loss of the life of my baby. To mourn my marriage and to find my way back to what drove me to say 'I do' to Cal."

"Let's talk about the last one. What do you mean, mourn your marriage?"

Cal audibly swallows before answering. "Because there was still infidelity."

Dr. Powell gasps even as Cal's arms around me tighten from where I'm still perched on his lap. He does nothing to avoid Dr. Powell's accusatory expression. "I thought you said..."

"I didn't." Cal's voice is firm and strong.

"I'm confused."

I spin so I'm facing Dr. Powell a little more fully while allowing Cal to hold the things most precious in his life—me and his child. "Some people would say I'm crazy for saying this, but Cal had an affair with Alliance."

The confusion washes clean away from Dr. Powell's face, leaving nothing but understanding. "Go on, Libby."

"The reality is, my husband cheated on me from the moment we met by lying. And that, combined with the trauma I'd just endured, left me feeling like nothing. I felt like it might be better if I just wasted away," I conclude softly.

The baby bumps hard against my stomach. Cal rubs the spot gently but doesn't say anything. During counseling sessions with Dr. Rhumed, we've had this discussion numerous times throughout the years. And the answer is I belong right here in his arms where my heart beats in cadence with his. "There's a feeling of being unable to trust your deepest emotions after a trauma. I wanted—no, needed to know that I could trust everyone around me. So, in order to live again, I had to live without Cal because I couldn't trust him anymore."

I turn in his arms. "I'm so sorry." Even though we're long past this, saying it still feels like I'm punishing him. Tears are coursing down my face at a rate more rapid than he can wipe them. He stops trying and just presses his forehead against mine.

Without lifting it, he addresses Dr. Powell. "Let's be clear, Doctor. We were both wrong for very different reasons. I kept secrets; Libby wouldn't listen. But it was due to my actions that our communication was damaged beyond repair. We make a conscious effort so that mistake won't occur again." He straightens, tucking me against him. "People all over the world have heard our story and judged each of us saying one or the other of us should have capitulated, forgiven sooner, forgotten what occurred before, or walked away." He shakes his head against mine. "No one should judge us or our life together. Not unless you've lived it, actually walked through every moment with us. There is so much this woman had to forgive me for that I understood she had to let go to heal."

"It was you my heart reached out for though." I sink one hand into his hair and cup his cheek with the other.

His smile—my smile—breaks across his face. It comes so much easier now. He brushes his lips across each of my cheeks before kissing me softly. "I'm the luckiest man in the world because I got you to fall in love with me twice."

"I never stopped loving you," I counter.

"Hmm." Cal steals another kiss. "You have to admit, it was better the second time around."

"That's because I taught you to woo me. You had the inside playbook," I tease.

Cal reaches up and touches his thumb to my bottom lip. "I hope when we're a hundred, I get to kiss the sass off your lips. I don't think I can live without that."

"I don't think I can live without your smile." I trace it with my forefinger. It comes so much easier these days, as if he's given himself permission to be happy now that the lies and the subterfuge are gone.

Dr. Powell clears his throat. A light flush hits my cheeks. Cal grins, which temporarily scrambles my brain cells. "I'm sorry, Dr. Powell, you were asking?"

"Well, I was asking about your goals," he begins.

Right. "Dr. Rhumed helped me identify a safe environment to recover from what happened, where I could find out who I was again. It might seem silly, but I couldn't do that here in Charleston."

"Why not? I would think with your family, you'd feel safe."

"I felt smothered, well intentioned as it may have been. But it caused me to forget what I was working toward and frankly—" This is difficult to say. "—my family triggered memories by constantly asking how I was. No one meant any harm, but it still brought me back to the bar on the *Sea Force* when I needed to be safe on dry land."

"Where did you go?"

I lean back against my husband. "All I did was wait for Cal to find me," I say secretively.

Dr. Powell looks at Cal in confusion. "I don't understand."

Cal kisses the top of my head before sliding me off his lap and tucking me next to him. "I didn't either. I even knew she was leaving. I had a text telling me where she was."

"And it still took you two months," I huff.

Cal smacks his hand to his face before shaking his head.

"Where was safe, Libby?" Dr. Powell asks again.

"There was only one place I remember where I knew in my heart Cal wanted me more than Alliance."

"Akin Hill?" Dr. Powell picks up his notes and flips through, guessing.

"No, only one. And it was the place where he broke the first date with me. Fortunately, the apartment wasn't rented since the owner had been remodeling it when students were looking for housing at the beginning of the semester."

I've managed to shock Dr. Powell. "But, you reconnected at Akin Hill, got married there. That wasn't where you felt him the strongest?"

"I needed the knowledge there was a time and a place he wanted me where he forgot about"—I air quote—"'the other woman.' Even if it was just for a moment. That was it."

Dr. Powell turns his head to Cal. "How on earth did you figure it out?"

Cal growls. I smile beatifically up at him. He shakes his head. "It wasn't easy. And since she prohibited me from using my job to track her, I had to figure it out the old-fashioned way."

"How's that?"

"With my heart," my husband of the last eleven years says.

78

CALHOUN

YEAR SIX - FIVE YEARS AGO FROM
PRESENT DAY - FEBRUARY

L ife is not always about shitty timing, Cal. Sometimes it's about shitty things being done or said. In my heart, I know there's a part of me you've always wanted to come back to. I know all the secrets and the lies. I wish you had trusted me enough to tell me, but all you did was lie. Over and over. I need to figure out how to trust you again; how to believe you'll stop hiding. I don't know how to open a door you won't walk through. And so do you. Once you've figured out where you said that to me, come find me. You should know where to look.

Her text has haunted me for two months since she left her parent's care. If it wasn't for the regular updates I've received from her parents and Josh assuring me Libby's safe and healing, I'd have lost my mind.

Confession is supposed to help people move forward. With the way Libby held me so close to her after her ordeal on the *Sea Force*, I hoped she would understand the motivation behind my work. And God love her, she did.

What she didn't understand was the lies.

"I would have loved you, Cal, if you'd been a professor, a lifelong military man moving us from pillar to post, or the businessman you claimed to be." Her bruised hand was clutching mine in the sick bay of the *Lassen* at the time. Her swollen face was turned away from mine as my heart began to understand the emotional desolation she's been living with the last several months. "Right now, I just can't trust myself to never know if you're lying to me," she carefully explained. IV fluids were being pumped into her so there was enough liquid in her for tears. "It's almost more crushing than what happened over there." She waved her arm in the wrong direction of where the *Sea Force* was.

I didn't correct her. I was too busy trying to rein in the emotions. I knew I promised myself I'd let her go, but I just couldn't. "Libby..." I choked out.

"I'm not the woman you married, Cal. I'm not sure if you ever were the man I did."

I couldn't hold back the wetness. I just didn't want it to burden her then. Pushing to my feet, I whispered a kiss over her lips. "Let's get you home. Celebrate with your family. Then..." I let the word hang there. In my head, I was pleading, *Before you make any decisions.*

She tipped her head back. "All right."

Exiting the sick bay, I leaned back against the cold metal of the bulkhead. This was the part where I told myself it would be okay, where I loved her enough to give her what she was going to give me.

Freedom.

But I'm a selfish man who needs the sun to survive. And I haven't seen it in months. Glaring at my shadow showing on the driveway outside the home I shared with Libby, I don't notice the other car until I almost walk into it.

Sam. And he brought Josh with him. I don't know whether to curse or be cautiously optimistic they have some news as to where Libby might be.

"Hey, man. Iris talked to Libby today," Sam calls out.

I grit my teeth before I respond. "That's great." If there's one thing I'm happy about, it's that my wife has cautiously forgiven her best friend. Then again, it wasn't Iris lying to her every single moment of every single day.

Josh shoves Sam before reaching out a hand, "Cal," he says warmly.

I grasp it firmly. "Good to see you, Josh." My brother-in-law and I have never been closer, our love of Libby bonding us in a way nothing else can.

"You're a moron," he tells me cheerfully, and not for the first time.

"I know," I say mournfully as I let them both in the house that feels like a tomb every time I walk into it.

"Why don't you just track her?" Sam demands a few minutes later after he's snagged beer for the three of us from my fridge. He kicks up his feet onto the coffee table. Josh does the same.

I pop the cap off mine, flicking it next to his feet. Libby would have a coronary if she saw the three of us, I think with just a touch of amusement. Then a vein of bitterness runs through me. "She'd have to be here to have that coronary."

I don't realize I've spoken out loud until Josh answers me. "If you don't go Sam's route, then you have to dig down deep, Cal. You're a trained investigator, for Christ's sake. Before computers, what the hell did you do?"

"I was in school, I was in the military. There wasn't a time when I didn't have a computer at my disposal," I growl.

Sam laughs. "Man, I remember back in college days when we couldn't write a paper with all of our references being online sources. Even your class, Cal. Why did you have to be such a dick?" Sam throws a pillow at me I don't even attempt to catch.

I'm too busy trying to breathe. "What did you say?"

Sam's brow furrows. "I said, back in college you were a dick of a professor..." I surge to my feet.

Could it really be that simple?

"God, my life? It's always about shitty timing."

"Sam," I say woodenly as I make my way toward the stairs. "I need you to cover at the office for a few days."

"What? Why?"

My foot on the bottom step, I turn and face them. Sam's expression is confused whereas Josh looks proud.

"Figured it out, finally?" he asks me.

"She went back to the beginning—to our beginning. And now, if I want to make it there before dark, I'd better get on the road."

Taking the stairs two at a time, I burst through the door of the master bedroom—it won't be ours until Libby is back in it. Quickly heading into the closet, I throw together a bag of clothes, enough to last me a week. "Fuck it, the town's big enough I can buy anything I forgot."

Tossing the bag over my shoulder, I step back into the bedroom. Sam's in the doorway. "Well? Where is she?" he demands. "If I go home and tell Iris you found her without letting her know how you figured it out..."

I rush past him. "Sam, she's in Athens."

He gapes at me. "And you expect to get to Greece tonight?"

There are times he's so brilliant that common sense is shoved out to make room for the rest of his brain. It's what makes him and Iris work beautifully together. "Think about what you said to me and you'll figure it out." Bounding down the stairs, I give Josh a warm clap on the back. "Thanks for not giving up on me."

"Thanks for not giving up on her. Now, go see if she's ready to come home." With a one-two slap, Josh releases me just as Sam yells from the top of the stairs.

"Holy crap! What the hell is she doing back at college?" Then he barks like a dog.

There are days I wonder why in the hell I ever recruited him, and then I remember he's the best man I know, and I give him a pass. With a shake of my head and a wave, I race out the door. Even though they waited for me to come home before they entered, the guys can lock up.

I need to get on the road.

FOUR HOURS AND FORTY MINUTES LATER, I'M PULLING UP TO THE OLD house Libby and Iris used to rent. And my heart settles.

Her car's in the driveway.

Leaving my bag in the car, I grab the cellophane-wrapped package I stopped for along the way and slide from my truck. I walk up the front flagstone path and ring the bell. There's music playing. I hear her tell the voice-controlled stereo to lower in volume.

"Just a moment," Libby's voice comes through the door.

My heart pounds in anticipation. The blood pumps even more furiously as I hear the chain rattle and the lock twist. The wood door swings open and there she is.

Everything I fell in love with.

"My life isn't always about shitty timing, Libby." I press forward as I shove the flowers into her hands. "Sometimes, it's about perfect timing. Like the moment I met you and realizing I will always be yours."

She gasps. But before she can respond, I yank her into my arms. "Any questions?" I demand belligerently.

A smile lifts her lips. "Just one."

I still. "What is it?"

"I thought you were supposed to be some hot-as-shit PI, detective, black-ops guy, or some crap. Are you trying to tell me it took you two damn months to figure this out? I thought I was going to have to go to the Georgia/Auburn home game next weekend. Was it going to take me holding up a sign on national TV declaring where I am?"

I decide the best way to shut her sass up in this case is to kiss her which is something I've been dying to do anyway. Dropping the flowers to the floor between us and wrapping both of her arms around my neck, Libby obviously agrees.

CALHOUN

YEAR SIX - FIVE YEARS AGO FROM
PRESENT DAY - FEBRUARY

"Are you ready to talk about it?" Libby draws her knees up, brushing them against mine. We're lying in the bedroom after an explosive kiss led me to dragging us here before she slammed the breaks on our physical reunion. "Nothing more until we talk, Cal. I just pulled myself out of the abyss. I can't drown again. Not because of you."

My arm covers my eyes. It's time for all the confessions, but I just got her love back. What's going to happen if...

"Cal, you can't stop my reaction to whatever you're going to say to me." Libby reaches her hand over. "But your silence has caused too many problems between us." She twists the ring on my left hand. "Think about the ripple effect of one misunderstanding. What did that almost do to us?"

Shuddering, I roll into her, tangling our legs together. "I don't know where to start," I confess.

"How about I start with this?" My heart lurches in fear. "Short of using the bathroom or food, we make a promise to not leave this house until it's all out—no matter how much we want to. If I need a time-out, you'll give it to me. But I won't go any further than the backyard."

"Not dressed like that you won't," I growl.

"Please," she scoffs. "I'm an old woman in comparison to the kids who live around here."

"You're the most beautiful woman in the world," I declare huskily. The rose color that infuses her cheeks lends credence to the fact I have a long way to repair the foundation that my marriage is built on. "I don't see any woman but you," I tell her honestly.

Taking a deep breath, she lets it out raggedly. "Can we start with the worst?"

"Yes." I brace, expecting her to ask me about Alliance, but my wife surprises me. Again.

"Tell me what happened with Iris. Even though she's called to apologize, I wouldn't let her discuss it. It should come from you. But I have to know." A terrible pain, the kind that is soul-deep, is emanating from her. Her closed-off face tells me she hopes I learned something in the time apart. I did. I learned the life I led wasn't worth the price I paid for it.

"It was spontaneous. I swear on my life. It was nothing more than a kiss of congratulations, Libby. Nothing more. Iris just retired. She said Rachel is getting too old to grow up without seeing her mother or their father. I was proud of her for making that decision."

"And that deserved my husband's lips on hers?" Libby's voice is a harsh crack in the otherwise quiet room.

"No."

Her chest rises up and down with the force of her breaths. "Was Iris the only woman you ever kissed, by accident or for work?"

"Yes, and I swear it wasn't intentional."

"How do lips just meet accidentally?" Her voice is like acid.

Even though I've had so long to think about it, predicting a perfect conversation and actually having one are two different things. I struggle to find the right words. "It was our anniversary and I'd knew I'd be gone—again—for an indeterminate amount of time. I was emotional. I was feeling things between us that I hadn't felt in a long time. Or was that just me?"

"It wasn't just you, but Cal?"

RIPPLE EFFECT

"Yeah?"

"I may have missed you, us, but I didn't break my vows." Libby starts to roll away.

I catch her behind the waist and pull her back. "Neither did I—not in my heart. It was a second out of time, Libs. It wasn't until I saw the picture you sent me that I understood how you felt, how it looked from your perspective. But I need you to understand. I don't—nor have I ever—thought of Iris that way. Sam was standing right there, Libs. Honest to God, I was talking to her, but my heart was with you. I'd just left our bed, and here was the woman closest to you who knew, well, everything. It was another level of relief knowing Iris would be there for you if something went wrong. And the next thing you know, I'd grabbed her face and kissed her. It was utterly sponta- neous; my intent was not how you interpreted it. Yes, we're all close. We've had to be. But not that way. Never that way." Her body is rigid against mine, but it isn't trying to get away. I plunge ahead, "Kid you not, it shocked both Sam and Iris as much as it shocked me as soon as I'd did it."

"Sam was there?" Libby's voice is carefully modulated.

"Yes."

"In the room?"

"He was on my computer fucking around with something. Why?"

"Move back, please."

I do as she requests, not wanting to let her go. I'm so afraid my simple yet honest explanation won't be enough, and the world will go dark again.

She wanders over to the window. I take the time to admire the strength in her gait. "You're stronger," I observe quietly.

"Much. I've been working with a psychologist your friend Thorn recommended."

"Thorn? When the hell did you talk with him?"

"On board the *Lassen*. He came to see me shortly before we flew home."

I'm incredulous when I ask, "What did he have to say?"

"He wanted to know if I'd managed to sleep yet. It was night three, and I still hadn't closed my eyes for more than fifteen minutes at a time. I was terrified to."

"What was it like when you tried?"

"Every time I tried, I'd wake up with my chest hurting—like I wanted to cry but didn't feel safe enough to."

"You were safe, Libby," I remind her.

"My head was, but my heart and mind weren't, Cal." Her words are like a knife sliding through my ribs, swiftly and effectively removing all traces of air from my body.

"Thorn handed me a card and said to call the number when I was ready—that I'd know when I was ready."

"So, what? He offered to be your sounding board?" Jealousy eats at me, bitter and acidic.

Libby whirls around, fire in her eyes. "If it weren't for that moment, I'd be in a different place. I wouldn't be able to have this conversation with you. I wouldn't even be speaking to you after years of being lied to. You owe more to your friend Thorn than you can possibly imagine."

"We're not exactly friends," I grudgingly admit.

"That's not the way he tells it," Libby says, shocking me with that before she says, "The card contained the direct line to the SEAL team psychiatrist, Dr. Rhumed. At first, our sessions were daily. Then we graduated to every other day. Now, I'm down to weekly. And I've worked through a lot. I am stronger. I'm not the same woman I was, Cal."

"No one would expect you to be." My voice is comforting.

"No, listen to me, Cal. I'm not the same woman I used to be." She walks back to the bed. There's a glow about her, but it's from the fire that burns deep inside. The light of innocence that was once there has changed. It's been affected by the lessons she learned. She's right. She's changed. I quickly learn how when she starts talking again.

"I wept for weeks over the lies, Cal. Flipping through my phone trying to pinpoint when it was you first lied to me and realizing there was never a time you spoke the truth. I cried because I allowed it, because I was done with it, done with you. And then I wondered what my life would be like without you."

Is this why everyone warned me to tell Libby all along? Not so she didn't get hurt but so I didn't end up crumbling? Or, had I changed as well? "Libby," I plead.

"The problem is, I can't. I can't blank out what I saw. And I'm left with so much conflict as a result." Libby stalks out of the room.

I count to ten before I follow after her. As she promised, she hasn't left the house. She's just standing in the kitchen. I approach slowly. "I can't say I didn't do it deliberately, because I did. I thought I was protecting this core of light in you that would die out if you spent day after day, month after month, worrying about where I was." I let out a ragged breath. "I was wrong."

"So, now what?" She runs a hand through her hair. It's her left one. It's still ringless. And after four months, all I can do is pray I'll see them back on her finger at some point.

"Can you forgive me? For so much, Libby." I step closer.

"You're going to have to be more specific."

"For the lies, for the pain, for not being open to the one person I should have known would have accepted me no matter what." I begin to pray in earnest.

She holds my life on tenterhooks while a million thoughts chase themselves across her face. I read the story of our marriage in a myriad of expressions: love, sadness, pain, hurt, love betrayal, defeat, and still love. "I forgave you before I left to come here."

I'm confused. Reaching for her hand, I rub my thumb over her ring finger. "Then tell me what it is you want. I need to know you. If there's one thing I'm certain about, it's that I can't live without you in my life."

Libby contemplates our fingers before she whispers, "Are you ready to let me in—all the way in?"

I'm about to open my mouth to agree when Libby interjects. "Be very sure before you answer. Because you're not obligated to stay."

"I want to stay. I choose to be with you. You are my life." And it hits me like a two-by-four that if I'd told her the truth, she'd have already known this. And never questioned it.

"I will always love you, Calhoun Sullivan. But my love isn't an obligation," she warns me. "I want it all—the good, the bad, the honesty I should have had from the first damn moment we stood here and you asked me out. If you can't give it to me, then there's the door." She points at the door behind me.

Slipping my hand into the back pocket of my jeans, I pull out my cell phone. I tear my eyes away from Libby's long enough to dial a number I have memorized by heart.

It rings once.

Twice.

Yarborough picks up on the third ring. "Cal? What is it?"

"I found Libby." My eyes go back to her mutinous face. "I need you to talk to your contact at DoD and get her clearance paperwork expedited so we can read her on."

I barely hear, "It's about fucking time," in my ear because I'm already hanging up the phone. I slip it back into my pocket.

"Even if I can tell you most of what we do, there will be times I still can't get into detail," I warn her.

"I've lived through what you do, Cal. I think I'm in a good position to set up a scoring system now for how bad things are going to be," she drawls.

"That mouth." I just shake my head. "From the moment I first saw you, you made me want to smile, you taught me to laugh. I never knew until I almost lost you that you could make me cry, Libby."

"Same goes."

"So." I hold my hands out to my side. "Where do we go from here?" I hold my breath, afraid of the answer.

"I get over missing the man I thought you were while learning the man you are. And somehow, we find a way because the kind of love we have is worth fighting for." Bashfully, she looks away. "You taught me that."

"I did?" I'm incredulous.

"Yes." Libby comes into my space. "The entire time I was on the *Sea*

Force, I kept remembering you trying to get through to me, and I realized if you didn't love me, you would have just walked away. So, I know there's a reason to fight. It's right here." Libby lays her hand on my chest.

"Christ, I love you." I pull her tight against my body.

Then, I hear words I never thought I'd hear again whispered in my ear. "I love you too, Cal. Always."

PRESENT DAY

CALHOUN

D r. Powell puts the file in front of him on the coffee table and sits back. "Is there any difference when you look back on it now?" Dr. Powell asks Libby.

"Every year that passes, I feel more blessed to have the life I do. There were so many things before I used to be worried about— everyday stressors—that are meaningless now."

"Can you give me an example?"

"Who's coming home late, who's making dinner? Did my dry cleaning come back with any stains? Did a client pay me on time? Hold on. Can you edit out the last comment? I really need my clients to pay me on time," Libby says cheekily.

All of us laugh. Dr. Powell leans forward and makes a note on his pad. "I'm surprised you haven't asked for much else to be edited out before now," he admits.

"Probably because I remember your integrity from the first time you interviewed Cal and me. I truly suspect, Dr. Powell, you wanted to know how we were doing as much for your own comfort as you wanted footage for the anniversary special."

The network interviewer, a renowned psychiatrist, twists his head toward me. "You married a smart woman, Cal."

"I'm well aware. I'm blessed, but not because of that," I respond.

"Why?" Dr. Powell asks.

I brush my lips across the top of Libby's head. "Somehow, I managed to get her to fall in love with me twice."

"It wasn't that hard," Libby murmurs.

"After everything?" Dr. Powell's voice is incredulous, echoing the sentiment in my heart.

"Not really. Because at his core, it wasn't superficial things that made me fall in love with Cal. It was the knowledge that I knew from the beginning he was the missing piece to my heart. Once I knew our marriage was his first priority and the communication issues between us were resolved, I was still in love with the same man."

I don't know if it's possible to hold her any tighter, but I try. "Like I said, I'm blessed."

"What are you doing now, Cal? It was mentioned your company was sold?"

Shifting, I drop my arm from Libby. "I may need to stop some of your questions," I warn.

"Of course," Dr. Powell agrees.

"It took about a year. Karl and I worked with the team to split off our part of Alliance—which included most of our team and part of the administrative staff. We sold it to an investigation agency based out of New York. I now head up their DC office."

"Are you still doing the same kind of work that brought you aboard the *Sea Force*?"

I hesitate. "I'm using the same skill set. I'm sorry, I really can't say more than that."

"That's fine. Does it give you the same kind of satisfaction the work you did for Alliance did?"

"Yes," I answer unwaveringly. "The work helps people on a more local level, so I see the impacts much closer to home, though there are still occasionally the instances where I have to travel internationally. And I can talk about 90 percent of my work with Libby. If I'm having a bad day, she knows. If we solved a case...oops." I grin sheepishly. "Can we strike the last part?"

Dr. Powell grins. "Of course. But continue. I like where this was going."

"Something as simple as talking can save not just something as defined as a marriage, but something as critical as a heart," I conclude.

"Well said, Cal. Libby, what about you?"

"Love can be taken from you in an instant. Sometimes we need to remember that in order to appreciate the gift of it. In the process of breaking, I learned the process of healing and forgiveness." Libby's voice is rough with emotion.

"And you're happy? Both of you?"

We simultaneously answer, "Yes."

Leaning forward, Dr. Powell rests his hand on top of the one I have wrapped around Libby's. "It couldn't happen to two people who deserve it more."

"Damn you, Doctor. I'm pregnant." Libby swipes her free hand beneath her eyes.

He just smiles at us both before leaning back. "Let me do the sign-off, and then I'd like to give you both a message."

Libby and I exchange confused looks while Dr. Powell faces the camera to his left. "Five years ago, today, twenty people were rescued from the *Sea Force*, including Elizabeth Sullivan and Lincoln McCallister. Their lives are bound by these tragic events for all of history. And now, I've learned they're all bound by something else—a newfound appreciation for things we may take for granted every day: love, faith, and freedom. It has been astounding to listen to their journeys. I wish them nothing but the best in their futures. This is Dr. Bern Powell with *The Truth*."

"And, we're out," a voice calls.

We all let out a collective sigh. "Libby," Dr. Powell says.

"Yes?"

"I went to see Linc last week in Texas. He asked me to pass on this message to you." Dr. Powell reaches into his folder and pulls out a tamper-evident envelope. I recognize it immediately from my work at Alliance. "It hasn't been read," he assures us quickly.

"I would never think that," Libby chides him. Tearing open the top, a plain white envelope falls into her hands. It has her name scrawled on it. "Do you mind if I read it here?" she asks me.

"Go ahead, honey," I encourage her. I know Libby worries about Linc. Our reunion has only one dark spot for my wife—knowing that Camille McCallister died on the *Sea Force* and Linc will have to wait years to be reunited with her.

Libby flips open the letter and begins to read. As her eyes dart back and forth, I take a leisurely study of her face. Her dark lashes practically touch her rose-colored cheeks. Her perfectly plump lips part in pleasure. "Oh, Linc." She folds the letter back up and slips it back into the envelope before handing it to me.

I know she'll tell me what's in it later.

"He seemed to be doing better when I talked with him. I hope that eases your mind some," Dr. Powell murmurs.

"It does. Thank you." We all stand.

"I'd like to wish you nothing but happiness, Libby, Cal. Time, it's a fickle thing. It fades the memories of those who don't have heart behind their memories. I don't know if we'll meet again."

I hold out my hand, and Dr. Powell shakes it. "Your story helped more people than you know."

"Even so, thank you for caring about more than just the story. Thank you for caring about us," Libby whispers. She leans forward and gives him a quick hug.

"Be happy, Libby."

She nods, too overwhelmed to talk. Guiding her away, we head back toward the green room to have our mics removed so we can head back to Akin Hill for the rest of our visit.

IT'S DONE.

Eight hours after walking into the local Charleston TV studio, Libby and I exit the building just before sunset. We're hand in hand, both of us surviving not only what we endured today but what happened five years ago. I squeeze her hand, still unable to believe that despite the millions of reasons I gave her in the early years of our marriage to give up and walk away, it happened only once.

And somehow, I found the path to bring her back home.

Love. Honesty. Trust.

Tucking Libby tightly against my side, I feel her stop in her tracks. Right in front of us is an amazing view of the Atlantic Ocean laid out in front of us. "And right there is the reason that calls to me each year why I should keep remembering the past. But now, I have a brand-new one that's going to keep me focused on the future." Her voice is almost serene as her hand drops to cover our child.

Carefully, I murmur, "Nothing we do will bring them back."

"No, but it helped keep their spirit alive in the hearts and minds of those who forgot." Even as I hold her, Libby's mind goes to only places she can go. After a minute of doing exactly what she's needed me to do from the very beginning of our relationship—just be there for her —she blinks. And smiles.

I turn her more fully into my arms. "Each time you smile, my heart falls in love with you all over again."

"Aren't you lucky I've been blessed with so much to smile about?" she teases.

But there isn't anything resembling laughter in my voice when I choke out, "Yes. And I thank God every day you still consider me one of them."

Libby presses against my chest tightly, her own wrapping around my back. Her head rests just over my heart. "And I thank God you were brought into my life." I feel her warm breath through my shirt.

Each beat of our hearts is louder than the slap of the waves against the sea wall next to us.

After first speaking with Dr. Rhumed after Libby and I first reconciled, he reminded me about a quote attributed to Buddha—that the two mistakes we make when it comes to telling the truth are not doing it or only doing it partially. I shudder. I have little doubt my wife was able to come out as adjusted despite what happened on the *Sea Force* because she was in the middle of an alternate trauma all because of my arrogance and narcissism and my inability to recognize that the strength of convictions of the woman cradled in my arms.

I could have lost it all through my deception and half-truths. Instead, I found the right reason to go to battle—love. I wasn't about to give up without the fight of my life.

"I love you, Libby. Always," I conclude, my breath moving the fine pieces of her hair.

Libby's head tips back. "And I love you, Cal. I always will."

When our lips come together, I taste the salt air between them. Or are those my tears as the emotions overwhelm me?

In the years since we started over and rebuilt our lives on a foundation that will withstand the battering that life's day-by-day will throw at it, I've learned life is precious; love is a miracle. And protecting it by lying is harming it from the inside out. And the harm will continue to spread just like a ripple effect.

EPILOGUE

CALHOUN - FIVE YEARS LATER

I'm sitting at my desk when the video comes through as a text to my phone. Pressing Play, the air rushes out of my lungs in a single whoosh. Her sweet voice comes through perfectly clear over the screeching laughter of the other children at the playground. "I love you, Daddy!"

Then, the camera pans over to where Libby's pushing the swing in a ray of sunshine, her body gently ripe with our next child, who's due in a couple of months.

Before I can send a text to thank Ali for sending me the video, my boss strolls through the door as if he owns the place. Well, since he and his best friend actually started the company and still own the majority of it, I can understand why his attitude wouldn't necessarily change. It doesn't mean I have to like it.

My counterpart in our Connecticut location tells me it's worse for him. "At least you don't have to deal with him stealing food on a regular basis just because he used to work in your office. You've got a sweet new one," Colby grumbled good-naturedly.

"I didn't, until Keene happened to be here for a routine visit last quarter," I retorted.

A chair creaked in my ear. "What happened?" Colby asked curiously.

"Libby baked my favorite cake for my birthday. She surprised me with it at work. I was gone for ten minutes to answer a question on the floor. Half the cake was gone!"

Colby laughed in my ear.

With a bemused smile, I face the man who a lifetime ago told me I'd find him when the time was right. He made it easy and sought me out instead.

"Are the girls having a good time?" Keene drops his tall frame into the chair opposite my desk.

Holding out my phone, I show him the video. His normally stern countenance softens when Leah's sweet little voice calls out to me. "She's getting so big, Cal," he tells me as he passes the phone back.

"I know." Shaking my head, I admit, "I'm in awe every single day."

Keene taps the file he came in with against his leg. "There's a million reasons why none of this should exist for either of us." Pushing to his feet, he tosses the file on top of the others on my desk. "And there's one why we have it all."

Curious as fuck what Keene Marshall—who normally embodies the term "sanctimonious prick"—has to say, I ask, "Why?"

"Because for some incomprehensible reason, they love us as much as we do them." Making his way to the door of my office, he smiles. Something I've learned he does as rarely as I do unless he's talking about his wife and daughters.

Just like Libby's love managed to pull mine out of me.

Even as Keene's closing the door behind him, I'm dialing Libby's cell.

She picks up breathlessly on the third ring. "Hey, honey."

"She has to go to daycare at some point, Libs," I admonish her gently.

Libby's peal of laughter warms all the spots of my soul that are swamped with guilt when I still have to travel or work keeps me late at the office. I never want us to ever get back to that place we were at ten years ago.

When I voiced my concerns in our bed late one night, Libby scalded me with a glare that should have filleted the skin from my body. "That won't ever happen again. That, I can assure you."

"It's one day, Cal. Besides, all of Ali's girls are here. Truth be told, it's like we're running our own daycare."

Laughter roars out of me. "And there's that sass."

"You know you love it," she replies pertly.

"I know I love you, Libs. Always."

Her husky "I love you too" only temporarily derails me. "Leah is never going to get potty trained, Libs. You were the one so adamant about sending her to this daycare because they had a 'potty whisperer.' How can Agnes work her magic if our child isn't there?"

"Fair point," she concedes. "But it's two days, Cal."

"Two days where she's going to wet the bed," I mutter.

"Fine, I'll be the one to change the sheets," Libby sighs.

I stand up and pump my fist up and down, grateful the glass that takes up an entire wall of my office so I can monitor the ops center is one-way. "Good. Do you need me to get Jax from school if you and Ali have all the girls?"

"No, honey. We have two cars. Ali said she'll follow me to the school and then to the house."

Sitting back down, I muse, "I never thought I'd be on a double date with my boss on a night like tonight."

"Me either, but I'm definitely not complaining. I'll see you at home by four?"

"Absolutely. Drive safe."

"Will do." Libby hangs up, and I dive back into work so we can be finished by the time I have to leave to head home.

"I'M SO NERVOUS." LIBBY TWISTS HER FINGERS TOGETHER AS WE ALL SIT in the back of the car taking us to the Harman Center for the Arts where the annual Premier Design Awards are being held. Deja Vu is nominated for the complete overhaul of the 80,000-square-foot space that now houses the mid-Atlantic headquarters of Hudson Investigations.

"You shouldn't be," Keene declares.

"Normally I'd tell Keene to stop being so arrogant, but he's right, Libby." Ali reaches over and pats Libby's knee. "It's a spectacular space."

"It must pain you to say Keene's right," I joke.

"To no end, Cal." Ali beams a smile at me.

We all laugh, but I still feel Libby's anxious movement. "Libs? Aren't you the one who told me just being nominated is a huge honor?" I slide my arm over her shoulder and squeeze.

She rests against me. "It is. It's just...I don't just want to win just for me."

"Is it because of all the people you had working on the building?"

"Something like that," she says mysteriously.

I frown but don't get the chance to say more as we pull up. Our door is opened by a helpful valet. Keene helps Ali from the car. Quickly, I slip out and hold my hand out for Libby, who looks brilliant in a black maternity suit with a shiny silver camisole beneath it. My heart quickens. Silver? She hasn't worn anything silver since she was pulled from the ocean after she was aboard the *Sea Force*.

What's going on?

Taking her hand, I feel the fine trembling she's trying to hide. I squeeze it. Just as we enter the glass doors, I lean down and whisper, "I love you, Libby. Always."

Her hair is pulled back from her face with a pair of combs. It's rippling down her shoulders like perfect mahogany waves. But her eyes are filled with every minute of love we've ever shared since the moment we've met. "I love you too, Cal." Turning, she lets out a nervous breath. "Let's do this."

A LITTLE LESS THAN TWO HOURS LATER, THE AWARDS FOR DESIGNS IN the 60-100,000-square-foot space are being announced. It comes as no surprise to me when "Project: HI DC Headquarters" is announced as the winner. Nor am I terribly surprised when Libby's hand claps over her mouth as she's overcome with emotion.

She and the members of her design and construction team stand to head toward the stage to receive the award. I'm applauding and whistling as Libby takes the stage. She's handed a black frame that almost dwarfs her luscious frame. And the spotlight catches the light off the silver camisole peeking above it.

"Thank you all so much." Everyone sits down as Libby starts to speak. "You all know the pressure to go through the blind bid process; imagine my surprise when I found out exactly what I was bidding on! I didn't know who the client was, only to find out it was my husband's company." She's interrupted by the titter of laughter around the room. Leaning back into the microphone, she tacks on, "Trust me, it's much harder than you think to design this kind of space knowing the kind of work your husband does every day. Because it has to be perfect. Lives are on the line. I should know. At one point, mine was one of them."

Silence descends upon the room. Out of the corner of my eye, I see Ali reach for Keene's hand. Libby keeps talking. "Ten years ago, the week we cut the ribbon on the DC headquarters of his new office, my husband and some of his colleagues saved my life and the lives of twenty other people on the *Sea Force*. The work they do requires long, arduous hours. And it often requires sacrifice as these men and women often spend time away from their loved ones to save people they've never met. People like you and me."

My eyes begin to sting as Libby continues. "When I designed HI DC, I knew the workspace had to be slick, but there had to be places to unwind. Technology was paramount as were state-of-the-art training facilities. And above all, I wanted to create a space where the men and women who worked there would always remember who they were fighting for." Libby takes an enormous breath. "So, I designed the saltwater reef in the lobby. After all, water is probably the best demonstrator to remind people that no matter what happens, you can recover from the effects of what happened to you. Rippling water is always moving, always changing—just like life is. And these men and women are determined to alter the course of people's lives for the better."

From my seat in the fourth row, I'm certain Libby can't see the tears I can taste on my face. She goes on. "What made the HI DC project even more special was the contractor I had the pleasure of working with. Again, as if it was meant to be, this contracting firm had only recently expanded their business to the mid-Atlantic from Texas. It must have been fate when she put her bid in. Then again, maybe it took her father that long to be able to let her out of his sight considering she looks so much like her mother." Libby smiles. There's a tinge of sadness to it.

The anxiety.

The silver.

The woman standing just behind my wife who she beckons forward has long blonde hair.

And I don't know how I know, but I do. And I want to run up on stage and kiss my wife senseless for her vast pride, her overwhelming courage, and her constant ability to show the world she's a survivor.

And so is Linc's family.

"If it wasn't for the incredible wisdom of McCallister Construction about all the necessary security requirements, headed by the amazing project lead, Bethany McCallister"—Libby confirms my guess as her voice moves on and gets stronger—"the things we wanted to accomplish would never have been possible. So, my profound thanks to them. To my own design team—Stacie, Jennifer, and Milicia, every day I'm grateful for each and every one of you. Deja Vu DC would not be the same without your brilliance. And of course, none of this would have been possible without the support of our family and friends." Holding the frame aloft, she calls into the microphone, "Thank you all very much!"

Everyone stands up again as the entourage leaves the stage. Before I can do more than lay my lips to Libby, they're announcing nominees for the Pinnacle Award.

"Oh, God," Libby whispers.

I take the frame from her and just hold her hand.

"Our first nominee, CMML, Baltimore, MD."

"Their design is amazing, Cal," Libby hisses. "I drove by it the other day."

"Why would you do that?" I mutter back.

"I was curious."

"You wanted to scope out the competition."

"Maybe, but..." She doesn't get to finish as the next nominee is announced.

"B+B, Arlington, Virginia."

"So brilliant! Their design team turned this old hotel into a high-class shopping mall."

"How much did that recon cost me?"

Libby just smacks me in the arm.

"Simon, Harley & Hurst, Washington, DC," the announcer proclaims to loud applause.

"They're the favorite. You should see the corporate headquarters they redesigned." Libby names the company, and I whistle aloud.

I earn an elbow to the ribs and a turned-up nose. "Next time, hire them."

"There won't be a next time," I murmur into her hair as I inhale the fresh scent of Libby's shampoo. "Libs, relax. You already won."

Slowly, her head twists until our noses are touching. "I know. I won the first time you asked me out. I won the day you came back, the night you first kissed me."

I interrupt. "You told me you loved me first."

"Semantics. I was under fear of dying if you'll recall."

I grin against her lips. "I'll never forget it." I'll never forget any of it.

"I kept on winning the day you proposed, the day we married. So, we hit a losing streak." She shrugs as if the years our marriage was on thin ice weren't the worst of both of our lives—when the lies I told almost did us in. "We came back in the bottom of the ninth and hit a home run with bases loaded."

"You're watching too much baseball lately," I chide gently.

"You can't say that about the Nats, honey. It's impossible." But her smile broadens.

As does mine.

"And no matter what, no matter what, as long as I have you, Jax, Leah, and this little one." She rubs her hand over her stomach. "I don't need a piece of paper to validate everything we went through was worth it." Cupping my jaw as her lips brush against mine, she whispers, "I love you, Cal."

"I love you, Libby. Always."

"And the winner of the Pinnacle Award goes to Deja Vu DC!"

We're still kissing as Libby wins the award of her career. We're too busy reminding each other that for almost twenty years—since the moment our eyes met across a bar and I gave in to what I had been feeling for her—the ripples of awareness have never stopped.

Not once.

"I guess I can't lose tonight." Libby's face is wreathed in smiles when I finally let her up for air.

My lips curve in a smile down at the woman who taught it to me. "Try not to get so mushy this time, okay?"

"Now look at who's throwing sass?" Plucking one last kiss from my lips, Libby strides her way confidently back up onto the stage but not before I see the tears pooling in her eyes.

And all I can do is stand, applaud, and smile—God, I can do nothing but smile at the woman who taught me how to do it—knowing that our lives may never be completely without storms, but as long as we have each other, we'll be able to weather them.

As Libby's eyes find mine, I know what she's thinking. Our lives haven't been perfect. They've been riddled with the kinds of storms that would have broken a love weaker than ours. We learned to cherish every moment, to ride the waves as they've come up. Because in the end, our love has been the end result neither of us would change. I mouth to her, "I love you."

And I always will.

THE END

ALSO BY TRACEY JERALD

Standalones

Close Match

Ripple Effect

The Amaryllis Series

Free to Dream

Free to Run

Free to Rejoice

Free to Breathe

Free to Believe

Free to Live

Coming Soon

Return By Air - June 2020

Also coming soon, keep a close eye on the Lady Boss Press site! Tracey is honored to be writing as part of the Kristen Proby's Boudreaux universe!

Title and release date to be announced very soon!

ACKNOWLEDGMENTS

To my husband, Nathan, every day I fall in love even more with the man you are. Thank you for being the true strength in our family. Your love is the kind worth fighting for. I love you.

To my son, my dreamer, you always ask me what my favorite part is and quite simply, it's you. Never lose your curious mind or your incredible capacity to love.

Mom, really, this book is your fault! You and Dad took me on so many cruises as a kid, it sparked my imagination. I can't thank you enough for showing me the world and telling me I can, even when there were days I thought I couldn't. You're the absolute best.

Jen, there's no way I can travel this journey without you. There'd be no joy, no laughter. And after close to three decades of friendship, no magic of sisterhood. I love you.

My Meows, I can survive anything as long as I have all of you. I love you.

Petr, who would have thought signing up for that class would change my life? Thank you for the decades of friendship and for consulting with me. Until next time, my friend...

To Sandra Depukat from One Love Editing. Hallelujah! I finally gave you one of the sacred recipes! I know, stop writing this and get back to more words. I love you, too.

To Holly Malgeri. My twin, I know the extra effort you used for this story. It means more to me that you did this then you can possibly imagine. I love you.

To my amazing cover designer Deborah Bradseth of Tugboat Design, I am blown away by the beauty and brilliance of this cover!

To Gel, at Tempting Illustrations, you created works of art that still give me the shivers.

To the amazing team at Foreword PR, you continue to astound me with your brilliance. Alissa, thank you for everything! You could ask for the moon and I'd be happy to do it.

Linda Russell, you're right. No, that's not the first time I've said it, nor will it be the last. But specifically, screw the bat phone. We're scary together, we're scary apart, so, let's just be scary together. I love you, lady!

To Sue Henn, Dawn Hurst, and Amy Rhodes, I can't express how much you saved me! Thank you for being gracious with your time and wisdom.

To the amazing people in Tracey's Tribe, MUAH!

To all of the bloggers and readers who take the time to read my books, from the bottom of my heart, I can't express how humbled I am. I am overwhelmed by your emails, your comments, and reviews. Thank you for your continuous support.

XOXO

ABOUT THE AUTHOR

Tracey Jerald knew she was meant to be a writer when she would re-write the ending of books in her head when she was a young girl growing up in southern Connecticut. It wasn't long before she was typing alternate endings and extended epilogues "just for fun".

After college in Florida, where she obtained a degree in Criminal Justice, Tracey traded the world of law and order for IT. Her work for a world-wide internet startup transferred her to Northern Virginia where she met her husband in what many call their own happily ever after. They have one son.

When she's not busy with her family or writing, Tracey can be found in her home in north Florida drinking coffee, reading, training for a runDisney event, or feeding her addiction to HGTV.

Made in USA - North Chelmsford, MA
1057366_9781733086158
03.19.2020 2124